Vacationland

ALSO BY MEG MITCHELL MOORE

The Arrivals

So Far Away

The Admissions

The Captain's Daughter

The Islanders

Two Truths and a Lie

Vacationland

A Novel

Meg Mitchell Moore

HARPER LARGE PRINT

An Imprint of HarperCollinsPublishers

VACATIONLAND. Copyright © 2022 by Meg Mitchell Moore. All rights reserved. Printed in the United States of America. No part of this book may be used or reproduced in any manner whatsoever without written permission except in the case of brief quotations embodied in critical articles and reviews. For information, address HarperCollins Publishers, 195 Broadway, New York, NY 10007.

HarperCollins books may be purchased for educational, business, or sales promotional use. For information, please e-mail the Special Markets Department at SPsales@harpercollins.com.

FIRST HARPER LARGE PRINT EDITION

ISBN: 978-0-06-324190-9

Library of Congress Cataloging-in-Publication Data is available upon request.

22 23 24 25 26 LSC 10 9 8 7 6 5 4 3 2 1

For Sue Santa Maria and Cheryl Moore

It goes so fast. We don't have time to look at one another. I didn't realize. So all that was going on and we never noticed.
—THORNTON WILDER, *OUR TOWN*

June

1.

Kristie

The Greyhound from Altoona, Pennsylvania, to Rockland, Maine, takes twelve hours and thirty-three minutes with three stops, all of them in places where you don't necessarily want to use the bathroom but may find you have no choice. Even so, the first part of the journey isn't too bad—Kristie Turner has two seats to herself. But in New Haven, six hours into the journey, she gains a seatmate in the form of a sixty-something named Bob who wants to talk with Kristie about the granddaughter he is going to meet for the first time, and also about his abiding love for Creedence Clearwater Revival. Never mind that the bus left Altoona at eleven at night, so by this point it's five in the morning.

Can't you see I'm tired? Kristie wants to say. *Can't*

you see I'm grieving? But, of course, Bob can't see that. Grief is not something you wear on a vest, like a Brownie patch. She rolls up her sweatshirt to form a pillow and angles her body away from Bob's, falling deeply asleep.

Along with her grief, Kristie is traveling to Rockland with $761 in cash—the very last of her tips—a duffle bag that fits beneath the seat in front of her, her phone, a trucker's hat from the last restaurant she worked at, $27,000 in medical debt, and an envelope her mother gave her the day before she died. The envelope contains a letter, and even though Kristie has the letter memorized, she knows it is something she will carry with her at all times, or at least whenever it is practical, like a lucky coin or a rabbit's foot.

Two days before she died Kristie's mother, Sheila, emerged briefly from her morphine haze, becoming, for less than a minute, the woman Kristie remembered: nervy and resourceful, if a little worn at the edges by life.

"I know it was hard on you, honey. I wish I gave you more. I'm sorry if I was a disappointment."

Kristie lay down in the hospital bed and curled into her mother the way she used to, when she was little, when it was just the two of them. Sheila felt different by then. Cancer had whittled her, she of the gorgeous breasts, tiny waist, and curvy hips, down to fewer than one hundred pounds, all of it bone.

"Stop," Kristie said. "Just—*stop*." She'd been more of a disappointment to her mother than her mother ever could have been to her.

When the bus pulls into the Greyhound station in Rockland Kristie wakes. She'd been dreaming, she realizes, about Jesse, whom she'd left three years ago passed out on their sofa in Miami Beach, coming down from whatever it was that had brought him up the night before. In the dream Jesse was in her mother's hospital room, pulling all the plugs out of all the outlets. Kristie tried to stop him, but then Nurse Jackie came in, with her blue scrubs and her stethoscope and her attitude, and told Kristie it was okay. "Sometimes we just have to let go," Nurse Jackie told her. "It's the circle of life."

Bob is gone—he'd been on his way to Portland; she must have slept through that stop. She gathers her belongings, feels in her pocket for the letter, checks her bag for her envelope of cash, and walks down the three steps from the bus and into the great unknown.

Immediately the smell of the harbor assaults her. It's a friendly assault. The water smells different here from how it did in Miami Beach, and, of course, in Altoona there is no ocean. Here it's more—briny. More alive than in Florida. The Greyhound terminal is some sort of ship terminal too. There are boats everywhere. She sees boats dry-docked in a parking lot; she sees boats in the water, and a sign that says FERRY TO VINALHAVEN. She sees an American flag. She sees a man in overalls looking at her.

"You look at little lost there," he says. "Can I help you find what you're looking for?"

I doubt it, thinks Kristie. Can he help her find her way out of debt? Out of sorrow? The man's eyes are kind. "Where can I find coffee?" she says. Her voice is dry.

"Fancy or not fancy?"

"Either."

"Dunkin' Donuts that way." He points to the right. "And downtown is that way." To the left. "Atlantic Baking Company or Rock City."

"Thank you." She takes a deep breath and turns toward downtown. And then, for the first time since she lay in the hospital bed, pressed against her mother's razor-sharp clavicle, she feels like everything might be okay. Maybe not right away, but sometime. It could be the man's kind eyes that make her feel this way, or the possibility of fresh adventure. Or something more nebulous.

Over a small coffee at Atlantic Baking Company she answers an ad in the free paper for a furnished apartment and arranges to see it that very day. It's on Linden Street, which her phone tells her she can walk to from the coffee shop—a longish walk, with her bag, but doable.

"Most of my other places are gone," the landlord tells her when they meet outside the building. "You really need to start looking in April if you want one of the good ones." He's wearing jeans over which a soft belly pouches, and he has a Maine accent like those she's heard on television.

"I don't want one of the good ones. I want one of the cheap ones."

"Well, all right then. I guess it's your lucky day."

The apartment is crummy, the top floor of a two-family that is crying out for renovation. In the driveway there's a truck with lobster traps stacked in the back. Two little kids, girls, are running around the front yard, and a woman in a tank top and cutoff shorts is sitting on the steps watching them.

The included furnishings are a double bed, a couch, a rickety wooden coffee table, and a recliner that looks like it's been through two world wars.

"I'll be tearing this down soon," the landlord says. "To rebuild. But it's yours for now if you want to put down first and last."

She talks him into taking one month's rent instead of

first and last, and a security deposit in installments, and then she says, "What about the family downstairs?"

"You don't bother them, they shouldn't bother you."

"No, I mean when you tear it down. What'll happen to them then?"

He shrugs. "They'll go someplace else."

Outside a bike leans against the house. The landlord inspects it. "Last tenants must have left it," he says. "It's yours if you want it."

The bike is a three-speed, not a vintage-cool three speed, just old. Kristie wants it. In Miami Beach Jesse drove a motorcycle, and Kristie used to ride on the back. She loved that. Motorcycles are glamorous, and dangerous, like Jesse himself, like Kristie used to be— like a Technicolor movie. Abandoned old bikes are like black-and-white television with rabbit ears you have to adjust by hand.

Still, it's something. She rides the bike around most of that first week, putting in applications at North Beacon Oyster, Rockland Cafe, Archer's on the Pier. One by one they tell her that they're covered for the summer. All set, they say. All set, all set, all set. They hired everyone they needed by Memorial Day, a week ago. She hears the same at The Landings, Cafe Miranda, In Good Company. She can leave her number on the application, they all say. They'll call her if anything changes.

Two doors down from her new apartment is a house full of college kids. Lots of cars with stickers that say MIDDLEBURY and UNIVERSITY OF VIRGINIA and even HARVARD. These are the kids who have the jobs that Kristie needs, and they probably don't even really need them, not the way she does. In the early afternoons they sit outside and drink craft beers from cans, toss a Frisbee back and forth. The girls all have long straight shiny hair and smooth brown legs and complicated sets of bracelets. The boys take off their shirts to play. Their bodies are hairless and slender and at the same time muscular. Kristie feels nostalgic watching them, even though it should be impossible to feel nostalgia for something you never experienced. Those years, the years when she could have been doing what these kids are doing, are lost.

By day she applies for jobs, and at night she eats the cheapest food she can find: Dairy Queen, Subway. She can survive without eating a lot. She can survive without most things. Sometimes, when she's eating her cheap food, she takes out her collection and looks at it: the printout of Louisa McLean's bio from the New York University website. The press release from the Maine Supreme Judicial Court, announcing Martin Fitzgerald's retirement. The directions to the house from downtown Rockland, and the Google Earth printout of the aerial view, and the Zillow page. The photo of Matty McLean winning a cross-country race.

By the fourth day of June she's worried she'll run out of money. She's also bored; there are no more restaurants to apply to. And maybe *that's* why she decides finally to bike to Ships View. It's three and a half miles from her apartment. She wonders if the bike will make it that far; she supposes there's only one way to find out.

Google Maps did not mention the hills. The ride is basically all rolling hills once she hits North Shore Drive, and she's really starting to sweat. The glimpses of the water in between the houses, and the houses themselves, are all glorious, but the sky is gray, and it's humid. She wishes she'd brought water. She passes the turnoff to the Owls Head airport, and then there are more hills, up and down, up and down. She knows she has to take a left on Hidden Beach Road but she has forgotten what comes before it; she worries that she's missed it. She wonders if she should pull over and look at her phone but she doesn't want to lose momentum on the hills. And then, yes, here it is, a dirt road, bumpy, uneven. And then the smaller lane turning off the road. And then the house.

She pulls her bike over near a playset with a green slide so she can look at the house without revealing herself. *The house.* She has Wazed it and googled it and mapped it; she's thought about it and dreamed about it, but now that she's standing here looking at it it's both more and less intimidating than she expected. Gray shingled, five windows across the top, five across the bottom, a semicircle of a garden that's a riot of color. Cars parked around the circular driveway: a minivan, a Mercedes sedan, a green pickup with the words GIL'S GARDENS stenciled on the side. She takes a deep breath, lets it out slowly. She can't go any closer than this, not now, not the first time. She just wanted to see it. There's a long porch on the back of the house; she knows this from her research. It wraps around one side, and that's the part she can see. She hears the voices of children farther out, maybe near the water, and as she watches a little girl runs across the lawn, arms pumping.

Kristie's heart constricts with something complicated and indescribable, but also with a very basic, very primal feeling. The feeling is envy. The people who live in this house have money. Old money. Real money. She has felt like an outsider plenty of times in her life, but never perhaps as she does right now.

"Can I help you?" Kristie jumps, turns around. There's a man there, a man about her age, maybe a year or two older; maybe five years older. He has long-ish hair curling a little in the back, and he's wearing a Portland Sea Dogs baseball hat. His eyes are dark green, almost olive. "You a Peeping Tom?"

"No!" She gestures toward her bike. "No. Not at all. I was out on a bike ride."

"On *that?*" He nods at her bike, but he's smiling. "Can't believe you got very far. What's that, a one-speed?"

"Three," she says. "Not to brag or anything." He smiles harder. "I took a wrong turn. I was just—trying to figure out where I meant to go. Are you Gil?" She points to his shirt, which says GIL'S GARDENS, just like the truck.

"Nope. Gil's my boss. I'm Danny."

"Kristie."

He holds out his hand, then pulls it back. "I'd shake your hand, but I've been pulling weeds all day. And maybe you're allergic." He points to the sky, which is darkening quickly, storm clouds racing across. "I'm no weatherman," he says. "But I'm guessing you don't want to be stuck out here too long."

As if on cue, the sky opens up, and the rain comes down.

2.
Louisa

Every summer the McLean family spends two weeks in Louisa's family's home on the coast of Maine, in a little hamlet called Owls Head. Louisa has never seen an owl here—she's been coming since she was a milky-eyed newborn, and actually before that, as a dividing egg; now she is nearly forty. Local lore has it that eighteenth-century explorers saw the shape of an owl's head in the promontory, so it's possible she'll never see an actual owl at all. But she keeps looking, and now her children, who are twelve, ten, and seven, look too. Matty, Abigail, Claire.

The house is called Ships View. Rightly so: from the window in the dining room they see all manner of ships pass, schooners out of Camden and yachts with Caribbean flags and pleasure boats from Rockland or

Rockport or farther afield—up from Brunswick or down from Deer Isle or Stonington. And presumably those on the ships can see the house as well.

This summer Louisa has come for ten weeks; Steven, her husband, may come for one, or part of one, at the very end, or may come for none at all, as per their agreement. She might be okay if he doesn't come at all.

The drive from Brooklyn was long, with traffic at the beginning and then toward the end, as they wound past and through the tourist-clogged towns like Wiscasset and Bath. They left at six in the morning but Louisa was up at four-thirty, packing, worrying, organizing, mainlining coffee. She is tired already, and the thought of dragging in the children's suitcases, pulling them up the stairs, unpacking the clothes, fills her with an even greater exhaustion: bone deep. After she greets her mother, Annie, Louisa walks directly into the dining room, at the rear of the house, to look at the harbor through the vast picture window. Across the harbor sits the town of Rockland and the Samoset Resort, where Louisa's parents were married more than forty-five years ago. Louisa and Steven were married in the yard she's looking at now, in a big white tent, on a windy day in May with a hard, bright sky. She feels her heart begin to lift, picks up her phone, and texts Steven: Got

Here Safely. Her fingers hover over the phone's screen for several seconds, and then she adds, Miss You.

In the harbor she sees two lobster boats, as well as the ferries to Vinalhaven and North Haven. The sliding door to the back porch is open, and as she smells the ocean she feels the energy return to her body. Brooklyn is where she lives most of the year, yes. But this is home.

The children run immediately down to the water, bringing Otis, her parents' golden retriever, with them. Otis can hardly stand the excitement. Children! *Three of them!* After such a long winter of near silence, holed up in the little house in Portland, with only a small scrap of yard. The children cross the wide lawn and go through the rickety wooden gate, scampering across the flat rocks to where the water breaks against them. Louisa watches them slow their progress as they reach the seaweed-strewn rocks, closer to the water's edge, and she watches them as they arrive at last at the frigid water.

In Brooklyn, the only body of water nearby is Prospect Park Lake, which sort of counts but doesn't really. Here, the harbor meets the Atlantic, which then stretches on interminably, at once standoffish and welcoming, mysterious and utterly familiar. Louisa loves this house all the way down to its bones: every carpet and pillow and rug and table; every damp scent and old board game and quilt; the creaky seventh stair and the tiny forgotten extra bathroom with the oddly shaped shower that nobody ever uses, so Louisa knows she can hide there with her secrets and her heartbreaks and her expensive shampoo that the children will waste if they come across it. She loves the handprints on the wall of the half bath off the kitchen, with the names and dates of the children the year they stamped them, and with Louisa's own tiny handprint too, from the summer she was five. She has loved this house at the age each of her children is now and in the years before that, and in the years after too. To see her children embrace it the same way she always has—well. She can think of no purer joy.

"Looks like they've made themselves right at home," says Annie, coming up behind her daughter and touching Louisa on the shoulder. "I'm glad to see it. I can't tell you how happy I am to have you here for the whole summer. Now let me have a look at you. Are you thin? You look thin."

"Oh, please," says Louisa, laughing, patting her tummy, which is mostly invisible, at least to others. "I've put on three pounds since last summer!"

"I think you needed those three pounds."

Louisa snorts and then looks more closely at her mother. "It's *you* who doesn't look right, Mom. Are you eating?"

"Like a horse."

"I doubt it. Sleeping?"

Annie looks away. "Mostly. Sometimes."

"How is Dad?"

The question hangs between them for a moment, waiting for Annie to wrestle with it. "The same," Annie says finally. Her voice is brisk but the purple crescents under her eyes seem to grow deeper. "Good days and bad days, you know, as usual. Thank goodness the agency has sent us Barbara. She's so good with him."

Twenty-two months ago Louisa's father, Martin, the retired chief justice of the Supreme Judicial Court of Maine, was diagnosed with Alzheimer's. Martin is "Dad" to Louisa, "Martin" or "Sweetheart" to Annie, and "Chief" to everyone else. Now there are days when the Chief recognizes Annie and days when he rails at her for some imagined transgression; there are days when he is clear-eyed, calm, and quiet, sitting at his desk among his papers and his books, and days when he can't find his way out of the bathroom. Two weeks ago, a Rockland police officer discovered him walking on North Shore Drive wearing nothing but a raincoat and bedroom slippers. Annie had gone to dress for the day when he slipped out. The whole thing would have been funny, except that naturally it wasn't. It was awful.

"Can I see him?" Louisa asks. She's asking, but she's not sure she wants to hear the answer. She's of two minds about her father, and of two hearts too. In Brooklyn, absorbed in her own life and her daily worries and tasks it's easy enough to pretend that none of this is happening, and to think of Martin Fitzgerald the way she's always thought of him, incandescent wit, blue eyes flashing with intelligence and warmth, but here she is, about to face daily—hourly—reminders of decline. No hiding. The realization makes her palms itch.

Something passes over Annie's face: sadness or worry or a combination of both. "Not yet. He's resting. Late afternoons and early evenings are the hardest. That's common. The mood changes . . ." Her voice trails off and she rubs at her temples. "He'll be ready to see you at dinner. We've got the Millers coming. I'm sorry about company on your first night, but when I asked them I didn't know you'd be arriving today and I couldn't very well un-ask them."

"Of course you couldn't," says Louisa, although she wishes that Annie had. Louisa had moved their departure date up by a week. Abigail and Claire didn't mind one bit but Matty groused—for the first time probably ever, he'd rather be in Brooklyn than Maine. The curse of the almost-teenager, worried about missing out. When Louisa was young she had her own life well established here, with friends, and sometimes boyfriends (Mark Harding, when she was sixteen), and she'd never wanted to be elsewhere.

"Pauline is making cod," Annie adds. Pauline has worked summers for the Fitzgeralds for years. She has a daughter Louisa's age, and two sons besides, but she was a young mother—still a teenager, for the first boy, and maybe for Nicole too—so she's much younger than Annie. One long-ago summer, the summer they were sixteen, Louisa and Nicole were briefly, intensely friends. "I should be able to do without her, I've been thinking lately," says Annie. "It feels like an extravagance."

Louisa feels a drumbeat of apprehension at Annie's words. Is Annie worried about money? No, she decides. It's just that famous New England frugality— you might live on waterfront land valued at well over a million, but you're still going to frown at the electric bill and buy extra bananas when they go on sale at Hannaford.

"Mom. If she's helpful, use her. You have to take care

of yourself. You're no good to Dad if you're exhausted. You can't pour from an empty cup, you know." This is a piece of wisdom she once gleaned from a SoulCycle instructor, but its origins don't make it any less true. Louisa should know, she's been trying to pour from an empty cup for a year now. "And who's that in the garden?" she says, looking out the window.

"Oh, that's Danny. He's new this year. He's been doing handyman work as well as landscaping. Technically he works for Gil, who's always done the work here, but we hire him on the side to do a bit of this and that. I'm ashamed to admit what a staff I have this summer. There's just too much for me to manage on my own."

"Of course there is, Mom."

Annie glances to the east, where the sky is darkening. "Looks like there's rain coming. Should we call the children in?"

"I think they'd rather stay out," says Louisa. "They're mostly waterproof."

"I suppose they are." Annie takes Louisa's hand and squeezes it. "Louisa, what it does to my old heart, to have children in the house. Are you really and truly staying for the whole summer?"

(Annie says nothing about Steven coming or not coming, and Louisa offers nothing.)

"I'd stay all year if I could," says Louisa, squeezing

back. "I'd stay forever." Louisa is a tenured professor of history at New York University, finishing up a sabbatical, during which she was supposed to have completed a book: *The History of the Seventh-day Adventist Church on Pitcairn Island.* A working title, not the snappiest. Steven is one of the two founders of a podcast start-up in Brooklyn called All Ears. He works long hours alongside beautiful, tireless millennials with fantastic eyebrows, and he's compensated mostly, at this stage, with hope and promise.

Annie has stepped out on the porch and is frowning at the sky. "Are you sure we shouldn't call in the children?" she asks through the screen door. "I can't believe how dark it got, so quickly."

Before Louisa even has a chance to answer there's a low grumble of thunder, like a warning from an ill-tempered dog, and almost immediately after that the rain comes.

3.
Kristie

Danny looks at Kristie with his olive eyes. "Come on," he says. "I'll give you a lift. You don't want to ride home in this."

She hesitates. "I don't know." But her top is already soaked through, and she thinks about all of the hills between here and Linden Street. She doesn't even know if the bike tires will work on the wet road; they're pretty bald.

"I'm a good guy," he says. He opens his arms, then shrugs, like he's apologizing for that. "Ask my mom if you don't believe me. I live with her." Kristie must have looked shocked because he laughs and says, "It's not as weird as it sounds. I mean maybe it is. I just sold my place, haven't found a new one yet. And what can I say? I'm pretty good company. Come on. Let me throw your bike in the back of the truck. I have a tarp I can cover it with. I'm done for the day anyway."

"Well, okay. Thanks." She watches Danny load her bike in the truck, and she climbs in the cab.

On the way to Linden Street she tells Danny that she's been looking for a job, with no luck. Danny tells her that he does all the landscaping for the house but that he also does handyman work for the family, as requested. She feels a shiver go up and down her body when he says this, and carefully she asks, "Do they need a lot of handyman work?"

He shrugs. "Average amount. Older home, older owners. They need lightbulbs changed, showers regrouted, that sort of thing. The exterior is going to need a coat of paint soon, so there's lots of prep to do. I'm happy to help. They pay well too."

There's a lot she wants to ask, but she says, "That's good," and leaves it there, not wanting to seem too eager.

"Hey, I have a joke," he says. "Want to hear it? It pertains to the matter at hand."

"Sure."

"What's the difference between a poorly dressed man on a tricycle and a well-dressed man on a bicycle?"

She thinks about it. She's never been good at figuring these things out. "I don't know," she says finally.

"Attire!" That makes her laugh really hard. "You're laughing!" he says. "Nobody ever laughs at my jokes."

It's corny, but it's legitimately funny. She's still laughing when she says, "Turn here. It's this one, on the right."

The rain has stopped and the sun is trying to peek through the clouds. The lobsterman's kids are in the front yard, attempting to use a Hula-Hoop without success. Someday maybe Kristie will show them how. She was a really good Hula-Hooper back in the day— much better than she is at figuring out jokes.

Danny lifts the bike out of the back and sets it on the ground. He knocks three times on the seat, ratatat-tat, and smiles at her. There is a smudge of dirt on his right cheek. She wants to wipe it off, but obviously she doesn't. Just the fact that she wants to is strange, though. She doesn't even know this guy!

"Hey, can I give you my number?" he asks.

"My phone battery died."

"No problem." He pulls his phone out of his pocket. "Give me yours. I'll text you right away and you can save mine when you go charge yours. Maybe I can tell you another joke sometime."

"Okay," she says, punching in the numbers. "Sure, another joke."

She pulls her bike around the back and parks it under the stairwell.

When her phone is charged she sees a text that says, See You Around, Bicycle Girl. She smiles. She's never had a nickname like that before. There's a voice mail too. Someone named Fernando at Archer's on the Pier, one of the places where she dropped off an application. They just lost one of their servers to a better offer on Cape Cod. He says *Cape Cod* like it's a curse. Can Kristie come in at two-thirty for an interview?

It's twelve minutes past two.

She calls back and tells Fernando she'll be there.

Fernando is compact and impatient. All the men Kristie has ever worked for or with at restaurants are compact and impatient. They sit at the bar. In the middle of the restaurant is a curving staircase made of light blond wood. Kristie can see two servers rolling silverware at a table near the kitchen. She hears prep cooks yelling at each other. The bartender, a woman maybe ten years older than Kristie, probably in her late thirties, is counting bottles of sauvignon blanc and marking numbers down on a piece of paper. "You want something?" she asks Fernando, then Kristie.

"No," says Kristie. "Thank you." She is so nervous!

"Ice water," says Fernando. No *please*. He jerks

a thumb toward the bartender and says, "Amber." Amber nods at Kristie.

Fernando studies Kristie's application, moving his finger as he reads, like a child just learning to sound out words. He doesn't look up when he says, "Miami Beach, huh? Hmmm . . . And—Altoona?" Now he looks up. The last place Kristie worked was a late-night place on Thirteenth called Tom & Joe's, which was billed as "family friendly." Miami Beach was not, for the most part, family friendly.

"Yeah," she says. She clears her throat around the lump that has just formed. "I mean, yes. That's where my mom lives. Lived. I was taking care of her. Until." The lump becomes a boulder and she can feel her eyes starting to fill. She whispers, "She died," around the boulder.

For a second Fernando's face softens. He takes a long sip of his ice water and crunches a piece of ice. Kristie can't stand that, the sound of ice crunching between teeth. Jesse used to do it all the time. Fernando is talking around the ice when he says, "So what brought you up here?" When he squints at her little lines shoot out from the corner of his eyes.

Oh, Fernando. The answer to that is probably more than you want to hear at two forty-five on a summer afternoon. It's more than I want to tell.

She shrugs. "Thought I'd try something different."

He doesn't believe her, but it probably doesn't matter. "If I called people at these places what would they say about you?"

"They'd say I'm a hard worker," she says. "They'd say I know how to hustle." These things are true. "They'd say I'm reliable." Also true. Fernando won't call anyone, though. She knows that. People in the restaurant business don't have time to call around, especially in a tourist place, especially in the summer.

"Amber." The bartender turns. "What do you think? Does she look like she knows how to hustle?"

Amber shrugs. "Sure."

"Come in tonight for training. Black pants on the bottom. You got black pants?" She nods. "We'll give you a shirt. Come back at four."

"Okay." She smiles. "Great, okay, thank you very much."

"Don't thank me yet. Let's see how you do first." He points at her arms. "You're going to have to keep that covered, okay?"

He means the tattoos. The ivy, the interwoven flowers, covering much of her left arm, from her wrist past her elbow. She got the first one on the one-year anniversary of being sober, and she's added one every year since. Three years, three sections of vine.

"Of course," she says. "No problem."

She stands outside and looks at the water. Far, far in the distance, she can see a breakwater, and at the end of it a lighthouse. Right in front of her is a tiny stretch of beach, but it's not really a beach—the sand is made up of small pebbles. She pictures the turquoise water off Miami Beach, the sand like spun sugar. It went on forever, that sand. Forever and ever and ever, like the days and nights and days again.

Well, Dorothy, she tells herself. *You're not in Florida anymore.*

Her first instinct is to text her mother to tell her she got a job, to tell her Kristie is going to be okay. Her fingers hover over her phone screen. She can't text her mother. But she wants to tell someone.

What's the difference between a poorly dressed man on a tricycle and a well-dressed man on a bicycle?

Bicycle Girl Here, she texts. Guess What?

4.
The Children

After the rain stops, the children spend two hours down on the rocks, hardly noticing time passing. They are full of frenzied energy, the inevitable car squabbles forgotten. (Abigail "squishes" Claire into the middle seat, which they need because the third row is folded down to make room for a summer's worth of gear; the boy odor when Matty takes off his shoes is offensive. And nobody likes anybody else's music, which they all can hear through the headphones or earbuds each of them employs.)

Now they are talking about all of the things they will do while they are here this summer. The *whole* summer: a blessed eternity. They love everything about the Owls Head house; nobody, even Matty, admits to missing anything about Brooklyn, where summer is stilted and unforgiving and the air in July always feels too heavy.

They lay their wishes out like beads on a string. Claire wants to kayak all the way to Rockland Harbor, which Matty and Abigail both know she's not capable of, but in the spirit of the first day of vacation they refrain from pointing this out. Matty wants to eat a hot dog at least twice a week from Wasses, and Abigail wants to see the Oreo cows at Aldermere Farm in Rockport. She wants, she discloses, to touch one. Which isn't allowed.

They haven't been called yet for dinner by the adults. Nobody has a watch, and their electronic devices are still in their bags from the car. Every so often a snippet of grownup noise travels from the wide back porch down to the rocks—their mother's laugh, the loud, somewhat forbidding voice of their grandparents' neighbor, Mr. Miller. Dinner at the Owls Head house is always at six o'clock sharp, and cocktail hour can start as early as four-thirty. It's the only real time constraint in the welcome unscheduled strings of hours that make up their days in Maine. Thinking about these days—so *many* days, this summer, so many more than previous years!—each child is filled with their own particular brand of excitement.

It is Claire who sees it first. She is thinking about

the cheese plate that often appears with the cocktails. Claire is wondering whether it's worth it to clamber up from the rocks to check on the contents. It sort of depends on what crackers might be available. In this house the children aren't allowed to rummage through the cupboards for snacks, the way they do in Brooklyn, and while this stricture sometimes seems as though it might be an impediment, it usually turns out to be something of a relief. More surprises are in store if you don't know what's in the cupboards. Claire is also thinking about the small pickled onions she sometimes purloins from the cocktail tray, and she is prodding at the water with a stick she has found, balancing carefully on the slippery rocks and pretending she is Percy Jackson, controlling the water, when her eye falls on something just out of reach from her stick, floating.

Matty is far down at the other end of the rocks, thinking about his grandfather. It has all been explained to them by their mother, in great scientific detail; she even went so far as to go online and show them side-by-side images of a healthy brain and a brain with Alzheimer's, the second one shrunken and oddly colored, almost tan. He can't get the image out of his head; it makes him feel sick to his stomach, the thought of the two brains, and what might be happening inside a person's skull while they go on about their business. At the same time it makes him feel oddly exhilarated, to know the specifics like this.

His mother spared nobody the images, not even Claire—his father said sharply that Claire was too young to look at the pictures of the brains but Claire said, breathlessly, "I want to!"

"They need to understand why he's different than he used to be," his mother said. "It's less scary this way, if you make it about the science."

"It's more scary," his father persisted, scowling. His mother bit her lip and kept looking at the computer screen and his father went off into his small study, the slam of the door like an exclamation point on the evening.

Matty is wondering how memories can live inside the coils and hills and valleys in the healthy brain and, in the unhealthy one, where they go when they depart. His mother told them that their grandfather may one day know them and be able to have a perfectly respectable conversation, and the next day he may not know his own name or that he once presided over some of the most famous court decisions in the state. Good days and bad days, that's what she told them.

This is what he's thinking when he hears Claire yelling about something in the water. He feels something in his stomach knot up, tight as a fist. It's fear, probably, but he doesn't give it that name.

Abigail has been brave enough to go knee-deep in the water, even though the water is always frigid in June and the small rocks you have to get past to reach the sandy ocean bottom hurt their winter-tender feet until they've been in Owls Head at least five days.

"You go see, Abigail," he says bossily, trying for an authority he doesn't truly feel. "I'm sure it's nothing. You know how Claire is."

Abigail obliges (she does know how Claire is) and makes her way toward her sister. She holds her arms out like a tightrope walker. She almost goes down on the seaweed but she catches herself; in Brooklyn she takes gymnastics, and she's not excellent at it, but she's good enough to have balance.

"It's not nothing!" Abigail calls back to him. "It's not nothing, she's right, it's something dead!" He hears the note of triumph in her voice, not so different from what he heard in Claire's, and he is vexed by a fear that visits him often, that both of his sisters, though younger, are bolder and braver than he is. He feels both a duty and a dread as he follows Abigail's path over the rocks, much less gracefully than Abigail traversed it.

The thing in the water, maybe ten feet out from the rocks, is tan, or brown, with speckles of black, and rounded where it comes out of the water, like the top part of a homemade loaf of marble bread. "I think it's a buoy . . . ?" says Matty uncertainly. It could be a buoy, for sure it could. A few lobster boats drop their traps not so far from here. They see them all the time, from the big picture window in the dining room. Sometimes the buoys come loose from their lines, go off floating. They found one two summers ago, red, black, and blue; it had washed up against the rocks.

"It's a seal," says Claire.

Matty's sharp intake of breath comes before he has time to stop it. A dead seal can signify sharks, and although there has never, ever, been a shark in these waters, the very thought makes Matty's heartbeat pick up, his blood rush too fast through his veins. Matty is scared of sharks. No, that's an understatement if ever there was one: Matty is *terrified* of sharks.

The rise and fall from the resulting waves brings the thing closer, turns it somewhat on its side, and now they can see half of a face, an eye, some whiskers, a single flipper.

"It's a seal." Matty whispers. "It is." They all wait, breath bated, to see if by any chance the seal might be merely sleeping.

"It's dead," pronounces Claire, with certainty. "It's definitely dead." She reaches out with her stick again.

"Don't touch it," says Matty.

"Not even with my stick? I can almost reach it. I won't fall in, promise."

"Definitely not with your stick. Don't touch it at all. We need to tell the grown-ups. That's what we need to do. And they have to call—the authorities."

"What authorities?"

"I don't know," says Matty. "The . . . mammal authorities." Claire tosses him a glance so skeptical it almost makes his cheeks burn. Claire does skeptical really well for someone who is only seven. "There are authorities!" he says, holding fast. "I know there are. Mom will know, or Granny. Abigail, want to run up?"

"I got it," says Claire. She makes fists out of her hands and puts them by her side and straightens her arms and lets out *such* a bloodcurdling scream that every grown-up on the porch turns toward the children, and the children can see their faraway startled faces, the drinks in their hands.

Claire gets things done.

5.
Louisa

Annie knows what to do. She calls the Marine Mammal Reporting Hotline, whose number she keeps on the bulletin board in the kitchen, and speaks to the dispatcher, and within the hour a responder and an intern have arrived and loaded the seal into a jet sled and transported it to their facility. Claire follows the responders like a flower girl does a bride and asks a *lot* of questions. What will they do with the seal? A necropsy? What's *that*? What's the difference between a necropsy and an autopsy? How long will it take? Who will do it, and when? Will it smell? She reports all of the answers over dinner, which does not take place at six o'clock, and the conversation serves to make Pauline's baked cod less than appetizing to some in the family.

Pauline clatters extra loudly in the kitchen to show her dissatisfaction.

At bedtime the children, worn out by the fresh air and the excitement, fall quickly asleep, Abigail and Claire in the Bunk Room, and Matty in the corner bedroom with its own tiny bathroom. Louisa's father is asleep too, having been helped into his pajamas by the caregiver, who has departed. Louisa loves the house like this, silent and brooding, in the hours after the children's bedtimes and before her own. And if she's being honest with herself it's a relief to have her father off to bed; she can pretend, for a moment, that everything is as it always was, that time isn't passing, that her children aren't growing up and her parents aren't growing old. She has always loved to be awake while others are asleep; even as a child, in this very house, she used to sneak downstairs at midnight and turn on a solitary kitchen light and read her book, sometimes staying awake until two or three in the morning. One summer here she read *Bridge to Terabithia*, just as Abigail will do this summer. Louisa cried herself to sleep at the end, and Abigail probably will as well.

"I'm just going to sit on the porch for a few minutes," she says to her mother.

"Shall I join you? We can have a nightcap! Unless you want to be alone?"

"No," says Louisa decisively. "I don't want to be alone. A nightcap sounds lovely."

It does sound lovely! Everything sounds lovely. Her responsibilities already feel lighter here than they do at home, and also, at this particular juncture, the absence of Steven feels like a lightness too. When the children were young any trip undertaken as the solo parent was more difficult, but now that the kids are older—sometimes even bordering on self-sufficient—she can see how this summer some parts of her might feel less tempestuous, more at peace.

The moon is almost full, and they keep the porch lights off to deter the bugs. They can hear the water slapping at the rocks, and, in the distance, the foghorn at the lighthouse, low and mournful. The light flashes intermittently. Her mother brings two snifters of whiskey and hands one to Louisa. Annie sits in the wicker rocking chair and Louisa on the love seat, her legs tucked underneath her.

She hears a far-off sound of crickets. "Is Pauline okay? She seems quiet, or sad. Did I do something to upset her? Or did one of the kids?"

"No, no," says Annie. "Not at all. She's heartbroken over a sick cousin, a very close one. And her own daughter hardly ever comes back, while here you are for the whole summer. I could see where that might be rubbing her the wrong way. But it's not your fault, of course."

"Nicole Pelletier," says Louisa. "I was just thinking about her today. We were really close that one summer, remember? When we were sixteen? Why doesn't she come back more?"

Annie shrugs. "She moved to Nashville a long time ago, you know. I suppose she likes it better down there. I suppose there's not too much for her to come back to up here anymore. I don't think it would kill her to bring the granddaughter up every so often though."

"I'd die if I couldn't come up here every year, and let it renew me." The bright dot of the stars against the dark sky, the chill of the air like a cool hand laid against a hot cheek. "I don't know how Steven's going to stand it in Brooklyn."

"Nicole lived here year-round for most of her life. Maybe she's had enough." Annie shrugs—Annie's shrugs are delicate and graceful, as is everything about Annie. "Steven will come up, right? Didn't you say he'll come in August?"

"Sure. Maybe. I'm not sure." *I hope so, I don't hope,* thinks Louisa.

"Claire said you've been fighting a lot."

Louisa groans. *Claire!* "How'd that come up?"

"She just offered it, when I went in to say good night. She's something, Claire." Louisa can feel her mother's smile in the darkness.

"Not fighting. Discussing. Figuring things out."

"Figuring what out?"

"Work. Life. The combination thereof."

Back in April, Louisa broached the two weeks in Maine: mind you, these were two weeks they'd marked on the calendar in the fall. Steven had gone into a full-blown panic. He couldn't leave All Ears! Not even for a long weekend. Not even for a minute, not really. The way he talked about the company it was a house made of Popsicle sticks balanced one on top of the other with Steven's hand the base holding the entire thing up.

"But you've been working like this all year!" she'd said. They were unloading the dishwasher.

"You've been on sabbatical. It was the right time to focus on the company. We talked about this." Steven filed the silverware neatly into the drawer.

"Sabbaticals are supposed to be for working, not for cleaning toilets and hanging out the washing." A misrepresentation, obvious to both of them: nobody cleaned the toilets in their home all that often, and they had a clothes dryer. "And I'm behind on my book, because you've been working so much. We decided on these two weeks in *September*, remember?"

"September was a long time ago. Things have shifted. I can't leave for two weeks. I just can't. I'm sorry, Louisa. I thought we'd be further along than we are now. It's really hard to predict how long each step in the process is going to take. And while we're trying to get funding—I can't be gone. What if we send them to camp? Then you could work, and I could work."

"*Camp*? Steven. It's *April*. People signed up for camps in *October*. We can't find a camp now. And it would cost, like, *thousands* for three kids. And Matty would feel too old to go. And plus, I don't want them to experience camp. I want them to experience Maine."

"Right," said Steven. "Okay. Sorry. Yeah, camp isn't the answer. We don't have thousands right now. Unless we use the Emergency Fund . . ."

"No," said Louisa. "Definitely not. That's not what EF is for."

They gazed at each other over the steaming glasses. This, Louisa realized, was what could appear in a dictionary next to the word *impasse*: two married people, arms folded, waiting to see who might blink first.

Finally Louisa blinked, and the situation had been resolved thusly: Louisa would take the children to Owls Head for the whole summer, removing them all, Louisa included, from Steven's hair so he could work his sixteen- or nineteen- or twenty-seven-hour days without guilt or compunction. Louisa would use the relatively relaxing atmosphere of Ships View, where her children could roam more freely, to get the bulk of her book complete, so that by the time school and routines started again the whole McLean family could return to some semblance of normalcy.

She traces the arm of the love seat with her fingers. Can she say any of this to her mother? Her parents' marriage is as steady as the tides, solid as a rock. Annie might try to understand, or she might not try, but either way she wouldn't really, truly get it. When Louisa was growing up, Annie was always home. "I won't bore you with the details," she says. She yawns. "I need to get on a good schedule while I'm here. I have so much to do on the book!"

"How much?"

"Most of it," she confesses.

Annie tsk-tsks. "Oh, Louisa. You poor thing. Where'd your sabbatical go?"

This is an *excellent* question. Where *did* her sabbatical go? In the fall she was just getting used to her new life and routines, and there were so many things around the house she and Steven simply couldn't get to with both of them working so much. Once everyone was off to school and work, therefore, Louisa allowed herself the luxury of tackling one small home project per day, culled from a list she kept tacked to the bulletin board. But! As anyone who has ever undertaken a home organization project in a perennially disorganized home knows, there is no such thing as a project that exists in a vacuum—setting the pun aside. One project begets another, begets another, and onward into eternity. So when Louisa found *one of Claire's socks* in the junk drawer in the kitchen, naturally this led her to Claire's room, which was a morass in the best of times and a certifiable federal disaster site in the worst. And let's just say this was not the best of times. Louisa spent forty-seven minutes organizing the sock drawer, another eighteen looking online for replacement pairs for all of the socks that had undergone a conscious uncoupling. By then her coffee had grown cold, and why not just make a fresh pot? Wasn't this the point of working from home, to allow a moment here or there for domestic conveniences? Anyway, think of what she was saving by not purchasing her usual morning coffee outside the house. And the disposable cup she was not using besides!

Which reminded her, she needed to order a fresh bag of coffee beans after she had found the right socks for Claire. She might just do that very quickly before she went back to work.

Days went by like this, then weeks. Every day began

fresh, full of endless possibilities, and ended on a sour note, all hope annulled.

In November, Abigail came down with the flu. Just as she got better, Claire contracted strep. Then Matty's school began a week of half days for parent-teacher conferences. After that, the holidays were upon them. There were cards to address, and gifts to shop for and hide. Lights to string. In past years Steven and Louisa might have shared some of these tasks, but with Steven working so many hours at All Ears and Louisa at home, it seemed silly not to take on the greater burden herself. She baked cookies; she attempted, and failed at, homemade marshmallows to go in the Christmas morning cocoa. Two of her stay-at-home mom friends, who thought *sabbatical* and *vacation* were synonymous, took to stopping by unannounced.

January came. A productive month! Sort of. Well, she got started, anyway. Except she had to travel to San Francisco to give a talk at a conference, and the jet lag set her back three days after she returned. January became February. February slid into March. In March she had to do two peer reviews of papers and read a graduate student's dissertation. March bled into April. Once she decided to spend the summer in Maine, there was no point in settling down for long stretches at home. She knew she'd get so much more done in Owls

Head. The breeze flowing off Penobscot Bay would clear her cluttered mind, allow her to work untrammeled. Come September, she'd turn in her book. It was simple, really. It was just time arithmetic. Sixty-four pages down, out of an expected three hundred. Two hundred and thirty-six pages to go, over—how many days? Ten weeks. Seventy days. Two hundred thirty-six divided by seventy. Well, she couldn't do math in her head, which was why she taught history and not calculus. But it seemed doable. Right? In Owls Head she'd get up early; she'd stay up late. She'd cut down on her alcohol consumption so her mind would be sharp for evening work. She'd work after the kids were tucked in.

She takes a sip of her whiskey. It goes down smooth and easy, the way she imagines a front-porch lemonade in summertime Kentucky might go down.

She will start her new schedule tomorrow. The day after, at the very latest.

6.
Kristie

Kristie *is* a fast learner—she wasn't lying to Fernando—and after two training shifts she's on the floor. The bill collectors have begun employing some new tactics: they call at different times every day, they call from different area codes. They have a lot of tricks, but what they don't have yet is Kristie's new address on Linden Street. She figures it's only a matter of time before they find it, but for now, yes, she will just turn off her phone.

At the end of her first shift she's released early, leaving more tips to the more established servers. She gets it; that's how the restaurant world works. She rolls silverware with a girl named Natalie. Natalie has long blond hair with enviable natural curl. She's going into her junior year at Northwestern. Her parents have owned a summer home in Owls Head forever, and this is the third summer she's worked at Archer's—first as a bus girl and now as a server.

"It's pretty good," she tells Kristie. "Fernando can be an asshole sometimes but the tips are good, especially if you're out on the deck."

"Everybody can be an asshole sometimes," says Kristie. "There's nothing Fernando can throw at me that I haven't already seen."

Natalie looks at Kristie, dazzled. "*Yeah,*" she says loyally. Natalie's life could not be more opposite from Kristie's. While they roll she tells Kristie a story about her boyfriend, who is doing a service project in Peru that he hopes will get him into medical school. The story is long and involved and has something to do with a shaman and a two-day hike. Eventually Kristie loses the thread of the tale because all she can think is, *who are these people? And where did they get these lives?*

"How about you?" asks Natalie. "What's your story?"

Kristie thinks about volunteering the time Jesse smoked a bad batch of K2 and ended up in the ER. "No story," she says. "I was living in Pennsylvania until recently, and I wanted to try someplace new. So here I am."

Natalie wants to see Kristie's tattoos, which are

impossible to hide all the way, even with the long-sleeved shirt Fernando has told her to wear underneath her official Archer's T-shirt.

"I love those." Natalie sighs. "I wanted to get one on my ankle, just a tiny peace sign, and my mom *flipped out*. It wasn't worth the battle, so I gave up."

A *peace sign*! thinks Kristie. A peace sign is so innocuous. Who would flip out about that?

"Did your mom care? When you got yours?" Natalie is looking earnestly at Kristie. She's so bright-eyed and unsullied; she looks like a golden retriever.

"She, ah," says Kristie. She blinks down at the silverware and shakes her head, not trusting herself to speak. "No," she whispers finally. "She didn't."

"Wow," says Natalie. "You have that kind of mom, huh? You're so lucky!"

When she's all done Kristie walks outside, tip money in her pocket. Soon she'll have to open a local bank account. She sees someone standing at the edge of the parking lot, looking out at the water, past the pebbly beach, toward the lighthouse. His hands are in his pockets. He turns when he hears her footsteps. It's . . . Danny! Gil's Garden Danny; Ships View Danny.

"Bicycle Girl," he says. He's grinning widely.

"What are you doing here?" She's grinning too; she

hardly knows him, but somehow he seems already like an old friend.

"I was in the neighborhood. I thought I'd take a chance and see if you were working. I peeked inside, and some guy with a goatee told me you'd be getting off soon."

"Fernando."

"I thought maybe we could get a drink."

Kristie doesn't want to go into the sobriety thing now, with this guy she doesn't know, so she says, "Ahhh . . ."

"Or a not-drink. A walk?"

"Maybe ice cream," she offers.

"Ice cream!" His face lights up, and she likes that. "I know a great place. But it's not in Rockland. It's in Camden. Is Camden too far?"

"What's Camden?"

"You've never been to Camden?"

She shakes her head.

"You have so much to learn! You'll love it."

Camden's downtown feels bigger than Rockland's, and livelier, though Danny explains to Kristie that it's actually smaller in both geography and population. There are people everywhere: people talking in clumps on the sidewalks, and sitting on restaurant decks, and walking their dogs and pushing strollers with sleeping children in them. Driving in they pass a small green on the side of a church with a tall white steeple. Danny parks on a side street, and they walk to an ice cream stand called River Ducks. Danny orders coffee ice cream in a cup and Kristie orders black raspberry in a sugar cone. She can't remember the last time she's eaten ice cream in a sugar cone. It's probably been fifteen years.

Danny leads her to a bridge over a small river. All along the bridge hang bright plants, and benches line the edge of the bridge. Danny explains that the plants are tended to by the hotel on the other side of the bridge. He touches a few of the plants, gently, identifying them: zinnias, lantana, million bells. He tells her that he wants to own his own company one day, or maybe take over for his boss, Gil, when he retires. They sit on one of the benches.

She asks if he's from here, and he says, "Sure am. Can't you *heah* it in my accent?" He leans hard on the second syllable, the *ah*. Then comes the question she has been expecting, and also dreading. "So, Bicycle Girl," he says. "What's your story?" While he eats his ice cream he presses his knee against hers. His knee is soft and warm and her heart jumps at the feel of it. *Calm down, heart,* she tells it. It's just a knee.

"No story," she says, same as she said to Natalie not so long ago. She concentrates on licking the drips of ice cream that are making their way down the cone.

"Everyone has a story," he says. That knee again. She presses back; it's like their knees are speaking their own language.

She tells him that her mother just died, bladder cancer, and that she wanted to start over somewhere new. She almost gets the whole sentence out without a wobble but then she thinks about this one time toward the end when her mother lifted her hands up like she was pulling at a rope. For some reason that was the saddest part of the whole thing, the pulling at the imaginary rope. Then her voice goes.

"I'm sorry," she says. She can't get the image of the hands out of her head. What were the hands reaching for? She'll never know. She turns her head away from his, blinking hard in the direction of the hotel, wondering if she can keep the tears in. "She had a hard life," she says. "And then at the end it started to get better, and then it was over."

Danny says, "Hey, hey." He puts his hand under her chin and turns her face toward his. He's so gentle that the tears come out. He takes a clump of the skinny ice cream napkins and wipes under her eyes. Then he kisses his own thumb and presses it carefully onto the spot where the tear was.

There's a little girl, maybe four or five, crossing the bridge, holding her mother's hand, probably on vacation; probably excited to be up past her bedtime. The mother also has a baby in a front pack. Kristie looks down at the girl's blue sandals but still she can feel the girl staring at her. It's disconcerting and fascinating, seeing a grown-up cry when you are a child. Kristie remembers being young and knowing that.

"I'm sorry," she says again. She doesn't look up until she's seen the blue sandals move along.

"No," says Danny. "Don't you ever apologize for being sad in front of me. Sad doesn't scare me." These feel like the nicest, most intimate words anyone has ever said to Kristie. She pulls herself together, and they finish their ice cream and walk back to Danny's truck.

The whole way back from Camden to Rockland the moon follows them; Kristie can see it out of the truck's window. She watches the moon and wonders what the catch is. There has to be a catch with this guy. There *has* to be a catch. People aren't nice like this for no reason. They just aren't. Jesse was nice sometimes, maybe a lot of times, mostly when he was wasted. Nice until he was not nice. As far as she knows Jesse is still in Miami Beach, still bartending, still partying, sleeping on the beach or in their condo, doing it all over again the next day, rinse, repeat, rinse, repeat.

Danny pulls up in front of the house on Linden Street. He remembers where it is without having to ask. The downstairs apartment is dark and quiet. *Lobstermen get up before dawn*, the landlord told her. *They'll be quiet by eight p.m.*

"Okay then," Kristie says. She doesn't want to get out of the truck; the truck feels like the best place she's been in years. She can still feel Danny's thumb on the delicate skin underneath her eye. Danny's hand finds hers and he ropes their fingers together.

She opens her mouth to tell him the truth, to tell him why she's there, to tell them that she wasn't lost the day they met. But nothing comes out. She can't say it. She can't even really think it. She just wants this moment, the innocence and first-timeness of it, to go on forever.

And then he unropes their fingers and kisses her. One hand on her back, the other hand tangled in her hair. They kiss for a really long time, then his right hand moves low on her thigh, then higher—then higher still.

When they come up for air, Kristie feels an ache deep in her groin. It's almost indecent, how turned on she is. She hasn't felt like this in a very long time. "You want to come in?" she whispers.

7.
Louisa

Time at Ships View is elastic, just as it's been since Louisa was little. An hour of reading on the porch can pass slowly, infinitely glorious, and yet the days stack quickly on top of each other, accumulating into a pile before you've even noticed. Louisa's room, the Pink Room, has two single beds and faces the ocean; it's always been her favorite room but she hasn't been here as a singleton in a long time. It's a treat to return to it every night. She falls asleep to the gentle moaning of the foghorn at the end of the Rockland breakwater and wakes to the sound of the waves slapping lightly at the rocks. She sleeps like a baby here, and her babies sleep like babies too, and time goes by and by and by.

Steven texts more often than he calls, which means that mostly she can deliver one-word answers, or answers in the form of emojis, or no answers at all. No, Louisa didn't pay the June electric bill before they left. Yes, the recycling needs to go in the building bin on Friday. How's her book going? If she doesn't want to answer it's easy enough to pretend she's been somewhere else—easy enough, in fact, to *be* somewhere else, without her phone: lying in the sun on the rocks, walking Otis in Owls Head Park, taking the kids into town for ice cream, sitting with her dad when Barbara isn't there.

The first week rolls by like this, and then the second. Louisa often wakes before everyone, fills one of the Damariscotta mugs with coffee, and sits in the quiet dining room, at the long table. She looks alternately out the giant picture window at the water, pinkish at this time of day, sometimes misty, always breathtaking, and at her mostly empty Pitcairn notebook. She has the idea that the notebook will allow her to move freely in or out of the house while capturing her brilliant thoughts, which she will then transfer to her laptop. Sometimes she writes a few words or—when she's feeling really ambitious—a sentence, but she almost always turns back to the water before going any further. *That's okay,* she tells herself. She has until September. It's only June!

One morning Louisa finds a letter addressed to Steven on the table where they put outgoing mail; they bring the mail to the Owls Head post office at the top of the hill once a day, and collect theirs at the same time. The envelope is addressed in Abigail's cursive—she must be the only kid left on the planet who writes in cursive—and the flap isn't sealed all the way. Before she has time to acknowledge what she's doing Louisa has slipped one finger inside the flap and pulled out a sheet of flowered paper that she recognizes as the paper she bought Abigail for Christmas, along with the fountain pen she had asked for. (Abigail definitely belongs in another century; she told Louisa recently that she wants to learn to whittle. *Whittle!*)

Dear Daddy,

When are you coming? I know you have to work and make your podcasts and blah blah blah but it isn't the same here without you. It's still better than Brooklyn in the summer though and I have been in the water every single day even though the warmest it has been was sixty-one degrees and usually it's colder. If you put your face right under immediately without even thinking it's bareable [sic] and that's the only way I can do it but Matty always goes in really slowly which is why he hardly ever goes under. It's so much harder if you let yourself feel the cold. Speaking of water, how is Gavin? Please tell him I said hi. He's a really good goldfish and he's been alive for thirteen months which is a pretty long time so please please please take really good care of him and don't over-feed him because overfeeding is deadly for goldfish. Just ask Claire. Remember her goldfish only lived for two weeks and even though I warned her about the food she didn't listen.

On our VERY FIRST day here you will NOT BELIEVE what happened. We found a dead seal. We had to call the Mammal People and they came and took it away on a stretcher.

We didn't see a shark bite, but that doesn't mean there wasn't one there somewhere.

See what you're missing by staying in Brooklyn? I bet you haven't found any dead bodies.

If you don't have time to write back can you please email and I can read it on the iPad. I will continue to write to you the old-fashioned way because I think that's CLASSIER.

Love, Abigail.

Louisa puts her hand on her heart and taps it twice. Children. She sticks a stamp on the envelope.

When Louisa is in Maine she takes pleasure in small tasks. In Brooklyn, small tasks plague her. (A birth-day gift for Abigail's friend Janey! An oil change for the minivan! Matty's checkup with the optometrist!) One morning Annie says she needs someone to stop by the post office to pick up the mail and then buy the lobsters for dinner from the Owls Head Lobster Company at the dock. Louisa offers to go. She's extracting her car keys from the detritus on the telephone table— Abigail's turned-over copy of *Summer of the Swans*, Claire's *sandwich crust?*—when her father comes down the stairs and says, "Are you off somewhere?"

"I am, Daddy." Louisa studies her father. He's wearing a navy-blue polo shirt and a pair of khakis. His hair is parted neatly on the side. He's freshly shaven, and he smells like the Royall Muske he's always worn. He looks . . . well, he looks normal. His eyes are clear and bright; his spine is straight. "I'm going to the post office, and then the lobster pound." She hesitates, then chastises herself for hesitating. "Do you want to come?"

He nods. "Yes. Sure, the post office and lobsters. I'll come."

The post office is only one mile away, but even so Louisa is nervous. Louisa and Martin have made the trip to the lobster pound, how many times together? A few times per summer times thirty-nine summers . . . but now she's not sure which Martin she's going to get.

They drive up the hill, passing the entrance to the

old logging roads, passing the homes—more modest than Ships View—that sit on the opposite street from the water, and Louisa finds herself thinking about her eighth-grade social studies teacher, Mrs. Wolf.

When Louisa was in her final year of middle school at the Waynflete School in Portland, Mrs. Wolf asked the Hon. Martin R. Fitzgerald to visit the eighth-grade classes to talk about his work on the Maine Superior Court, where he served before he was appointed to the supreme court. The judge was busy and could afford only forty-five minutes, so Mrs. Wolf gathered all the classes in the arts center for him to speak to everyone at once from the stage. Louisa remembers how she was horrified by the whole event—no eighth grader wants to call *more* attention to herself, for any reason. But Mrs. Wolf had been so happy to have Martin there. (Looking back from the vantage of adulthood, Louisa is pretty sure that Mrs. Wolf, a divorced single mother of eight-year-old twins, was flirting with her father.)

What does Louisa, driving now toward the Owls Head post office, remember of her father's visit to her school? She remembers that he cut an imposing figure. She remembers that his voice was deep, steady, sure. She remembers that the moment he began speaking her classmates were rapt with attention. She remembers that Clay Hansen wanted to know if any judges ever showed up to court wearing only underwear under their robes, or nothing at all! (Not that Martin knew of.) She remembers her dad's advice, which he has repeated over and over again, and that he actually believes and actually lived in his time on the courts: *Leave the world better than you found it.*

She decides to give it a try. "Daddy? Remember when you came to talk to my class in eighth grade?" She glances at him. He's nodding—but is he really remembering?

"Sure," he says. "On stage at Waynflete." He grins.

"That's right," she says. "That's right, Daddy!"

"I remember when there was a moose there," Martin says. He points to the small pond across the street from the post office. Louisa pulls into the parking lot at the little general store next to the post office and turns to her father. He remembers the moose in the pond! Her heart begins to lift.

"I remember that too," she says. "He tied up traffic for the whole day. He was *so big.* So much bigger than I ever realized a moose is."

Mail, the drive to the pound, the man in waders who doesn't even need to weigh the lobsters because he's been doing this since he was knee-high to a grasshopper and can tell by sight within a quarter-ounce what any lobster weighs. They're driving back up the hill from the harbor when Martin says, "How's Steven?"

How's Steven? Her heart lifts further. This is the first time since Louisa arrived that Martin has mentioned Steven. This is a positive sign—right? Her father remembers the past *and* the present. Maybe—and Louisa understands that this thought is contrary to decades of Alzheimer's research and basically to all of science—maybe he's getting better! Maybe his brain is untangling itself.

"He's doing pretty well," she says. "He's super busy at work." She almost considers telling Martin the whole story about Steven and their agreement. What a relief it would be, to be a child again, instead of a parent, to have somebody solve her problems instead of presenting theirs for her consumption. She rolls down the minivan's window and takes in the smell, the mix of pine and harbor and silt, and feels, for the first time since April, truly hopeful.

"When do you think you'll think about children?"

Her heart plummets. She glances at Martin.

"Daddy—" How can her father remember the name of Louisa's school from more than a quarter century ago and not his own grandchildren?

"I suppose there's plenty of time for all of that," Martin says pleasantly. "No hurry, no hurry."

"Daddy," she says.

"What?"

"Never mind." She takes the turn onto the gravel road too fast, throwing them both to the left.

She delivers her father to Barbara and finds her mother in the playroom. Her mother is working on a cross-stitch of the Owls Head Lighthouse. She's sitting in the chair by the window, but soon, Louisa knows, she'll move to the bench in the dining room, where the light gets better as the day wears on.

"Steven called while you were out," Annie says, glancing up.

Louisa's stomach clenches. "On the house phone?"

"On the house phone. He said he'd tried you a bunch of times on your cell but hadn't gotten you."

That, Louisa knows, is because she hasn't answered Steven's last few calls. She's walking a thin line between irritation at the intrusion—she's got the kids, she's got her dad, she's got her work—and fear that if she tries to lean on Steven to talk about her father she'll lose the tenuous strength she's trying to build up. Worse, what if she tries to lean on him and he's not really there? He probably has only a few minutes to talk between recording sessions or an editing marathon. He's probably so busy with All Ears he has No Ears left for her.

There's a commotion outside the playroom door and

Abigail and Matty come trooping in, followed closely by Otis, who is wearing a pair of goggles, pushed to the top of his head like ladies' sunglasses, and a life vest, the kind that are stored with the kayaks under the back porch.

"Oh, come on now," says Louisa. "Otis, you poor thing!" Otis manages to look both shamefaced and stoic. "Oh, honey," she tells him. "You're a very, very good dog to put up with everything you're asked to put up with."

"I told them not to," says Claire, bringing up the rear. "I told them he wouldn't like it." She is quivering with the injustice of it.

"If I was allowed to have a phone, I could definitely make Otis TikTok famous," says Abigail. She looks pointedly at Louisa, who says, "Forget it. Not until seventh grade."

"I could use Matty's but he won't let me."

"It's mine," snarls Matty, uncharacteristically grumpy. Hormones? He *is* almost thirteen. Louisa isn't equipped to handle boy hormones on her own. Now she's irritated with Steven all over again. "I don't have to share it if I don't want to. Use the iPad if you need to use something."

"I don't have a TikTok account. Mom, can I get one?"

"Definitely not." They've been over this, but Louisa is too tired of talking about it even to say, We've been over this.

"Otis doesn't want to be TikTok famous!" says Claire. "He just wants to be himself, you're making him *miserable!*" She makes little cooing noises at Otis and eases him out of the goggles and the life vest. Otis, exhausted from the ordeal, melts to the floor and puts his chin in his paws with a great and long-suffering sigh. Claire rubs his ear, and Louisa thinks about her father and feels the fissures in her heart expand.

8.
Kristie

Danny doesn't officially move in with Kristie so much as he stops sleeping at his mom's house and starts keeping his toothbrush, all of his Gil's Gardening shirts, and his special beer mug from the 2011 Rockland Lobster Festival at the Linden Street apartment. He's still looking for another place to buy, but he's not in a hurry. Kristie hopes Danny never finds a place to buy. She could go on like this forever! Some days she almost forgets why she came here in the first place.

One morning halfway through June she finds an envelope with money in it on the little kitchen table when she gets out of bed to start the coffee. (Even this— coffee for two! Waking up next to somebody without a hangover, without shame or regret—feels like a little gift every single day.) She turns on the coffeepot and climbs back into bed, snaking her arm around Danny's back, pressing the envelope against his bare chest.

"What's this?" she asks, half worried that Danny is paying her for sex.

He turns to her, opens one eye and smiles. "My share of the rent," he says. "Want me to make eggs?" Danny has a real way with eggs—he chops scallions and melts cheddar into them, or cooks them with tomatoes and minced basil. He fries them with a perfect crisp of olive oil and puts them between wedges of ciabatta from Atlantic Baking Company. Kristie, who has worked so long in restaurants, subsisting mainly on family meals made for the staff before shifts started, isn't much of a cook.

She peeks in the envelope. "No way," she says. "This is way more than half. Take it back."

"Utilities, then."

"Utilities are included." She wants Danny to be able to save enough to become his own Gil, the way he wants to be. And yet. She's worried about money all the time. She's working as hard as she can at Archer's, and the tips are good, but she's not sure how she'll ever get ahead. She doesn't understand how anybody gets ahead who didn't start out ahead. She thinks about the kids running across the grass at Ships View, from the massive house to their very own stretch of water. *Those* kids started out ahead. Everybody in that house started out ahead. Kristie started out behind, and behind she remains.

"I'm not taking it back," says Danny. "So either you keep it, or I guess I could throw it out the window."

"Thank you," she whispers into his shoulder. In Miami Beach she paid most of the rent for her and Jesse's apartment. Jesse made a lot of money bartending, more than she did as a server, which was saying a lot, but money flowed out of Jesse like water out of a bucket with a hole. When he was wasted or high he bought round after round for people he didn't know. He bought expensive drugs. He bought motorcycles and clothes. Tears prick her eyes at Danny's thoughtfulness, at his not-Jesse-ness.

There's more. The kitchen faucet breaks, and Danny fixes it. There are bare spots in the lawn and Danny sprinkles grass seed on them, watering them diligently until they begin to grow, even though the lawn is not Kristie's responsibility. He asks her if he thinks the landlord would mind if he planted a row of begonias along the front of the building. Gil had extra from one of the houses on North Shore Drive and he gave them to Danny. "I'd just hate to see them die," he says. "They're hardy. They're survivors, that's why I like them."

"Go ahead," says the landlord, when Kristie asks him.

She watches out the window as Danny puts the plants in the ground, settling the dirt gently around each of them, giving them a comforting pat. She thinks, *I am falling in love with this man.* She knows that is not what she came here for—but knowing that doesn't appear to be stopping her.

On Kristie's nights off they watch Netflix—Danny has a subscription. They make it through season one of *Ozark* and begin season two. Sometimes they go out to dinner. They've been to Ada's Kitchen and In Good Company and Claws, where you order at the counter and eat at picnic tables looking out at the harbor. Kristie can't believe that she's only been in Maine a little over three weeks. She can't believe she's the same person who once lived in Miami Beach, underrested, undernourished, overpartied.

They spend a lot of time in bed. Danny's the first lover she's had for any length of time while she's been sober, and she marvels at the time they take with each other. She marvels at the way she can feel each of his quad muscles; she marvels at the strength of his back and biceps from all of the time he spends working outside. She marvels at how much he admires her body, and how much she wants him to.

The house Danny recently sold, she learns, he had

shared with his ex-girlfriend, Elizabeth, who cheated on him with Danny's best friend, Stu. How could *anyone* cheat on Danny? she wonders. He is *perfect*.

When they lie in bed waiting for sleep he traces circles on the inside of her elbow and tells her stories about all the houses he works at with Gil. There's a six-bedroom in Rockport that used to be a Methodist church, and a waterfront Owls Head beauty with a barrel-vaulted-ceiling porch looking out over a quarter-acre annual garden edged against a sandy beach. There are homes in Camden with Olympic-size swimming pools and harbor views. Kristie tries to ask questions about all of them, but, of course, the only one she wants to know about is Ships View. What is the family like? How about the matriarch, Annie, what's *she* like? And her husband? Danny has said he's not well, there are health care people about, but he doesn't know the specifics. The family is private.

"But what do you think he's sick with?" she asks. "If you had to guess."

"Hey hey, Nosy Nellie," says Danny. "Why so fascinated?" He kisses her on the top of the head, and her heart starts to beat faster, and she reminds herself to be careful.

"Rich people are interesting," she says. "I'd just love to see that house again, that's all. It really spoke to me."

"One rich person," Danny says, "has more problems than people like us put together. I guarantee it."

"I don't know about that," says Kristie.

One day they are planning to shop for groceries at Hannaford, but Danny gets a call from Mrs. Fitzgerald, who wants him to come and work through yet another to-do list. There's an outdoor lightbulb that's burned out and requires a trip up a long ladder; there's a hornet's nest under the porch; the latch on the gate that leads to the water is broken. The money the Fitzgeralds pay Danny is too good to turn down—but, he says, he's sure Gil wouldn't mind if Kristie used the truck while Danny works. She can drop him off, do the grocery shopping, and swing back by for him after.

"Really?"

"Sure. You're a good driver, right?"

"I'm an *excellent* driver. And my sense of direction is known the world over." She pulls down the gravel drive at Ships View and idles, waiting for Danny to get out.

"Do you have a second? I want to show you something."

Her breath quickens. "Here? At this house?"

"In the garden. The peonies are blooming, I want you to see them. They bloom early in the season, and then they're gone. Poof."

She puts the truck in park and follows Danny around the side yard. She can't believe she's *this close* to *this house*. She also can't believe, now that she's seeing more of it, how near this house is to the water. She imagines that from the upstairs bedrooms you might not be able to see the slender stretch of grass that lies between the house and the rocky coast; you might feel as though you're on a ship. Just imagine, waking up every day in a house like this. Just imagine. These people have problems?

The garden Danny leads her to is on the far side of the yard and is encircled by gray rocks. "Here," says Danny proudly. "These are officially called Peonia Sonoma Welcome. I've been trying to grow this variety forever, but I've never gotten it to take." The flowers are the palest, palest pink, nearly white, on the outside and a darker pink toward the center. They are really lovely. Danny crouches down and gently touches one of the leaves. He's as tender with it as one might be with a newborn, with a kitten.

"They're beautiful," says Kristie. "They really are." Then she has an idea. "Danny?" she says. "I'm sorry, this is awkward, but I really need the bathroom. Really badly. Do you think I could pop inside the house quickly? Before I go to the store? I drank too much coffee." She waits—has she gone too far? Danny is still inspecting the peonies. His brow is furrowed. "Danny?"

"Sure," he says, looking up. "There's a half bath right inside the door on the other side of the house. Here, I'll show you." He walks her around the house, past the wide porch that faces the water. The land dips and then rises again. There is a garbage can back here, and a large green recycling container, and a separate bin that says BLACK EARTH COMPOST on the side. Danny points to a plain wooden door tucked inside a little nook and says, "Right in there."

"You sure it's okay?"

"Of course."

"I'll be quick," she says.

She enters the bathroom and closes the door behind her and takes a deep breath. She's here! She's in the house. The bathroom is tiny—there's just enough room for a sink and a toilet and a towel rack that holds a towel with lobsters printed on it. She can't believe it, but she's here.

There are handprints on the wall in primary colors, named and dated in black ink. Louisa, 1987, red. Matty, Abigail, Claire, 2016, in red, yellow, blue. Claire's handprint is *tiny* in 2015. Kristie knows she should hurry out of there before she's discovered, but she can't help taking a little longer to stare at the handprints;

she finds them mesmerizing, all the lines and whorls in each palm, all the *life* stamped there on the wall.

My mother has been in this house, she thinks.

She's not sure if Danny is waiting for her outside, so she flushes the toilet, runs the water, and opens the door. What will she say if anybody sees her? She'll say the truth—that she's with Danny, and he told her it was okay to use the bathroom, that it was an emergency.

Kristie's brain tells her to go right out the door she came in, but her heart—her heart tells her to turn the other way, into the kitchen. She sees wide, gleaming countertops and shiny stainless appliances. She sees a deep farmhouse sink. She sees a loaf of bread on a cutting board; she sees a wicker basket full of nectarines. She sees no people. She listens carefully. She doesn't hear anyone either. She sees a doorway that must lead to the dining room, and she sees one end of a wooden table. Before she can stop herself she's walking into the dining room, and she sees that the table reaches the full length of the long room, all the way to the giant picture window that looks out on the rocks and the water. From here she can actually see the pier attached to Archer's. There's a pair of binoculars on the end of the table nearest the window, and her hands itch to pick them up and lift them to her face.

But, no, that would be going too far. Already she's

gone too far! Then she hears footsteps on the stairs, and a voice call "Anything else from Hannaford? Mom? I'm going right now." *Louisa.*

Kristie hightails it back through the kitchen and out the door she came in, her heart hammering.

"You okay?" says Danny, coming around the side of the house. She jumps. He's holding a trowel and grinning. "You look like you saw a ghost."

I did, she wants to say. *I saw ghosts everywhere.* But, no, that's not quite right. What she saw inside that house wasn't so much a ghost as it was an outline, a sketch of everything she herself doesn't have. Kristie's feelings at this moment are so complicated, and their roots run so deep and spread so far, that she can't possibly illuminate them to Danny even if she wants to, even if she tries.

She hurries back to the truck and waits in it until she sees Louisa walk out the front door of the house with a straw bag slung over her shoulder. Finally Kristie gets a good look at her. Louisa Fitzgerald McLean looks just like she looks on the faculty pages of the NYU website: thick dark hair, thin pale face, small frame. She's frowning now, while in the photo she was smiling. Kristie watches from Gil's truck as Louisa climbs into a minivan with New York plates and pulls out of the driveway. Thirty seconds later, Kristie follows her.

In Hannaford Kristie makes an art out of trailing Louisa without being seen. Kristie thought Louisa would be an organized shopper—she is, after all, a mother of three, and she has brought reusable grocery bags—but, no, she's haphazard. No list, no apparent rhyme or reason to what she picks up: two lemons, four tomatoes, asparagus.

In the bakery section Louisa selects a baguette. Her phone rings, and she stops near the muffins, pulls it out of her bag and looks at it, then puts it back in the bag without answering. Louisa pauses by the seafood, staring for a moment at the lobsters clambering over each other in the glass case, but the smell here makes Kristie feel queasy so she has to take a detour into the pharmacy. She puts a couple of items in her own cart— she's low on shampoo, and Danny has asked for razor blades, potato chips, and cereal—and by the time she finds Louisa again Louisa's phone is ringing once more. The ringing stops and starts again.

Kristie thinks about the woman who worked in billing at UPMC Altoona, who'd shaken her head when Kristie went to see her two days after Sheila died.

"I can't pay these," Kristie said, holding out the stack of bills.

The woman had soft brown eyes and the pallid skin of a person who rarely goes outdoors. A tired smile.

She had pictures of grandchildren on her desk, and a Big Gulp with a straw she sucked on as she looked at the bills. "I'm sorry, sweetie," she said. "There's nothing I can do to help you. You can run, but you can't hide. They'll find you eventually."

Kristie gets in the checkout line behind Louisa, and knows—she absolutely *knows*—she shouldn't do this, but she lets her cart bump into Louisa's, and not gently either. Hard enough to spark a reaction.

Why? Why does Kristie Turner, formerly of Altoona, Pennsylvania, now of Rockland, Maine, by way of Miami Beach, Florida, want Louisa McLean to turn around? Kristie wants what we all want—it's one of the most innate, most human desires there is. She wants to be seen.

Louisa turns around. She's annoyed.

"So sorry," murmurs Kristie. "My mistake."

"No worries," says Louisa. She doesn't smile, but she doesn't frown either. Louisa McLean's eyes, a very light blue with a dark rim around them, would have been startling had Kristie not known them so well: they are her very own eyes.

That evening Kristie is waiting to pick up her chowders for her three-top when Fernando comes up to her. He's standing too close, his hip actually touching hers. She moves away, and he moves close again.

"Don't forget to garnish the specials," he says.

She looks at him. "I never forget to garnish the specials."

She drops the chowders at the three-top and goes back for the entrées for her two-top. He's there again, lurking near the silverware setups. Natalie is waiting to pick up her order too.

"You never stay for the shift drink," Fernando says. "How come? Don't you like us?"

"I guess I have better things to do," says Kristie. Her elbow bumps the silverware tray.

"Watch it, New Girl," says Fernando.

Natalie rolls her eyes on Kristie's behalf.

9.
The Children

On the day of the summer solstice Granny announces that she'd like to treat everyone to lunch at her favorite restaurant in town, Archer's on the Pier.

"All of us?" asks Matty. He's worried that his grandfather may come along. What if his grandfather takes off all of his clothes and walks naked on the pier? What if he starts talking about something that happened in, like, 1903, and they all have to pretend to be interested and attentive?

"Most of us," says Granny. "Your grandfather will stay behind with Barbara."

Claire, who is still wearing her nightshirt, doesn't want to put on shorts. Abigail is reading on the back porch and doesn't want to put her book down. Matty would prefer to eat lunch at home—he was hoping to take a peanut butter and jelly sandwich down to the rocks alone. But one look from their mother and they decide not to mention their individual desires. She has her don't-you-dare face on.

"Sounds fabulous, Mom," says Louisa, in her fake-cheery voice.

Annie sits in the passenger seat, next to Louisa. The children crowd into the middle row even though the minivan has a perfectly respectable third row that is no longer taken up by luggage, and almost immediately the squabbling begins. Claire shrieks when Abigail tells her that because she's the smallest she should have the middle seat all the time.

"Then sit in the third row," says Abigail. Claire wails that she gets carsick in the third row. It isn't fair—it's never fair. The youngest always gets the short end. Nobody understands, is what Claire thinks. Nobody ever, ever understands.

In general the children get along better in Owls Head than in Brooklyn—without the distractions of school and friends their vast differences in age, gender, and temperament seem less pronounced. They play cards; they play outdoors; on rainy days they build elaborate forts in the living room by draping blankets over the stalwart furniture. When they do turn on the TV in the playroom they hardly argue over what to watch.

But in the car the gloves come off. Their mother shoots them a warning glance in the rearview mirror.

At Archer's they are seated by the hostess at a table on the deck, with a stellar view of the pleasure boats moored and docked. It's a postcard-perfect day, the kind of day they all dream about through the long winter. One by one, they start to feel more festive. It is, after all, a treat to be out here. The deck is covered by a canopy. A slight breeze travels off the water. The restaurant is busy. The hostess pours their water and tells Granny and Louisa that their server, Kristie, will be with them in a minute. After a few minutes have gone by the hostess returns.

"I'm sorry," she says. "We just got slammed. I'm going to take your drink order, and *then* Kristie will be with you."

"I'm fine with the water," says Matty. Abigail and Claire each order a Shirley Temple, casting a sidelong glance at their mother to see if they will be shot down. Matty's mom opens her mouth and raises her eyebrows, but Granny says, "Oh, *let* them. It's summer vacation." Then she orders two glasses of wine, one for herself and one for Matty's mom.

"She'll be right with you, I promise," says the hostess. "You're the very next table she'll be coming to." She points to a server three tables away, writing down an order on a small white pad. "In the meantime, I'm going to grab your drinks."

"She looks familiar to me," says Louisa. "The server she pointed to. I swear I've seen her somewhere before."

Abigail and Claire have made it through half their Shirley Temples by the time the server arrives.

"Louisa, go ahead," says Granny. Louisa asks for the fish tacos. Granny orders the crab club with no mayonnaise. Matty: the farmhouse burger. Abigail and Claire both order grilled cheese off the children's menu.

"Are you sure you don't want something a little more sophisticated, girls?" asks Granny. "After all, this place is known for its seafood, about as fresh as you can get."

"No thank you," say the girls in unison. They are back to coloring their children's menus very intently.

"I'll get this order right in," says the server. Her eyes flick back and forth, and she's tapping her pen against her ordering pad in a way that makes her seem nervous. Matty doesn't blame her. Granny makes him nervous too.

"I'm sorry, dear, what did you say your name was?" Granny asks.

"Kristie. If you need anything."

Claire looks up from her coloring and says, "What's your name if we *don't* need anything?" Matty kicks her under the table and Claire says, "*What?*"

"Are you here for the summer, Kristie?" Granny asks. "Or are you a local? I don't believe I've seen you before." Abigail rolls her eyes; it's just like Granny to assume she should know everyone in town, in every restaurant.

"I—uh. I just moved here, actually."

"Oh, how interesting." Claire thinks that from the way Granny's lips are pinched together it doesn't look like she thinks it's very interesting at all. "From where?"

"Pennsylvania."

"Lovely. What part?"

The server chews her lip.

"Mom," says Louisa. "I'm sure she has other tables to get to. Look how busy it is."

"You wouldn't know it," says Kristie. "It's a small town."

"I might know it."

"Altoona."

"Ah," says Granny, her eyes darting away. "Altoona's not so small. I know it." She drains her glass. "Two more glasses of the Whispering Angel, Kristie." (Claire notes that Granny forgot to say "please," which is an unforgivable transgression when *Claire* forgets, but nobody says anything to Granny. Oh, the world is unfair! But Whispering Angel sounds lovely. Who wouldn't want to be told a secret by an *angel*?)

"She *really* looks familiar to me," says Louisa when the server has departed.

By the time the food arrives Matty's stomach is legitimately grumbling. The farmhouse burger looks delectable—it features an over-easy egg along with bacon and Swiss cheese—and Louisa's fish tacos, just as good. Abigail and Claire are delighted with the grilled cheese. Only Annie is frowning at her plate.

"I ordered this without mayonnaise," she says.

"Oh, I'm sorry! That must be my mistake. I'm new. I'm still learning the computer system. Would you like me to bring it back to the kitchen?"

"Yes please," says Annie. Her lips are pressed together so hard they've almost disappeared, and her words are clipped.

Abigail shoots her eyebrows to the sky and glances at Matty. *Granny never talks this way to service people,* is what Abigail is thinking. Right? Matty agrees silently, reading her glance. If anything, Granny is kinder than she needs to be to grumpy Pauline. And she's very polite to Barbara, and Danny, who does the yard work. She's polite to everyone!

"Sorry," says the server. She scoops up the plate, flustered. "I'll have them put a rush on this. It won't be long."

At the end of the meal, Kristie brings the check and explains that the manager took off Annie's meal because of the mistake with the mayonnaise.

"You didn't have to do that," says Louisa, and at the same time Granny says, "Thank you," and hands over a credit card. When Kristie returns with the slip for Granny to sign she says, "Thank you, Mrs. Fitzgerald."

"I don't like when they do that," says Granny as she signs the slip.

"Do what?" Louisa asks.

"Say your name like that when they hand the credit card back to you. Like they know you!"

"Oh, Mom." Louisa rolls her eyes. "Privacy is over, didn't you know that?" She says she needs to duck into the bathroom before they head home, so it is only the children left for Annie to address when she says, "I should hope that's not true."

10.

Kristie

Two of Kristie's two-tops get sat at the same time. Kristie takes a deep breath: she's still shaking, off her game. She mixes up the specials with the first table and has to go back and tell them it's halibut, not swordfish. She delivers the drinks to both tables, the meals to her four-top, and tells Natalie, who's working the other station on the deck, that she's going to the bathroom.

She splashes cold water on her face and dries it with a scratchy paper towel. Her hands are shaking and she presses them to her cheeks to make them be still. She considers herself in the mirror.

It's not such a ridiculous coincidence that the McLean/Fitzgerald clan would eat at Archer's while Kristie is working. Rockland is lousy with restaurants, sure, but Archer's has one of the best outdoor seating options, with beautiful views of the harbor, the moored sailboats, the occasional one-hundred-foot-plus yacht.

Louisa, of course, she recognized from Hannaford, from the house, from all of the research she'd done before that; Matty she recognized from the photo of the cross-country race. The two little girls she's never seen—Louisa's Instagram is private, and Kristie was not bold enough to submit a follower request. But the person Kristie really wanted—needed—to see wasn't here. Martin Fitzgerald. Why did he not join his family for lunch? Danny has said he is ill, but he hasn't said what kind of ill, or how serious the illness is.

Does Annie Fitzgerald know who Kristie is? She did press her to say Altoona—but maybe she is the kind of person who always wants to know where a server is from. If she knows who she is she wasn't exactly happy to see her.

Well, what did Kristie expect? A welcome wagon, a kiss on the forehead, an invitation to Sunday supper?

Suddenly grief for her mother rolls over her in waves and she worries she'll start crying again. She needs to get out there and serve the halibut. But thinking about the halibut her grief is replaced by a roiling nausea. She turns into one of the stalls and is sick in the toilet. She hears the door to the bathroom open, and then the door to the other stall. The person in the other stall uses the bathroom, then flushes. Kristie steels herself and opens the door of the stall, emerging at the same time as . . . Louisa. Of course. They head toward the sinks together, as if they are dancers in a choreographed number. Kristie splashes more cold water on her face and reaches for a paper towel.

"Hey, you okay?" Louisa asks.

"Yeah, I just—yeah. Yes. I'm fine, thank you."

In the mirror they regard each other. Louisa's blue eyes are softer and kinder than they were at the grocery store. Maybe this is because of the wine she had with lunch, or maybe she's simply in a better mood.

"I got it." Louisa snaps her fingers. "You looked familiar to me and now I'm remembering . . . I saw you in Hannaford, right? Last week?"

"Maybe," says Kristie. "I'm not sure."

"And, oh, hey, by the way. I'm sorry if my mom was rude to you. She's not usually like that." Louisa looks down and tells the sink, "She's been under a lot of stress lately. My dad's sick—well, I won't bore you with the details, but she's not herself."

"Don't worry about it," says Kristie. "Hazard of the job. I'm used to it."

"You *sure* you're okay?"

Kristie nods. "I'm just tired. Thank you. I've been working a lot. But I'm not sick. I don't want you to think that I served you food while I have like a stomach flu or something."

"Maybe you're pregnant."

"No!" says Kristie, horrified.

Louisa shrugs. "I mean, I don't know you from Adam, but if you're tired, and you got sick for no reason—if I were you, I might take a pregnancy test. If nothing else just to rule it out. Trust me. I've been through it three times." She swings the door open and steps back into the restaurant.

Kristie waits a beat, then leaves the bathroom herself. Fernando is waiting for her. "You're not supposed to take a break when you have tables," he says.

"It was an emergency," Kristie says. "A female matter." That explanation typically renders men quiet.

He considers her. "Your pretty eyes are all red. Either you were crying in there or getting high."

"I'm not high," she says, trying to move past him.

"You smell nice," he says. "What's that perfume you've got on there?" He sniffs at the air around her neck. He's so close that she can see the little dark hairs he missed when he shaved.

"Eau de Kitchen," says Kristie. It's a joke, obviously, but she's not smiling and Fernando doesn't smile either.

"You'd better watch yourself, New Girl," he says.

"I have a name."

"Not to me, you don't." He puts his hand on her arm.

To keep from smacking him, Kristie bites the inside of her cheek so hard she thinks she's probably drawn blood. Restaurants are full of Fernandos. Another one is nothing she can't handle. She shakes his hand off her arm and stops short of telling him to screw himself. She needs this job.

11.
Louisa

As she drives home Louisa's eyes flick to her children in the rearview mirror. Matty and Abigail are each looking out their respective windows and Claire, in the middle seat, always in the middle seat, is looking straight ahead, her lips tucked and her eyes narrowed, as though she is concentrating on memorizing a physics equation. The wine has made Louisa sleepy, almost slipping over the edge into cranky; she's already behind on her three-plus pages a day, but she won't get any work done without a nap first. They probably should have stayed home and given the children peanut butter and jelly sandwiches to take down to the rocks after all. The day has grown darker: clouds scudding by in front of the car, the air through her cracked window carrying an unexpected chill. Maybe it's those slight alterations in mood and atmosphere that feel portentous, or maybe it's something more nebulous and internal, but either way when Louisa pulls the minivan into the driveway and the door opens and Barbara comes out of the house—not running, not exactly, she doesn't seem like someone to whom running would come naturally—but moving quickly, holding the cordless house phone, what happens next seems like it might have been inevitable all along.

"Oh, no," says Annie. "No."

"What?" says Claire. Annie shakes her head and opens her door, out of the car in an instant. Abigail's eyes go wide, and they all see now that Barbara is crying. One by one, they disembark.

"I only went to visit the ladies' room!" says Barbara. Her cheeks are red and her voice is wobbling. "Not even thirty seconds, and he was *gone*. I've looked everywhere. Everywhere."

"Did you call the police?" Annie asks.

"I was wondering if I should. But I thought, he must be somewhere in the house. He couldn't have gone far! So I started with the downstairs—"

"Of course you should have called the police," snaps Annie. "Here, give me the phone. I'll do it."

First to come out to the house is a deputy officer—

so young, he can hardly have had time to earn a high school diploma, baby pudge still visible in his cheeks, kind blue eyes, short-sleeved dark uniform with the name TREMBLAY over the right pocket.

Then the doorbell rings again, and Louisa opens the door, and her heart thumps twice, then a third time, because although it's been more than twenty years, she recognizes the chin dimple and the brown eyes and for a second she's sixteen again, riding on a Boston Whaler, the wind blowing back her hair and the ocean spray salting her face.

"Detective Mark Harding," says the owner of the dimple and the eyes, putting out his hand. "I know there's a deputy officer on the scene responding to the missing person call. I'm here to coordinate a more thorough investigation, should one be needed."

"I know your name," she says, putting out her own hand. "Mark, it's Louisa."

He squints at her. He stands back, looks up at the house, then back at her, and it sounds corny and cliched to say a smile spreads across his face, but that's exactly what it does, taking its sweet time to get from one end to the other.

"Louisa Fitzgerald," he says. "I didn't make the connection, when I first heard the address. Louisa! It's been a long time."

"Yeah," she says. "It's been a really long time." She's grinning, despite the gravity of the situation. "Sorry, where are my manners? Come in. Come in! Meet the kids."

"Hey, kids," says Mark Harding, nodding at Matty and Claire, who are standing near the telephone table. (Where is Abigail?)

"My mother is with Barbara, my dad's caregiver, and the officer, outside," says Louisa. "They're going over where my dad was last time this happened. This is Matty, and this is Claire. And Abigail is—guys, where's Abigail?"

Claire shrugs; Matty shrugs. "Well, there's one more around here somewhere," says Louisa. "The middle one."

"Three kids!" says Mark. He turns to Louisa, and she arranges her face in a way that could either say, Aw, shucks, it's nothing, in my spare time I care for foster puppies and read to the blind, or, I know! It's not what I would have predicted for myself either. "It's great to meet all of you, even under these circumstances. I'm sure we'll find your grandfather quickly. Not to worry." The past sits between Louisa and Mark on a sturdy invisible table, and each waits to see if the other will pick it up first. The boat; a kiss; a teenaged love triangle. "Your mother and I used to know each other, when we were teenagers."

"Mommy wasn't a teenager," says Claire immediately.

"Of course I was a teenager," says Louisa.

"Why aren't you wearing a uniform?" asks Matty, looking suspiciously at the chinos and tie.

"I'm a detective," Mark says. "It's the sergeants and deputies who wear the uniforms. Sorry to disappoint." He smiles. "But I have a badge. See?" He points.

"What about a gun?"

"Matty!" says Louisa.

"What? I'm just curious."

"It's not a problem," Mark tells Louisa. To Matty he says, "Yes, sir," patting his jacket. "A concealed firearm is part of the job."

"Do you ever have to use it?" asks Claire, and Mark hesitates.

"You don't have to answer that," says Louisa.

"Yeah, okay. I think I'll plead the Fifth if you don't mind."

"Well, what's the plan for finding Grandpa?" This is one of Claire's favorite phrases, picked up somewhere along the line from grown-ups and sometimes employed in unexpected ways: *What's the plan for finding my other sneaker?* Or, *What's the plan for ever getting a puppy in this household?* She's looking at Mark Harding.

"Well," he says. "If the officers don't locate him

right away, which nine times out of ten they do, we'll coordinate a search. First thing we might do is bring in a K-9 to attempt a track."

"A police dog!" Claire breathes. "I'd like to meet that dog."

"What if the dog doesn't work?" asks Matty. His face has the terrified look he gets before cross-country races.

"If the search becomes prolonged, we would utilize other options."

"What other options?" Louisa's heartbeat picks up. She imagines her father wandering around, confused. She thinks about the tangles in his brain.

"We'd call in the Maine Warden Service to set up a command post. We'd get some planes in the air and coordinate search teams and volunteers to conduct grid searches. But like I said, I don't think we'll get to that point." He looks at Louisa and says, "Really, I don't."

Louisa takes a deep breath and tries to calm her mind. She wants to believe Mark. "Well, here," she says. Her voice sounds shaky. "No reason to gather by the telephone table. Come in the living room, at least."

Mark sits on the couch, with Claire sitting right next to him. She must be securing a top spot in case the police dog arrives. Mark says, "I can't believe our summer paths have never crossed before this."

"I know. But we're not usually here for the whole summer, usually just a week or two."

"This summer we're here for a long time," explains Claire. "Daddy stayed home to work." And then, although nobody has asked for elaboration, "He works for a start-up. In Brooklyn. He works all the time. She takes a breath. *"All the time."*

"I see," says Mark. He smiles again. When he smiles the corners of his eyes crinkle up in a way that is unfairly more attractive on a man than on a woman. "What's he starting up, then?"

Both children look at Louisa expectantly.

"Oh, it's sort of complicated," says Louisa. That's not true, so she continues, "It's not really that complicated. It's a podcasting company. It's pretty simple actually. They make podcasts. They're looking to be acquired, so it's a lot of long hours . . ." Her voice trails off. "They're in a delicate part of the process, with funding and all of that. And suddenly everyone and their sister is making podcasts, so there's a lot of pressure to stand out."

"Also you've been fighting a lot," adds Claire unhelpfully.

"Claire!" say Matty. Instantly Louisa flushes.

"What?" says Claire, unperturbed. "It's only the truth."

"Not *fighting*," says Louisa. "Discussing." She frowns warningly at Claire.

Mark Harding, Knox County detective, laughs—a startling, full-throated laugh that is instinctively as familiar to her as the eyes and the dimple. They'd laughed all the time that summer, Louisa and Mark and Nicole. "I'm twice divorced," he says. "Believe me, I get it."

"Twice!" She doesn't mean to grimace, but it happens anyway.

"I know," he says, shaking his head. "It's at least once too many. One divorce can be the other person's fault—two, well, you might have to look in the mirror."

If I keep talking, thinks Louisa, *I can distract myself from worrying about my father.* So she keeps talking. "Your family was only ever here for the summer, just like mine. How'd you end up here full-time?"

"Wife Number One got me used to the winters."

"And Wife Number Two kept you here?"

"Something like that." A wry smile.

"I'm on sabbatical from my job," Louisa says. She feels the need to make sure Mark doesn't see her as a mother who doesn't work while her husband puts in impressively long hours. "I'm writing a book, actually. I'll be doing a good amount of work on that this summer. Or at least that's the plan, assuming the cooperation of these angels." She looks around. "Speaking of the angels, where *is* Abigail? You guys, where's your sister?"

Matty and Claire both shrug.

"Is that her?" asks Mark, turning to point out the long rectangular windows that look from the living room onto the porch and the lawn beyond. "Out there? Louisa, is that your father with her?"

The next morning Louisa finds this letter waiting to go out:

Dear Daddy,
We had a lot of excitement when we got back from lunch at Archer's today. Grandpa was gone!
Barbara who is Grandpa's aide was crying. She said she had only turned her back to go to the bathroom, and when she did Grandpa was dozing on the porch. She was positive she had time to VISIT THE LADIES' ROOM as she put it. But when she came back from the bathroom he was gone!
Poof!
Naturally everybody went crazy. Granny called the police. You know how there are all of those woods right across the street? The old logging roads? One of the police went to look for him there. Barbara got in her car to drive up toward the post office.

But guess what? In the end it was ME who found him!

I had what I guess you could call a HUNCH and I walked down the grass and through the gate and down the stairs, and there was Grandpa, sitting on a flat rock. It was a rock you couldn't have seen from looking out the window so that's why nobody saw him.

He wasn't doing anything. He was just looking out at the ocean with one hand on each knee. Have you ever looked at Grandpa's hands, Daddy? They are absolutely COVERED with AGE SPOTS. I hope that doesn't happen to you when you get old.

I approached WITH CAUTION. I was thinking of the diseased brain Mommy showed us online, with all of the tangles.

I said, "Grandpa?"

He turned his head toward me. I wasn't sure if he'd be confused but he gave me a smile and said, "There you are!"

Then he said the most surprising thing. He said, "It's you I've been looking for all this time."

Well, I couldn't help but feel flattered about THAT.

"Here I am," I said.

Then he said, "Sit here, young lady, beside me."

So I sat.

Then Grandpa said, "You know I never meant to hurt you."

And I was like, "Whaaaaaa?" Inside my head. But what I said out loud was, "You didn't hurt me. You've never hurt me at all." I tried to make my voice soothing, the way Mommy does, and Granny too, when they're talking to him. I had the feeling that Grandpa had me confused with someone else. At that point I stopped being flattered.

Then you know what Grandpa said? He said, "In the end, you see, there was simply too much at stake. I had no choice."

I felt it was very important at that moment to say exactly the right thing. Mommy has said that if Grandpa is confused about something it's better to JUST GO WITH IT rather than try to correct him.

Grandpa looked so sad that I said, "I understand. It's okay."

Then he said, "What's your name?" I thought about saying one of the names I wish was mine. Tallulah. Brittany. Clarissa. But in the end I came out with the truth.

And you know what Grandpa said? He said, "A lovely name, Abigail. I feel as though I knew someone else with that name once . . ."

And I was like, "Duh. You do. Me, your oldest granddaughter." But I didn't say that out loud because I was still trying to GO WITH IT.

Then I remembered that everyone would be looking for him so I said, "We need to go, Grandpa." And I stood up and held out my hand and he put his spotted old hand into mine and I tried to be okay with that and not look too closely at the skin.

I reminded him to be careful on the rocks. You know how slippery it can get, with the seaweed.

Then hand in hand we went up the steps and across the grass and to the back porch.

Phew! Sorry this letter is so long! As Granny would say, we had ourselves a day.

When are you coming? Please ELUCIDATE.

ELUCIDATE means to EXPLAIN OR MAKE CLEAR. I learned that from Granny's dictionary.

Love,
Abigail

This is how the story begins. In 2006 Steven McLean was visiting his college girlfriend, Aggie Baumfeld (Boston College, go Eagles!), at her apartment in Boston's Back Bay, where she lived while procuring her MBA at MIT's Sloan School. Aggie resided on the corner of Newbury Street and Clarendon, in a sweet two-bedroom with an eat-in kitchen. *Nobody* in grad school had an extra bedroom and an eat-in kitchen, but Aggie's rent came straight out of the pocket of her grandfather in Minnesota, a real estate magnate.

On this particular Friday night Steven McLean, a copy editor at the *Village Voice,* left New York on the 4:05 Amtrak Acela—a splurge, he usually took the bus, and if he took Amtrak it was never the Acela—which landed him at Back Bay station at 7:16. Approximately seventeen minutes later he was using the spare key Aggie had made for him to let himself into her apartment; thirty seconds after that, he was listening with shock, dismay, and *possibly* (but really only later would he realize this) a modicum of relief to noises of ecstasy coming from the larger of the two bedrooms, where Aggie and her fellow corporate finance proseminar classmate, Mikhail, were working off some steam after a successful presentation.

Where to go, after such a discovery? His Acela ticket was a super saver fare, nonrefundable, no changes allowed.

As luck would have it, three of Steven's Boston College buddies—Murph, Finn, and Scooter—were living in a train wreck of an apartment in Brighton. Steven exited Aggie's place just in time—he knew her well enough to know that she was close to orgasm—and put out a distress call. Of course Steven could crash with the Brighton guys! Murph, Finn, and Scooter—that's right, those were their names, like a trio out of a sitcom—took Steven in, propped him up with three shots of Jägermeister, and repaired to the Venu, where a group of six Fordham girls were knee-deep into an evening celebrating the bachelorette party of the first of the group to get married, a Cambridge resident named Marissa. They'd started, of course, with dinner at Dick's Last Resort, because that was what you did if you got married before the age of twenty-seven in those days in Boston.

The maid of honor was none other than one Louisa Fitzgerald, one of the most promising students in the history Ph.D. program at Columbia University. The bride-to-be was wearing—wait for it—a white visor with a shoulder-length veil attached. Louisa had donned her favorite boot-cut jeans and a 1930s blouse she'd bought at a vintage shop on Broome Street. And yes, thank you very much, she *would* like to dance to "Hips Don't Lie" by Shakira, featuring Wyclef Jean, with the brokenhearted, adorable *Village Voice* copy editor she met in line for the bathroom.

At the end of the night, phone numbers were exchanged.

Fast-forward through Aggie's tearful, unaccepted apology, the phone calls between Louisa and Steven, the courting, dates one through fifteen, the meeting of each other's families. Louisa's father, a justice on the Maine Supreme Judicial Court, was intimidating; her mother, Annie, was classy and warm. Steven had a big, close family in Philly: three brothers who worked with their father at his plumbing company: McLean and Sons. (The oldest brother, Robbie, joked that when Steven decided to go white-collar on them Steven's dad thought about naming it "McLean and Sons Minus One.") The second oldest, Joe, had married his high school sweetheart and produced three sons. Nick, a year younger than Steven, never told Steven that when Steven brought Aggie home for Thanksgiving junior year she'd put her hand on Nick's thigh under the table during the dessert course, before the Kennedy-esque football game the brothers, their father, and a peloton of cousins played every year.

New York City, 2007. Steven and Louisa got an apartment in a postwar building on West 111th Street. Louisa finished her classes at Columbia and taught undergraduates while she worked on her dissertation. These were busy, blissful days—Louisa was on a fast track; she was going to be one of those students, as rare as a Bornean orangutan, who completed her course work and her dissertation on time and was ready for the job market.

Steven took the 1 train downtown every morning to Christopher Street and walked to the *Voice*'s offices in Cooper Square. Once he was gone Louisa made a second pot of coffee and sat down in the postage-stamp-size kitchen to work. Two afternoons a week she exchanged her slippers for shoes with actual soles and taught an intro lecture to Columbia undergraduates.

At a wedding that September for one of Steven's BC buddies Louisa finally met the infamous Aggie Baumfeld. Aggie gave Louisa a cool, assessing glance and offered her long-fingered bejeweled hand to Louisa; for a brief, horrifying second, Louisa thought she was supposed to *kiss Aggie's ring!*

A proposal in late 2008, Christmas Eve. Accepted, with glee. Champagne, phone calls home. More champagne. Of course they'd get married at Ships View! Louisa wouldn't consider doing it any other way. Steven had visited Owls Head with Louisa the previous summer, placed in the Bunk Room, while Louisa had the Pink Room: reasons of propriety. And while perhaps he wondered if all of their future vacations would take place in this very house, with Louisa's parents in residence, Steven certainly didn't voice any doubts aloud. After all, he was in love! And the view of the water from the picture window in the dining room was as stunning as promised.

They set a May date.

2009. The day before Louisa Fitzgerald went before the committee to defend her dissertation she threw up in a bathroom in Fayerweather Hall. Nerves. Perfectly normal; who *wouldn't* be uneasy? All that work, all those hours, whittled down to one terrifying afternoon.

Three days later, she and Steven went out to Louisa's favorite restaurant, Pisticci Ristorante. When the server placed in front of Louisa her favorite dish, penne pisticci, her queasiness returned. The chunks of homemade mozzarella in the yellow and red vine tomato sauce turned her stomach. To the bathroom she repaired. The Duane Reade on Broadway was open twenty-four hours.

Only she and Steven knew why the seamstress had to let out the bodice of Louisa's wedding dress ever so slightly, and why Louisa took a twenty-minute power nap before stepping into her open-toed, three-inch white shoes with a sprinkle of diamonds across each forefoot. There was a collection of cells inside her uterus, multiplying mightily, on their way to becoming Matty McLean.

2010, a mild winter day, Matty in a BabyBjörn, Louisa taking her daily walk through Morningside

Park, a call from her advisor about a job at Reed College in Portland, Oregon. Her advisor had talked her up to his colleagues; she should apply. (*I can't possibly fly across the country, can I?* thought Louisa. *I have a baby!*)

Well, but. This was academia. You had to be willing to go where the jobs were. You flew when you were asked to fly.

A flight; a breast pump packed in a sleek black bag. Louisa *loved* Reed. She loved Portland. She loved the idea of living on the other side of the country, with the open spaces for Matty he'd never experience in New York. A series of interviews, an offer put forth by phone, Steven opening the apartment door just as he ended his own phone call.

"I have news," Louisa said, brimming with excitement and pride.

"I do too." Steven's eyes were panicked.

She swallowed and said, "You go first."

"That was Joe on the phone," he said. "He's at my parents' house. My mom is sick." He blinked and looked suddenly both younger and older than he actually was. "Really sick. She had a massive stroke."

Louisa turned down Reed; Nancy McLean died six months later.

Louisa was devastated about the job—tenure track

positions in history did not exactly fall from the sky; they didn't fall from anywhere—but Steven was more devastated about Nancy, so she tamped down her disappointment. She joined a playgroup, but she wasn't sure anyone else ever picked up a book or thought about anything other than organic teething rings and mastitis. She did some adjunct teaching at Columbia, but only one class. Her friend Franklin from her program, single and gay, got a job at the College of Charleston. He had no strings tying him down. Louisa tried not to be envious—although she was. She spoke at a conference; she published a single paper. But she could feel the new grads nipping at her heels.

Things at the *Voice* got rough. Everything was political; it was hard to rise. Steven wanted to get into radio. There was an opening at NPR.

The days go by slowly, someone once told Louisa about motherhood. *But the years fly.*

2011, a call from Louisa's advisor, with whom she had remained close. "I have great news," he said. "No, wait. I shouldn't say that. I have very somber news. There's been a death in the history department at NYU. Gary Rosenthal?"

"That's *terrible,*" Louisa said. Her heart fluttered. Gary Rosenthal had sat on Louisa's dissertation committee; her work was considered an extension of his.

"I'm so sorry to hear it." She waited a long, long minute.

Gary Rosenthal had suffered a heart attack in his office. A grad student found him with his head tipped forward onto Doris Kearns Goodwin's *Team of Rivals*, which he was reading for the sixth time. Possibly, Louisa thought, there was no better way for a legend like Gary to go.

Louisa, as an only child herself, told Steven early on she didn't want to *have* an only child. It was too lonely! Steven wasn't afraid of chaos—look at the home he'd been raised in. One semester into her position at NYU Louisa began feeling the telltale queasiness that signified Abigail. A home search; a three-bedroom on Prospect Park West, a breath-snatching price tag; a move.

Two children for female professors was rare; three was almost unheard of. And yet! Here came Claire, in November 2014. The cost for a nanny was astronomical; when Annie and Martin Fitzgerald offered to contribute, Louisa and Steven couldn't say yes fast enough.

The days go by slowly but the years fly? Untrue. The days and the years both flew.

A BC buddy got divorced, remarried at the Chatham Bars Inn on Cape Cod. Again, Aggie was at the wedding. Did Aggie go to every wedding of every former Eagle? It seemed so. While Louisa was battered by motherhood—she felt like she was losing the battle *and* the war—childless Aggie seemed not to have aged at all. She was the Benjamin Button of BC alums. She looked like she was getting younger!

"I'll call you about that thing," Louisa heard Aggie say to Steven.

"What thing?" she asked.

"A business thing," said Steven. "A question I had for Aggie."

2015. "Listen to this," said Steven. He placed one earbud into each of her ears and sat Louisa down at the kitchen table. "Marc Maron interviewed Barack Obama! In his *garage*. For this podcast."

Louisa hadn't seen Steven look so smitten since he moved aside the striped newborn blanket in the hospital to count the fingers and toes of each of their children. "Look at what they did with *Serial,* too. There are so many stories waiting to be told this way. This is what I want to do. I want to start a podcasting company."

Claire was cruising on all of the furniture, you couldn't take your eyes off of her. Abigail was having nightmares; Matty needed glasses. Louisa was teaching a full-time course load and working on her first book. If she didn't get tenure, she'd be out. If she didn't publish, she wouldn't get tenure. The academic world was brutal like that. The nanny decided to go to school to become a physical therapist; they needed another nanny.

For Steven: investor meetings. Long hours, a small staff, a studio in Brooklyn. Content, content, content.

Louisa. Tenure, finally, in 2017. She thought the pressure would ease up then, but it only increased. She needed to publish another book. Every now and then, taking the F train from Prospect Park, walking past a urine-soaked person sleeping outside the Broadway-Lafayette stop, looking at the website of the private school she wanted to send Matty to and gasping out loud at the price, Louisa still thought of Reed's campus and the open, manageable spaces of Oregon, the relative affordability.

2019. Martin and Annie made their annual visit to Brooklyn—they came on the long October weekend, when summer in Owls Head had wound down, and they stayed for three nights. On the last night Martin and Annie always treated the McLeans to dinner out at a local family restaurant, or, if a sitter was available, a fancier dinner for just the adults. That year the high school junior they sometimes employed was free, so Louisa made a reservation at Fausto. The meal was lovely and decadent. At one point, Louisa noticed her father staring into space while Steven was talking. This was unlike him; Martin was an accomplished conversationalist.

They finished their espresso; Annie went to the ladies' room. Martin was frowning at the bill.

"Dad?" Louisa said. "Everything okay?" Her father's brow was furrowed. He took off his reading glasses, frowned more, rubbed his eyes, put them back on.

"The tax—" Martin's voice trailed off. "I can't figure out the tip, that's all. The tax is off . . . this doesn't make any sense. Can you have a look at this?"

Steven and Louisa glanced at each other. Martin was a whiz with math. He did his own taxes; he claimed that in college physics problems relaxed him. Louisa studied the bill. The dinner had been expensive—no wonder she and Steven would never dine at Fausto on their own!—but the tax was perfectly correct, and the tip was easily figured, even by a numbers-challenged history professor like herself. "Fifty-two," she said. "The tip should be fifty-two dollars, Daddy."

"Of course." He smiled. "Of course it is. Fifty-two." Just then Annie reappeared, her lipstick freshly applied. "There she is!" said Martin, his brow smoother, his eyes bright. "My lovely bride. All is well." He reached out his hand for Annie's as she regained her seat.

"All is well," said Annie. Something in her glance

unsettled Louisa. A knot of concern bloomed in her stomach, another in her ribs.

Slow days, fast years? No. Annie called seven months later, to tell Louisa that she was taking Martin in for evaluation with a neurologist at Maine Medical, and she called again when they had the diagnosis in hand. No, that wasn't right, that the days were slow. It was *all* going fast.

12.
Pauline

When there's a week left to go in June Pauline brings two containers of soup—one, her famous chicken noodle, and the other a fish chowder, new recipe, she'd gotten it off the Internet—to her cousin Marilyn, who lives off South Shore Drive down a funny little road called Cripple Creek Lane.

Marilyn's husband, Eddie, lets Pauline in. He's on the quiet side by nature, but now Pauline can see by the way he keeps his eyes down, hardly greeting her, he's gone positively silent. He captains a lobster boat just like Billy, but he didn't even put the boat in the water this April so he could care for Marilyn after the cancer budded in a kidney, then jumped to the liver, and has now spread itself out through her body.

What not having the boat in the water must mean

for their finances Pauline can't even begin to imagine. She knows how that muscle in Billy's jaw moves after just one bad week on the water, never mind a whole lost season.

Marilyn lies in a hospital bed in her front room. It's the sort of bed the patient can lift or lower at will, and Marilyn has it set halfway between upright and lying down. Pauline sits in the straight-backed chair angled in a certain way beside the bed so Marilyn doesn't have to turn her head to look at her.

"I brought soup," says Pauline. "Two kinds, both labeled. I put them in the fridge. But I can go warm you up some, if you want. Do you think you might eat a bit of soup, Lynnie?"

"Oh, Pauline," Marilyn says. "Thank you. Thank you so much." Her small gray eyes are wet. "I'm hardly eating at all. But this will mean the world to Eddie. I know he misses my cooking."

"Maybe just a spoonful," says Pauline, starting to rise from the chair.

Marilyn is three years older than Pauline, but now the difference between them could be a dozen years, or more. Marilyn's face, always smooth and small and brown, has become shriveled and old, with new dips and crevices, more walnut than acorn.

"Not now," says Marilyn. "Sit, sit. Really, I couldn't

take even a bite right now. And it's been so long since I've seen you, Polly."

"Oh, come on now," says Pauline sharply. "I was just here a week ago. On my day off." She sounds sharp because she's scared. She doesn't like seeing Marilyn like this, one week worse than she was the last time.

Marilyn smiles slightly in that vague, almost secretive way she now has. Pauline noticed the strangeness of the smile last time she was here.

"I thought I was dreaming that," she says. "Time is running together."

"I suppose that can happen—" says Pauline. She stops herself before saying, *in the end*, the way she almost did. "I mean, that happens to all of us," she says instead. "Half the time I don't even know what day it is." This is not true. Pauline always knows what day it is, and what time too. She thinks about the Chief, who recently asked her if his suit was pressed for court. There's a man who doesn't know which end is up.

"I don't think it will be long now," Marilyn says dreamily. Pauline sees that there's a tube coming out of Marilyn's arm and the tube runs away behind her back to something that Pauline can't see. Another piece of the tube goes to a small black button on the side of Marilyn's bed. Every now and then Marilyn presses the button with her thumb and afterward she sighs.

"For the pain," whispers Marilyn, when she sees Pauline watching.

There was a time—oh, early high school, or perhaps earlier than that, seventh or eighth grade—when Pauline looked up to Marilyn with such ardor it felt almost like a hurt. Marilyn used to pick up Pauline in her daddy's pickup truck and drive them into Rockland or out to Camden. Radio on, windows down, wind in their hair and on their young skin. Joyriding, it was called back then. Cruising.

"Does it hurt very much?" Pauline asks Marilyn.

"Sometimes."

"Well. I'm sorry to hear that." Pauline thinks about taking Marilyn's hand but it's like a stranger's hand, so small and curled up, and she's frightened of it. Pauline pauses, then releases the question she really wants to ask. "Are you scared?"

"Sometimes," says Marilyn. Pauline notices the answer shoots right out of her. "Sometimes if I wake in the night, you know? Sometimes I feel this—well, it's a terror, I'd have to say. A black terror, squeezing on my heart like a fist." She folds her small newly unfamiliar hands in front of her on the bed and looks at Pauline expectantly. For an instant she's the old Marilyn, with the wide-leg jeans, the short-sleeve shirt tucked into them, keys to the pickup dangling from one hand. *Let's go,* she used to say to Pauline. *Come on, Polly, let's see what's happening.*

"How's it going at the Fitzgeralds'?" she asks.

"They treat me well enough," says Pauline, still thinking about the terror squeezing at her cousin's heart. "Really pretty good, actually. The pay is good, the hours are manageable. They still like my food, after all these years. It's a heck of a lot more work with Louisa and the kids there all summer, I'll tell you that. I never saw people make a mess quite so fast."

"It's a long time you've been working there."

"Long time," says Pauline. "Making their food. Keeping their secrets." She waits for Marilyn to ask, and she thinks if she does she might just tell her.

But Marilyn is asleep. Pauline sits with her for several minutes more—so many, in fact, that she can see the way the light begins to change in the small front room, the sun edging its way past the center of the sky. It's getting on toward midafternoon.

At long last she rises. She'll tell Eddie to say her goodbyes for her. But as soon as she's standing Marilyn is awake again, looking at Pauline with those small gray eyes. *Come on, Polly, let's see what's happening.*

"I have to go, honey," says Pauline. "Billy will be coming home soon. I've got dinner to fix and a list of chores a mile long at my own house."

"Oh, Polly." Marilyn sighs. "I'm so glad you're here. You'll come back again, won't you?"

"Of course I will. Every Wednesday, on my day off. And Eddie can call me if you need me sooner than that. They can manage without me at the Fitzgeralds', if you need me. Okay? You tell him that. Anytime. Never mind, Lynnie. I'll tell him myself, on my way out."

"Bye for now," says Marilyn. "See you soon."

"Soon," says Pauline. She stands for a long second, not quite sure exactly what to do from here, and then she leans over and touches her lips to the dry, cracked forehead belonging to Marilyn, her favorite cousin, this familiar stranger.

How happy Pauline is to get out in the fresh air, back in her car. How *alive* she feels, in comparison to Marilyn, regardless of her joints that ache at the end of the day, the sagging skin at her elbows. How alive. She's just pulling into her own driveway when her phone, lying on the passenger seat, begins to ring. The sound startles her. She never uses the cell phone. She has a limited plan, and only Annie Fitzgerald and her family members have the number.

"Hello?" she says. She's always cautious when answering the cell phone, like it might explode if she says something wrong.

"Hey, Mama."

"Nicole?"

"The one and only." A hint of a laugh in her daughter's voice.

"Well, well, well," says Pauline.

"How's everything? How're you and Daddy? How're the boys?" asks Nicole. She means her brothers; Cliff is two years older than Nicole and Will two years younger, both captaining their own boats now, Cliff in Owls Head and Will not so far away in South Thomaston.

"Fine," says Pauline. "Good. Busy, you know. I'm just coming from seeing Marilyn."

"Marilyn! How is she?"

"Not good," says Pauline. "I'll leave it there. Drains me to talk about it any more than that." She thinks about Marilyn's hands.

"Oh, well that's a shame," says Nicole. "That's a real shame. I'm sorry, Mama."

"Not your fault."

"Well I know it isn't my f—"

"How's Nashville?" Pauline cuts her off, because she's starting to feel the hot press of tears behind her eyes.

"Oh, it's good, I guess. Let's see. I'm going to see Chris Stapleton at the Ryman next week."

"Well, la-di-da."

"You know Chris Stapleton?"

"No," admits Pauline.

"Ha! I didn't think so. You should listen to him, though. He's really amazing. A-mazing. I'll send you some clips." Pauline doesn't know what *send you some clips* means.

"Is that why you called, Nicole? To tell me about this person named Chris Stapleton?"

"No! Of course not. I called—well, just to say hi, really."

Pauline waits. Fat chance of that. She waits some more.

"And also." *Here we go,* thinks Pauline. "Things aren't going so great between me and Richard, Mama. I just need some time to figure things out. We're— separated. For now." The rest of the words come out all in a rush, tripping over each other. "I was wondering if maybe I could send Hazel up to you all for a bit. So I can clear my head. So she can get out of what has, frankly, become a toxic environment."

"Toxic environment? What's that supposed to mean?"

"Would that be all right, Mama?"

Well, hell. Would that be all right? Can a coon cat stalk a mouse? Pauline knows the answer to both questions, but for some reason she makes Nicole work for it.

Richard is Nicole's third husband. *Three husbands!* First there was Hazel's dad, Cole. He was a singer. "Singer-*songwriter*," Nicole always used to correct if on accident you just said *singer*. Not that it matters now; they split when Hazel was three. Cole is writing songs about someone else now. "Come on back home," Pauline had told Nicole at the time. "Live with me and your dad. You'll have your brothers nearby." But, no, Nicole didn't think she was cut out for life in Maine; Nicole thought she was meant for bigger and better things, warmer winters. After Cole came Gary the concert booker. It seemed to Pauline as though you couldn't throw a stone in Nashville without hitting a concert booker. Eighteen months that marriage lasted. Then a period of being single, years, and onto Richard. Richard the record producer, making the big bucks. They live in a mansion, Pauline has seen photos, although to hear Nicole tell it's just a regular house. Those are Nashville standards, Pauline supposes. Pauline doesn't understand this impulse of Nicole's, to marry again and again, this inability to let things stand as they are. Pauline loves Billy to the moon and back and needs to change husbands like she needs to change into an evening gown to boil corn. One is plenty. One is more than enough.

"Let me think about it. Okay, Nicole? How long are you thinking?"

"I don't know—a few weeks? A month?"

"A month!" Pauline sounds grumpy but her insides are skipping along like a girl on the way to a birthday party. Her granddaughter! For a visit! For a month!

"I mean, maybe not quite a month. Could be three weeks, three and a half."

"Can she fly by herself up to Portland, do you think?"

"She's thirteen. 'Course she can fly by herself. And Daddy can pick her up on the other end. Right? Would that work, for him to go down to Portland? She could arrive in the evening so he doesn't have to miss a day of hauling. When it's time for her to come back I'll fly up and fetch her home."

"Now when would this be?"

"I was thinking—day after tomorrow."

"Day after tomorrow?" So soon!

"I bought the ticket already. I probably should have asked you before doing that. I'm sorry. I just—I didn't know what else to do. I need some time to think, Mama, that's all. I need some air."

"Isn't that expensive?" Pauline asks. "To book last minute like that?"

"I'm not concerned about *that*." Nicole's laugh is

a tinkle, a wind chime, the high note of a xylophone. "Believe me, the cost of a ticket I paid for with Richard's credit card is the very last thing on my mind right now. The very *very* last thing. Ha! After what he—oh, never mind."

"Let me think about it, okay? Let me just figure a few things out."

"Okay. I'll be here."

"I'm hanging up now."

"Bye, Mama."

Ninety seconds later Pauline calls Nicole back. "I thought about it," she says. "We'd be so happy to have her."

"Oh, Mama, thank you. *Thank* you."

"But I work a lot in the summer. Your dad too."

"I know. I wish you didn't have to work so hard, the both of you!"

"If wishes were horses," says Pauline. She notices Nicole stops short of offering the record producer's money to make this wish come true. Not that she would take it. "Anyway that's not my point. You know, me I'm an ox. I've got years' more work in me. What I meant was that Hazel'll be left to her own devices most days. I'm off Wednesdays and the weekend, that's it. And you know how your dad's hours are. She good at entertaining herself?"

"She's *so good* at entertaining herself," says Nicole. "She won't have any problems with that. She'll be happy for a change of pace, you know? It's so hot here in the summer. Maybe Daddy can take her out on the boat one day."

"What, hauling?"

"Of course, sure. Yeah. Hauling. Why not? She'd love it. She's skinny, but she's strong. The way I used to be." Nicole stopped going out on the boat the summer she turned fourteen. Suddenly she couldn't stand the smell of the bait, the motion of the waves, the earliness of the hour.

"Why not?" says Pauline. "Maybe. Send me the information on the flight, will you?"

"I will. Right away, once we're off the phone, I'll text it."

"Okay, then. I'll look for it." Pauline hates texts. She can never figure out how to make them get off her phone's screen once she's done with them. "Bye, now, honey."

"Goodbye, Mama. And thank you."

"Yup," says Pauline.

Sometimes Pauline feels like she has never been quite so exasperated by anyone in her whole life, and at the same time like she hasn't loved anyone quite so much either.

13.

Louisa

Louisa loves the Farnsworth Art Museum in Rockland, and she's trying to feel excited about the trip Annie has proposed, but she's having trouble summoning her usual enthusiasm. She's trying to think *summer summer summer* and *family family family* but instead she keeps thinking *book book book*. June is slipping away; despite its initial promise, time is as elusive as a bar of soap in a bubble bath, and she's written eleven and a half pages when she should have written sixty-eight. July had better be some kind of productive. She agrees to the trip mostly out of guilt—she doesn't want to disappoint her mother, and she doesn't want to disappoint Abigail, whose devotion to the museum is highly unusual for a contemporary child. Louisa is trying not to smother Abigail's ardor with her own ambivalence.

Also, there is the promise of a sandwich after from Atlantic Baking Company when they are finished, and she really loves those sandwiches.

While Annie is showing her membership card Abigail slips out of sight. A guard says, "Looking for the little girl? She's up there." He nods toward the Hadlock Gallery. They climb the short flight of stairs from the lobby and find Abigail in front of an Andrew Wyeth painting called *Her Room,* which depicts a room with a wooden desk or table holding a conch shell just off center. Light pink diaphanous curtains are pulled back from either side on each of the two windows. A door stands open, with a diagonal splash of light across it.

"This is a very plain room," says Abigail sternly, acknowledging her mother's and grandmother's appearance on either side of her. "But, oh! Look at the seashells lined up on the windowsill. In order from biggest to smallest. I love that." She has her hands clasped together behind her back and looks for all the world like a miniature professor.

Louisa, who hadn't even noticed the shells on the windowsill, leans in. "Very observant of you, Abigail." She touches Abigail's hair, done in two French braids by Louisa herself that morning. Abigail's hair is thick and tends toward unruliness, like Louisa's, and tamed in this way it gives her a clean, old-fashioned look that Louisa loves. Claire's hair, by contrast, is fine and straight and falls like a cap around her face, and Matty's—well, Matty has boy hair, subjugated every six weeks by a Brooklyn barber. Their eyes are all different too: Abigail's are sapphire blue with a dark rim, like Louisa's and Martin's; Matty's are brown, like Steven's, and Claire's shift between blue and green depending on what she's wearing. The McLeans are their very own Punnett square.

"I wonder whose room this was?" asks Abigail.

"There's a whole display with information about it," Annie tells her. "Early sketches and so forth. You can see the different versions the artist worked through before creating the final. See? Just over there." She takes Abigail by the shoulders and turns her gently around. "You can read all about it."

"I don't think I want to read about it," says Abigail, turning back to the painting. "I don't think I want to know for sure. I prefer to imagine."

"She's just like you were," says Annie to Louisa as they move out of Abigail's earshot, leaving her to take her time in front of the painting.

"Oh, no. I was never such a dreamer, was I?"

"You were," says her mother, "Oh, you were. Always talking to your dolls, setting them up with their own little worlds and circumstances. Sometimes they'd have arguments, and you'd be in charge of settling them. That part came from your father, I suppose. The desire for order in the face of disagreement. I always thought you'd go to law school yourself."

"I don't remember anything about doll arguments," says Louisa.

"I figured it was the curse of the only child, left so often to your own devices, that made you that way. But here's Abigail, sandwiched between the other two, with her head in the clouds. Who knows? Maybe she'll become an artist."

"No thank you," says Abigail primly, appearing beside them without warning. "I think I'd like to be a vet."

Abigail has so far shown a total of zero interest in science, though it is a fact that her devotion to dogs has always run strong and true.

"I think you should be a pianist," says Louisa. "If you would just practice more, you'd be really good." Abigail's talent for the piano seems to have fallen onto her long, cool fingers from the clear blue sky, none of the rest of them having ever played at all. She doesn't like to practice, so her teacher says she'll never be as good as she could be.

"Absolutely not," says Abigail.

They take their time walking through the rest of the

museum, then, when a sufficient amount of time has passed, Louisa mentions that Atlantic Baking Company often sells out of the sourdough pullman bread, her favorite.

"But we haven't gone in the house yet!" cries Abigail. She means the Farnsworth Homestead, just behind the museum, the former home of the museum's benefactor, Lucy Farnsworth. For some reason—it's beyond Louisa, who finds the home on the fusty side—Abigail loves to go into the homestead, insists on it every year, even as her siblings, when they come, race through the museum and ask if they can wait outside in the sunshine, all done with the past. "*Please?*" begs Abigail. "I'm not even a little bit hungry yet. Can't we go in?"

"Of course we can," says Annie, and Louisa sighs and puts a hand on her grumbling stomach. She steps outside to call Barbara, who reports that her father is doing just fine, sitting with his newspaper on the back porch. She texts Matty to ask if everything is going okay, and he replies, Yes.

Is Claire with you, she texts back, and again: Yes. So, with no other excuse at hand, off they go to the homestead.

In the house they are greeted by a female museum employee, tall and stern, with an out-of -season cardigan, a faint mustache, and the kind of short gray hair

Louisa hopes never to have but fears sometimes is inevitable. Louisa is familiar with the lore: Lucy Farnsworth, the last owner of the house, lived to the age of ninety-seven, a spinster who wore all black; the neighborhood children thought she was a witch. When she died, her entire estate went to the creation of the art museum.

Abigail takes Annie's hand and leads her through the first doorway into the sitting room. So many competing prints, the wallpaper, the drapes, the carpet. It makes Louisa dizzy.

Abigail has an endless supply of questions for the museum employee. What used to happen in this room? What about that one? Did children live here? How old were they? Is there any tea in the teapot that sits on the table in the drawing room? No? Why not? And then, one for Louisa: Can they get carpets like this in their house in Brooklyn?

"Definitely *not*," says Louisa. When they renovated their Brooklyn apartment a few years ago they paid through the nose for old carpet to be torn up, revealing parquet that they then replaced with white oak, and somebody will have to carry Louisa out feet first before they do anything else to those floors.

The kitchen is the room on the first floor that holds the most fascination for Abigail—she stands forever in it, staring at the coal stove along one end, the farm-house sink, the butler's pantry with the orderly shelves of crockery and glasses. Once finished there, she wants to examine both sets of stairs, one carpeted and one bare. "For the servants," she says philosophically, studying the back staircase.

They go up the front stairs, treading on the bare carpet where so many others have trod before them. At the top hangs a drawing of horses in a pasture, sur-rounded by ducks and sheep. Even this Abigail gives her time to, as if she knows the horses personally.

"You know," says Annie, "once I came up here from Portland at Christmastime, and they held a candlelight tour of this house."

"You *did?*" Abigail's eyes are shining. "You really got to do that? By candlelight?"

"I did. They took us through all the rooms, and talked about the family that used to live here. Do you know that of the six children in the family, only three survived to adulthood?"

"*Six!*" says Louisa. "I'm guessing their mother was not a tenured professor of history."

"Three died? That's awful!" says Abigail, but her eyes are still alight and fascinated. "And was it all decorated for Christmas, when you came?"

Annie looks around, lips pursed, trying to remember.

"The town was, and the museum was, and they had the lobster trap tree up on Main Street, you know, in the square. But the house looked just like this. Only candlelit. Oh, it was so pretty. At the end we had cocoa over at the museum."

"*I* never knew you did that," said Louisa, feeling petulant. "You never told me!"

"I guess I don't tell you everything," says Annie shrewdly. She winks at Abigail.

"I want to live in a house just like this one day," Abigail says. "Just exactly like this. Decorated the same way. In fact I think I'd like to live in *this* house." She is lost in a painting of the Last Supper that hangs in one of the bedrooms, which only makes Louisa think again of the sourdough pullman loaf across the street. If they've sold out of it, she's going to be devastated.

"I need some air," Louisa tells her mother and her daughter. "I'll wait for you outside."

Between the sidewalk and the house stands a white picket fence, outlining the tiniest front yard there ever was. Where on earth did the six children who used to live in this house play? Simpler times, Louisa supposes. They probably played in the street, darting around horse-drawn carriages. Or maybe children didn't play back then; maybe they were too busy taking care of younger siblings and beating laundry clean against a rock. She doesn't realize Annie has snuck up beside her until she hears her say, "How much longer are you going to let Steven leave you all alone up here?"

"*Let?*" says Louisa irritably. "There's no letting. We have an agreement. I told you. He needs a little more time to get through the work stuff. And I'm not alone." Louisa's sunglasses had been perched on the top of her head; she drops them over her eyes, the better to remain inscrutable.

Her mother gives her the look that she used to give her in high school, the look that says I-know-this-bottle-of-vodka-used-to-be-fuller-than-it-is-now. "Well, but. Surely he could make time for a short visit, if he cared to. It's not like he's in New York and we're in Vancouver, or Timbuktu. One can be here in a matter of hours from Brooklyn!"

Louisa is balanced on the knife's edge between composure and agitation. She can feel herself tipping the wrong way. "It's not that simple."

"I don't see why not. You hop in the car, and you come to see your wife and children."

"For one thing, Mom, we just have one car. And it's up here. For another, he's working day and night. The company needs this other round of funding to keep going forward. They're *so close* to making it, but if they don't get another round, it could all go pffft.

He can't do it when we're in his hair. Believe me, I'd rather have him here! But I'm giving him the summer, and when they sort this piece of it out, we'll go back to sharing the responsibilities the way we used to." She blinks back unexpected tears, hoping the conversation can end here.

"Well," says Annie. "That's not—" She pauses, and Louisa fills in the pause with what she thinks Annie might say. *That's not an agreement your father and I ever would have made.* Or, *That's not the way to run a marriage.*

But with an unforeseen empathy Annie says, "That's not an arrangement that's making things very easy on either of you." She frowns. "It must be difficult, with both of you working so hard."

Louisa squints at Annie. Relief floods through her, nearly weakening her. Her mother understands! "Yeah. *Yes.* It is." Her beloved Pitcairn, always calling to her, and she not able to answer. Fifty-two days left in Owls Head, which means that she now needs to write five pages per day to stay on track.

The door to the house opens and disgorges two women. Louisa has the sense that she's falling off the knife's edge here, and she goes ahead anyway. She wants to honor her mother's life, her work, yes, but she also wants to question it. "I mean, Mom. It *is* different.

I agree that it's different. For you guys, Dad's career took precedence over everything. You gave and you gave . . . and, I don't know."

"And what?"

"And what did *you* get in return for all of that? Do you ever think about that, Mom?"

Suddenly Abigail is there, a bright blade of grass among the mushrooms. She takes one of Louisa's hands and one of Annie's, and Louisa marvels at the coolness of her daughter's fingers, and thinks again about the piano.

"Now I'm hungry," says Abigail. "Can we eat?"

Annie meets Louisa's eyes over Abigail's head—or would have, if Louisa had lifted her sunglasses, which, for a variety of reasons, she leaves in place.

"I got this," says Annie. "I got to be your mother, and grandmother to your children."

14.
The Children

Matty is stretching his right quad just outside the front door when Louisa says through the screen door, "Do you mind keeping an eye on Claire while Granny and I take Abigail to the Farnsworth?"

Matty drops his right leg to the ground and lifts his left. He can feel how taut the muscles of his abdomen are; he can count his ribs when he looks in the mirror wearing only his running shorts. His heart, tight as a fist, and strong as one, is an efficient machine. His resting heart rate is fifty-five. His long run is up to eight miles. He'll get it to twelve before summer is over. "Why do I have to?"

"Because I'm asking you to," says Louisa. "Unless you were hoping to go to the Farnsworth too."

"*Definitely* not." He says this because he knows his

mother loves the Farnsworth, and he is angry with her. Even though nobody has come right out and said it, he knows it's her fault his dad isn't here.

"All right then. Claire doesn't want to go either. So, you don't have to rearrange your day around it, just be here in case she needs anything."

"Why me?"

"Because neither of you wants to go to the museum! And I can't ask Grandpa." A muscle in his mother's cheek twitches when she says this.

"What about Pauline?"

"Child care isn't in her job description. She'll make you two lunch, but I can't ask her to *babysit.*"

Matty bristles. "I don't need a babysitter."

"Exactly. And anyway, you and Claire usually have fun together. I'm not asking you to pull out your own toenails, or anyone else's either."

Matty wants to argue with this, but he can't. He and Claire *do* get along, often better than Abigail and Claire get along. She can be a pest, sometimes, and she's *so much* younger than he is, but he can see a time in the dim, distant future, when they are adults, or when Claire is in college, that they'll hang out in bars or whatever. Claire will probably turn out way cooler that Matty—*she'll* probably tell *him* where the good bars are. That's Claire for you.

"I was going for a run." He's talking now from upside down, his upper body hanging over his lower.

His mother eases herself out the screen door and stands next to him on the little front stoop. He straightens, and all of the blood rushes from his head back down to his feet. "So go for your run. We won't leave until after you're back. Okay?"

"Okay."

"Thank you, kiddo." She touches him on the shoulder and he flinches, on purpose, to throw off her hand. He tries not to notice the hurt look on her face, but he can't help it. His mother when she's hurt looks a lot like Abigail before she starts crying. Their light eyes fill up fast: it's like looking into a swimming pool.

"*Matty*," she says. "That was harsh."

"Sorry," he mutters.

Not long after their mother and grandmother and sister go off to the Farnsworth Matty and Claire sit in the dining room, making a plan for the day. They are playing UNO, but not putting much effort into it. They haven't shuffled well enough and all of the cards are coming up green. Should they have gone to the Farnsworth after all? No. They both find museums so boring. They don't understand Abigail's interest.

Annie and Louisa and Abigail will be gone through lunch and into the early afternoon. They'll eat in town.

Matty and Claire will get their lunch from Pauline. They hope for grilled cheese, which Pauline has a knack for.

"You two," says Pauline, coming in with a rag to wipe the breakfast crumbs from the table. "You're underfoot. Go on and play outside."

"It's foggy—" begins Claire.

"Come back at lunchtime, how about that? But clean up these cards first."

They slouch together out to the porch and sit for a minute. It *is* foggy. They can scarcely see the water from here, and if a boat were to glide by they wouldn't see that either. They can hear the foghorn on the Rockland breakwater.

Through the fog Matty thinks he sees movement on the rocks. Claire sees it too. She stands. "Someone's down there," she says. "I'm going to see."

"Don't—" says Matty. He's thinking of the dead seal. Why isn't Claire thinking of it; why isn't she scared to push her way through the fog? Reluctantly, he rises and follows her.

The fog begins to part like a curtain, the way fog sometimes does in Maine, and now Claire can see more clearly. There's a girl on the rocks: there's a girl on *their* rocks. Claire scampers over the rocks nimbly, fearlessly, and Matty does his best to keep up.

For a moment, brother and sister study the girl: a stranger, an interloper. Phone in the back pocket of her short-shorts, ridiculous platform flip-flops. Stick-straight hair, the finest, palest blond, a nose that turns up slightly, deliciously, at the end. A strappy tank top, out of which rise actual breasts, the real deal. She's a very pretty girl.

"Who are you?" says Claire, combatively. She feels like another species in her pajama pants, with her Hogwarts pride T-shirt, with her bare feet.

"Hello to you too," says the girl merrily. "I'm Hazel." There's a slight southern drawl to her voice, *I'm* becoming *A'hm*. It's beautiful."

"Where'd you come from?" demands Claire.

"Nashville."

"But right now, today. Where'd you come from right now?"

Matty can't say anything. His voice has vanished. His heart is pulsing.

Hazel jerks her head away from the water. "My grandparents live up the road. My grandma works for your grandma."

"*Pauline*? Pauline is your grandma?" Matty can't square Pauline, with her long gray braid, the thin set of her mouth, and this lovely creature before him.

Hazel nods.

"How come we've never met you before, then?" Claire challenges. "We're here every summer. This is our very favorite place in the whole world. We grew up coming here. It's in our blood." This last part is a slightly edited version of something she's heard her mother say. "And we've never met *you* before."

"My mom and my grandma don't get along so good," the girl says. "I'm not always invited. But this time, my mama didn't know what to do with me. So here I am." She shrugs.

Here you are, thinks Matty.

"I'd be careful here, if I were you," Claire says authoritatively. "I found a dead body here a couple of weeks ago."

"A *seal's* body," Matty corrects, and Claire glares at him.

"My grandma told me about that," says Hazel. She smiles. She has braces, which somehow make her even more beautiful. "That must have been scary."

"Not really," says Claire. "Not for me."

"Well then," says Hazel. "I guess you're very brave." She smiles harder, and dimples pop out in her cheeks. "My granddad works pulling traps and he said if I get bored while he and my grandma are both at work I can come down here. I hope that's okay?"

Matty locates his voice, prepares it for use. "Anytime," he says. That word comes out croaky so he clears his throat. "We don't own the water."

"We own this part," says Claire. Matty shoots her a look. Claire hates that look of his. "Well, we do."

"We don't. Not the water."

"The rocks, then."

"No, Claire, I don't even think we own the rocks."

"So she has a name!" Hazel says. "Hi, Claire."

"And I'm Matty." Matty pushes his glasses up; a futile gesture, as they only slip back down again.

"You should take those off," Claire says to Hazel, looking at her flip-flops. "Before you fall on your face. The rocks get really slippery."

Hazel shrugs. "I have great balance." She makes a graceful, unattainable movement with her arms. "I used to be a gymnast." She smiles even more broadly at Claire—there are elastics too, in the very back of her mouth, bright green—and says, "I like your Hogwarts T-shirt."

Matty watches Claire pull the word out of herself carefully, like a shard of glass from skin: "Thanks."

"I love Harry Potter," says Hazel.

"No you don't," says Claire. "There's no way. You're—how old are you?"

"Thirteen."

"Older than you," Claire tells Matty pointedly, unnecessarily. Then, turning back to Hazel: "So you're too old for Harry Potter."

"I haven't always been thirteen," says Hazel. "Once I was your age, and I loved Harry Potter. All the way until sixth grade I loved Harry Potter. In fact I still do. I just don't tell everyone, that's all. I only tell people who will understand."

Claire presses her lips together and looks closely at Hazel. "Are you wearing makeup?" she demands.

Hazel laughs and says, "A little. Are you?"

Claire looks shocked. "*No,*" she says. "I'm seven. I'm not allowed."

"Maybe someday you can use some of mine," says Hazel. "When nobody is looking."

Claire shrugs and tries not to feel tempted.

Hazel sits on one of the wide flat rocks and puts a hand in the water. "I might go for a swim," she says. "Anyone want to join?"

"No thank you," says Claire virtuously, not saying that she's not allowed to swim without permission from a grown-up, and that she isn't about to go ask Pauline.

"I'll go with you!" says Matty, scrambling to his feet. His face feels warm under Hazel's cool and appraising glance.

"We have *plans,* Matty," says Claire. "Remember?" They're supposed to play Egyptian Rat Screw, and they're supposed to spy on Pauline, and they're supposed to work on the jigsaw puzzle with the three sailboats that they have dumped out on the puzzle table in the living room. (They've found only three out of the four corners so far!)

"We can do our plans later," says Matty. "We have all day. They won't be back for hours."

"Who's 'they'?" asks Hazel.

"Our mom and our granny and our sister," says Matty.

"She's ten," says Claire. "And she *likes* museums."

"I like museums," says Hazel.

"Me too," says Matty.

Claire rolls her eyes so hard they feel like they might pop out of her head. "I have things to do inside," says Claire, kicking angrily at a rock.

She stomps across the rocks, slipping once then righting herself, and marches all the way up to the house. Matty watches her tiny angry body cross the porch and go in through the sliding door. He should go after her, but he can't. Hazel is a Nashville sun, and he's a planet, caught in her orbit.

15.
Louisa

A day after the visit to the Farnsworth Louisa gets home from picking up the mail at the post office and sees an unfamiliar car in the driveway. She plonks her keys on the table in the front hallway and says, "Hello?" Her father's study door is closed. Otis comes galloping in from somewhere, tail wagging. "Mom?" says Louisa.

"In here." Annie's voice is coming from the dining room. She's sitting on her cross-stitch bench.

"Where is everyone? Who's here?"

Annie tips her head toward the water. "Kids, out there." She peers closely at her cross-stitch and frowns. "Pauline, grocery shopping. Danny is working on the retaining wall around back, you know that one that's been falling down for ages? Barbara is finishing up some of your father's laundry. And Nina Dawson is here, visiting your father. They're in his study." Annie is like Keith Lockhart minus the sweat; she's got no instrument to play herself, and yet without the flow of her batons the entire orchestra would come to a halt.

"Judge Dawson? Really? I *love* Judge Dawson." Louisa sits in the chair in the corner of the room, next to her mother's bench. When Martin left the court there were two female justices, and Judge Dawson was one. She's younger than Martin by eight or ten years and still holds her seat; there's talk that she's in line for the next chief justice appointment. At a summer barbecue Louisa once attended with her parents when she was home from college Judge Dawson beat every single person, kids included, in badminton, wearing a knee-length skirt.

From where they sit Annie and Louisa can't see the door to Martin's study but they hear it open and close and soon enough Judge Dawson enters the room. She rivals Annie for the award for Most Elegant Older Woman, in her sundress and sandals, with her dark hair swinging around her chin and her gold hoops and her lipstick just so. How is it, wonders Louisa, that she's surrounded by women who look like they stepped out of a J. Jill photo shoot while she can scarcely find a clean bra? She likes to imagine that she too will age into such grace and composure, but she fears that one can't add after the baking something that wasn't in the recipe in the first place.

Annie and Louisa both stand. "Nina!" says Annie. "How did it go?"

Judge Dawson's eyes are damp. She hugs Annie long and hard and says something so quietly and so close to Annie's ear that Louisa can't hear it. Whatever it is makes Annie smile. Louisa's father was on the court for twenty years; the other justices were his best friends and colleagues, and the spouses of the justices became close with each other too. It really was a family.

"Oh, Annie," says Judge Dawson. "Annie, Annie Annie. And you, Louisa." She takes Louisa's hands in both of hers and squeezes them. "How lovely you are. How grown-up."

"Oh, well," says Louisa, feeling embarrassed and undeserving and actually not so grown-up after all—her insides are somehow just as chaotic as they were when she was in her teens and twenties. "I mean, thank you, but." (She wonders if by "grown-up" Judge Dawson means "aging poorly.")

"A tenured professor! Writing a book, your mother told me when I arrived. I'm not a bit surprised at all you've accomplished, you know. I'm just impressed."

What Louisa wants to say is, *If by writing a book you mean avoiding writing a book, then yes, I am writing a book.* What she actually says is, "I'm so glad you came by. I know how much my dad appreciates it, even if he doesn't always show it."

Judge Dawson's skin is milk white—a combination, Louisa supposes, of extremely responsible sun care and all of those hours spent indoors, in chambers, reading briefs and writing responses and *thinking* and doing Very Important Work. Louisa remembers reading once that Ruth Bader Ginsberg, may she rest in the most peaceful peace imaginable, got by on only a few hours of sleep almost every night. It's easy to forget, sometimes, the commitment these judicial careers have required, the brainpower, the sacrifices. On the superior court and then later as chief on the state supreme court Martin was a relentless advocate for Maine's drug courts, which allowed nonviolent drug offenders to receive substance abuse support and judicial oversight instead of jail time. How many naysayers had called Martin soft on crime in those early days? How many fights did he have to wage to get the funding? How many people did the drug courts keep out of the state prison system, where they would have languished for decades? Martin had attended the court graduations of some of these people; he'd told Louisa and Annie with tears in his eyes about young mothers being reunited with children who had been removed from their care.

"Sit down," says Annie. "Visit with me for a few minutes. Won't you have tea or coffee?"

"Tea would be perfect," says Judge Dawson.

"I'll get it," says Louisa. "You two catch up."

Teapot, the burner, mugs, and tea bags. Milk and sugar set on a small plate. She balances the plate on her forearm while she holds a mug in each hand. When she enters the dining room Judge Dawson is telling a story.

"—that time when somebody organized a spouses' lunch while we had our annual meeting?"

"I remember," says Annie.

"And Robert went, of course, because he's always so good about these things, even though sometimes he has to take the day off work to do it. And somebody thought it would be a good idea to organize something after the luncheon, remember that, for the spouses? This was before Sandy Lopez joined the bench, so Robert was the only husband, among all those wives." She holds her sides and leans over, practically shaking with mirth. "And they chose *knitting!*"

"*Knitting!*" repeats Annie, reaching across the table and laying her hand on Judge Dawson's arm. "Oh of course, I remember the knitting! That woman with the Christmas sweater that she'd made herself, yes, I'll never forget it. And what a sport Robert was about it. His yarn got tangled almost immediately, and there he sat, not a hint of self-consciousness on him, just working away at it! Oh, Robert." She shakes her head. Then, "Thank you, sweetheart," when Louisa sets down the mugs and the cream and sugar.

There is one of those pauses that happens sometimes in a conversation between two people who are comfortable enough with each other not to fill in the spaces just for the heck of it, and in that pause Louisa is overcome by a sense that Judge Dawson and Robert have it right. Robert is a judge's husband, yes, but he's also a school principal. Maybe *this* is how you build a life, a marriage, a history, a legacy. Maybe you go to the luncheons, and you try your best to knit, whether you know the difference between a moss stitch and a stocking stitch or not, and you don't let it bother you if you are the only person at the table with tangled yarn. Maybe you work as a team.

"Sit with us, Louisa," says Judge Dawson. "Where's your tea? Didn't you make yourself one?"

Louisa can't bring herself to intrude. Also, she doesn't drink tea. To Louisa tea is a last resort if you're all out of coffee.

"Oh, I wish I could," she says. "But I want to check

on the kids. Make sure they're not drowning each other, you know."

"I'll say goodbye now then," says Judge Dawson. "I'm having lunch with my Radcliffe roommate at Archer's, can you believe it? And then I've got to go straight home after for a reception tonight. You remember how it is, Annie. The obligations."

"I remember," says Annie. "I certainly do." She smiles; there's a hint of sadness in her smile. "Sometimes I miss all of that, for both of us. And then sometimes I don't miss it a bit."

Judge Dawson stands and opens her arms to Louisa, and the way she embraces Louisa—not like a mother, not like a friend, but somewhere in between—makes Louisa's throat ache, and she's glad, after all, when she walks down to the water, that it's hot and sunny by the rocks, and that Claire and Abigail are squabbling over the lime-green raft that Matty has blown up and anchored within spitting distance of the shore, because the children give her something else to think about, besides her father, besides the delicate balance of her marriage and her work, both of which lead her somewhere she doesn't really want to go.

After Nina leaves, and Louisa is back up at the house, Pauline returns from the grocery store and announces that she put in an order for two pounds of lobster meat at Jess's that she'll have to go back for; it wasn't ready on her way through town. She's making her famous bisque.

"I'll do it!" says Louisa. "I'll get it, I'd be happy to. I want to walk the breakwater anyway. I'll pick up the meat on the way back."

"If you're sure—" says Pauline. She says it in the Maine way: *sho-wah*.

"Positive." Louisa sees now that Hazel has joined the raft party; all three of the girls are crowded on it and Matty is still on the rocks, the bend of his shoulder suggesting—what? Shyness? Sadness? Deference? The loneliness of being the sole male in the household, excepting Martin? Hazel, Louisa can tell, is a southern force, circling like a cyclone around Matty's heart. She considers asking him to go with her but she's sure he'll say no, and also the breakwater is just an excuse—what she wants as much as the walk is the opportunity to sort through the complicated thoughts Judge Dawson's visit has left her with.

She stops at the parking to the breakwater and makes the short walk to the rocks, thinking about the story of the knitting luncheon. It's a funny story, but it's also not, because behind each justice is an invisible spouse, like an elf in the workshop, toiling away with all the drudgery of toy building while Santa gets to drive the sleigh. Her mother's sole job was being that elf. Her phone rings as she begins to make her way onto the breakwater. It's Steven. She's glad to see his name of the screen; she'll answer, and she'll tell him what she's been thinking about. She'll tell him that they each need to knit for the other person sometimes. Metaphorically, obviously. They would both be terrible knitters.

"Hey. You answered!" He sounds rushed. "I have something to tell you. Well, not tell you. Ask you."

Louisa's heart lifts, and hope unspools. "Are you done? Are you coming up? My mother will be so happy. She thinks we must be headed for divorce court, to be spending so much time apart." Maybe they can knit together in person! Metaphorically, again. She edges past a family walking slowly on the rocks. Too many years of being a New Yorker have made a leisurely pace impossible for Louisa Fitzgerald McLean.

"Oh, no. It's not that. I can't come up. It's not even July yet. We've got miles to go before we sleep, you know that."

The wind makes pleats in the water, and gulls circle, screaming. "I know," she says. "I know, I know." She keeps walking, and she thinks of the young woman with the amazing eyebrows who works in the front office. An absurd envious part of her that she typically tries not to give voice to asks, "How's Greta?"

"Greta? Fine, I guess. I don't know. Why?"

"No reason. I was just wondering." Steven clears his throat, and Louisa keeps walking, and the water is dazzling in the sunlight, and she wishes she'd worn a hat.

"The thing I'm wondering about—Louisa, there's something that I need. I mean, there's something that All Ears needs, to get us through the final stretch."

"*No*," says Louisa instantly. She's positive she knows what Steven is asking. "You can't have more time after August. You can't! You *promised*, Steven. You promised. My book is due and my sabbatical is ending and *you promised* that ten weeks would be it."

Louisa is sure that Steven's hand not holding the phone is lifted, palm out, in the universal sign for *don't freak out*. "It's not more time, Louisa. I'm not going back on our agreement. It's something else." She waits. What could it be? "I'm not sure how to—well, I'll just come right out and say it. It's the money from the Emergency Fund. EF. One investor pulled out, last minute, and we need to fund the next few months to get us in the best possible position to be acquired." Steven starts speaking more quickly, like one of them has a stopwatch on the conversation. "We need to pay salaries, and we've got three different shows in production—we have to finish those. There are travel expenses, to talk to potential buyers. It's a lot, and without that investor we just don't have the cash."

Louisa takes a deep breath—she's almost at the end of the breakwater now, at the lighthouse, and she can see Ships View across the way. She imagines she even sees the green dot of the raft in the water, and her three children plus Hazel.

"The Emergency Fund! Steven. You may as well have said you wanted one of Abigail's kidneys. The Emergency Fund isn't for this kind of thing!" Long ago, newly married, struggling then (in truth, as life became more expensive, the children more plentiful, they struggled still, sometimes struggled more) they'd birthed the fund. Ten percent of each paycheck, always: in the fund. Significant cash gifts from Annie and Martin on the occasion of each of the children's births: in the fund. A medium-size inheritance from Steven's childless aunt, who had remembered all of the McLean brothers in her will: in the fund. They put the fund in the hands of Murph, Steven's Boston College buddy, who, whatever his faults (and faults he had aplenty), was in fact a solid money manager. The Emergency Fund has grown under Murph, grown a lot in fact, to $150,000, and there it sits, inviolable, untouchable, a nest egg they never want to crack. "No," she says.

"No?"

"We don't touch the Emergency Fund. It's for *emergencies!* Like, an unexpected medical situation. Or if we get sued. Or if one of the kids needs to go to rehab someday."

"Louisa! Who's going to need to go to rehab?"

"Hopefully nobody. My money would be on Claire, if I had to pick. But probably not. Anyway, we didn't use the EF when we redid the floors, and that's why it took so long to get to them. We're still living with the appliances that came with the apartment, waiting until we save enough to replace them. That stupid fourth burner that you have to light with a candle lighter. I hate that burner, but we said we'd wait and save up. We didn't use the money for camp. Our kids have never been to Disney World, which is practically a rite of passage for an American child, and now Matty's too old for it."

"He's not too old for the scary rides."

"Well. But he won't like the scary rides. My point is, we held back on all these things because we said we wouldn't touch the Emergency Fund. We said we'd let it keep growing. We never said we'd invest it in a start-up! Where we could lose it!"

Steven's voice cracks. "It's not *a* start-up. It's *my* start-up. And we're not going to lose it. I'm talking about moving it from one investment to another. It's just to tide the company over, and I'll put it right back as soon as we have another investor, or when we sell."

It's true that All Ears is making itself attractive to big media companies. But it's also true that bad things happen all the time to start-ups with good intentions.

"But it's in the stock market—we pay taxes if we take it out!"

He's silent for a moment, and she watches the Vinalhaven ferry pass by. "We only pay taxes on the profit."

"How much is that?"

"I don't know. I'd have to ask Murph."

Dazzling sun on the outside; incandescent rage on the inside. This feels like a betrayal, as certain as if Steven had put his hand to Greta's breast, stroked her perfect eyebrow. First the time, and now the money. What next?

"No. Don't ask Murph. It doesn't matter. I don't want to do it. I don't agree. The emergency fund is for emergencies, and this doesn't feel like an emergency."

"It does to me."

"Well, it doesn't to me." She softens her voice. "I mean, yes, I see that it is a *company* emergency. But it's not a *family* emergency. And there have to be other places All Ears can go for the money, not to your own personal fund. Our own personal fund." She pauses, then says, "I have to go. Pauline is making her lobster bisque, and I'm bringing home the lobster."

"Fine," he says. "Enjoy your lobster." His voice is clipped.

"I will." Hers too.

On the way back, she tries to find herself in the memory of the girl who danced to "*Hips Don't Lie*" at the club in Boston, making, without knowing it, the first tentative movements toward tying her life to Steven's. Marriage, children, the quotidian details that make up a life, an Emergency Fund built from scratch. And now this: a screaming gull, a husbandless summer, a blooming resentment, just when she was ready to start knitting. She and that Ph.D. student in the boot-cut jeans feel like two entirely different people, unrecognizable to one another.

When she gets home, Claire is lying on a beach towel in the side yard, fast asleep. Louisa fears she's burning. She pokes Claire's leg with her toe, and when Claire startles awake she helps her move to a shadier spot.

Claire rubs her eyes and lets her forearm fall across her face. "Mommy?" she says. "What's a love child?"

"A *love child*? Where did you hear that?"

"I heard Pauline say it," says Claire sleepily. "When I was listening from the bathroom to the kitchen."

"Who was she talking to?"

"I don't know. I think she was on the phone."

Louisa studies Claire, with her fair hair and her fair skin, both hiding a fiery spirit. Claire is not yet eight! Louisa hasn't treated her to the Facts of Life talk. "A love child is a child who is loved very much," she says.

"Oooh, that sounds really nice," says Claire. "So I'm a love child." She turns on her side on the beach towel and goes back to sleep.

16.

Kristie

Kristie has half the deck for the lunch shift, and Todd, who tends bar when he's not serving, has the other half. It's a fine, clear day; Kristie can see well across the harbor, all the way to the breakwater. The boat traffic is steady: not just the bigger boats coming from Camden, but the smaller boats in their slips are coming in or going out, and all along the pier she can hear fragments of words or sentences and the cries or laughter of children and the squawking of gulls.

At table three, one of Todd's tables, sit two women in their sixties, one with dark hair, and one with a blond-silvery mix. It's a four-top and Kristie can tell by the seats they've chosen, next to each other rather than across from one another, that they are close.

"It's the saddest thing," the woman with the dark

hair says. Something in her voice makes Kristie stop and listen. "It's enough to break your heart. Corinne, believe me when I tell you that Martin Fitzgerald had one of the finest minds I've ever known, in all my days on the bench, and before that, all way back to clerking, and law school. If it weren't for him there would have been, I don't know, *countless* people withering in the jails after a drug—" The woman turns her head toward the water and the rest of her words are lost to Kristie.

Kristie takes a painfully long time clearing the plates from table six—so long that she sees Fernando glaring at her from the doorway—but then the clatter of a bus tray from across the deck drowns out the rest of what the woman is saying. *Martin Fitzgerald.* She wants to sit down. Her heart is beating fast, and her fingers are quivering. Table seven signals for the check, which, owing to the setup of the deck and the way the tables are numbered, brings her back in orbit with the two women.

She delivers the check to seven, then she drops a napkin near table four and bends to pick it up. She makes herself busy folding a clean napkin in thirds to put under an imaginary wobble on one of the table legs so she can study the women more closely. They are drinking white wine and eating salads. They have expensive haircuts and expensive perfume and each wears a single expensive-looking bracelet (one silver, one gold) and even the way they tip their heads toward each other looks expensive, like they've been trained in a special expensive school to do so.

"It's a terrible disease," the blondish one says. "Simply awful, Nina, I know. Oh, I'm so sorry to hear it."

"Kristie!" says Fernando sharply. He's right next to her.

"I'm sorry," she says. "This table was doing that thing again."

A few minutes later, at the bar, Kristie and Todd are both waiting to pick up their drinks. Kristie says, "Who's that woman? At table four? The one with the dark hair?"

Todd shrugs. "Girl, how should I know? You think I know the name of each and every one of my customers?"

"Right," she says. "No."

He smile-smirks at her and garnishes a seltzer with a lime. "Do you know the names of *your* customers?"

"No! No, of course not. I just thought she looked familiar, that's all." Her knees feel unsteady. Maybe she misheard the name.

At the end of her shift she's rolling silverware, thinking about the thing she has to do as soon as she clocks out. She knows Danny is working at the Fitzgeralds' today after his work for Gil is done, so she has time. He won't be back for a couple of hours.

"Earth to Kristie!" says Fernando. How is it that he's *everywhere*, constantly popping up like a Whac-A-Mole? She braces herself and looks up. Fernando is holding a clipboard, has a pen behind his ear. "Any interest in a double? Lexi called in sick."

"I can't today," says Kristie. "Sorry, Fernando." She knows Lexi isn't sick. Her boyfriend is visiting from Atlanta and they're going out to dinner in Camden. They have a reservation at Peter Ott's; Kristie was standing right next to Lexi when Lexi made it. Seven o'clock on the deck. There is nothing a server likes more than going out to another restaurant to be wined and dined. Kristie understands this, and she likes Lexi, but this is not her problem. Kristie is so, so tired. She can't imagine taking on a dinner shift.

"Plans?" says Fernando with a slight sneer. "Big night out?"

"Something like that," says Kristie. "Not that it's any of your business." More Netflix; maybe a pizza. Plus the thing she has to do.

"Your loss," says Fernando. "Lexi was in station one." Station one is the best one. You walk with at least two hundred after a busy night in station one.

"I guess it is," she says, shrugging, but not too hard.

It's a lot of money she's giving up by saying no. She got another call from the collector on her way to work—her phone said *private number,* so she didn't answer, but she knows they'll catch up with her. When she thinks about how many baked stuffed haddocks she'll have to serve to get to $27,000 she wants to lie down on the stack of napkins and go to sleep while somebody else figures out her problems.

"You should smile more," says Fernando, when she's clocking out. "You're a lot prettier when you smile, you know."

Go screw yourself, she says in her head. She can't let herself say it out loud.

It's only a half mile from Archer's to the Walgreens on Park Street but if feels like a half marathon as she's walking it. She hews close to the water as long as she can, along the Rockland Harbor Trail, by the yacht club and the harbormaster hut, watching the boats bobbing in the harbor, passing people and dogs who don't have to do what she is about to do, before cutting over to Main Street and then to Park. By the time she arrives she's sweating and thirsty and the air-conditioning in the store is sweet, blessed relief.

She skirts down the hair accessories aisle and toward the pharmacy, where she finds what she's looking for next to the condoms. Irony notwithstanding. She shuttles it into her basket and hides it beneath a box of Triscuits and a greeting card, blank inside, with a photo of a black Lab puppy on the front. Kristie has nobody to send the card to, but she's always wanted a black Lab puppy. She adds a bottle of cold water from the cooler near the checkout line and waits behind a pale family covered in sunscreen and rash guards.

When it's her turn to approach, Kristie doesn't meet the cashier's eyes—she's a grim, middle-aged local with fine lines around her mouth that suggest a lifetime spent with a cigarette between her lips. But when Kristie pays and takes the bag from her, she inadvertently catches the woman's gaze and sees something there that could be pity. Or curiosity.

"You take care now," the woman says, and tears spring to Kristie's eyes. Maybe what she saw in the woman was just good old-fashioned kindness.

Kristie walks back to Linden Street, drinking the water, ignoring her phone when it dings with a text from Danny. He'll be done in the next thirty minutes; maybe they can grab a bite at the Fog Bar? He'll see her at home, and they can figure it out.

Kristie picks up her pace. She'll have to take the most direct route; no meandering by the water. She passes the fancy boutique hotel on the corner of Park and Main; she passes the Time Out Pub and the Rock City Café. She passes the turnoff to the Y, and she keeps walking until she's home.

The lobsterman's daughters are in the front yard, arguing over a doll. One of them has it by the hair and the other by the legs and they're pulling it back and forth between them, saying, "Mine, mine, mine," rhythmically, almost as though they're reciting a poem to each other. When they see Kristie they drop the doll and stare at her, wide-eyed, until she waves, and then they both smile.

Kristie locks the door behind her. She pees on the stick, sets the timer on her phone and paces, not allowing herself to look at the screen or the stick until she hears the bell. Instead she looks out the window, at the clear blue sky. When the sun starts to go down and the air cools station one will be hopping. She thinks about Lexi and her Atlanta boyfriend; she thinks about Danny pulling out of the Fitzgeralds' driveway; she thinks about her mother's face, small against the big pillow.

And then the timer goes.

It's not a surprise. The nausea, the breast tenderness, the fatigue—but still it *feels* like a surprise, and she's immediately faint and flushed and wobbly in the knees. Two pink stripes, side by side, parallel, the two ends of an *H* without the crossbar connecting them. H for *help*. H for *hopeless*, for *hell*, for *how*.

It's the oldest story in the book. A tale as old as time, etc.

A knock on the door. Danny. "Kristie! Kristie. Are you in there? Sorry, babe! I left my keys on the table this morning."

She shuttles everything into the bathroom garbage, then takes a deep breath. She swings the door open.

July

17.
Louisa

Dear Daddy,

Hazel is mine and Claire's sworn enemy. We are UNITED on that. We don't think she knows because she is always extra friendly to us. She is going home on the first of August. If she's still here when you come can you try to be not exactly perfectly friendly to her? EVERYBODY loves Hazel except for me and Claire so it would be nice if you could be on our side. Even Granny likes her, and YOU KNOW that Granny is a tough customer. I promise you Hazel is NOT ALL SHE'S CRACKED UP TO BE.

Sufficey to say Matty is probably going to fall in love. If he hasn't already.

Daddy, I think we've lost him.

Write back.

Love, Abigail

The Pitcairn Islands, for those who don't know, and truly, Louisa understands, many people don't know, and fewer probably care, comprise four volcanic islands in the Southern Pacific. The Islands are the sole British territory in the Pacific Ocean. Only one of the islands, Pitcairn, is permanently inhabited, by about fifty people. Pitcairn is the setting for the final book in The Bounty Trilogy, a slew of self-published books, an exposé about the dark secrets on the island, and a *Vanity Fair* article. To this body of work Louisa is going to add hers, which will compare the Seventh-day Adventists with the evangelical movement in the United States.

At one time—indeed, when she proposed the topic—this seemed a subject that was suitably interesting to keep Louisa working fruitfully during her sabbatical. At one time she felt great passion for the island of Pitcairn, which is rife with drama and intrigue and beauty. (The island is only about the size of Central Park! Most of the houses don't have doors! You can watch humpback whales in the surrounding water, which is the clearest, least polluted water anywhere!) She has written four pages since she and Annie visited the Farnsworth. Recalculating the math tells her that she must write between five and a half and six pages per day between now and their departure in mid-August.

Now here she is, at the Rockland public library while at Ships View her children try out her new plan for increasing her own productivity.

Her phone, set on silent mode, shows that she missed a call from Franklin in Charleston. She loves Franklin, but sometimes he's so tapped into the history professor scene that talking to him makes her feel anxious. Better to leave it for now.

She checks her watch. It's eleven o'clock. Too early for lunch? Maybe, but Louisa's stomach says otherwise. And the Rockland library, though an indisputably stunning building, is hardly NYU's twelve-story Bobst. It's perfect for parents and children and browsers. She packs her laptop and her notecards into her work bag and slings it over her shoulder. She'll walk around a little bit, just enough to get the juices flowing again, and then she'll grab a bite to eat and perhaps find somewhere else to work.

On the wide green lawn in front of the library two kids are throwing a Frisbee back and forth. This warms Louisa's heart—she didn't know that kids still threw Frisbees. She thought they had all switched over to virtual reality Frisbee-adjacent games. But here in Rockland, maybe time has stood still. As she's crossing Route 1 to head toward Main Street she entertains a short vision of bringing the children up here. The children can attend Rockland public schools and grow into cleaner, happier, Maine-er, more wholesome versions of the kids they would otherwise.

Then she remembers that the Owls Head house isn't winterized. Abigail would never want to leave her gymnastics classes. Matty is at a precarious age— nobody cares to start over in eighth grade. And she and Steven, and this is the most salient fact, don't have jobs here. (Claire would probably come.) On Main Street, she peeks into Atlantic Baking Company and Rock City Café. She chooses Main Street Markets, where she orders a hummus wrap that she can carry down to eat somewhere close to the water. She'll find a bench! The day is temperate; the sun is out but it's not too hot, and there's a light breeze coming from the water.

She has just paid and is heading out the door when she feels her phone buzzing. She looks down. Steven.

"Hey," she says, answering in her I'm-super-busy voice. "What's up?"

"I had a break," says Steven. "So I thought I'd check in, see how everyone is."

Louisa grits her teeth against the memory of their last conversation, about the Emergency Fund. Since then they've exchanged only texts. "Everyone is fine," she says. She has one goal, and it's to get in and out of this conversation without a fight.

"I've got to be back in the studio in ten, but I wanted to say hi to the kids. Can you pass the phone around?"

"I can't, I'm actually not with them."

"You're not? Where are you?" Tiny bit of something in Steven's voice—a morsel of judgment, perhaps? Or maybe merely curiosity. Louisa wriggles around for a moment in the middle of a paradox: what she has wanted for much of the past year for her and for the kids too was more of Steven's attention. Now here it is, and it's come at a time when she wants to eat her wrap and look at the water and imagine she's on Pitcairn, so she resents it.

"I'm in town working, and the kids are at home. In fact, let me tell you about my genius scheme. I can't believe I never thought of this before. Listen to this. I pay Matty ten dollars to keep an eye on Abigail and Claire. I pay Abigail seven dollars to watch Claire, and I pay Claire four dollars to get watched by Matty and Abigail so she doesn't complain. But the super genius part is that unless they compare notes nobody knows about the other two."

A long silence, and then Steven says," Per *hour*?"

"No! No, of course not. I'd go broke. For the morning."

"What about your mother?"

"Oh, well, really she's driving the whole bus, obviously. But she's never been the get-down-on-the-floor kind of grandmother, and she has a lot going on. This way I'm hoping they don't bother her."

"Are you paying *her* too?"

"*No!*" This conversation has taken a left turn when she expected it to go right. "Of course I'm not paying my mom, Steven, that would be so weird."

"I agree."

"My mom's not a babysitter."

"Of course not. But isn't that one of the main reasons you're there? So she can help out while you work?"

She shifts her bag onto her other shoulder, puts the hummus wrap on top for safekeeping. She's flustered now. It's not fair for Steven to make her feel flustered! "One of the main reasons we're here, Steven"—she leans hard on the first syllable of his name, a sure sign to both of them that she's irritated—"is so *you* can focus on your company without us in the way."

"Well sure," he says reasonably. "But your plan was also to work on your book while your mom is there to help. I'm just not sure that paying the kids to watch each other is the way to teach responsibility."

"Responsibility?" Is this conversation really happening?

"Yeah. Fiscal responsibility, and also personal responsibility. First of all, you're way overpaying them, which isn't teaching them the value of money—"

"*Four dollars* I'm paying Claire!" she protests.

"—And personal responsibility too. My parents never paid us to watch each other when we were kids. We just hung out. It's not really a job, to keep yourself occupied when your parents work, is it? It's just something you have to do sometimes. I don't know if this is how we want to go about it."

"*We* are not going about it in any way right now," she says. "*I* am going about it, because I am the one who's here." She glances at her watch. "Oh! Looks like your ten minutes are up. You'd better get into the studio."

When she finds a bench, she releases the wrap from the bag, unwraps it, and chews it harder than she needs to.

Upon Louisa's return all three of the children are near the water, screens nowhere to be seen. Vitamin D is flowing. Her father is working in the garden, with Barbara hovering nearby. Danny is backing the mower up the ramp and into his pickup. (He seems to be here every other day. Does the grass grow *that quickly*?) Louisa's mother is lying down in her room. See? She wants to tell Steven. My genius plan *is* genius! Instead Louisa sits on the back porch in the white rocker and calls Franklin.

Louisa and Franklin were Ph.D. students together at Columbia—they listened to each other's dissertation defense practices, they drank pint after pint of dollar drafts at the 1020 bar, they bitched about their thesis advisors and other students in their program who published papers in journals before they did. When Louisa met Steven, she called Franklin at two in the morning to tell him she thought she was in love. When Franklin married Beau, Louisa served as Franklin's best woman, opposite Beau's sister, Shonda.

"Lou Lou!" Franklin is the only person ever in the whole world who can get away with calling Louisa this, and only sometimes.

"Franklin," she says. "I'm sorry it took me a few days to call you back. I'm in summer mode, which means I'm getting nothing done except worrying about what I'm not getting done."

Franklin and Beau live in Charleston, South Carolina, in a gorgeous, brick-fronted three-bedroom condo on King Street. Franklin teaches at the College of Charleston and Beau works at the Gibbes Museum of Art. They have no children, which means that Franklin has published at almost twice the rate that Louisa has. Okay, maybe that's not *just because* Franklin doesn't have children. Franklin is also incredibly smart and really, really hardworking. But certainly his mind is less cluttered than Louisa's on any given day.

"Sure, sister. I hear that. I'd ask how you are and all that other bullshit but actually in fact I think I'm just going to get right to it."

"Get to what?" Louisa's heart goes zip zip.

"To what I have to tell you." It would be hot in Charleston, and humid, but Louisa imagines Franklin dressed in some sort of dapper seersucker number, sockless feet in fashionable loafers. He's probably sitting in his air-conditioned living room, whose floor-to-ceiling windows look out on King Street, sipping a glass of sweet tea. "Somebody else is writing about Pitcairn."

No. *No.* "Wait, what? What do you mean?"

"They're reexamining the Pitcairn sexual assault trials of 2004 in light of the #MeToo movement. I was asked to peer review a paper that I'm pretty sure is on track to get turned into a book. I just read it, and I texted you as soon as I was done."

Louisa's stomach drops. Of course she's going to address the trial, when six men, including the mayor, were convicted of sexual assault offenses. But a whole book about the trial, with the added context of the #MeToo movement, is guaranteed to get attention.

It's an important topic! Relevant. And Louisa didn't think to write it herself.

"Who is it? Who's writing this?" She searches her mind. Which school would produce a scholar who would produce this work? She should know this. Think, Louisa. *Think.*

"You know I don't know, Lou. It's a blind review."

Louisa lets a little wheedle enter her voice. "Come on, Franklin. We all know blind reviews aren't really blind." They are, ostensibly, but academia is a small world. Once you'd read enough work written by your peers—in journals, in conference papers, in books or chapters of books—you started to recognize a person's writing style, and the reviews became not so much blind as slightly blurry.

She hears a whoop from down on the rocks—it's Abigail, going all the way under the water and emerging triumphant, arms above her head.

Franklin sighs. "Lou Lou Lou. I can't even hazard a guess. I couldn't possibly."

"You can hazard. You can *definitely* hazard." She waits. She knows she has him.

"But if I had to? Like, with a gun to my head had to take a guess?"

"Gun to your head," says Louisa. "Big, big gun."

"Then I suppose the name Phoebe Richardson might come to mind. Possibly."

Louisa makes a little noise of dismay. Phoebe Richardson is twenty-eight, maybe twenty-nine, newly minted out of Berkeley. Phoebe Richardson is poised to be a superstar. Louisa met her once, at a conference last year. Louisa was prepared to hate her and irritated to learn that she was actually sort of nice. And a little bit funny. And very pretty.

"No," she says. "That can't be true. That doesn't even make sense." Pitcairn was so very, very remote, so small and unpopulated. Why is anyone besides Louisa even thinking about Pitcairn?

"I'm not saying it's definite," says Franklin. "I'm saying gun-to-my-head guess. I could totally be wrong."

"You're never wrong about these things, Franklin. Your sense for other people's writing styles is uncanny."

"Well," says Franklin modestly. "Obviously I don't want to blow my own horn. But, yes, that is one of my talents, along with folding fitted sheets and restarting tape rolls when the end of the tape slips off the thingy that holds it."

"Pitcairn is *mine*," says Louisa. "It's *mine*. Phoebe Richardson can't have Pitcairn." She remembers devoting at least three minutes at last year's conference to staring at Phoebe's shoes, which had a spiky heel and a narrow toe and a complicated lizard pattern.

"You might be okay, darling." There is a pause, during which Louisa is certain Franklin is taking a refreshing sip of his sweet tea. "It's a submission for a conference paper. It's not a book yet."

"But you said she might be turning it into a book."

"She might! Then again, she might not."

Louisa hears a shriek from the direction of the rocks. "Franklin, I have to go," she says, with a small measure of relief. "Emergency here." She disconnects, drops her phone onto the side table, and runs across the grass.

Claire is coming through the gate up to the yard. Her knee is bloodied and there are tears running down her face, mixing with the dried yogurt left there from breakfast. She wipes savagely at her eyes and says, "I slipped on the stupid, stupid seaweed."

"Oh, honey," says Louisa. She crouches down and opens her arms. Claire puts her wet face into Louisa's neck and her whole body shudders with a sob. "That seaweed *is* stupid," says Louisa. "Come with me. We'll get you all fixed up." She puts her arm around Claire's spindly shoulders and leads her up the porch steps and into the house. She may not be able to keep fancy-pants

Phoebe Richardson from reexamining the Pitcairn trials of 2004 in light of the #MeToo movement. But she can get a Band-Aid and some Neosporin from the medicine cabinet in the small downstairs bathroom, the one with the handprints, and she can patch up Claire temporarily at least, and that's something.

18.
Kristie

After Danny leaves for work Kristie stays in bed. He has left her a cup of coffee on the nightstand, placed carefully on top of a coaster. He is so thoughtful; she can't believe how lucky she is. Will his thoughtfulness change when he learns about the pregnancy?

She can't drink the coffee. It turns her stomach, and anyway it's not good for the baby. She places her palms on her stomach and thinks, *Baby.* She goes over the timing of her last period. It was in the middle of May, before she left Altoona for Maine. It was right after her mother died. She remembers because she had cramps when she was talking to the woman in the billing department at UPMC Altoona. She met Danny in early June. So that timing tracks; she would have gotten pregnant right away. Probably the first night they slept together, after the ice cream at River Ducks.

Then she got so caught up in her new life here, in Danny, in her job, in watching the house in Owls Head, that she didn't even notice her missed period.

She reaches for her phone and pulls up a pregnancy calculator, inputting dates. The calculator spits out the answer almost immediately. She is five weeks pregnant, almost six. How big is a baby at six weeks? She googles again. The baby is the size of a pomegranate seed! So tiny. By the next week at this time it will have become the size of a blueberry.

Kristie falls back onto the pillow and stares at the ceiling. How can something as tiny as a pomegranate seed make her feel so tired? She closes her eyes. The next thing she knows her phone is ringing and sunlight is streaming in the window. She fumbles for the phone. It's Fernando.

"Kristie—what the hell? You were supposed to be here fifteen minutes ago to set up for lunch. You're out on the deck. It's sunny as all fuck today. We're going to get slammed."

"Ohmygod. Fernando. I'm sorry. I'm so, so sorry." She's working a double today.

"Get your ass over here ASAP if you want to keep your job."

"I do. I do want to keep my job." Kristie's hair is sticking to the side of her face, and the sheets are sticking to her body. The coffee has grown cold on the nightstand, the cream congealing in a slick layer on top of it. Her stomach turns. She's out of bed, peeling off her pajama shorts with one hand and holding the phone with the other.

"I'm on my way," she tells Fernando. "I'm almost there." Toilet, toothbrush, cold water on her face. No time for a shower. Ponytail, lipstick.

She gets through the lunch shift. It isn't pretty, but she gets through it, even though the entire time her limbs feel like they're moving underwater. While she's rolling silverware she pulls up a map of the apartment in her mind, tries to figure out where to put a crib. But surely a new baby doesn't need a crib. They can hold off on that for a while, right? The baby can sleep in a bassinet. How much does a bassinet cost? She fumbles the silverware and drops a setting on the floor.

"What's eating you, Princess?" Fernando asks her as he picks up the silverware and puts it in the dirty dish bin. "You look terrible."

"I hate that expression," she says, irritated. "And: nothing." Fernando calls all the female servers Princess except for the one he's sleeping with, Sarah, whom he calls Babygirl. Both names are misogynistic and insulting, but that's the restaurant business for you. It was worse in Miami Beach. Harder to complain there, though, because the tips were so good.

She has ninety minutes before she has to be back for dinner setup. She naps for eighty-six of the ninety minutes, not changing out of her work uniform. "You look even worse," Fernando tells her when she returns. "Freshen up, why don't you." She puts on lipstick in the bathroom and feels a little better.

It's a full house almost from the start. Good. She needs the money. More than ever, now, she needs the money. She hopes every adult at every table orders a cocktail before peeking at the wine list. Fernando has her out on the deck, where there's a wait by five-thirty. She's doing her best to keep up, but her mind is lagging. She orders the wrong bottle of wine for one table, opens it before she realizes it, has to have Fernando take it off the bill. Amber will use it behind the bar, but still. This is supposed to be her fresh beginning, and she feels it slipping away.

By seven-thirty the sun is still vigilant. There's a breeze off the water, which is nice, but Kristie feels like it's midnight. Fernando gives her a four-top. Two couples, not much older than Kristie. Men in golf shirts, suntanned faces and arms, women in sundresses and wedge sandals. Twenty bucks says they came from a sailboat docked in Camden and Ubered down here. She can smell the women's expensive perfume. Their fingers are lousy with rings; their earrings are square diamonds.

When she does her bit—Fernando makes them say it this way, *I'm Kristie, and I'll be taking care of you,* one of the men says, *Thank you, Kristie,* and gives her a cheesy smile. He's looking at her tattoos and she can bet he's thinking, *I'd like to have you take care of me.* People always make assumptions about tattoos and sex. One of the women has dark hair pulled up in a perfect high bun; the other has expensive honey highlights.

A round of cocktails: Dark and Stormys for the men and vodka tonics for the women. She bets she can talk them into a nice bottle of sauv after.

They order. House salad topped with crab. Caesar salad topped with haddock. Delmonico rib eye. Seafood pie. Okay, now they're cooking with gas. The Delmonico is thirty-two dollars and the seafood pie, a house specialty, thirty-four. No appetizer, but they go for two bottles of wine, the sauv she suggests and a red blend.

She tends to her other tables. It's such a nice night, everyone is lingering. That means less tip money, but she's okay with that; she's having trouble catching her breath. She keeps thinking of the pomegranate seed.

She's only known Danny a little over a month. This will scare him into leaving.

She opens both bottles of wine while she waits for the entrées. She brings fresh napkins to one of her other tables and recites the desserts to a two-top. The party of five at table seven is still perusing the menu. Just before entrées for the four-top come up, they're ready to order. She writes everything down on her notepad; she'll enter it into the computer after she delivers the entréees.

"Come on, Kristie, my girl," says Joe, who's running the kitchen. He's sweating through the bandanna he wears to cover his head; he's as bald as the day is long. "That pie's my pride and joy, don't let it dry out."

"Got it," she says. Her arms feel shaky. She nods to the food runner to take the Delmonico and the pie and she grabs the two salads. Through the dining room, out onto the deck. Her legs feel shaky too. She can't remember what she ate today, or even if. She'll have to be more careful about her nutrition, with the baby.

The word *baby* stuns her, even in her head. She puts down the salads—these go to the women, of course—and reaches for the seafood pie. But there's a disconnect between her hands and her brain, or between the food runner's brain and Kristie hands, and the seafood pie slips out of her hands and lands in the lap of High Bun lady before flipping over onto the floor of the deck, landing with a terrific crash, so loud that it seems to reverberate over the harbor. High Bun Lady screams, and everyone on the deck falls silent and turns to look. From somewhere unseen comes a long, low whistle. There is always some asshole who whistles like that when somebody drops something in a restaurant. Every time.

High Bun Lady is livid. Who wouldn't be? The plate is hot, and it's heavy. The pretty dress is ruined— definitely for tonight, if not forever.

"I'm sorry," Kristie says. "I'm so, so sorry." She wants to curl up into a ball and disappear forever. She doesn't even know where to start cleaning up the mess. Someone alerts Fernando, who sends the busser out, then Fernando works overtime in the appeasement department. Napkins to cover the summer dress, dry cleaning assured. A replacement for the dress if the dry cleaning doesn't take care of it. Fernando removes all four entrées from the bill and brings a fresh round of cocktails. Kristie stands near the walk-in, stupid tears popping into her eyes.

"Kristie," says Fernando, whipping through the kitchen to tell the chef to expedite the pie order. "You just cost me a hundred and eighteen dollars, before the cocktails."

"I'm sorry," she whispers. She wants to sink down onto the kitchen floor. "I'm just having a really bad day." She can't help but resent Fernando's choice of words; surely he is not footing the bill for the entrées from his very own pocket! But every restaurant manager she's ever worked for has used personal pronouns in the same way. She could offer to pay for the entrées herself, but she can't afford it. She probably hasn't even made one hundred and eighteen dollars so far today. And she needs to hang on to every penny. Crib, she thinks again. Formula. Diapers. Diapers. Diapers.

Fernando whistles through the gap in his front teeth, and his brown eyes rove and then settle on hers. "Kristie. You were late for lunch today, and now this. If you don't want to be here maybe you shouldn't be here."

She doesn't want to be here, but also, she needs to be here. "Wait," she says. "Do you mean I shouldn't be here tonight, or—forever?"

"Either. Both." Fernando crosses his arms and studies her.

"Are you firing me?" she says. "Fernando, are you fucking firing me?" One of the line cooks whistles in the same way that the person on the deck whistled when she dropped the plate. She knows the curse was a mistake as soon as it comes out of her mouth, but it's too late—she can't get the word back.

"I wasn't before," Fernando says. "But now? Yeah, I think I am. I don't like when people talk to me that way. I don't put up with it."

"Good," she says, taking off her apron. "Saves me the trouble of quitting."

"I had high hopes for you, Kristie. I thought you were going to be one of the good ones."

It bothers her more than it should that she's disappointed Fernando. "Good luck finding a replacement."

Fernando snorts. "You think I can't find a replacement? I've got a stack of applications a foot high in my office. I've got college kids coming out of my ears right now."

"Okay," she says. "Well, that's good for you then." He's probably right.

She folds her apron and leaves it in the back room. She collects her credit card tips for the night from Amber at the bar, who gives her a fist bump and a sympathetic look. She hugs Natalie, who's standing at the bar, waiting on her drinks. She leaves the order for table seven on her notepad, not entered in the computer. She takes the notepad with her. Good luck, table seven.

She tries to slam the door on the way out, but it's the kind of door that doesn't actually slam.

She should have told Fernando she's pregnant. She's pretty sure you can fire someone for shitty work or careless dropping of a seafood pie onto a woman with a perfect high bun but if you fire someone for being pregnant it's most likely illegal, and she could fight it. Would she even want to fight it, though? She's tired of summer people who can order thirteen-dollar cocktails without a second thought, and she's tired of people asking her where the spiral staircase in the middle of the restaurant goes (nowhere!), and she's tired of rolling silverware into napkins, and she's tired of coming home smelling like the Captain's Platter, which has four different types of fried seafood. Beyond all that, mostly she's just really, really tired.

She stands for a minute in the parking lot, looking out at the water, at where the pier stretches out into the middle of the harbor. In the short time since the four-top sat, the sun has begun to set; the moon is on the rise. She can hardly see the boats tied up at the end of the pier. The moon shimmers beyond the breakwater, and it lights up the water in a way that would normally lift her heart.

But not now. Her mother is gone. Danny won't stick around once he learns about the baby. When Danny leaves, her connection to Ships View will vanish, and that's the only reason she's up here anyway. Where will she go next? How will she start over once more?

She trudges home, following Ocean Street to where it briefly becomes Scott, and then back to Ocean, hooking a right on Linden. There's a light on in their apartment but the lobsterman's house is quiet and dark. Danny has told her that lobstermen haul every day but Sunday. She pictures the little girls with their heads on their pillows, their eyelashes long against their cheekbones. Their place can't be much bigger than Kristie's; the girls must share a bedroom. Maybe they sleep separately, in twin beds side by side, or maybe they share a single bigger bed. Sisters. Her heart constricts, then expands.

She climbs the stairs, each lift of her leg like picking up a log from mud.

Danny is understanding about her losing the job at Archer's—Danny's cousin Amanda once worked at Archer's, and his mother's ex-boyfriend's son was a line cook two summers ago, and neither had anything good to say about Fernando—and also optimistic that she'll find something else. In the meantime, he says, he's happy to cover more of their expenses.

But Danny doesn't know about the money the debt collectors are after, and he doesn't know about the pregnancy, and he doesn't know Kristie's real reason for being in Maine.

The day after the firing, Danny is working for Gil in a house in Rockport—he might be late getting home because they are putting in some new trees, and you can never predict how long new trees will take. He's so excited about the trees that he wakes her up early and they make love. In bed she's not tired, but everywhere else in the world she's exhausted.

"Wow," she says, after. She kisses him on the nose and then once on each eyelid. "I guess you really do get excited about planting trees."

"It's my favorite part of the job," he says. He's like a kid about to look inside his Christmas stocking. He talks about the trees: two eastern redbuds and four Fort McNair red horse chestnuts. All flowering, but they won't bloom until next spring.

As soon as Danny leaves, her exhaustion returns, covering her like the weighted X-ray vests the dentist uses.

By the time Danny's trees bloom she'll have a baby.

After Kristie drags herself out of bed and showers she revisits all of the restaurants where she dropped off applications at the end of May. If nobody was hiring before, twice as many nobodys are hiring now.

"We're coming up on the middle of July," says the

manager at Cafe Miranda. "I'm not anticipating any changes."

She's right back where she started.

"Nope, sorry. Nothing."

"All staffed up."

Rustica. Time Out Pub. Brass Compass Cafe: all the same.

"Sorry, hon," says the woman at Rock Harbor Pub & Brewery.

"No, I get it," says Kristie. She feels like she should apologize for even asking. "I totally get it."

She's walking out the door, feeling the doleful slump of her own shoulders, and that new, vicious fatigue, when the woman calls her back. "Hey, hon. This isn't a restaurant job, but I know they need someone down at Renys. My brother-in-law's cousin works there, she was just telling me over the Fourth."

"Renys?" says Kristie.

"Don't you know Renys? On the road to Camden. It's like—it's sort of like a department store. They sell everything under the sun, at great prices too." She points. "Thataway."

"Oh," says Kristie. "Camden. Thank you. But that's too far. I don't have a car. I can only work at places I can walk to or maybe bike."

"Bus goes right by there." The manager shrugs.

"Up to you, of course. But if you go, ask for Diana, and tell her Mary sent you."

"Mary," she said. "Diana. Renys. Got it. Thanks." She needs to get to Renys before some other fired server gets there, so she treats herself to an Uber. Twenty-five minutes after she walks in, she walks out with a job. "Okay," she tells her belly. "Okay, little guy or girl. This is something. It won't be what we were making at the restaurant, but it's something."

She calls another Uber and puts her address in the app. After this, no more Ubers.

"Linden Street?" says the driver.

"Yes." Kristie roots around in her backpack; all of this excitement has made her thirsty. She imagines her little pomegranate seed is thirsty too. She drinks until all of the water in the bottle is gone, and then she unzips the small front pocket and sees the small pad of paper and pen she keeps there for emergencies.

"You know what?" she tells the Uber driver. "Change in plans. Can you take me out to Owls Head, please? I'm going to give you an address, but I'd like you to drop me before you turn off the main road."

"Put the new address in the app," says the driver.

Kristie puts the new address in the app. She starts writing.

After she walks down the dirt road and approaches

the house her eyes fall on the flower garden where Danny once showed her the peonies. Their bloom time has come and gone, but now there's a crowd of other colors: oranges and yellows, some reds. Daises are the only ones she recognizes. In the middle of it all is an old man in a hat. Every so often a handful of something—weeds, Kristie supposes, or hopes—flies out of the garden and lands on or near a large sheet spread out on the grass. Well, there he is. The man himself. Your Honor. His honor. Kristie's honor. She's gripping the note in her right hand; she worries that the sweat from her hands will make the ink run, so she puts it in the back pocket of her interview pants.

Just as she gets close to the garden: "Hey!" A woman comes marching down the steps that lead from the long back porch to the grass. "Excuse me there. What do you think you're doing?" The woman has a long, half-gray braid and a wicked scowl. This must be Pauline, who Kristie knows from Danny cooks for the family. "Chief, you don't know this person, do you?" She has a deep crater in the center of her forehead, and frown lines around her mouth.

"I do," he says. "Yes, I believe I do." He looks wonderingly back and forth from Kristie to Pauline. "It's Louisa, isn't it?" He's wearing sunglasses along with the hat, so it's hard to read his expression, or even see much of his face.

"No," says Pauline gently, her face relaxing and softening. "No, Louisa is inside with the children. I don't think you know this woman. I think she might be bothering you." She looks sternly at Kristie. "I don't know what it is you're selling, the Good Book or the Good News or whatever it is—"

"Oh, not that," says Kristie. This woman thinks she's a Jehovah's Witness! They used to get them going door to door in Pennsylvania. "No, I'm not here to—I just wanted to . . ." Words elude her, and she shoves her hand in her pocket, reaching for the note. She has to leave the note.

"Whatever you're selling, we're not buying it. And this man has Alzheimer's. He is in *no* condition to talk to strangers."

Time slows down. Kristie looks out at the water. A speck of a sailboat glides by. Closer, a kayak. She can see the breakwater and the lighthouse and the buildings of Rockland. She can almost see the deck at Archer's with the pier reaching out like a finger. It's low tide; the expanse of rocks between the yard and the water is covered with seaweed. Far, far off is a stately white vessel that Kristie knows now is the ferry to Vinalhaven.

She looks back at the man in the garden. She's too late. All the time, all the effort it took to get here, and she's too late. Her heart is a stone, sinking, sinking to the bottom of her body. She has come too late.

Then she feels a touch on her shoulder. And then: "How'd you know I'd be here?" *Danny.* Her palms are sweating even more now. Danny isn't at the house in Rockport with the red horse chestnuts. Danny is right here. "How'd you know I'd be done with the trees?"

"The trees!" Kristie pivots, and feigns frustration with herself. "I forgot all about the trees. I figured you'd be here—because you're always here."

Danny smiles. "Pauline, this here's my beloved, Kristie. Kristie, Pauline." He puts his arm around Kristie. He smells like sweat and freshly mown grass. "We were done with the trees early, and Mrs. Fitzgerald let me know that there were a few jobs here at the house if I wanted. So here I am!"

"Here you are!" says Kristie. "I wanted to tell you my good news right away. I got a job, at Renys."

The way Danny reacts to this Kristie might have told him she'd won an all-expenses-paid cruise around the Greek Islands and she's chosen *him* to be her plus-one. He picks her up—picks her *up!*—and swings her around once before setting her back down. She worries he might do a handstand or a heel click. "Look away if you don't want to see me kiss my beloved, Pauline," says Danny, and he gives Kristie a kiss so deep and searching that, when they pull apart, Kristie knows she is blushing.

"I should introduce you to the Chief, while you're here," says Danny. "Chief, Kristie. Kristie, the Honorable Martin Fitzgerald." To Kristie he says, "The Chief likes to help me out with some weeding every now and then."

"Keeps him busy," says Pauline. "Out of trouble." To the judge she says, "Barbara'll be here at two o'clock, okay, Chief?"

"Okay." The Chief looks up and meets Kristie's gaze. His expression is vacant and pleasant. "Thank you for coming," he says.

"If you can wait twenty minutes," says Danny. "I'll drive you home."

"You never said it was *Alzheimer's* that Judge Fitzgerald has," says Kristie later. "You just said he was sick." She's trying to keep the accusation out of her voice but she knows a jagged edge of it is breaking through.

Danny shrugs. "Honestly I'm not sure I even knew for certain. It's not like they keep me in the loop. I'm just the help." He grins. "All I know is that they need a *lot* of help and I am here for it."

19.
Louisa

Dear Daddy, says the letter Louisa finds the next morning.

Thank you for the picture of Gavin. He looks happy.

Last week I went to the Farnsworth with Granny and Mommy and also out to lunch at Atlantic Baking Company.

They were out of sourdough.

During lunch I asked Mommy when you are coming to Maine and she used her clipped voice and said STOP ASKING ME THAT ABIGAIL I DON'T HAVE AN ANSWER FOR EVERY-THING. I said she didn't need to have an answer for everything just the one thing I asked and she said YOU DON'T ALWAYS NEED TO BE SO

LITERAL ABIGAIL. I had to check the dictionary even though I was pretty sure I knew what she meant.

LITERAL means TENDING TO CONSTRUE WORDS IN A VERY STRICT WAY.

Do you think being literal is a bad thing? I DEF-INITELY DO NOT.

Are you and Mommy going to get a divorce? When Shelby's parents got a divorce Shelby got an Apple Watch and an iPhone for Christmas because her parents were NO LONGER COMMUNICATING and they were trying to BUY HER FAVOR. But even if I got an Apple Watch and an iPhone that wouldn't be worth it to me. I would like everything to stay the way it is with no divorce. Don't forget the lobster festival is in the first week of August.

Love,
Abigail

Every summer Annie purchases two mugs at the Damariscotta Pottery—one for Louisa to bring home for her own personal collection, and one to add to the open shelves in the kitchen in the Owls Head home. They have to make their Damariscotta trip on the early side of the season, because the stock sells out fast; by August there'll be nothing left.

"Something on your mind, Louisa?" Annie asks as they drive out of Owls Head and onto Buttermilk Lane toward Route 1. When she was a child Buttermilk Lane always made Louisa crave pancakes. Come to think of it, she could go for a pancake right now.

Yes, thinks Louisa. *Phoebe Richardson is on my mind. My book is on my mind. My career is on my mind.* "Not a thing," she says. She'll write her pages (seven per day are now required) when she gets home. They'll be back by early afternoon, and Pauline has agreed to keep an eye on everyone in their absence. (Feeling rebellious, Louisa has raised Matty's wages to eleven dollars for the morning; Claire's and Abigail's have remained stagnant, and she hopes they don't decide to unionize.)

The coast of Maine is littered with potteries of all shapes and sizes: some are tiny mom-and-pops, some are just moms, some are tourist traps. Damariscotta, with its giant splashes of color, its intricate floral designs, is truly one of a kind. Louisa can tolerate a certain amount of chaos in her life—she learned long ago that life with three children meant thinking of most of their possessions as disposable—but her Damariscotta mugs are sacred. She treats them as though they are made of spun glass and eggshells. The children are not allowed to drink from them. Not until they are at least thirty years old, is what she tells them. What will happen if one of them breaks? they ask. I'll never recover, she says. I'll never, ever recover. She's joking, but only sort of.

Pottery first, then the bookstore, then lunch at King Eider's. This is always the way they do Damariscotta. Louisa leaves Phoebe in the car as she searches for her new mug. It has to fit her hand exactly and be capable of holding the perfect amount of coffee. The design has to be something not too similar to what she already has, but similar enough to fit in with its friends.

In the bookstore they browse the new release table, all of the books with their bright summer covers. Women in sun hats looking out at oceans. Women on beach chairs. Women poolside, telling secrets. (Did only women celebrate summer? Did only women tell secrets? You had to wonder.)

There's a short wait at King Eider's; they squeeze near the hostess stand, and Louisa studies her mother. Annie is wearing light pink lipstick and a sundress that goes to her knees. Flat sandals, a bracelet, earrings she bought from the Sissy Yates trunk show at the Knox Museum last summer. Louisa knows the earrings' origin because her mother bought her a pair that day too—although today, like many days, she has forgotten to put in any earrings at all. Annie's hair is perfect, while Louisa's is in her summer bun, which means she hasn't washed it for a few days. Next to her mother Louisa feels frumpy and unkempt, full of turmoil inside and out.

They sit; the server appears; they order. The blackened haddock sandwich for Louisa and the Pub Club for Annie. No mayo, obviously. Two iced teas. Annie is rummaging in her pocketbook, looking for her phone to check for messages from Barbara, when a piece of paper falls out and pinwheels itself to the ground.

"Never mind that, Louisa," she says, though Louisa is bending already. "Just leave it." Her voice, suddenly sharp, startles Louisa, and she picks the paper up anyway. On the front of the pamphlet, she reads these words: GREEN PASTURES: MEMORY CARE FOR THE ONES YOU LOVE. Under the words, a silver-haired woman in a cardigan is staring off into space with a pleasant, vacant expression on her face. Behind her stands a man with a tidy haircut—former military, maybe—and his hand on the woman's shoulder. The woman's hand is covering the man's hand; they look very cozy, like the pot roast is in the oven and they have just enough time for a cocktail before it comes out.

Louisa studies the pamphlet, her heartbeat picking up. She glances at Annie, who has her eyes narrowed and a strange expression on her face, part recalcitrance, part terror.

"Mom," Louisa says. "What's this?"

Just then their food arrives. They make themselves busy with accepting it and Annie spends some time centering her plate on her place mat. Finally she rearranges her face into something grave and says, "I put down a deposit."

Louisa's stomach plummets. She turns the pamphlet over. "Where is it?"

"Portland. The doctors think by this time next year your father will be—more comfortable with round-the-clock residential care. And there's a place I can live there too, a separate residential area, so I can be with him."

"Next *year?*" Louisa feels like someone has snatched her breath. "That soon?"

"Yes. It's not all that soon, when you think about it. One of the issues for patients like your father is getting him in before he *really* needs the care but not so soon that he's unwilling to accept the change in circumstances."

A long pause ensues. Louisa picks at her sandwich, not wanting to meet her mother's eyes.

"Louisa."

Louisa looks up.

"There's something related to this that I really need to talk to you about. I've been avoiding bringing it up because it's uncomfortable—" She takes a deep breath, closes her eyes briefly, opens them.

"What is it?"

"It's money. That's it. It's money. This place is *very* expensive."

"What do you mean by *very expensive?*"

Annie hesitates. "Upward of nine thousand dollars a month."

"A *month?*" Nine thousand dollars a month is . . . almost one hundred and ten thousand dollars a year. More than all of Louisa's salary, pretax. Nine thousand dollars is three average Brooklyn mortgages, two expensive private schools; nine thousand dollars is getting one and a half children a new set of braces every single month.

Annie nods. "Your father's father lived to the age of ninety-two . . . so we could be talking—well, we could be talking well over a hundred thousand dollars for *years*, Louisa. This place is the best around, and I want the best." She pauses, and takes a sip of her iced tea. "I'm going to have to make some changes in order to afford it, and that's something I've been meaning to talk to you about. I guess now is as good a time as any."

Louisa braces herself. "But—you have money. Right?" The *right* comes out in a whisper. She's always thought of her mother's money as a creek that will never run dry. There's always been money—for gifts for the children, for Ships View, for Pauline and Danny and expensive dinners out in Brooklyn when Annie and Martin come to visit.

Annie clears her throat and shifts her eyes toward the door. "Yes. I have some money. But there are the vagaries of the market, which hasn't always been kind. I put money into the college accounts for the children. You know that. I was glad to be able to do that. There's upkeep on the Portland condo. Condo fees, utilities. Then taxes and maintenance on our house here. Yes, we own this house outright, but you'd be astonished by how much it takes to keep it running. The roof will need replacing before the winter. The water heater is going to go. There's paying for Barbara, and for Danny. The lawn and gardens alone . . ." She shakes her head. "There's Pauline. I'm sure I could manage without Pauline, but what am I going to do, put her out on the mean streets of Rockland after all she's done for us? She depends on this job. And Barbara will only be able to help us for so much longer. She's a caregiver, not a nurse. We really should have a nurse . . . we need someone who can dispense medications, and so forth.

Help more with toileting." (Louisa wants to wince at the word *toileting*. It is simply not a word you want to think of in the context of your father, and yet, there it is, sitting on the table with the condiments.) "An actual nurse is double the cost of Barbara." She looks straight at Louisa and says, "I'm going to have to think about some very specific changes to make all of this happen."

Louisa feels a vise tighten around her heart. "What specific changes are you talking about?"

Annie fiddles with her wedding ring, twisting it around and around. It's looser than it should be. "One option is to sell Ships View." In a smaller voice she says, "That's the best option, really. The only option. I should be straight with you. That is the option. The plan."

Annie may have well been telling Louisa she intends to swim across the English Channel without a wet suit. And that she wants Abigail to swim next to her, watching for sharks. Louisa feels lava made out of confusion and rage rise into her throat, threatening to spill out. "*No!* Mom, no. You can't."

"Louisa—"

"*No.*"

"Listen to me. Please. What I'm saying is that I've already come to terms with selling. I just need to figure out the whys and wherefores, you know. Get the ball rolling before next summer. I know this feels sudden for you, but it's not so sudden for me. I've been thinking about it, running the numbers, for a long time now. And I've become resigned to the idea, as much as it pains me to say that."

"Where will *you* go next summer?" (*Where will* I *go*, Louisa is also thinking.)

"The Portland condo, for now. But before too long I'd like to move into one of the residential places in the facility, to be near your father."

"You can't do that, live in some tiny apartment . . . You'll shrivel up and die."

"Don't be ridiculous, Louisa. Of course I won't shrivel up and die."

Louisa stares at her sandwich, and the sandwich stares back at Louisa. She knows that she's doing nothing to make this conversation easier for Annie— but she also feels like the rug has been ripped out from under her, and that under the rug, it turns out, there's a giant hole, and she's about to fall into the hole. She thinks about someone painting over the handprints in the half bath off the kitchen, maybe ripping up the peonies or putting ugly lawn furniture on the spot where Steven and Louisa got married. She thinks she might throw up.

The drive home is long and painful and very, very

quiet. When they finally pull into Rockland proper Louisa says, "How much would you need to keep from selling it before next summer?"

Annie's eyes behind her sunglasses are inscrutable, but her lips are pressed together, a thin pink line. "Louisa. It's decided."

"Fifty thousand? One hundred? Half a million? How much?"

"At this point, sweetheart, it's a matter of putting everything in place. I thought maybe you could help me find a Realtor, while you're here. You know how terrible I am about searching for things on the Internet."

Louisa concedes this point with a nod; her mother *is* terrible about searching for things on the Internet. But: "No, Mom. Don't. Not yet."

As soon as they get home (but home for how much longer?) Louisa calls Steven at the office. Greta answers. "He's in production," she says.

"This is an emergency," says Louisa. "Can you get him *out* of production?"

"Easier said than done, but I'll try. Hang on, okay?" Four beats of silence, then Greta returns. "Hey, Louisa. Sorry. He's in the studio, so I had to wait until the light went off. He wants to know if it's like an *emergency* emergency, like someone broke a limb or is bleeding profusely, or if it's an emergency that can wait like twenty minutes."

Louisa sighs, considers lying, then thinks better of it. "It can wait like twenty minutes," she says eventually. "Nobody's bleeding or broken. But *please* have him call me as soon as he can. Please, Greta." She sits in the rocker and puts the phone on the small table and stares out at the water for a moment and tries to imagine someone else on this deck. She picks up the binoculars that one of the children (her money is on Claire) has left illegally outside and trains them across the harbor on the breakwater. The fog has rolled in from the east, shrouding the white buildings of the Samoset, but with the help of the binoculars she can see the outline of the lighthouse; she can even see a solitary figure making its way down the breakwater. She thinks about the safety net she's always assumed was there—and how it's now floating out to sea.

Her phone rings and she lunges for it. "Steven. Hi. I'm glad you called me back—I'm really really sorry to bother you at work. But it's important, and I had to talk to you about it right away." She takes a deep breath and goes into it: the lunch, the pamphlet, the conversation. She doesn't specifically describe the potential fracturing of her heart into many little pieces but she assumes that's implied along with the rest of the details. She expects to wait a bit while he processes this, but his answer comes too quickly.

"I'm sorry, babe. I'm really sorry to hear that." (Is Steven *chewing* something?)

"Um," she says. "You're sorry? That's it?"

"Yeah. Sure. I love that house too. We've had some really good times there."

"*Good times?* We got married here!"

"Right. Of course. But maybe it's all for the best. I mean, it must be expensive to run that house. All those constant repairs! The salt water does a number on the shingles. And think of all the places we can start to visit instead, sometime in the future, once Owls Head isn't our only option. I've always wanted to do two weeks on the Cape. Or even Nantucket, or the Vineyard! Someplace with lots of sandy beaches, maybe with surfing."

All for the best? Has someone absconded with her actual husband and left this stranger in his place? Sandy beaches? *Surfing?* Steven doesn't surf. "You don't surf," she says.

"No. But I've always wanted to. And the kids could learn! Abigail has amazing balance. And Claire's fearless. They'd love it." Louisa feels like this conversation has crossed three lanes of traffic to take an illegal left where she didn't intend it to go. "And you said recently you want to take them to Disney. Or Europe! I always wished I grew up in the kind of family that could afford to go to Europe. I still haven't seen the Eiffel Tower."

"I've seen it," Louisa says. "It's not that great. But what I'm thinking is something different." She steels herself, tightens her core. All hard things, the exercise people tell you, start with the core. "What I'm thinking is—what if we use the Emergency Fund for *this*—to save the house for my mom, and for us, and for our kids."

"No," says Steven. "*No.*"

"You should see them up here, Steven."

Even from so many miles away and with no visual cues Louisa can sense a tightening in Steven's aspect. "I see them up there all the time," he says.

"But they've never spent the whole summer here, the way I used to, until this summer. You've never seen *this*! They're so . . . settled in. They're so happy. Abigail hasn't asked me if she could get TikTok for *days*. They hardly ever turn on the TV. Claire's helping Danny, the lawn guy, with the garden. She asks him every day if she can weed! Matty practically has a girlfriend, did he tell you? And besides that . . . you know how much this house means to me." This feels like a dramatic understatement, like calling the 120-foot yacht that sailed in the day before out of Cayman a cute raft. "It's part of me, Steven. It's part of my family. I can't lose it." The pause that follows is so big Louisa wonders if it's pregnant with triplets. "Hello?" Has Steven hung up? But no—she can hear his little huffs of breath, the kind he makes when he's stressed. She endures another fifteen seconds, listening to the huffs, and then she says, "Are you still there?"

"I'm here."

"So—what do you think? Do you think we could consider it? The Emergency Fund?"

"Well, no. I don't."

In a voice that sounds like it belongs to someone else—a visiting mouse, maybe; a tiny, squeaky voice— she says, "You don't?"

"No. I don't think *this* happens to be an emergency, Louisa. You love it up there, I get it. But we can always rent a place for a week or two, if it's that important to you to be in that area. I'd totally be on board with that. Maybe not every summer, but who knows? Every other."

"*Rent a place?*" She'd rather pull out each of her eyelashes with a pair of tweezers and then feed them, one by one, to Otis. Steven doesn't understand the gravity of the situation, and her blood is beginning to simmer. "I'm not *renting a place* in Owls Head. Steven. I grew up here! In *this house*. I'm not going to *rent a place, every other summer.* We're not just going to find a house like this on VRBO!"

Steven sighs. "You can find anything on VRBO. Seriously, Louisa, will you listen to yourself? I'm sorry, but if you think the Emergency Fund should stay untouched, and that's what you thought when *I* had an emergency, then it should stay untouched for all the same reasons, when you have an emergency too."

"But this is an actual emergency!"

"To you."

She bites her lip. "But—you wanted to put money into a business. You have other ways to find money for that. I don't! This is home, and family. Our family. We can't just, like, *find an investor* to help my mom pay for my dad's care. It doesn't work that way."

"Listen, Lou." His words are clipped. "I've got to get back in the studio. They're waiting for me. Okay?"

"Okay." She waits for Steven to end the call, then puts the phone on her lap. "This," she says, to nobody, or everybody, "is what's known in the business as a stalemate." She feels her heart grow hard and unyielding, like a rock.

20.
Matty

Matty enters the kitchen cautiously, scared of Pauline, not wanting to admit his fear. But nonetheless really wanting a banana. The kitchen is empty so he scurries over to the fruit bowl. Then, like a ghost, she's there.

"Hey there, Mr. Matty," she says. He jumps back; the banana drops to the floor. "What are you up to?" She's carrying bags from Hannaford, the straps straining around her wrists.

"Nothing," he says. Then, because he knows this is what his mother would want him to do, he says, "I can help you with those."

"No need." She hefts the bags onto the counter and begins to unload them. "You don't need to be scared of me, you know," she says. "Hazel says you're a nice boy."

"I'm not scared of you." His voice, which lately has a mind of its own, cracks on the last word. She looks at him appraisingly, unloading tea bags, crackers, olives, broccoli.

Matty and his banana leave the kitchen. He eats it quickly, putting the peel in the pot of summer flowers outside the front door to be retrieved later. He laces up his running shoes and heads up the gravel drive-way, then up again—a slight incline, up the fire road, nothing like the hills that are coming for him later in the run.

By the time he's back at the house he's logged six miles no problem, it's noon, and he's thoroughly soaked in sweat. He douses himself with the gardening hose and drinks from it too, wanting to avoid another Pauline kitchen encounter, and walks around to the back of the house. His sisters are on the rocks near the water, which means his mother or grandmother or both are there too because his sisters aren't allowed to swim without supervision. He looks hopefully for Hazel but doesn't see her.

He climbs the steps to the porch, and there, moving slowly back and forth in the swing, is his grandfather.

"Hi, Grandpa," he says. He never knows if he should introduce himself again, never knows how tangled the brain is at any given time.

"Sit here, young man," says his grandfather, and Matty hesitates—there's the copious sweat, then the dousing from the hose—but sits anyway, leaving space between his body and his grandfather's. His grandfather has a piece of paper in his hands. He's folding it in half and in half again, then unfolding it and repeating the same actions. He's looking out at the water, not down at the paper, while he does this.

Matty searches for something to say. A sailboat glides by, far out in the harbor, and he squints to see it. "Looks like the *Lazy Jack II* out of Camden," he says.

"Ah!" says his grandfather. "So it is. So it is." All the time continuing the gentle rocking and the folding and unfolding of the paper.

Eventually Matty says, "Whatcha got there?"

"Oh, this paper." He considers it. "A young lady brought it to me."

"A young lady? Abigail? Claire?" Maybe it's a drawing. Claire is young enough still to give her little drawings out as gifts. Just yesterday she handed Matty a smiling turtle with a neon-pink shell.

"Maybe." He holds the paper out to Matty, who takes it. There's no drawing, just a parade of words across the center of the page, small block letters that Matty has to work to read. His glasses were so foggy from the run that he'd left them on the big flat rock in the garden when he hosed off and he forgot to pick them up.

"You can have it," says his grandfather. "I don't understand it."

"Okay," Matty says. "Okay, Grandpa. I'll take it." He narrows his eyes at the letters until he can see them.

MARTIN,

MY NAME IS KRISTIE TURNER. I JUST WANT TO TALK TO YOU. I'M NOT LOOKING FOR ANYTHING MORE THAN THAT.

Then a number with an 814 area code.

Matty folds the paper along the lines that his grandfather has already created. It folds easily, the divisions already worn in the paper. He stands, still dripping water or sweat onto the ground, and says, "I'm going to take a shower, Grandpa." He and Hazel are going to take one of the kayaks out.

"Okay, then," says his grandfather. "Off you go, young man. Off you go."

"Should I take this with me, Grandpa? The note? Or do you want it back?"

His grandfather waves his hand at him. "Yes, take it, please. It's not meant for me."

"It has your name—"

"It's for you."

Matty puts the paper in the top drawer in his room, underneath the stack of running shorts, where nobody, not even Claire, who tends toward sneakiness, will look. He stands for a long time in the shower, letting the water run over him.

Now Matty has a secret. Now Matty has *the responsibility* of a secret. But he doesn't know what the secret is, so what does he do with that responsibility?

21.
Louisa

Dear Daddy,
Will you please come soon????? All Matty does is
hang around with Hazel. All Claire does is follow
Hazel and Matty around until they see her and
Matty tells her to go away. Granny mostly sits on
the porch with her book or does her cross-stitch or
goes on errands with Mommy and when Mommy
isn't doing errands with Granny she's working on
her BORING book. Grandpa is only interesting if
he goes wandering off because at least then there is
the excitement of looking for him but that doesn't
happen very often because Barbara is with him most
of the time or Pauline or Granny are watching him

or he's sleeping. They are VIGILANT after what happened last time. That is a word I just learned.

Yesterday Claire had to sit in the naughty chair in the dining room for ten minutes for saying a bad word. I won't write the word here because I'm not allowed but I will tell you that it starts with F and ends with K and rhymes with an animal you see mostly in the water. She was so mad about it that she kicked the wall and made a mark on it and then she had to stay for an extra ten minutes and then she had to clean the mark off the wall. I am glad I have outgrown the Naughty Chair.

Love,
Abigail

On Friday morning at 8:00 A.M. Louisa stamps Abigail's letter. She has given up on her book math because she doesn't like the way the numbers are coming out. Her new plan is to start the day with some exercise—she'll do something active in the morning, thus getting her creative juices flowing. For her first adventure she has chosen Ash Point Preserve.

She checks on the members of the household one by one. Claire is eating a yogurt on the back porch. Matty and Abigail: still sleeping. Her mother is up and dressed, reading the *Portland Press Herald* in the dining room while she drinks her coffee. No, she doesn't mind at all if Louisa goes for a walk but would she mind taking Otis with her? "He's got energy to burn," she says.

Otis, sleeping deeply under the dining room table, doesn't look like he has energy to burn, he looks like he wants to slumber until noon, but Louisa rouses him anyway. Sneakers on, out the door, and she's lifting Otis's big blond hindquarters into the back of the mini-van when Abigail comes running across the yard.

"Where are you going? I'll come with you," she says.

Louisa shakes her head. "Not this time, sweetheart. I'm just taking Otis for an outing."

"Why can't I go?"

"You're not ready, and I'm leaving now." Abigail is sleep-tousled, still in her jammies. "I bet you haven't eaten or brushed your teeth."

"I can be quick. And I won't take up any room. I'll walk very small, I promise."

But it wasn't the physical space children took up—it was the mental space. The children could roll themselves up small enough to fit inside a peanut bar jar and still their presence—their delightful, infuriating Abigail-ness or Claire-ness or Matty-ness—would be bigger than a lion's. Louisa needs to think through some of the broad themes in her book, she needs to figure out how to make the Seventh-day Adventists as relevant as #MeToo.

"Next time, okay? Do something with your brother and sister. I'll be home before you know it."

"Matty only wants to do things with *Hazel* now!" cries Abigail. She crosses her arms over her chest.

"With Claire then." Louisa climbs into the driver's seat and lowers the window so she can wave at Abigail.

"But Claire's just a baby."

"She's wise beyond her years. Give her a shot. I'll see you soon. Granny or Pauline can get you some breakfast." She waves and watches Abigail's small disappointed face grow smaller in the rearview mirror as she crunches over the gravel and up the hill.

Ash Point Preserve is only four miles from the house and yet somehow Louisa has never stopped here. She passes the elementary school, and the community center, and the tiny airport. She almost drives right by the small parking lot for the preserve—blink and you miss it. She pulls in, and who does she see parked two cars over? Mark Harding!

"Hey!" says Mark. "Fancy meeting you at this preserve."

"Mark! What are you doing here?"

"Same as you, presumably. Walking? It's my day

off. Also, looking out for birds. Last time I was here, I saw a northern harrier."

"Wow," says Louisa. "Imagine that!" She pauses. "Is that good?"

"Very good. I'm a bird-watcher now, if you can believe it. I've been looking for quite some time for a northern harrier. They're elusive little guys. Do you like birds?"

"Sure," says Louisa. "Birds are good." Otis leans against Louisa's leg and pants, reminding her not to forget him. She points and says, "I got assigned to walk the dog today."

"Otis," he says, formally. "Also nice to see you again." Otis's plume of a tail waves back and forth like a fan. "Do you want to go together? Or were you hoping to be alone?"

She thinks briefly of Abigail and feels guilty. But Abigail is not a grown-up.

"Together," she says.

The walk is easy, even for Otis, who is no endurance athlete. It's a flat trail bordered by trees on both sides. Spruce? Fir? Birch? Honestly Louisa isn't sure. For most of the walk the path is framed by a low stone wall, the stones covered with moss. Tree roots are everywhere. Louisa trips on one and Mark catches her by the elbow, saying, "Whoops-A-Daisy." (*Whoops-*

A-Daisy? thinks Louisa. This is something a grandfather would say. What happened to the teenager with
the Whaler?)

In no time at all they've reached Penobscot Bay, and
even though, yes, this is the same water Louisa sees
every day from Ships View, she never tires of it, and it
looks different from this angle. Louisa unclips Otis's
leash and remembers the collapsible water bowl she
packed. She fills it from her water bottle and offers it to
Otis, and he drinks until it's empty.

"It's so quiet here," says Louisa. "Nobody is asking
me for a single thing. Heaven." She runs her hand along
Otis's soft side. Is this a betrayal, saying these words?
In case it is, she says, "I love my kids. Of course. But
everyone needs a break sometimes."

"Your kids are great, Louisa. So funny and smart."
He stops for a long moment, looking at the water.
"I always thought my life would end up more like
yours. Loud family. Kids everywhere. What's it like?"

She thinks about this. "Chaotic," she says. "Over-
whelming. Intoxicating. I wouldn't trade it for anything. I talk about them like a collective, you know?
But each is an individual, a particular entity, with their
own desires and foibles and specifics."

"Like what?"

"Oh, I don't want to bore you. Talking too much

about your kids is like describing your dreams. Only interesting to the person who has the kids or the dream."

"I'm not bored. I promise. Tell me about them."

"Really?" He nods. "Well. Let's see. Matty is most likely to bring a Band-Aid to a grown-up with a paper cut. Abigail has the best understanding of sarcasm, both how to deliver it and how to receive it. Claire gives the warmest hugs." Otis shifts on the rock, flattening himself out on one side, sighing but not waking. The McLeans don't have a dog in Brooklyn—it's unfair to dogs, Louisa thinks, the walking regimen, being cooped up in an apartment all day—and she sometimes forgets what peace there is in watching a dog sleep, untroubled and imperturbable. "Why didn't you ever have kids?" she asks.

Mark makes a noise somewhere between a puff and a sigh. "I wanted them really badly. But she—my second ex-wife—didn't. It turned out to be an irreconcilable difference, as they say. So we divorced. And now here I am, no wife *and* no kids." The crinkles at the corner of his eyes pop up just as they did that first day. "Good thing I like my job. I guess one out of three ain't bad."

"I'm not a mathematician," says Louisa. "But those aren't great odds."

He laughs. "No, not great, you're right."

"Where's your second ex-wife now?"

"Seattle. She's very happy. She was always a city girl. The backwoods of Maine never did it for her."

"I don't consider *this* the backwoods," says Louisa, gesturing at the water. "This is the midcoast!"

"I don't consider it the backwoods either," says Mark. "But she did." A couple of minutes go by. Louisa traces a divot in the rock. At the very bottom of the divot is a pool of water.

"It's my favorite place in the world, Owls Head," says Louisa. Then she feels the catch in her voice, and all of a sudden she's telling Mark the whole story. She tells him how her mother needs to sell the house to pay for her father's care; how she wants to use her and Steven's Emergency Fund to pay for the house, and how Steven doesn't agree that that's the best use of the money. She even tells him about how she said no when Steven wanted to put the same money into his business, and how she put her foot down. "In fact I put my foot down *so hard* that I can't believe I didn't get a stress fracture," she says.

Mark laughs so enthusiastically at this he snorts. "I forgot how funny you are, Louisa."

"You think I'm funny?" Louisa asks. She's felt many things so far this summer, but funny isn't one of them.

"Yes! *So* funny. I always thought you were *hilarious*. We used to laugh all the time, remember?" Does she remember? Yes, she remembers. It was such a long time ago, and also yesterday: all of them laughing, Nicole too, the way you do when you're young and the consequences of everything feel small and far away.

Mark stops smiling and looks at her. "I completely understand how you feel about your house."

"You do?" Blessed relief! Someone understands.

"Of course. It's a phenomenal home. Not just because of the views and all of that. You grew up coming here. I get it. And it's been in your family for how long? More than one generation?"

"My mom's parents had it built," she whispers. "So, yeah. I'm the third generation. My kids are the fourth. I always figured they would keep coming here, then *their* kids would, and someday I'll be a wrinkled old matriarch sitting on the porch while people bring me great-grandchildren to hold, and I'll be looking out at the same view of the breakwater with my rheumy eyes until I can't see anything any longer . . ." Her voice trails off, and Mark waits a bit before picking up the conversation again.

"That's tough, Louisa. It really is. I'm sorry. Honestly I can't think of a better use of an Emergency Fund." Her spirits lift so high she wonders if they'll float over Penobscot Bay. It feels so good to be understood! "But keep in mind my statement is coming from someone whose emergency fund went to divorce lawyers and alimony. And every marriage is different, I get that."

They walk more slowly on the way back, and Mark stops to point to a bird high up in one of the trees. "That's a black tongued east coast warbler, you know."

Louisa can't see much of it, just a corner of a wing. "Really? Is that a particularly rare bird?"

"Probably not. I made it up." This time *she* snort-laughs.

Two more cars have arrived nears theirs, and the small lot is now full. A family of four is putting on bug spray, and two young parents are packaging a baby up in a sling. They're working together, heads bent in concentration, and Louisa feels a ping of recognition and sadness, watching them. That could be her and Steven with Matty, all those years ago. "That was a really nice walk," she says. "And it really helped to talk things out. Thank you." She unlocks the minivan and motions Otis inside. The dog looks at her balefully, and she says, "*Fine,*" and lifts his hindquarters to help him. "Lazy boy." When she has closed the car door she leans against it and squints at Mark, and, yes, there he is: now she finds the teenager in the Whaler, sun-tanned, with salt on his skin that she could taste. All of these memories: she feels like she's living inside a Taylor Swift song.

"We should grab a drink or something sometime," Mark says.

"Sure," she says. *I can't do that,* she thinks. An accidental hike is one thing. A purposeful drink is a bridge too far. Is it? "Maybe," she says.

She pulls out of the parking lot and drives along, past the airport, past the community center. When she looks in the rearview mirror she sees that Otis is scrutinizing her with his black button eyes. His expression, if a golden retriever can be said to have an expression other than serene affability, is serious. "I don't know why you're looking at me like that," she says. "I didn't do anything! We just happened to run into each other. It wasn't *planned.*" Otis blinks. "I'm not going for a drink with him, so you can calm down about that. It's just nice to have someone understand my side of things. Okay, Otis? I just wanted someone on my side, just for a few minutes. That's not a crime, is it?"

When she gets home she writes four and one-quarter pages like it's nothing.

22.
Kristie

Kristie has been waiting tables for so long—lunch shifts, dinner shifts, cocktail hours, marathon doubles—that she finds a surprising comfort in *not* waiting tables, in the ease and order of working at Renys. She spends an hour or two at the beginning of each shift stocking shelves, mainly in the grocery section, or straightening children's pajamas in the clothing section. The people she works with, mostly women, all middle-aged or older, all locals, are friendly but not too friendly. This, Kristie is learning, is the way of true Mainers, and the attitude suits her. She comes to think of the women collectively as "the Renys." The Renys have teenaged children or adult children and young grandchildren; they have husbands who haul lobster traps out of Rockland or Rockport or Owls Head, or who work construction or for plumbing companies. They're not afraid to comment to one another about summer people and their attitudes, but, by gosh, they'll wrap their jars of blueberry preserves in enough paper at the checkout so that they can be sure nothing will break on the way back to their waterfront homes.

The best part about getting to know the Renys is that one of them, Elaine, lives on Marine, just three streets over from Kristie's apartment. She offers to drive Kristie home when they work the same shift, sparing her the hassle of the public bus.

Kristie wonders what it would be like to be a Reny. She finds herself imagining being married to Danny, living in their own little house in Rockland, working long, peaceful hours stocking shelves. In her walks around the downtown area she has even picked out her favorite street, Summer Street, and her favorite house, a little yellow Cape with a square of garden that Danny could go to town on. The yard is crying out for a low stone wall.

According to the online pregnancy calculator her baby will be born at the very end of February, or maybe early March. This baby will be a Pisces: empathetic, mystical, romantic. Sheila was a Pisces, and the connection gives Kristie comfort. Kristie is a Scorpio: passionate, stubborn, resourceful.

How cold will it be in Maine in late February? Kristie shivers just thinking about it. Although she is coming around to rocky coast over miles of spun-sugar sand, she doesn't really like the cold. That's why she stayed so long in Miami Beach; that's why she couldn't wait to get the heck out of Altoona in the first place. Will their yellow Cape be well heated? Kristie hopes so. It is always there that the fantasy stops, because in order to live in a bungalow with Danny and a child she'll have to actually tell Danny that she's having a baby.

On a Wednesday toward the middle of July Elaine offers Kristie a ride home. The lobsterman's children are drawing with chalk on the street. As soon as she closes the door of Elaine's car her phone rings.

"Hi!" says a friendly, unfamiliar voice. "Kristie?"

"Yes. This is Kristie."

"It's Sierra!"

"I'm sorry," says Kristie. "I don't know anyone named Sierra."

"I'm calling to see how I can help you today by helping you consolidate and begin to pay off your debt."

Oh, no. No. She shouldn't have answered. She remembers the woman in the billing office: *I'm sorry, sweetie. You can run, but you can't hide. They'll find you eventually.* She wants to hang up; she wants to throw the phone into the harbor. She never should have taken the call: she knows better than to answer an unfamiliar number. She has grown careless.

"Kristie?" says Sierra. "My goal is to get you in a better financial situation. Not to judge or implicate you. In fact, if you'd like, I can be an ear for you. I can listen to your story." Kristie can tell Sierra is reading from a script because she trips over the word *implicate*.

"Well, Sierra," says Kristie. "Do I have a story for you."

In third grade, right after Sheila and Kristie moved to Altoona, Kristie made a best friend by the name of Twyla Ambrose. Twyla had recently broken up with her former best friend, Nelly Friedman, and she took Kristie under her considerably expansive wing almost immediately.

Sheila was working long hours as a legal assistant at Goldstein, Heslop, Steele, Clapper, Oswalt and Smith. Twyla's father, Ken, owned a small fleet of dry cleaners in Altoona; her mother, Helen, took care of the house, Twyla, and Twyla's little brother, Zachary. Each morning Helen did Twyla's hair in two French braids with a perfectly even part. When Kristie spent the night at Twyla's, which she was invited to do nearly every weekend, the girls watched *Sabrina the Teenage Witch* in the rec room and Helen brought them giant bowls of buttered popcorn made in a pot on the stove and not in the microwave. While the girls took over the rec room, Helen and Ken sat next to each other on the wraparound couch in the living room, eating vanilla fudge twirl ice cream out of matching white bowls and watching television. When Kristie walked upstairs to use the bathroom—it wasn't until 2005 that the Ambroses added a three-quarter bath to the lower level—she'd peek at Twyla's parents and report back to Twyla what they were watching (usually *Who Wants to Be a Millionaire*).

Twyla didn't care. "They. Are. So. Boring," said Twyla. "That's all they ever do."

"Yeah," said Kristie. "Boring." To her, though, it seemed exotic. Two parents sitting on a couch side by side, there when you went to bed at night, there when you woke up in the mornings. On the mornings after sleepovers, after they'd eaten pancakes, Helen Ambrose would French braid Kristie's hair too, apologizing if she was pulling too tight. But it never felt too tight to Kristie. (Sheila had to leave for work right after Kristie climbed on the school bus, and she never had time to do anything with Kristie's hair.)

It was one of many injustices, some big, some small, that Kristie would never, ever tell her mother about, because her mother was tired, and because she was always working so hard, and because her feet hurt at the end of the day from the office shoes she wore, and sometimes she missed the teacher conferences, and sometimes they ran out of bread so there was no toast in the morning, and because it was clear that she was trying her best.

Anytime Kristie asked about her father, Sheila's answer was always the same: *We don't need to talk about him. We don't need him at all. We have each other!* This was the answer in second grade, in third, in fourth and fifth and sixth.

In seventh grade they were assigned a family genealogy project. Kristie got a pit in her stomach as the teacher was reading out the assignment. Of course she wasn't the only person in the entire grade with an unconventional family. Bolin Jeffries had been adopted as a one-year-old from China; Sarah Popperdam had two moms and no dad; Myles Furtada was conceived from a sperm donor. But this was all public knowledge and each of these kids knew their personal origin story. Kristie didn't know hers.

Twyla turned her project in a day early. It was done on a hunter-green poster board, with a cutout of a big brown tree pasted in the center. Every branch of the tree had a name on it, and each of the names was accompanied by a small photograph. Kristie hadn't started hers. She'd been reluctant to broach it with her mother. When she did:

"You put 'deceased' for father," said Sheila. "You know that."

"What about the rest of that side?"

"Leave it blank."

"All of it?"

"All of it. But look! I have identical twins on my side, my cousins once removed. That's something interesting you can add!"

"Were you in love with my father?" Kristie asked, her frustration making her bold.

Sheila looked at her long and hard; even in her tender youth Kristie could tell this was a question Sheila had been bracing for during Kristie's whole life. "I thought I was," said Sheila. "I mean, yes, I was. But I was young and naive, and I didn't understand back then that love isn't enough. You need more than love, sweetheart. You need to be smart, and resourceful, and in charge of your own destiny."

Love isn't enough. Kristie didn't heed these words in time to avoid leaving Altoona without a backward glance when she was eighteen, nor her lost years in Miami Beach, nor her unhealthy relationship with Jesse. Restaurant to restaurant, bar to bar, flitting here and there like a sparrow, floating on the current of her life rather than doing the strong backstroke or butterfly—that was Kristie. No post–high school education. No real skills.

Love isn't enough.

Before the rest of it, before the handing over of the letter and the clawing at the air and the dying and the leaving of Kristie with $27,000 in debt, Sheila finally met the love of her life, the owner of a local HVAC company named Glenn. They'd met when the water heater blew in the basement on West Chestnut. It was nine o'clock on a Sunday night, and Glenn had stayed until nearly midnight, helping Sheila mop up the mess.

Three years after Sheila met Glenn he started getting dizzy spells. Night sweats followed. He was so tired he couldn't get out of bed, and then he, a man who had always walked the line between "strong" and "beefy," dropped twenty pounds like they were nothing. It came out that for part of Glenn's life his father had been leasing his farmland to a fracking company. Four months later Glenn was dead from lymphoma. Then, because one tragedy doesn't produce antibodies that protect you from the next tragedy, Sheila got her own kind of cancer, and eight months later she was pulling an imaginary rope above her hospital bed.

Kristie doesn't tell Sierra all of this, of course—but she gives her the broad brushstrokes, an outline, enough so that Sierra is momentarily quiet. "Do you want to hear something else about my mom?" says Kristie, into the silence that she herself has created.

"Um," says Sierra. "Sure?"

"We had bad schools in Philadelphia, where I was born, okay? So my mom—my single mom, worked as a legal assistant, my smart and beautiful mom, who should have gone to law school but never got the chance even to get her bachelor's—moved us to Altoona, because she saw it on a list of safe places to raise a family. And you know what she got in return for that? I left her as soon as I could, because I thought Altoona was too small-town for me, and I thought I was meant for better things."

"I bet you *were* meant for better things," says Sierra. She's definitely going off script now.

"I appreciate your saying that. But my mom was meant for better things too. And she had shitty luck. Some people just have shitty luck, right, Sierra? My mom was one of those people."

"Can we talk about a payment plan?" says Sierra. She's trying to claw her way back. Line, please, stage manager. "I'm sure we can figure out an option that would work for *you*, Kristie."

"We can talk all you want," says Kristie. "I still

don't have any money. And can I tell you one more thing, Sierra?"

Sierra's sigh travels from her phone, pings a cell tower somewhere in the vicinity, and lands in Kristie's ear. "What?"

"I'm pregnant."

"Um," says Sierra. "Congratulations?"

"You're the first person who knows that, except maybe the lady who was working the checkout when I bought the pregnancy test at Walgreens."

"Is this—good news for you?"

"The jury is still out on that, Sierra. The jury is most definitely still out." Silence. Kristie waits two beats, then says, "Is there anything *you* want to tell *me*, Sierra?"

"Actually—no, wait. I can't."

"Go ahead. You can tell me. I'm a vault."

"Okay." A pause ensues. "I hate my job," says Sierra. "I really hate it. I *hate* hearing people's sad stories and knowing that I'm supposed to get money out of them. I don't think I'm cut out for it."

"You seem really nice, Sierra."

"Thank you." Sierra's voice has lowered to a whisper.

"And I think you're right—you're *not* cut out for it. You're too kind. You have a good heart."

"Thank you for saying that. I *do* have a good heart."

"You seem like a really smart young woman. Let me guess—what are you? About twenty-two?"

"Twenty-three."

"I bet you could find another job."

"This job pays pretty well though. And I have school loans myself." She sighs. "So I know how it feels. Which should make it easier, but actually it doesn't. Actually, it makes it a lot harder."

"I bet. But I'm sure you could find something better."

"You think so?"

"I'm *positive*, Sierra. There's no way it's healthy for you to surround yourself with this kind of negativity. You know what I want you to do?"

"What?"

"I want you to march into your boss's office—"

"I can't," says Sierra. "I work remotely. From home."

"Oh, honey. Really? From like a home office?"

"Well, sort of. From my bedroom. In my parents' house." She sniffs.

"*Sierra*. Okay. Then I want you to hang up, call your boss immediately, and quit. Then I want you to find a job with people your own age, who go out for drinks or whatever on Fridays, and I want you to start living your life."

"That sounds really nice."

"So do it. Do it now, before you lose your nerve."

"Kristie?"

"Yes?"

"You know I can't close your file. I mean, I can make a note that we talked, and they'll consider that some kind of progress, but they're just going to pass your case along to somebody else, and that person is going to keep calling you."

"I know," says Kristie. "I know. The world keeps on turning, et cetera. I have to go now, Sierra, okay?"

"Okay," says Sierra. "Thank you. And good luck."

"You too." Kristie ends the conversation feeling better than she started it feeling—an unusual reaction to a bill collector call, to be sure. But sometimes she needs to be reminded that she's not the only one with problems.

Text from Danny. I'll be home soon. I'm taking you to Claws for dinner. Put on something warm. We're eating outside.

She thinks, This could be the night.

The only pants she has that still fit comfortably are the tan cargo pants she wore for her Renys interview; her jeans have become difficult to zip. When she's getting dressed she looks at herself in the mirror. Earlier that day, standing naked after her shower, she'd been able to see the slightest thickening around her waist. Her breasts, already tender and sore to the touch, looked fuller. Danny hasn't noticed these changes yet, or if he has, he hasn't commented on them—but soon enough they will be too obvious to ignore. Soon enough she'll have to tell him, or he'll guess, and he'll leave her, just as Martin Fitzgerald left Sheila. Kristie will find herself repeating a pattern already established, sliding into a pair of well-worn slippers set beside the door. And on and on it will go from here.

At Claws Kristie orders a lobster roll and Danny has the signature haddock sandwich. They get an outside table, under an orange umbrella, overlooking Lermond Cove, and wait for their number to be called. The lobster roll is Instagram-worthy, with the lobster meat, lightly sprinkled with paprika, overflowing its bun. Side of coleslaw, dill pickle. Seltzer water for Kristie, a can of Seadog Ale for Danny. The setting is picture-perfect, and the New England-y ocean smell is all around them. As the sun begins to set the air starts to get chilly, and Kristie pulls her sweatshirt more tightly around her.

"To summer!" Danny says, raising his beer can. "To us."

"To us," says Kristie. She could tell him now. She

could tell him everything. She could tell him why she came to Rockland in the beginning of June, and that it wasn't an accident that he found her in Ships View in the first place, and why she'd gone there a second time, and why she had so many questions about the Fitzgeralds. She could tell him about the baby, so that if he wants to walk away he can do it now, before she becomes even more attached to him than she already is.

She opens her mouth to speak, but all she can think about is her mother sitting at their little kitchen table, worrying herself over the bills. Her mother, going alone to the parent-teacher nights in elementary school, when so many other kids had two parents. Her mother, bravely moving them from Philly to Altoona because the schools were better. Her mother, always trying to catch up, never getting ahead because she started out so far behind. And even though Kristie's mouth is ready, her heart isn't—nothing comes out.

She feels in her pocket for the note she didn't leave with Martin Fitzgerald a week ago. Maybe she'll try again, get a better handle on Danny's schedule, do a better job of avoiding Pauline.

She moves her hand around. The pockets are deep, and she has to half-stand to feel the bottom of them.

"What's the matter?" asks Danny. "Don't you like

your lobster roll?" He's gazing at her with such concern and love, more of both than she deserves.

"I love it," says Kristie. "It's so good, Danny." She
sits back down and tries to slow the rush of blood to her
head. The note is gone.

23.

Louisa

Dear Father,
Thank you for your last letter even though if I'm
being honest you didn't do anything for me. Saying
that "life can be complicated when you're a grown-
up" and "I'll understand when I'm an adult"
ISN'T HELPFUL AT ALL. When I'm an adult I
probably won't care as much about this as I do now.
I'm sorry if it hurts your feelings to hear that but
it hurts my feelings to know that you are choosing
a stupid podcast company over your own fleshened
blood. I won't bother asking you when you're coming
to Maine because obviously the answer is capital N
Never.
Granny said that even people with jobs like yours

deserve a vacation and then Mommy said that it's
NOT THAT SIMPLE.

Yours (for now),
Abigail

Laundry, laundry, laundry. Even on vacation it never ends. The stack of Matty's running shorts is so high Louisa wonders if Matty is running more than once a day. She'll have to pay better attention, make sure he doesn't get an eating disorder—anorexia isn't just for girls! She almost leaves the shorts on the bed for Matty to put away, but she can foresee him not noticing the pile and knocking the whole thing to the floor, undoing her work. He is a boy, after all.

Plus, she's desperate to do something nice for Matty. He's been annoyed with her lately. Louisa can tell he blames her for Steven's absence. She pulls open the drawer, and she sees a piece of paper, folded carefully into squares. She picks it up, perplexed and curious. A love note from Hazel?

Louisa shouldn't look—she knows she shouldn't look!—but the same impulse that forces her to read Abigail's letters to Steven visits her here. She's a mother. Hazel is a very pretty girl. Louisa doesn't want Matty to get hurt. She wants to know if his heart is in danger. She unfolds the note.

MARTIN,
MY NAME IS KRISTIE TURNER. I JUST WANT TO TALK
TO YOU. I'M NOT LOOKING FOR ANYTHING MORE
THAN THAT.

There's a phone number too, with an unfamiliar area code, 814. Google tells her that cities served by the area code include Altoona, Bradford, DuBois, and Erie. Where has she heard someone talking about Altoona recently? She thinks back, and then—yes. She has it. Back in June. The same place she heard someone say her name was Kristie.

She finds Annie sitting with her cross-stitch.

"Mom?" says Louisa. "This was in Matty's room." Annie snaps the magnifying glass off her glasses, takes the note, and reads it. Her expression doesn't change. "I can't figure out what it means . . . ?"

"My goodness, how should I know what a note in Matty's drawer means?" Annie touches the necklace at her throat.

The moment feels wrong, or maybe not exactly wrong—momentous. Louisa holds her voice steady, but something in her is starting to wobble. "Well. I checked the area code for that number, and it's Altoona, Pennsylvania. The name there, Kristie, is the same name as that server at Archer's—and I remember that *she* said she was from Altoona. And that all seems like too much of a coincidence to be nothing."

Annie hesitates, then seems to gird herself for something Louisa doesn't understand.

"Do you want to tell me what's going on?" demands Louisa. "Because *something* is going on."

"Come with me," Annie tells Louisa. "Out on the porch. I need to talk to you. Alone."

"Why?"

"Hang on. We need to see where everyone else is first."

They peek into Martin's study. He's sitting at his desk, reading a law book. Barbara is in the chair near him, knitting. The children are playing Monopoly in the playroom, with Otis watching them and sighing every now and then at how long the game is taking.

Louisa follows Annie to the porch. "Sit down," says Annie, indicating one of the two wicker chairs that sit beside the swing. She takes the opposite chair. She gets back up almost immediately and says, "I can't do this without a drink. Do you want anything? I'll bring you something." She returns with two gin and tonics and hands one to Louisa. "Drink up," she says. "I have quite a story for you."

Louisa drinks. The drinks are strong; the gin burns going down. Her mother drinks too, then puts her glass on the table between the chairs.

"There's no easy way to say this," Annie says. "So I'm just going to come right out with it."

"Please don't tell me," Louisa whispers. "I don't want to know." She wants to stop time—no, more than that. She wants to travel back in time, to a safe age, when nobody has something they need to tell her, when she's not fighting with her husband, not watching her father slip away, not preparing to say goodbye to the house.

"Nonsense," says Annie. "Whether you want to know or not, I'm going to tell you." She takes a sip of her drink, and her hand, putting the glass back on the table, is steady. Louisa presses her knees together and braces. And her mother begins to talk. Once she starts talking everything else flies out of Louisa's mind: Steven and the money, Franklin and Phoebe Richardson, Detective Mark Harding standing wistfully by his car. "When you were nine years old, your father met a young woman through work. Her name was Sheila Turner."

"No," whispers Louisa, because she doesn't feel good about what's coming next. "No no no no."

"Yes," says Annie firmly. "Sheila Turner. She was from Philadelphia, but was up in Portland for school, working as a courier at a law firm. They began a relationship. It went on for a few months. Sheila Turner became pregnant. When you were ten, she gave birth to a little girl. That little girl, Kristie, wrote this note." Annie holds up the paper from Matty's drawer. "How Matty got ahold of it, I don't know. But I know that Kristie is in town. She waited on us that day at Archer's. She must have brought it by here with the intention of giving it to your father and somehow Matty ended up with it."

Louisa thinks back—it seems like that lunch at Archer's was a thousand years ago. "You were short with her, about the mayonnaise. So that's why . . ."

Annie sighs. "I wasn't *short* with her. She forgot, and I was simply letting her know. You know I can't eat mayonnaise!" She takes another sip of her drink. "All right, yes, Louisa. Perhaps I was less than gracious. I've known her name since she was born, but of course Kristie is not an uncommon name. I always wondered when she might come back into our lives. All these years, I've been half waiting. I heard her name, and I know she grew up in Altoona. Then I got a good look at her eyes, and I was certain. They're exactly your father's eyes, Louisa."

"*My* eyes are exactly Dad's eyes."

"Yes, I know. And Kristie's are too."

What Louisa cannot believe is how *calm* her mother is in the telling of this. "Why are you so *composed?*" she asks. "Why are you talking about this so *matter-of-factly?*"

"It's not new information for me, Louisa. I've known this for a long, long time. The girl must be twenty-nine years old by now."

Louisa is remembering herself at age ten. She remembers her tenth year with crystal clarity—she was just thinking about this, because in the fall Abigail will enter the fifth grade. Louisa's fifth-grade teacher was Mrs. Purcell. Mrs. Purcell had a mole on her chin out of which a coarse dark hair sometimes grew (bad) but she also gave out butterscotch candies to anyone who got all of the words right on the weekly spelling test (good). Louisa always got all of the words right on the spelling test. To this day she can't eat a butterscotch without saying to herself, *million, minor, modern, mountain.*

She also remembers fifth grade because her best friend at the beginning of the year was Bridget Backler. In October of fifth grade Bridget left the friendship to become best friends with Kimberly Cossack, who had a swimming pool with a twisty slide that dumped you off in the deep end. Then Chloe Jones moved to town, and instantly Louisa had a best friend again. Fifth grade at Waynflete Lower School was the best of times, it was the worst of times. And now, sorry, *what?* Now it turns out that while Louisa was making *cootie catchers* and learning to *Dutch braid* her father had not only an affair but also a *child?*

"How'd you know she lived in Altoona?"

Annie looks out into the harbor. The water is as calm as glass; there's no wind. The sailboat gliding by must be using a motor. "For eighteen years I sent a quarterly check to Kristie's mother. A sizable quarterly check. That was part of the agreement I made with your father."

Louisa bows her head and looks at her hands, clenched tight in her lap. She feels like her heart is clenching in exactly the same way. "You had an agreement? With Dad? To pay *hush money?* For a *child* that he fathered?"

"I think hush money is rather a dramatic term for it, Louisa." Her mother keeps talking, and Louisa can't stop listening. "Keep in mind, you don't get rich from being a judge. A judge is a public servant. All the rest of it, all of this"—Annie indicates the water, the rocks and garden, the house behind them—"all of this is because of *my* money, from my parents. All of this is mine. Your father and I made an agreement that if I decided to send the money, our lives could go on without interruption."

"But—you wanted to go on? Without interruption?"

"Of course. It would have ruined your father, if this came out. He would never have *made* it to the court, if this had become public, never mind everything he accomplished while he was there. An affair, an illegitimate child. Can you imagine what that would have done?"

Leave the world better than you found it.

These questions are not black and white—Louisa gets that. She understands how two lives become so entangled that picking each knot apart would be arduous, maybe even impossible. And yet.

"But—just as you said. Everything was yours. The money, this house. You didn't have to be tied to him after this . . . you could have left. Did you think about leaving? He betrayed you!"

"Would you? In my place?" Annie's voice is still calm.

"Maybe. Yes. I think so. I would have to."

"In my place, Louisa. Not in your place. This is easy for *you* to say, right now, when you have your own career. Do you know what *my* career was?" Now there is something in Annie's voice Louisa has never heard before—a bitterness, maybe.

"Yes," whispers Louisa.

"Yes, of course you do. Being a judge's wife. Being my parents' daughter. Being your mother. And you know who would have suffered if I'd had your father 'take responsibility'?" She puts little air quotes up. (Louisa didn't think her mother knew about air quotes; she's never seen her use them.)

Louisa doesn't answer.

"All of us. You and me along with your father. There would go his career, and his reputation. Down the drain, gone. And there too would go our stability, yours and mine. Our life, our neighbors, our friends. Perhaps your school. Maybe we'd have moved away, had to start over somewhere new. We had a happy life. We had a good life. I wasn't going to throw that away and suggest your father run off with a law courier and start a new family. I wasn't going to leave him and make my way on my own. People make sacrifices for their families, Louisa. They forgive things. Sometimes they help right the wrongs. That's what parents do. That's what adults do. That's what I did."

"But a *quarterly check*? That makes you complicit. You were a victim of it, and you became complicit."

"Life is messy and imperfect, Louisa! And to say forgiveness is a virtue is a cliché, yes, but it's also true."

"Not to me it's not," says Louisa. "Not in every situation. It shouldn't be. I can't *believe* this went on, all this time. And I'm finding out now—this way! This is—this is—" She doesn't know what to say, so what she comes up with is the thing she thinks will bother her mother the most. "This is *bullshit*," says Louisa. (Annie detests cursing.) "He betrayed me too, you know. It wasn't just you."

"I know," says Annie. "Believe me, I know."

It's hard to slam a sliding screen door in anger, that is true, but it's not impossible, and Louisa does her level best. She doesn't call to the children to tell them she'll be back soon; she doesn't ask around, as is customary, if anyone needs anything while she's out. She simply snatches her car keys off the table in the hallway, and she goes.

When Louisa was a kid they'd go to the Owls Head Lighthouse at least once each year. Louisa has been less disciplined about establishing these sorts of traditions for her children. Maybe that's because it's unusual for them to be here for the whole summer. Or maybe it's because it's harder to corral three children than it would have been for her own mother to corral one. Or maybe Louisa is simply lazy.

On the way to the lighthouse she hardly notices the beauty of the town wharf, which typically makes her heart stand still, especially at this time of day, when the lobster boats are coming in, filling in the moorings. She whips by the Owls Head Lobster Company like it's nothing special, even though it is. She doesn't look to see which of the beautiful water-facing homes between Main Street and Lighthouse Road have undergone extensive renovations over the winter. She can't see past her own anger.

Fueled by confusion and rage, she pulls into the parking lot at the lighthouse. Perhaps not exactly like a bat out of hell—the parking lot is lousy with tourists, and she doesn't want to hit anyone—but maybe like a bat leaving hell quickly, under less-than-ideal circumstances. She slams the door to the minivan as hard as she can and stomps across the parking lot. She doesn't stop to look at the picnic tables on the hill leading to the water where she happily ate many a peanut butter sandwich while her father, an esteemed lawyer, later an esteemed judge, *fathered another child*. She hardly notices the beauty of the water. The path to the lighthouse is pitted and uneven from a long winter of freezing and thawing, so it's hard to stomp, but she stomps anyway. She stomp stomp stomps past a bright young couple holding hands and walking leisurely, and she weaves around a boy of about six walking beside his father. When she reaches the lighthouse she runs up all fifty-two steps and arrives breathless and heaving at the top. Aside from having been lied to for *twenty-nine years* of her life, it appears she is also extremely out of shape.

She takes her phone out and tries to call Steven, but gets only Greta. "Let me guess," says Greta coolly. "Another emergency. You need him to call you back."

"Yes," snarls Louisa.

She looks around. The panoramic views of the harbor are almost enough to get her out of her funk. But not quite. When she was a child she used to stand in this very spot and think about all the ships that had depended on that lighthouse since it was first lit in 1825. She would think about the smallness of herself and her problems in this vast, vast universe—in the face of this vast, vast ocean. She tries to replicate that feeling now.

It doesn't work. She's *so* angry! She's angry at her father, yes, of course she is—although she's not sure how to be angry at someone who is no longer present. But she's also angry at her mother. She might be *more* angry at her mother, because her mother is more available to be angry at.

She takes it more slowly down the steps than she took it up. When a couple of teenage boys knock into her as she's going down she almost elbows them. She left her gin and tonic half full on the porch, and now she needs a drink. She drives home, still angry. She passes the post office and the general store that makes phenomenal egg sandwiches and eventually pulls into the driveway at Ships View. It's quiet inside the house; there's just some clanking from the kitchen as Pauline works on dinner.

She calls "Hello?" and nobody answers. The children might be in their rooms, or they might be on the rocks. The tide will be going out now. Then she hears her mother's voice from the porch: "Still here."

Louisa greets Pauline, then reaches into the refrigerator for a bottle of white wine. She pours herself a giant glass and carries it out to the porch. She sits on the rocker. Her mother has refilled her own drink. Her eyes dart over to Louisa's and then rest again on the water.

"I've got some questions," Louisa says.

"Go ahead." A small tip of the head, a concession.

"Were there others, before or after?"

"No."

"How can you be sure?"

"I'm sure, Louisa. Believe me. I'm sure."

Louisa takes a deep breath. "How much money did you send?"

Annie picks at a loose piece of wicker and says, "I don't want to talk about that. That was my concern, not yours."

"If you hadn't sent money all those years, would you need to give up the house now?"

Annie takes her time with this one. She sips her drink, and Louisa gulps her wine, and the rocker creaks gently back and forth, back and forth, and a sailboat has enough time to come from the east and disappear to the west before Annie answers. She puts her glass down on the table beside her. "I don't know. Maybe. But maybe not quite so soon."

"Okay, final question. How did you forgive him? I get *why*, I guess. But *how* is harder to understand."

"Here's how, Louisa." Annie holds up a thumb and a forefinger about an inch apart. "Out of more than forty years of marriage this relationship lasted a few months. That's how." Annie brings her thumb and finger closer together. Now they could hold a pencil. "It was this much time, in the middle of an eternity. That's how."

Later, after dinner, when Louisa is in her bedroom, sitting cross-legged on her bed, her Pitcairn notebook open on her lap, Annie knocks on the door. The house is quiet now, the children are in their rooms, either sleeping or pretending to sleep, and Martin is in bed for the night too. Louisa has been staring at the same sentence fragment for the longest time: *Pitcairn, with its wild, ravaged beauty,*

Oh, who cares. It's a relief to hear the knock. She says, "Come in," and when Annie enters she's carrying two glasses of whiskey, two fingers each. She hands one to Louisa and says, "I came to say good night. And I brought you this. This is the good stuff. Twenty-one-year-old single malt."

"'I'm not sure I'm worthy," says Louisa. Her parents have always ended their days this way, as long as Louisa can remember. Two fingers at night to "slay the dragons and settle the nerves," as her mother says. Well, at least Louisa now understands what the dragons were.

"You're worthy," says Annie. She kisses Louisa on the forehead, just the way she used to when Louisa was little. Louisa catches a whiff of Shalimar, and of something more nebulous and mysterious. Secrets.

24.
Matty

Matty is lacing up his running shoes outside the front door when his grandmother appears behind him. When he turns, she's dangling her car keys.

"I'd like you to come with me on an errand, Matthew," she says. (Annie is the only person in the entire world who calls him Matthew.)

"Me? Now?" It's an easy day, just four miles, recovery pace, but still he wants to get it done.

Annie smiles thinly. "I don't see anyone else around, do you?"

He surveys the yard. "No." Just Danny, always Danny. Today he's scraping old paint off a shingle on the side of the house.

"Well, then. Hop in the car."

Annie is not the type of person you tell that you were just about to go out for a run, and can you please do the errand with her later. Matty looks with dismay at his running shorts. They're *short*. With a slit up each side! Does he have time to change?

"No dawdling," says Annie crisply. "I haven't got all day. In the car, please."

Annie's car is a midnight-blue Mercedes with cream-colored leather seats. Annie drives a car for two years and then gives it back in exchange for a new car—this is called a lease, and Matty's father has told him that it's a fiscally irresponsible way to approach car ownership because you are never accruing value in something that you can sell later.

Matty breathes in and smells—nothing. The absence of odor is glorious. Their minivan smells like old potato chips, like Abigail's experiments with body spray, like feet. You could make a meal from all of the crumbs hiding between the seats and the door. All the parts of Annie's car—the dashboard, the gearshift, even the soft carpet under his feet—are immaculate. When their minivan moves, it sounds like an old man in an influenza ward. This car sounds like a very gentle cat purring.

"Where are we going?" he asks.

"You'll see." Annie has a secret smile playing at her lips. Her spine is perfectly straight. She's wearing sunglasses and a dress, even though it's just a regular weekday. Matty is not sure he's ever seen his grandmother in a pair of pants—and *definitely* never, ever in shorts. Or a bathing suit. Imagine living so near the water and never putting on a bathing suit.

At the end of North Shore Drive Annie turns toward town. Maybe they are going out to lunch!

"This may not be the most exciting errand in the world, Matthew," she says. "But I believe it is important."

Matty's heart sinks. An important, not-exciting errand does not sound like lunch. The water sparkles off to the right. He can see boats in the harbor. They pass a runner. As they get closer to town the houses are closer together. Here is the turnoff to Archer's, where they ate lunch earlier in the summer. Here is the Time Out Pub, where he heard somebody once died by falling backward from the upper deck. He shivers.

They keep going. Is Annie taking him to the Farnsworth? He hopes not. He hates museums. They pass the Farnsworth and continue on.

"I see you've become quite friendly with the Pelletiers' granddaughter, young Hazel," says Granny.

"Uh," says Matty. Is this a test?

She glances over again. "Don't say *uh,* Matthew. It makes you sound less intelligent than you are."

"Sorry," says Matty. "I mean, yes, a little bit. A little bit friendly. She's—" Here, words fail him. *She's perfect* is what he wants to say. *She's a goddess.* He finishes, lamely, with, "She's really nice." Then, because he thinks his grandmother will understand this next sentiment, he says, "It's good to have someone close to my age around. With Abigail and Claire being so much younger."

"That's fine. Just keep your wits about you, won't you?"

"Okay," says Matty. What does *that* mean? He doesn't want to ask, but he does want to know.

"Hazel's mother and your mother used to be friends long ago, did your mother tell you that?"

"No."

"Well! It ended badly. A skirmish over a summer boy when they were teenagers. If I recall correctly your mother was the victor and Hazel's mother—Nicole— never got over it." Matty casts a sidelong glance at Annie. "Nicole was always after a different kind of life anyway. First chance she got she was off to Nashville. I think she had it in her head that she had some sort of future singing country music." The noise Annie makes after that leaves no doubt as to what *she* thinks about country music. Hazel has mentioned nothing about her mother being a country singer. She hasn't said much about her mother at all, in fact.

"Anyway I think she got what she was looking for—money!—when she married her record executive. And I'd say that poor child has borne the brunt of that chaotic marriage." Annie shakes her head. "It never ceases to amaze me, what lengths people will go to when tearing up their families, instead of leaving well enough alone. It's good she's here with her grandparents—they've got their heads on straight, always have."

Matty thinks about his frazzled mother, her hair in a messy bun, bleary-eyed at the kitchen table over a stack of undergraduate papers. He supposes he's always known, sort of, that his parents had lives before they met each other, before they began their family and became the five McLeans. He knows that his father once had a very rich girlfriend named Aggie Baumfeld. There are photos all over Ships View of his mother as a young girl, and an awkward preteen with braces and glasses, and a high school graduate with a robe and a diploma. But Matty hasn't *really* contemplated her early existence. They pass the ferry terminal, and the Home Kitchen Cafe, and they keep going. His heart sinks again: they are heading toward Hannaford. Is

Annie taking him *grocery shopping?* He looks again at his shorts. Maybe he can wait in the car. There is *no way* he is walking around Hannaford in these shorts.

No. She doesn't take the turn toward the shopping center.

They drive north on Route 1, as though they are going to the Samoset. Or maybe they are going to walk the breakwater? That would be okay, although Matty isn't sure if it qualifies as an Important Errand. And Annie's shoes don't look appropriate.

Annie doesn't turn off at the breakwater *or* the Samoset. Instead she keeps driving and then pulls down a small gravel path, where she stops. They are surrounded by graves. It's a *cemetery.* The important errand is to a *cemetery.* Annie turns off the car—most cars grumble when they turn off but the Mercedes merely sighs blissfully—and reaches around to the backseat, where Matty sees there are two red roses lying on a towel. Annie hands one to him and holds the other herself.

"We're going to visit my parents," she says. "Follow me."

This is the errand? To visit Annie's dead parents?

Matty trails his grandmother through the cemetery. She walks fast, her pocketbook hanging from the crook of her arm, her low heels sinking into the soft ground.

He doesn't like to think of all of the bodies buried underneath where they're walking. The headstones look old; some of them are tipped forward or back, like crooked teeth. Isn't it true that hair and fingernails continue to grow after a body has died?

After a time—way too long of a time, if you ask Matty—Annie stops at a site where two headstones sit close together. "Here we are," she says. "I always worry that I won't find them, but then I always do." One of the headstones says WALTER LOWELL and the other says JEAN LOWELL.

Annie lays a rose on Walter's grave and looks significantly at Matty, so Matty lays his rose on Jean's grave and backs away. He waits to see just how much more uncomfortable this moment can get. Annie reaches into her pocketbook and pulls out a small package of tissues, the kind Matty's mother carries in her own giant bag. Annie extracts one and dabs at her eyes. Matty is shocked by this. Annie is *old!* Her parents have surely been dead *forever!* Is she still sad about them? Then he imagines his own parents dead. Will he still miss his parents when he is as old as Annie is now? Most likely he will.

He notices something about the headstones. They have different birth dates, but the date of death is the same: July 18, 1995.

"They died on the same date?" he asks. His question comes out in a whisper. (Are you supposed to whisper in a cemetery as though you are in a library?)

"They did," Annie says. "In a car accident, near Boston. They were on their way home after a week at Ships View, in fact."

Matty looks at his watch. "*Today* is July eighteenth," he says.

"Exactly," says Annie. "That's why I wanted to come today. This is the twenty-seventh anniversary of their death."

Matty inhales, exhales slowly. A sense of importance lays itself across his shoulders like a shawl. Annie could have taken Louisa or Abigail or Claire on this errand, but she chose *him*. She chose Matty. He reaches out tentatively and takes her hand. He says, "I'm sorry, Granny." He squeezes her hand once. "I'm sorry about your parents."

She squeezes his back and says, "You're a good boy, Matty. You're a very good boy." Annie points to an empty space next to her parents' graves and says, "Your grandfather and I will go here, when the time comes. We've had these plots reserved for some time." Now that she's finished dabbing at her eyes she seems sort of nonchalant about the whole thing; she might be talking about a dinner reservation for next Saturday night.

"There's one more stop I want to make," she says. "On the way back home."

The stop, it turns out, is at the public library. The *library!* Inwardly, Matty groans. He has brought his summer reading book with him—*Fahrenheit 451*—but that is all he is planning to read until school resumes. Is his grandmother going to make him check out books? "I don't know if I should go in," he says. "My shorts are pretty short."

Annie is unmoved. "They're supposed to be short. They're shorts. This will just take a minute, Matthew."

In they go.

"This building in a national treasure," she says when they are in the vestibule. "Andrew Carnegie donated the money to build it, you know." She waits expectantly at the glass door, and Matty realizes he's supposed to open it for her. When they are in the main part of the building Annie breathes deeply and says, "Smell. Isn't it wonderful? I love the smell of a library."

Matty inhales. He doesn't smell anything specifically, but Annie is looking at him so he says, "Me too." The other library patrons are grandmotherly types like Annie, and also young mothers with small children looking through books in the children's room to the right. Annie leads Matty the opposite way and stops in front of a display case. One shelf holds a book called

A History of the Maine State Supreme Court, and on the shelf above it is a framed photo of men and two women, all in black robes.

"Look," says Annie, lowering her voice to a respectful whisper and pointing at the glass. "Do you recognize this man?"

Matty peers at the photo. "No," he says. He can't help looking beyond the display case to a small court-yard outside the window, where there's a stone bench and a tree that looks like it would be really fun to climb. Matty is light for his height, but he's also strong, and both of these things make him an excellent tree climber.

"Look again."

Underneath the photo is a small gold square that says MAINE STATE SUPREME COURT, 2005. "Your grandfather is in the front row, third from the left," says Annie. Matty peers harder. "Before he was Chief." She pauses. "Do you know why I'm showing you this?"

Matty shakes his head.

"I couldn't hear your head rattle, Matthew."

"No, Granny. I don't know."

"It's because your grandfather's brain is so diminished now. I still see him in there but I know not everybody does, or not all the time. And I don't want people to forget who he was. In particular I don't want *you* to forget who he was. Do you know why that is?"

Matty starts to shake his head again and then catches himself and says, "No."

"Because you are the next male in line, his only living male blood relation. In the entire world. That's an honor and a privilege, Matthew. Do you understand? At one time your grandfather had one of the sharpest minds in the state. Someday, when you're older, you'll read more about him. You might even read some of his writings. But even now, even at your age, I should say *especially* at your age, I don't want you to forget where you come from. Do you understand?"

"Yes, Granny," he says. "I understand."

He follows her back through the glass doors and the vestibule and out to the car. There has been no mention of lunch. He says, "Granny? Do you think maybe we could go to Wasses before we go home? For a hot dog?"

The look on Annie's face is pure horror; Matty might have suggested lunching on songbirds. "Oh, Matthew," she says. "Surely a *hot dog* is not the type of cuisine you want to put into your body to fuel all of this running. Pauline was at work on a nice haddock chowder this morning. We'll go home and have some of that, why don't we?"

Matty doesn't want to have chowder for lunch; he closes the door to the Mercedes harder than he needs to, to show his displeasure.

"Right now, Matthew, with your father still in Brooklyn and you here with your mother and your sisters, and Grandpa not always himself, you are the man of the family." They turn by the Walgreens, pass the coffee shop his mother likes, then, on the outskirts of town, the fancy restaurant Primo. They continue on for a while, and then turn on North Shore Drive.

"My mom doesn't like that phrase," Matty says eventually. Mostly he's mad about the chowder, and about not having a hot dog from Wasses, so this statement, while true, is more a quiet act of rebellion than anything else.

Annie glances at him, then turns her eyes back to the road. "What phrase is that?"

"Man of the family."

If Annie in fact knew how to roll her eyes Matty is certain she would be rolling them now.

"Why doesn't she like it?"

"She thinks it's misogynistic."

A puff of air escapes Annie's lips and she turns off North Shore and bumps along the dirt toward Ships View. "There is nothing wrong with that phrase, Matthew. There is nothing wrong with *being a man*, for heaven's sake. Men have been doing it for thousands of years, and I expect they will do it for thousands more."

When they arrive home, a goddess in short-shorts and a strappy tank is sitting cross-legged on the big flat rock in the middle of the front yard. Hazel, like a visiting angel.

"Speak of the devil," says Annie, even though it was some time ago they were talking about Hazel.

Hazel unfolds herself from the rock and comes toward them. "Hi y'all!" She shields her eyes from the sun with her hand. "Hi, Matty. Hi, Mrs. Fitzgerald."

"Hello, Hazel," says Annie. "How can we help you?"

The question is so formal that Matty cringes, but Hazel doesn't seem to notice. "I was looking for Matty," she says. "Granddad says I can help him haul his traps day after tomorrow, and he says Matty can come too."

Matty's stomach somersaults. "Can I?" he asks his grandmother. "On Wednesday? Can I?"

"Certainly, Matthew," says Annie. "Clear it with your mother, of course. I can't imagine she'll have a problem with it. You'll have to be up with the birds, though."

"Maybe even before the birds," says Hazel brightly.

"Well. Perhaps," says Annie. "I'm going inside.

Don't dawdle out here. I'll have Pauline see about the chowder for our lunch. Hazel, of course you may join us if you wish."

"Thank you, ma'am. But I already ate."

When his grandmother has gone Matty asks Hazel, "Do I have to, uh, know how to do anything? Like in advance. For the boat."

Hazel smiles her smile of spun gold at him. "I can show you whatever you need to know. I've been out a couple times already. Don't worry about that. The most important thing is to dress in layers. *Layers*, got it? Especially on top. It's going to be *freezing* in the morning."

"Got it," says Matty. "Layers."

It's possible, it turns out, to get from the flat rock in the center of the yard all the way to the front door without your feet ever touching the ground.

25.

Louisa

"**Y**our father wants a lobster roll," says Annie.

Louisa looks up from her computer and says, "Okay." She's sitting on the couch in the living room, cross-legged with her computer on her lap. Her back is to the windows so she doesn't get distracted by the views of the water.

Annie waits.

Louisa says, "And . . . ?"

"And I thought you could take him down to McLoons to get him one."

"Me?"

"Yes. You."

"By myself?"

"If you're up for it. Or bring the children with you."

"Don't you want to come?"

"Not this time," says Annie. "I'm helping Pauline with some meal planning."

Louisa looks at her computer screen. She has typed exactly one sentence, and it's not even complete:

The reality of the Adventist Church on present-day Pitcairn is as mercurial as . . .

As what?

She saves her work—work being a generous term for the single almost-sentence—and closes her computer. "Okay," she says. "Sure. McLoons." McLoons is just past South Thomaston, nearly a twenty-minute drive away. Louisa hasn't been alone with her father since the post office outing—long before she learned about Kristie. She needs reinforcements. She invites Matty first. He's on his way to the rocks, a towel looped around his neck.

"I had a really long excursion with Granny yesterday," he says. "I think I want to hang here today." Hang here, Louisa thinks, is code for hang with Hazel.

"Fair enough," says Louisa. She tries the girls, who are on the porch, bent over the iPad and a bag of colored thread. "Abigail? Claire? Lobster roll at McLoons?"

"No thank you," they say in unison.

"We're trying to learn an ombre stripe friendship bracelet," says Abigail.

"We're concentrating really hard," says Claire.

That's it, then. No buffers. Louisa picks up the minivan keys from the front table and watches her father make his way down the stairs slowly, holding on to the handrail.

"Louisa," Annie says. "Come here a moment." She leads Louisa into the playroom and speaks softly. "You remember what Barbara always tells us? Be in the moment. Connect. Don't agitate him, okay, sweetheart?"

"Why would I agitate him?"

Annie gives her a long look: they both know why. "I don't think you would on purpose, of course. But inadvertently. I've done it, without meaning to. You just need to stay calm and centered. Deep breaths. Like you do in yoga."

"I don't do yoga," says Louisa. "I'm not patient enough."

"But you know what I mean. Like other people do in yoga."

"Be in the moment," repeats Louisa. "Connect. Don't agitate."

The parking lot is packed—and it's no wonder.

McLoons's lobster rolls are, in Louisa's opinion, the best in Maine, and she's eaten a lot of lobster rolls. And besides that, the views are seriously out of this world. When you're sitting at the picnic tables you can practically touch the working boats coming in to drop off their haul at the little red shack, and even though you'd think that in Maine you might tire of another harbor full of more boats with more outcroppings of rock, well—somehow you don't, because each has its own personality.

She sits Martin down at a picnic table and waits until her father has taken two bites of his lobster roll and thoroughly chewed and swallowed them before she lets everything her mother told her fly out of her mind like bees from a hive and she says, "Daddy. I found out about Kristie."

Martin meets Louisa's eyes and says, "I don't know anyone with that name."

Live in the moment. Connect. She can hear the chatter from the lobstermen pulling in, the ribbing.

"Kristie. Sheila's daughter. Your daughter, Daddy."

"I don't have any daughters," he says pleasantly. He takes a sip of his water.

Don't agitate.

"Daddy. Of course you do. I'm your daughter. Louisa. You know me, right?"

He wipes his mouth with the napkin and considers her more closely. "Are you sure?"

"Positive."

"Are you from Swords too?" he asks. "County Dublin?"

"No, Daddy. You know I'm not from Swords. I was born at Northern Light Mercy."

"I don't know where that is."

"In Portland. Ninety minutes south of here. You know that. I've only been to Dublin once. I was in middle school, remember? We took a trip there. You showed us Dublin Castle. You took us to Saint Stephen's Green. You and me and Mom. It was springtime. The daffodils were blooming. It was beautiful."

"Saint Stephen's," he says. "I used to go to Saint Stephen's with my brothers." His eyes take on a far-away look and she's wondering what he's remembering; she knows the longer ago memories are often more accessible to an Alzheimer's brain than the more recent one. A Christmas Eve with the seven of them crowded around the fire? His own father stumbling home from the pub? A snowball fight with his lads?

Be in the moment. Connect.

She could ask him more about his childhood with his brothers; she could let him ramble on about Saint Stephen's Green. She could let him think she was anyone he wanted her to be: mother, sister, aunt, niece, friend.

But she doesn't want to do that.

"Kristie," she says. "Kristie Turner. I know you know that name." Her voice is too sharp, and a woman at the next table, eating by herself, glances over. Louisa looks down, ashamed. "Sorry, Daddy." She takes a minute, and they both eat. Louisa opens her father's bag of potato chips and sets them beside him. "But you do have another daughter. Kristie Turner. Mom told me about her. Her mother is Sheila. Kristie is ten years younger than I am."

"I don't know what you're talking about."

"You do, though, Daddy. You do." She's pleading with him now, but she's also getting frustrated.

And: there. She can see the second she went too far; it's practically visible, a black dot on the day, a marker.

"I don't! Stop bothering me with all of this talk. Nonsense is what it is! Nonsense." He pushes away his lobster roll, and in so doing knocks over his water bottle. She rights the bottle but too late: the water has pooled on the table and is dripping into Martin's lap. "Goddamn," he says. "All over my pants."

"It's okay, Daddy. It's only water. It's okay. Come on, let's get back to the car." She mops up the spill and shuttles the rest of their food into the garbage and gets her father into the car. Her hands are shaking, and she can feel that her forehead is shiny with sweat.

The ride home is excruciating: Island Road has never felt so long, and Louisa can't enjoy any of the scenery through South Thomaston. Martin is silent, staring out the window, and because she can't see his face she can't read his expression. She knows better. She's read countless articles. Annie gave her specific instructions. Don't agitate. She knows better!

"What happened?" says Annie when they get home. "Louisa, did you say something to confuse him?"

"I'm sorry," whispers Louisa. "I'm sorry, Mom. I just wanted . . ."

"What? You wanted what, Louisa?"

"I don't know." An explanation? An apology? What?

"Here comes Barbara now," says Annie. The tires of Barbara's red Taurus chew up the gravel, and when Barbara emerges Annie motions her over.

"I want to change my pants," says Martin.

"Of course, sweetheart. Of course. Look, here's Barbara. She can help you with that."

When Barbara has taken Martin inside Annie turns to Louisa and hisses at her, "You brought her up, didn't you?"

"Mom, I—"

"I told you to leave well enough alone, Louisa. Didn't I tell you that?"

Annie disappears inside the house and closes the door behind her, leaving Louisa standing in the front yard. Her mother is right. She should have left well enough alone. She feels so bereft and so confused and, well, so ashamed, that when her phone rings and she sees Steven's name on the screen she answers it. Maybe she can talk to him about it. They haven't even had a chance to fully pick apart the bombshell that is Kristie's existence. Louisa didn't get through Greta the Gatekeeper until the day after she found out (was Steven now sleeping at the studio?), and so she'd had to tell him in a text. A text! She walks around the side yard. No sign of Matty on the rocks now, but Claire and Abigail are still at it with the friendship bracelets, so she moves over to the far side of the yard, near the vegetable garden, and fixes her eyes on the staked tomato plants.

"Hey," she says.

"Hey! You answered. Good. I have something I want to tell you."

"I have something I want to tell you too," she says. Her heart expands with hope. Steven will understand that she didn't mean any harm with her father—and

he'll also understand that she wants Martin to acknowledge the big secret. Steven will be on her side, and even
if he thinks she went too far with her dad he'll be kind
enough to keep that thought to himself. She looks up
from the garden to find a sailboat gliding west to east
and the Vinalhaven ferry gliding east to west. She takes
a deep breath.

In that breath Steven says, "I don't need the money
any more. The Emergency Fund. We figured it out
in-house. So I'm really sorry that I caused all of that
strife between us, Louisa. I really am. You're absolutely
right. We shouldn't touch that fund for anything. It's
sacred, only for absolute and true emergencies. It's for
the future."

"Sacred might be going one bridge too far—" says
Louisa. (If there are no other claims on the fund, she
might still be able to persuade Steven to agree to invest
in saving Ships View—maybe once he gets up here.
Once he sees.) "I think the main point I was trying
to make was that mixing business funds with personal
finances is dangerous. But we can talk about that later.
Tell me. How'd you figure out the money? Did everyone in the company commit to selling plasma and bone
marrow?"

"Ha! No. I didn't think of that. But we'll definitely
keep it in mind if we need another round."

"Did Greta decide to become a surrogate for a wealthy couple on the Upper West Side?" (Greta probably had gorgeous, untroubled eggs, brimming with youth and optimism.)

"Louisa!"

"I'm sorry. I'm joking. Obviously. What happened, really? Did you find another investor?"

Steven hesitates. Eventually he says, "Something like that."

Louisa feels a prick of suspicion. "Why are you being so cagey? What is this, Episode Six of a new podcast called *The Secret Lives of Podcasters*? I just had a terrible lunch with my father and I'm about to lose it. Just tell me some good news."

"Okay." Steven clears his throat in the theatrical way nervous people do when they do not actually have anything caught in their throat. "I got it from Aggie," he says.

Louisa's heart thumps and she says, "I'm sorry?"

"Igotitfromaggie."

"Aggie just gave you one hundred and fifty thousand dollars?" She can hear the incredulity—nay, the envy!—in her own voice. Every insecurity Louisa has ever had about Aggie rushes to the surface so fast she's surprised they don't collectively get the bends.

Steven sighs. "I was worried you'd be like this about it."

"Like what? I'm not like anything. I'm just a person standing near a garden."

"Like this. Funny about Aggie."

"Funny?"

"Yeah. Funny. But you don't need to be. First of all, to Aggie the amount of money we need right now is practically spare change."

"Well that must be lovely," says Louisa. "She just found it between the cushions of her couch, then? Under the floor mat of her car?"

Steven doesn't answer that question. "And second of all, it's not a gift. It's an investment. Vetted by her lawyers and everything."

Louisa pictures a team of men and women in pinstripes, sitting around a gleaming conference table, with Aggie at the head. "Does Aggie invest money in all of her ex-boyfriends' business ventures?"

"Does it matter?"

"Yes. No. I guess not."

"I don't know, Louisa. I doubt it. I don't think she has a lot of ex-boyfriends actually . . . she can be difficult, in a long-term relationship. Chaotic."

"Shocker."

Steven clears his throat and Louisa can tell he's trying to get her off the call. "So, anyway, I just wanted to let you know. That that doesn't have to be a thing between us anymore. It's sorted out. What was the thing you wanted to tell me?"

"I don't feel like talking about it."

"Louisa! No, come on. Tell me."

"Maybe next time. I'm tired, all of a sudden. I'll call you in a day or two."

"Okay. But super quick, before you go. There's one more part to the story."

Louisa chews her lip and bends down to examine an earthworm in the garden. The simplest animals with brains, earthworms. Impossible to overthink anything if you're an earthworm. "Is it about Aggie?"

"Yes. Super quick—"

"Sorry, Steven. I can't. I can't take anything else in right now. I'm full to the brim. I have to go, okay?"

She presses the disconnect button, and the urge seizes her to hurl her phone into the water—but obviously that would create more problems than it would solve. The closest Apple store is in Portland. So she settles for making a loud, aggravated noise in the direction of the harbor.

"Everything okay?"

She jumps. It's Danny, standing behind her with a

Weedwhacker. Geez, it seems like this guy is *literally everywhere!*

"Fine," she says. "All good, thanks for asking." This family is already messy enough. No need to get the yard guy involved.

Later that afternoon, before dinner, Louisa is prepping for battle with a hostile honeydew melon. After the honeydew (Abigail's favorite) she's got to face off against a cantaloupe (Matty's) and a mini watermelon (Claire's). It would be too easy for all three children to like the same kind of melon. She finds the big cutting board and the appropriate knife and stares for a while at the honeydew, trying to bend it to her will. She raises the knife just as Annie comes in, and for a few long seconds they regard each other, their conversation from after lunch standing between them.

"Louisa, sweetheart," says Annie finally. "Let me take over. You've got the knife angled all wrong. You're going to stab yourself if it slips."

"I'm almost forty, Mom, I think I can cut a melon." But the *sweetheart* is a balm on her tortured soul, and she relinquishes the knife, because she's actually not sure she can cut the melon. She buys precut.

Annie slices the honeydew expertly in half, then scoops out the seeds. "Hand me that smaller knife, the ten-inch over there, won't you?"

"Mom?" Louisa says, and Annie says, "Hmm?" as she separates the fruit from the rind, not a millimeter going to waste.

"How do you not do it?"

Annie looks up, startled. "Not do what?"

"How do you not lose your temper with him, ever? How are you always so calm? Where does it come from, this endless reservoir of patience?"

Annie laughs without mirth. "It comes from your imagination, I think." She makes a neat pile of the honeydew rinds, all of a size, and reaches for her next victim. Cantaloupe.

"No. No, it's real. I see you with him . . . you're like a saint."

"Hardly." Annie puts down the knife and studies Louisa. "I'm no saint, Louisa. You don't know, my darling. You don't know how I've raged, in private. There's such shame in me, for that." Her voice gets quieter, like she's talking only to herself now, herself and the fruit. "Such shame I have."

"That's okay," says Louisa—although she's startled by the admission. "That's okay. That's understandable! You need to go easy on yourself, Mom." She watches as the cantaloupe rinds stack up too. "We're all imperfect people. We're all making imperfect decisions all the time, every day."

Annie releases a half-smile. "Well, that's exactly it, Louisa. I can let the anger chew me to pieces, if I'm not careful." She sighs and snaps the cover on the fruit container. "I just need to figure out how to keep moving, one foot in front of the other, despite it all."

Despite it all, thinks Louisa. Truer words. Her mother kept their little family going through a tremendous upheaval, and again now, marching against a relentless disease, and here's Louisa, about to be undone by the demands of a podcast company, by an argument over an Emergency Fund.

Annie dries her hand on the dish towel and then covers Louisa's hand with her own. She squeezes once, as if to indicate that they'll now move on to another topic. "Shall we tackle the watermelon next?"

26.
Kristie

D ay off from Renys. Kristie is sitting on the front stoop, trying to use her phone's calculator to figure out how many hours at minimum wage it will take her to save $27,000. Taking into account what's held back for taxes, and what she has to pay for rent, and utilities . . . never mind what she needs to save for when the baby is born . . .

She peers at the number on her phone. That can't be right. *That* many hours? She doesn't know how she would fit that many hours of work into a week, into a life! Is Renys even *open* that many hours? She might have to go back to waitressing if any jobs open up.

But even if she finds a job, can she waitress all the way through her pregnancy?

She puts her phone down and lifts her face to the

sun and closes her eyes. When she opens her eyes, one of the lobsterman's daughters is staring at her. She is standing in that little-kid way with her back concave and her belly poking out. Her bangs are too long, and there's something that looks sticky around her mouth. "Hi," she whispers. "Are you sweeping?"

"No," says Kristie. "Just thinking." She scoots over to make room in case the little girl wants to sit down.

"About what?"

"Life," says Kristie. "How funny life is, I guess. About the past."

The little girl nods somberly, like she gets it.

The first time Kristie meets Jesse she's three years into her time in Miami Beach. He's bartending at Sweet Liberty; she's waiting tables at Stubborn Seed. She goes out with a group after service, and when she orders a Cuba Libre he smiles at her in a way that makes her stomach go whump. She orders another, and later a third: she stays at Sweet Liberty until he's off, and then they go dancing at Treehouse until closing time, which is five o'clock in the morning, which, of course, is already the next day.

She blinks, and she and Jesse are living together. Every night is a party; every day is a hangover. Rinse, repeat. Work, go out, sleep, work, go out. The time goes by. They make a lot of money, and they spend a lot of money too. Jesse likes to have fun. Jesse *is* fun— he's fun personified; he's everything Kristie wanted when she left Altoona. When Kristie is with Jesse she's fun too.

Sometimes they smoke weed. It's fine—Kristie can take it or leave it. It's whatever. She'll mostly stick with alcohol, she decides. Jesse wants her to try mushrooms with him. Will this bring them closer? She's not sure. Maybe! Okay, she says. Here goes.

Philosopher's stones, Jesse calls them. He did them once in high school in Michigan and has always wanted to try again. He had *such a good trip,* he tells Kristie. He wants her to experience what he experienced, and even though no two people experience the same trip, well, he thinks they should give it a shot. He knows a guy who knows a guy. Jesse always knows a guy, and all the guys know Jesse. He'll get them some, as a treat.

Kristie is tired and cranky when she eats the mushroom; she's worked four shifts in a row, had too much coffee, hasn't slept. Jesse forgets to tell her that your mental state at the beginning of a trip is important. They eat them in the early morning hours on the beach, as the sun is rising. They have the beach to themselves.

Jesse's experience is euphoric, textbook positive. Kristie's brain goes somewhere dangerous. Whereas Jesse looks at the sand and sees each grain magnified into a diamond, she looks at the Atlantic Ocean and sees a massive tsunami heading toward them, ready to wipe out the entire city. She sees people on the water—people swept up from other parts of the world, who will all crash into Miami Beach at the same time. Babies without their mothers, little girls on bicycles. She screams and screams.

It is the worst experience of her life.

Jesse's comedown is like dipping into a pool of warm water. Kristie's is like riding on a plane careening down a runway right before it crashes into Terminal A. She lies down on the beach blanket and covers her head with her hands. When it's over Jesse is standing over her with a joint.

"What happened?" she whispers. The tidal wave has receded.

"Just a bad trip, baby," he says. "It happens. Smoke this. It'll calm you down."

Kristie shakes her head. She doesn't want the joint. Enough. No more drugs, of any kind.

Jesse shrugs. "If you don't want it, I'll smoke it," he says. "No big deal."

She blinks again, and Jesse has moved to the harder stuff: cocaine, crystal meth.

The alcohol is where the danger is for her. Shots during a shift. Shift drinks after work, and barhopping after the shift drinks. They go to Repour Bar and Broken Shaker. They dance until dawn at Mango's.

One year goes by this way, then two, five, seven . . . a blur. The constant sun darkens her skin. People ask her if she's Cuban, or Puerto Rican, or Mexican. Yes, she says. Yes, yes, yes. All of the above. Whatever you want me to be. Yes.

Jesse gets written up in the *Miami New Times,* the *Miami Herald,* and a hot website called SocialMiami. com. He wins a mixologist competition at the Fontaine-bleau; contestants have to mix three traditional beverages, two cutting-edge drinks, and one cocktail of their own creation. She blinks, and Jesse is a celebrity!

She blinks again and sees Jesse kissing someone after his shift. She's drunk, so she's not sure if she made it up. She goes home and falls into bed: she has to work lunch that day. She's at a different restaurant now, then another one: Il Pastaiolo, Safron Grill. Everyone moves around a lot down there.

Another time she is 100 percent certain Jesse smells like a perfume that's not hers. He laughs it off. He's around women all night long! He works with women behind the stick; women press themselves up against the bar when they're ordering. Kristie knows how it is. It's the business. *You get it, right, baby?*

Yes, she knows how it is. She gets it. Baby.

One day she wakes up and her head is foggy and there are cobwebs in her brain and her eyes are burning like she rubbed sand in them, and who knows, maybe she *did* rub sand in them! She's not sure. She doesn't remember everything about the night before. Looking back, there's a lot she doesn't remember about a lot of nights, the one before that and the one before that and all of the others.

The sun is shining in the window beside her bed. It's relentless, and she knows the sidewalks will already be baking, and once she leaves the air-conditioning the air will be so heavy it will feel like walking through an endless sauna. There's only one word she can find in her muddled brain. The word is: *enough*. She calls the Altoona number and she says, "Mama. I want to come home."

"Come home, sweetheart," says Sheila. "Please come home. I want you to meet somebody. I want you to meet Glenn."

Back in Altoona Kristie gets back into the rhythms of a quiet life. She sleeps and wakes and eats and sleeps again. She gets jobs working lunch shifts and is home by four-thirty. She tries yoga and eating three meals a day instead of one, or none. She stops drinking and finds out what it's like to wake with her mind clear, her nerves steady. What it's like is, frankly, amazing.

She's never seen Sheila as happy as she is with Glenn. Glenn is a golfer and he gets Sheila out on the green. They go on vacations: Cape Cod, Isle of Palms, Orlando. They grill steaks and sit on the deck of the house on West Chestnut, chatting with the neighbors.

Kristie begins counting the days of her sobriety. One, seventeen, thirty, thirty-five. She's on day one hundred and sixty-two, just coming off a shift, when Glenn gets his first dizzy spell. She blinks, and he's gone. Her mother is ravaged, heartbroken. So much happiness she had, but for such a short time. Kristie blinks again, and her mother is sick, then she's gone too.

She blinks. She's on the Greyhound, heading north.

Was she a good daughter? In the three years she lived at home, through Glenn's illness and then through Sheila's, yes. She was a good daughter then. Uncomplaining, hardworking. Nobody could have asked for better.

But she can't ever forgive herself for how badly she wanted to leave once upon a time, and for how long she stayed gone once she left, and she can't ever ever forgive herself for how much, during those Twyla years, she wanted Sheila to divide herself into two and fill identical ice cream bowls and become Mr. and Mrs. Ambrose.

She looks down: the little girl is sitting next to her

still. She has her chin in her hand and she's squinting out at the yard. The calculator is still up on her phone's screen.

"What's on your phone?" the little girls asks.

"Just some numbers," says Kristie.

"Okay," says the little girl equitably.

"Tatiana!" The voice is coming from inside the house. "Getinhererightnow."

"You'd better go," Kristie whispers. "I don't want you to get in trouble."

"Me too," says Tatiana. She puts her chubby little hand on Kristie's shoulder for balance as she gets up, and maybe Kristie is imagining it, but her hand lingers for several seconds, and it's warm, and it feels like comfort, or maybe even absolution.

27.
Louisa

"There's an errand I need you to do for me please, Louisa." It's early, and Louisa is drinking coffee on the porch. Annie is uncharacteristically not yet dressed for the day; she's wearing her rose-colored robe printed very faintly with peonies. Her hair is as smooth and perfect as ever, but without makeup, without jewelry, she looks older, and tired, and not quite like herself. Louisa thinks of their conversation over the fruit and softens.

"Sure," says Louisa. "What is it?"

"I want you to find Kristie and give this to her." From the pocket of the peony robe Annie produces a plain white envelope, with Kristie's first and last name written on it in Annie's tidy script.

Louisa takes the envelope. "What's in here? A cease-and-desist?"

Annie turns and leans on the porch railing. Louisa rises to join her. The sky is a soft pink, bordered along the edges with violet. The Vinalhaven ferry hasn't started running yet, nor have the tours from Camden to Rockland. Louisa can hear the approach of a lobster boat, though, one of the few that drop their traps in this water, and when the motor cuts they can hear the voices of the captain and the sternman, every third word snatched by the wind.

Annie takes a long time to answer. Louisa waits and watches the lobstermen pull a trap. This is her favorite time of day out here, the pinking of the ocean, the gentle slap of the water against the rocks. Then again she also loves twilight. She loves to watch the sun setting over Rockland, when the sky catches fire. And midday, when the kids swim in the bright heat and the bay is busy with boat traffic and there are kayaks and ferries and sailboats. She loves waking in the night too, especially when it's foggy and the foghorn lulls her back to sleep. Each time of day is her favorite time of day here. The thought that this may be her last summer with all of these moments is unfathomable.

"It's a check," says Annie finally.

"A check for what?" Louisa's heart goes pitter-patter and she whispers, "A check for *how much?*"

"Never you mind how much," says Annie. "No more questions, please, Louisa, just bring it to her. Sooner than later."

Telling Louisa "no more questions" is like putting a plate of Godiva truffles in front of Abigail and saying, "No more chocolates."

"But for what?" Louisa asks. "Did she ask you for money?"

"No." Annie bites her lip and turns her head toward Louisa, and Louisa sees tears spring into her eyes. "I'd rather not go into it right now, Louisa, if you don't mind."

The motor on the lobster boat starts again, and off it goes.

"But I *do* want to go into it," says Louisa. "I want to know."

Annie pulls the belt of her robe tighter around her slim waist. Are her hands shaking slightly? Louisa isn't sure. "Sooner than later," she repeats. "In fact today would be wonderful. Thank you."

Annie walks—no, she *glides!*—to the screen door, and then she glides through, closing it quietly behind her.

Louisa stomps her foot once, then because it feels right, again. She's a full-fledged adult. She's almost forty! She has brought up three children almost half-way. She's been married so long her marriage has even had time to launch itself occasionally onto the rocks. And yet sometimes even then when you are home and your mother refuses to tell you something that you really really *really* want to know you might still feel like a child, chastised and excluded.

Besides. Louisa has a vested interest in the answer to this question! How much money *did* Annie give Sheila and Kristie over the years? How much is she giving her now? If there had never been a need for those quarterly checks—seventy-two of them!—would Ships View now be in jeopardy?

Louisa holds the envelope to the light. It's impenetrable. Annie of course would have folded a sheet of plain paper around the check, a relic from pre-Venmo, pre-online-banking days.

Later, Louisa gathers her sunglasses, her car keys, the envelope containing Annie's check, and a bottle of water. She heads out the front door. The day is hot, with very little breeze coming off the water. Each summer they have spent at Owls Head has been marked by some particular event. There was the summer Matty, age six, got sick at the all-you-can-eat pancake breakfast at the Lobster Festival. There was the summer Steven took the double kayak to Treasure Island with Abigail and had to wait four hours for the wind to shift before returning. She supposes that this summer will come to be known as the summer she confronts her father's daughter.

"Wait!" Claire is behind her. "Wait, Mommy, where are you going? I want to come."

Louisa turns. "I just have to do a little errand. Where are the others?"

"Abigail is reading. I don't know where Matty is. I can't find him."

"Well—make Abigail stop reading and play with you." (What kind of a mother tells a child to make another child *stop reading*? Louisa is officially beginning to lose it.)

"She won't. I tried." Claire's lower lip juts out and begins a slow tremble. "Are you going to town? Will you take me to Wasses? Pleeease. Please. We haven't been all summer. And I am starving." She flings herself dramatically on top of the large flat rock in the center of the lawn. Danny, weeding one of the side gardens, smiles at her.

"You're not starving—" begins Louisa.

Claire cuts her off. "I know, I know. Only people without food are starving. But I'm really hungry. Please please please take me to Wasses."

Louisa considers her youngest daughter, crossing

the fingers on both of her hands, waiting for Louisa to decide. How powerless children are, dependent on adults for the fulfillment of every wish! Wasses *is* a favorite summertime tradition. And Louisa *did* bring Abigail to the Farnswoth already. And she *had* felt bad, after the fact, about leaving Abigail behind when she went walking with Detective Mark Harding earlier in the month.

"Okay," she says. "Okay, but I don't want to bring a whole crowd. This has to be a secret little trip, just the two of us. I'll take you to Wasses after."

"After what?"

"Just after. Run and get your shoes, but be quick and quiet."

"Yessssss," says Claire. She disappears and comes back in a pair of rain boots that go up to her knees. They must be Abigail's.

On the way to town, Louisa lets Claire play with her phone so she can think. She's angry with her mother, and she's angry with her father. Is she angry with Kristie? Maybe. She's not sure. She's about to find out.

"Can I download an app?" asks Claire from the backseat.

"Sure." The minivan rises and falls along the hills of North Shore Drive.

Claire is so entranced in her new app that she doesn't

notice when Louisa turns off Main Street and hooks a right on Ocean to head down toward Archer's. By now, it's seventeen minutes past eleven; Louisa isn't sure what time Archer's starts serving lunch. Louisa parks and tells Claire, "We have to run in for a second. Then Wasses, I promise."

The restaurant is open. Louisa and Claire stand by the hostess stand until the bartender notices them and says, "Hi there. The hostess isn't in yet. Fernando will be right with you."

"Great!" says Claire, all hopped up on her recent app download. To Louisa she says, "Why are we here again?"

"Long story," whispers Louisa. "I'll tell you later."

When Fernando appears and says, "Two?" Louisa finds that her voice has gone elsewhere. She locates it, but it cracks and shimmies as she says, "Hi, yes, I mean, no, we're not eating. I'm looking for Kristie. Is Kristie here?"

"Who's Kristie?" asks Claire, very loudly.

Louisa nudges her and says, again, "I'll tell you later."

Fernando's expression is inscrutable. He looks from Claire back to Louisa and says, "Kristie doesn't work here anymore."

This, Louisa was not expecting. "What do you mean?"

Fernando shrugs. "I mean, she no longer works here."

"Did she quit?"

"Something like that," says Fernando, and the bartender clears her throat. "Can I offer you at a table for two? We open at eleven-thirty, but I can seat you now. Give you menus."

Claire says, "I thought we were eating at Wasses!"

"We are," Louisa tells her. To Fernando she says, "I'm sorry—where did she go?"

Again, the shrug. "I don't know. Not my concern."

"Okay then. All right. I'm sorry to bother you." Fernando seems like a short man with too much power. They turn to go. Outside they look out at the harbor, and Louisa shows Claire how you can see the breakwater from here. She points in the general direction of Ships View. They both squint and pretend that they can see it even though they can't.

They're walking toward the car when they hear someone call, "Hey! Excuse me! Ma'am?" Louisa bristles at the *ma'am*—she's not *that* old—but turns to see a server coming toward them. "Hi," she says. "I overheard you in there, but I knew Fernando would be pissed if I broke in." She looks at Claire after she says *pissed* and says, "Sorry."

"She's heard worse," says Louisa.

"I sure have," confirms Claire.

"I'm Natalie," the server says. "I keep in touch with Kristie." Natalie is tan and very pretty. She looks like she could be one of Louisa's undergrads, taking Intro to Western Civilization in sweats with a hangover and a messy bun. "She got a job at Renys." She looks over her shoulder and then says, "I think it's crappy, that she got fired. Fernando can be kind of a creep. If you see her, tell her I said hi, okay?"

"I will," says Louisa. She forgives Natalie the *ma'am*. "Thank you."

She knows she's pulling at the very last thread of Claire's patience, and that if she pulls any harder it will snap, and also, she was prepared to see Kristie but now that a hurdle has arisen, her nerves are slithering back in. So she turns into Wasses' parking lot. Claire gets the Everything dog, which comes with mustard, relish, and fried onions; Louisa thinks about the Western but in the end keeps it simple with just relish. She's too nervous for her system to handle the Western. Fries, obviously. Two Cokes. They eat in the car, as you do at Wasses. Louisa lets Claire sit in the front seat.

"Seriously, Claire," says Louisa. "Don't tell anyone

about any of this. Especially about the Cokes. If anyone asks we ate kale salad and drank mineral water."

"Got it," says Claire. Her face is smeared with mustard. "Kale salad." She squints at Louisa and asks, "Why is your face doing that?"

"Claire," Louisa says. She clears her throat and considers her hot dog. The *later* that she promised Claire is actually *now*. She will be honest with her children in the way that her own mother and father were not honest with her. "Do you remember earlier in the summer, when you asked me what a love child was?"

"Yes." Claire is deep into her hot dog.

"I didn't answer you as honestly as I could have. A love child is a baby born to parents who are not married to each other."

"Okay," says Claire.

Louisa pauses. She hasn't covered the Facts of Life with Claire yet. She knows that Steven has talked to Matty, and Abigail had questions for Louisa last year. But Claire is her baby, and she wants to put this conversation off as long as possible.

"Claire," she says. "When a man and a woman love each other very much—"

Claire puts down her hot dog and looks at Louisa. "If this is about how babies are made," she says, "I already know about that. Hannah told me at school."

It doesn't feel right that a seven-year-old has relieved Louisa of her parental duties, but Louisa is relieved not to have to begin with the basics. "Okay, good," she says. "That's a start. We can talk about that in more detail another time."

"Gross," says Claire. "No *thank* you."

"We'll see. Anyway. When you heard Pauline say something about a love child earlier in the summer she was probably talking about a specific person. There's a person named Kristie Turner who is the daughter of Grandpa—*your* Grandpa—and another woman who isn't Granny."

"Okay," says Claire.

"Do you understand?"

"I think so."

"What I'm saying is that a long time ago, when *I* was a little girl right around Abigail's age, Grandpa had a"—(What's the right word to use here? In the end she chooses the one Annie used.)—"a relationship with another woman. And they had a baby."

Louisa lets this sink in for Claire; they are both silent for a few moments. The traffic buzzes by on Main Street. Across the street the ferry parking is packed, and, beyond that, Lermond Cove is dotted with moored boats.

Louisa swipes a fry through ketchup. "There are a lot of grown-up things that I won't go into right now, Claire Bear, because frankly I think they would bore you. There are a lot of factors that make this a very complicated situation—factors that you wouldn't necessarily understand."

"I bet I would understand," says Claire.

Louisa sucks up the very last bit of her secretive Coke through her environmentally unfriendly straw and says, "Actually I'm sure you would. But I'm not going to go into all of it right now."

"It doesn't seem that complicated to me," says Claire. "She's your sister, right?"

"Technically, yes."

"An extra sister?"

"Well. I mean, I guess you could put it that way."

"I think if I got an extra sister I'd just be happy about it."

"It's not quite that simple," says Louisa. "You sort of have to know someone pretty well for them to be a *sister* sister. So she's a sister, but in name only." Claire looks skeptical.

Renys is busy busy busy, even with the sun shining so aggressively and summer crooking its finger at the world, asking it to come out and play. Louisa turns off the car and tilts the rearview mirror so she can see Claire. "I'm not sure how this is going to go," she says. "So just hang with me, okay?"

"Got it," says Claire. She gives two thumbs-up. When they enter the store, Claire says, "I love it here." She breathes in deeply.

"Me too," says Louisa. "It smells like bargains and happiness." Renys is like the best of CVS, HomeGoods, Woolworth's in its heyday, and the camping accessories section of L.L. Bean, all rolled into one. In the winter Louisa still dons striped socks she bought here when she was in college.

"Which one is your sister in name only?" asks Claire, studying the checkout women. One of the women looks over, alarmed. The other smiles at Claire. Older women historically love Claire.

"Neither of *those*!" whispers Louisa. "She's younger than I am. And keep your voice down, okay?"

"Okay," Claire whispers back. She puts a finger to her lips and nods conspiratorially.

They wind their way through the store, Claire creeping after Louisa like Pink Panther after the Inspector. Louisa loses her briefly to a display of children's pajamas and has to backtrack.

"Can I get some?" Claire asks when Louisa appears next to her.

"You have a thousand pairs of pajamas, Claire." Louisa's heart is thumping and she can't feel her toes—two sure signs that she's nervous.

"I don't have these," says Claire. The pajamas come in a set. The shirt says, I LOBSTER YOU VERY MUCH with a giant lobster forming a heart with its claws. The pants are dotted with smaller lobsters.

"Later, maybe. On our way out."

"Promise?"

"I said maybe."

"Please? Can you just promise?"

"Okay, yes. Fine. I promise."

Then, between the clothing section and the grocery section, Louisa spots Kristie—she is crouching down beside a cardboard box, sliding a box cutter along the tape. There's the flowering vine on her arm. Kristie stands, turns, registers their presence. She looks from Claire to Louisa and back again. Louisa watches the recognition cross her face.

"Hi," says Louisa. She is *so nervous!* "Kristie. I'm Louisa. McLean. Fitzgerald McLean."

"I know," says Kristie. Here are the eyes: blue, with a dark rim around them. "I know who you are." A long pause takes shape, giving Louisa time to study Kristie more closely. Her hair is a few shades lighter than Louisa's; her skin is darker. Louisa envies her that. She looks like she takes a tan, although she is not tan now. Kristie is taller and curvier.

"Hi," says Claire. She sticks out her hand the way Louisa has taught her to do when meeting an adult and says, "I'm Claire. Nice to meet you." This makes Louisa so proud she momentarily forgets her nerves.

"Nice to meet you too, Claire," says Kristie. They shake. "I like your boots."

"Thank you." Claire chews her lip and looks at Kristie. "I like your tattoos."

"Thanks."

Then Claire says, "Are you the love child?"

"*Claire!*" says Louisa sharply.

Claire says, "Okay, okay!" She holds her hands up in surrender and says, "Can I go look at the board games?"

"Yes. Just stay where you can hear me if I call for you. And don't talk to strangers."

After Claire goes Louisa and Kristie stare at each other. Louisa knows the responsibility to talk is on her, but her voice box feels suddenly frozen.

"How'd you know I'd be here?" Kristie asks.

"We stopped at Archer's first, and the manager said you didn't work there anymore. Short guy, dark hair, goatee?"

"Fernando," says Kristie. She makes a face.

"And one of the servers said she kept in touch with you and knew you'd gotten a job here."

"Natalie," says Kristie. "Natalie is nice. Fernando is a prick."

Louisa hears a kid screaming somewhere she can't see. Over the loudspeaker she learns that someone named Curtis needs to go to checkout four. An old lady toddles by, leaning heavily on her cart, which is full of beach towels.

"Natalie says hi," says Louisa. "And, here." She holds out the envelope with the check to Kristie, and Kristie takes it.

"What is this?"

"It's from my mom."

"Hate mail?" says Kristie. "Should I check it for anthrax?"

"Ha!" (How dare Kristie be *funny.*) "It's—it's money. It's a check."

"For what?"

Many answers dart through Louisa's mind, and the one she comes up with, disappointingly, is, "Um."

Kristie crosses her arms over her Renys vest. "Is it so I'll go away?"

Louisa hesitates. "Things are complicated in my family at the moment," she says. "My mother's been through a lot, and my dad's really sick." She squints at

Kristie. "It's not the right time for something like this to come up, that's all."

"So it *is* so I'll go away."

Louisa says nothing—she offers instead an infinitesimal shrug. "I don't really know," she says. "I'm just the messenger."

"I'm sorry about the timing," says Kristie. Her voice sounds like it spent the night in a deep-freeze. "But I didn't have a lot of control over when I found out about it. I didn't even know about your father . . . *our* father . . . until May. I never knew who he was. Not a name or anything."

"Mom?" Louisa turns. Claire is beside her, holding a game of Connect Four. "Can we get this? We don't have it."

"I love that game," says Kristie, in a kinder voice. "That's a good one. Old school. I can ring it up with my discount."

Why, Louisa wonders, couldn't Kristie at least have the decency not to be nice to Claire? That would make it much easier to tell her to take the hush money and run.

"No, thank you," Louisa says primly. "We don't need it."

"Pleeeeeease," says Claire. "I want it so much." She

hugs the game to her chest as if it's her firstborn child. "I want it so, so much."

"We have enough games," says Louisa. She knows her voice is growing sharp. "We have games that we brought up that you haven't even looked at this summer. There are stacks of games in the downstairs closet too." And then she cringes at how she must sound to Kristie. *We have so much! So many games in our big, big waterfront house. And you there, unpacking your sad little cardboard box, probably have so little. You probably have no games at all!*

"The games in the downstairs closet all have missing pieces," says Claire accurately. "They're about a hundred years old."

Kristie gives Claire a little smile and shrugs and says, "Sorry, Claire. Maybe next time." Maybe it's just a garden-variety shrug, but to Louisa it says, *I know your mother is unreasonable and probably also mean.*

"Wait by the pool noodles and boogie boards, okay?" Louisa tells Claire. "And don't talk to anyone."

"Not even if they talk to me first?"

"Especially not then."

When Claire is gone Kristie shakes her head and says, "I should have guessed from Danny that it would go like this, the first time we really talked."

"Danny?"

"Yeah."

"Danny at the house? *Our* Danny?"

Kristie looks briefly disgusted. "He's not *your* Danny."

Louisa's head is spinning. She thought she would be in control of this situation, but instead she's on her back foot. "I mean, Danny who works for us?"

Another look moves over Kristie's face, quick as a passing shower. "He works for a lot of people, not just you. We're together." Kristie gets two spots of color on her cheeks when she's upset, just like Louisa does: their father's Irish heritage.

"So you've been following us around, and now you're dating our *lawn guy?*"

"Following you around?" The spots of color grow brighter. "*You* came to *my* restaurant!"

"*You* came to *my* town!" Louisa spits back. "And you followed me in Hannaford. You bumped into my cart."

Kristie's head wobbles uncertainly. "That was an accident. I didn't mean to bump into your cart."

"You came to my house. You left a note."

"I didn't mean to. I didn't know that he's sick. The note fell out of my pocket. After I found out he's sick I wasn't going to leave it."

"Well, you *wrote* the note," counters Louisa. Kristie squeezes her lips together. "My son found it. When I asked my mother about it—that's when she told me about you. And it's, what, some sort of coincidence that you're dating someone who works at our house?"

Kristie seems to be weighing two different options in her mind. "It's not like that," she says.

"What's it like, then?"

"What it's like is, I met someone and now I'm with him. Which I don't need anyone's permission for."

"I know you don't need my per—"

"What it's like is, your father didn't do right by my mother. That's what it's like. What it's like is, my mother died. I've got nobody left in the world, except your father. *My* father. Ours. Whatever. Whose existence I just found out about. I'm just figuring things out. I didn't know where else to go. This is all new to me too! That's what it's like."

Louisa touches her throat, feeling for a necklace that isn't there—it's Annie's gesture, adopted. "Your mother died? When?"

"In May." Kristie flings the word *May* at Louisa like it's an arrow and she's going for the Olympic gold in archery.

A woman rushes by and says, "Kristie! That box isn't going to unpack itself, is it?"

"Nope," says Kristie. "It's not. Sorry, Diana. This is me, getting back to work." She waits for Diana to disappear and says, "I have to finish this up. So you should probably go. I can't afford to lose this job too."

Louisa stands there for another long moment, until Kristie crouches down by her cardboard box. Louisa wants to protect her family, of course, but Kristie's mother died in *May?* May was only two months ago, and so she wants to protect Kristie too.

"Okay," says Louisa finally. It's an inadequate response, and she knows that, but she's not sure Kristie wants anything more from her. If she does, Louisa can't figure out what it is. She goes to find Claire by the pool noodles. Keys, car, windows down. She turns onto Route 1 earlier than she should, and the driver of a pickup bearing down on her leans on his horn. She wants to curse at him but she holds her tongue, for Claire's sake.

"We forgot to get the lobster pajamas," Claire says sadly from the backseat.

"I'm sorry, Claire." Louisa does hate to break a promise. "Next time, really. We'll go back. Soon."

"That's okay," says Claire with resignation. "I didn't really need them." She emits a small, heartbreaking sigh. A few minutes later she says, "Are you mad?"

Louisa thinks about this. "Not mad, exactly. Maybe a little sad."

"I thought she was nice," says Claire.

"She was nice. Is nice. That isn't the problem."

(What did Kristie mean, that she "should have guessed from Danny that it would go like this"? What had Danny told Kristie about Louisa, or about any of the Fitzgeralds?)

"So what's the problem?"

"The problem, I guess, is that I don't think that was how I wanted it to go."

"How'd you want it to go?" asks Claire.

"I don't know," says Louisa truthfully. She sighs and takes the turn onto North Shore Drive a little too fast. "Claire Bear, I just don't know."

Dear Daddy,

I have really big news. We have a new aunt! She is a secret aunt who Mommy didn't even know she had as a half-sister. I didn't know you could get a new aunt at my age. My new aunt works at Renys and has tattoos. This is according to Claire, who met her in person. She was our server at Archer's at the beginning of the summer but we didn't know at the time that she was our half-aunt. I wish I knew. I would have gone to Renys too.

This is much more exciting than Sabrina's trip to Italy or Shelby's dad's new Tesla.

Last night Granny and Mommy had a FIGHT. It started off as a whisper fight but then it became a yelling fight. I was on the porch reading A BRIDGE TO TERABITHIA which let me tell you is a VERY GOOD BOOK and they were having their whisper fight in the living room so naturally I could hear everything. I don't think they knew I was there because I was lying down on the swing, which is how I most like to read.

I thought that it was only parents who have whisper fights.

During the whisper fight Granny said she wasn't supposed to tell Kristie the money was HUSH MONEY and that it all felt so TAWDRY now. I had to look that word up in the dictionary, but I waited until Mommy and Granny were done with their fight to do it.

TAWDRY means SHOWY BUT OF CHEAP OR POOR QUALITY.

HUSH MONEY is not in the dictionary although HUSH PUPPY is and did you know that they actually used to feed those to dogs which is how they got their name? I love hush puppies.

Mommy told Granny that if she had an issue with it maybe she should have brought the check herself. She also said that it was just like a man to leave everyone else to clean up from his DALLYINS.

I'm guessing that HUSH MONEY is money that you whisper about. We learned in fourth grade about figuring words out FROM THE CONTEXT if you don't know what they mean.

(I also learned from the dictionary that the word is DALLIANCE and that it means AMOROUS TOYING. Then I had to look up AMOROUS and learned that it means INCLINED TO SEXUAL LOVE.)

After that I accidentally dropped my book and Mommy said, "Abigail? Is that you?" so I had to pretend that I was on my way to the kitchen for a glass of water and that I hadn't heard a thing. I wasn't even thirsty but I drank the water anyway and as I was leaving the kitchen Mommy and Granny were coming out of the living room. They both had mad faces on and Mommy said FINE, MOM, FORGET IT, and Granny said, VERY WELL THEN, which is a fancier way of saying FINE.

They both went upstairs to their separate bed-

rooms and both of their doors went SLAM and nobody even checked to see if we'd brushed our teeth, which is how I got in to use the dictionary.

I did brush my teeth, if you're wondering, but Claire did not.

I was reading when Claire came in looking to see if I wanted to play a game with her. She said she wished we had Connect Four. I have never liked Connect Four because it takes about three seconds to finish a game and then you have to start all over and sometimes the pieces get stuck when you are trying to let them out. I have found most of the sets of Connect Four I have played to be VERY TAWDRY.

Please write back.

Love,
Abigail

28.
Kristie

Fifteen minutes after Louisa and Claire leave, Kristie takes her break in the break room, and she opens the envelope. The check is for one thousand dollars.

It's a lot of money. Yes. There's no denying that. But it's a fraction of what she needs.

Also, part of Kristie is seething. *Louisa's* mother has been through a lot? What about *Kristie's* mother? What about Kristie herself?

She takes out the letter from her mother, the one she carried with her all the way from Altoona, the one she had with her on that Greyhound bus, grieving next to Bob for all of those hours, and smooths it on her lap.

Dear Kristie,

This is a letter I have been wanting to write for a long time. It's also a letter I thought I might never write. I'm going to do my best to say the things I have to say.

You know I told you right along that your father was dead. I told you he died right after you were born. I told you I never put his name on the birth certificate because I was never married to him and he didn't intend to stick around anyway. Some of those things are true but not all of them. I wasn't married to him. He didn't intend to stick around. Those are the true parts. But he's not dead.

Let me back this up, Kristie. Let me back it up pretty far.

When I was twenty years old I was working for a law firm as a courier. My family didn't have enough money to send me to a four-year college, so I had moved to Maine to be a nanny for a family and take night classes at Southern Maine Community College. I did this for two years, and then the family didn't need me any longer.

I thought I might go to law school myself one day. I thought that could be in my future. Me, a girl from Philly, going to law school! I was the first person in my family to go to any sort of college at all. The thought that I would do something like that was almost inconceivable to everyone I knew growing up. But I was smart, and I was ambitious, and I was determined, and it wasn't inconceivable to me.

The courier job was perfect for me: it gave me a taste of the law, and enough money to pay my rent, and the right schedule to keep up with my classes.

There were two other girls in my office close to my age. They were law school students, interning for the summer.

Five o'clock on a summer Friday, my boss gave me a package to bring to another law firm. "Go ahead home when you're done with this," he said. "Weekend's here anyway."

One of the interns looked at the package, reading the name. "Oh, he's a charmer," she said. "Watch out for that one."

"The eyes!" the other one said.

"The eyes," the first one agreed. "Sapphire. Don't look at the eyes. It's like looking at the sun during an eclipse."

"Oh, please," I said. I'd had exactly one serious boyfriend, Jason Carpenter, and his eyes were dark brown, golden retriever eyes. Jason Carpenter broke up with me the month before I met your father. Do you know what Jason Carpenter said to me? He said, "I'm sorry, Sheila, I just don't feel a zing." Can you imagine somebody breaking up with someone that way?

Anyway, it didn't matter, about the eyes. I wouldn't even see the lawyer! You just drop these things off with the receptionist. That's how it goes.

When I got to the law office, which was a few blocks away from the one where I worked, the receptionist was gone. I rang the little bell on the desk, and a voice from down the hallway said, "Here, please!"

I followed the voice. I followed it all the way down the hallway to an office at the end. Inside the office, sitting behind a big wooden desk, with the early evening summer sun streaming in from a window behind him, was your father. I knocked on the door, even though it was open.

"Maryann has gone down to Kennebunk for the weekend," said your father. "She always leaves early on Fridays in the summer. And you know what? I don't blame her." He was looking down at papers on his desk and holding out his hand at the same time. "I'll take it." Didn't matter to him who brought it, as long as he got what he needed. That's how important men are, Kristie. That's how they've always been, and that's how they'll always be, no matter how much the world pretends to change.

I handed over the package, and he said, "Oh, this.

Okay. I've been waiting for this." He said, "Please wait, if you don't mind. I might need to respond to this right away." He looked up, and I thought, oh, the eyes. Now I get it.

He pointed to a chair in the corner of the office, and I sat. I sat for a while, looking around the office. It all looked very quiet and important. I think your father forgot I was there. It felt like a long time went by.

"I'm sorry," said your father finally. "I didn't think it would take so long. The least I can do is offer you a drink."

"Oh, no thank you," I said. "I'm on the clock."

But he was already standing and pouring from a carafe I hadn't even noticed on the far side of his gigantic desk.

"It's Friday night," he said. "The clock is off. I hope you like whiskey."

"Sure," I said. I had never had whiskey.

He poured two glasses, handed me one, and sat back down at his desk. He sipped his whiskey slowly as he looked through the papers in the envelope.

I sat back into the chair. More minutes went by. The whiskey warmed me up and also made me feel bold. I rose from my chair and took a walk around the office. Law books on the shelves. A tiny sliver clock that told me it was twenty past five. Framed diplomas. A photograph of a woman and a little girl smiling on a beach. The little girl was wearing bright pink sunglasses and the woman was wearing a floppy hat and lipstick. I thought, lipstick at the beach?

Finally, your father let out a big sigh and said, "Okay, here. I'm all finished. I'm sorry, but can you bring these back to your firm?"

He looked at me, and his famous charm was fully apparent in the way he smiled. The eyes, I thought again.

"Of course," I said. "That's what I'm here for."

There was a moment where I could have moved away, or I could have moved closer. One action led in one direction and one led in an entirely different one. I thought about Jason Carpenter saying "Sheila, I just don't feel a zing." I moved closer. I thought, I am twenty years old and I wonder what will happen if I do this.

I kissed him.

I felt a zing.

Immediately, and I mean, immediately, he said, "I'm so sorry." Even though I had kissed him, he apologized.

I'm proud to say I kept my cool. "Don't be," I said.

"I can't do that," he said. "I shouldn't have. I don't

know what got into me. I have a wife and a daughter."
His wife was the woman who wore lipstick at the
beach.

"I understand," I said. It was my first time drinking whiskey. It was my first time kissing a married
man. My stomach was on fire. My lips were loose;
my head was loose. I made myself wait for thirty
seconds. Someone once told me that if you leave a
silence of thirty seconds in an awkward conversation
the other person will feel compelled to fill it in. It's
human nature, not to let silence go on too long.

Twenty-nine seconds went by.

At the thirty-second mark he said, "Let me take
your number, Sheila. Just in case."

I didn't ask in case of what.

Two months later, I was pregnant.

Those are some of the facts of the case.

Here are the other facts of the case.

1. Your father's name is Martin Fitzgerald. He was,
   at the pinnacle of his career, the chief justice of the
   highest court in Maine. A brilliant man.
2. You have his eyes.
3. Your father met you one time, when you were
   very young and very small. He kissed you on the
   head, and he said hello, and in practically the same

breath he said goodbye. And then he left us and went back to his other family. His real family.

4. Your father spends summers in a big gray shingled house in Owls Head, Maine, right outside of a town called Rockland. I have been to this house once. It's beautiful there, Kristie. There is a chance, without going into too much detail, that you were conceived at this house.

5. I don't know the number of the house, or if it has one. It has a name, or it did. The name is Ships View, and it is painted on a small sign above the front door. The road you take to get to the house is called Hidden Beach Road. This is all I remember of it, but it is enough for you to find it if you want to.

6. An older man, a younger, naive woman. There's nothing new about this story. It happens ALL THE TIME. It happens so much it's a cliche, it's the plot of so many books and movies. But there's a part of me that still thinks our story is special, and different.

7. Don't feel sorry for me, Kristie—and don't feel sorry for yourself. Martin Fitzgerald gave me the most precious part of my life, and that's you.

8. I know I wasn't able to give you everything I wanted to give you. I tried, but I just wasn't able to.

9. The obvious way to tell this story is that a man
made a mistake, and when he realized his mistake
he returned to his true love. But that's not the way
I tell the story. The way I tell the story, who's to
say that you and I weren't the stars instead of the
bit players? Right, my darling? Who's to say that
we weren't the real loves?

10. What you do with this information when I am
gone is up to you. But I hope you go to Maine.
And I hope there you find all the things you've
been looking for.

Kristie would give anything—anything!—to spread
out a blanket and lie down in a corner of the break
room and go to sleep. She is hungry and nauseated at
the exact same time, and she's sad, and she's confused.

But her break is over, and she has to go back to work.

Sorry, Mom, she thinks. She folds the letter and puts
it in her backpack, and she folds up the check and puts
it in there too. *I know you tried. But I don't think it's
working out the way you hoped.*

29.
Matty

Billy Pelletier's truck rumbles into the driveway at five-thirty in the morning. Matty has been awake since just past four—once he woke, he couldn't get back to sleep. His stomach is jumbled and all of his organs feel like they're bouncing around.

The pickup has only one seat, a bench seat in the cabin of the truck, and Hazel moves closer to Billy to make room for Matty. She's already chewing gum. The smell of mint permeates the truck. She's wearing shorts and a Vanderbilt sweatshirt. Matty is wearing his cross-country sweatshirt. Hazel is sleepy-eyed, tousle-haired. Matty feels like Cupid is lifting his arrow and pointing it straight at his heart.

"Hi," says Matty as he slides into the truck. It's cold this early in the morning. He tries not to shiver.

Billy is wearing a Red Sox cap, a flannel shirt, and jeans. His face is gray-stubbled and intimidating, serious. The truck tires chew the gravel. Matty feels a twinge of longing for the warm, dark house, the sleeping inhabitants.

"You eat?" Billy asks.

Billy's question puts Matty into a deep freeze. Should he have eaten? Should he not have eaten? "A little," he says eventually (he had a banana), and that answer, met with silence, seems acceptable. The truck rises and falls over the hills on North Shore Drive. Everything looks different at this time of day. The sun has just begun to rise, and a hazy light hangs above the trees.

They turn at the post office, and the centrifugal force of the turn briefly forces Matty to slide closer to Hazel. The mint smell grows stronger. It is an exquisite form of torture, being this close to her. The truck rights itself, and he shifts back to his side.

"We brought coffee, in a thermos," says Hazel. "And muffins that my grandma made. Blueberry."

"Great," says Matty. He's never had coffee. Once last year Claire drank a whole cup when nobody was looking and stayed awake for fourteen hours after.

"You ever been lobstering before?" That's Billy.

"No sir."

"All this time coming up here and you've never been out on a boat?"

"Not that kind of boat."

"Shame," says Billy, shaking his head. Matty feels like he should apologize, but he doesn't.

Billy explains that a lot of the boats will be out already. "I earned my stripes long time ago anyway," he says. "I can come and go as I please." They pull into the parking lot at the wharf, next to the other trucks. There's a man fiddling with a trap in the back of his truck. Billy, who's first to the boat, says, "Hey, Brendan."

Matty slides out of his side, and Hazel right after. Brendan calls out, "Hey, Billy, you hire yourself a new sternman?"

"Yuh," says Billy. He smiles, and his eyes crinkle at the corners. "Got two for the price of one. My lucky day." Hazel rolls her eyes at Matty. She squeezes his hand, then lets it go. *I could die happy,* thinks Matty after the hand squeeze. *Right here, right now.*

Billy's boat is called *Pauline,* after his wife, Hazel's grandmother. It's an honor, Billy says, to be the most important woman in a fisherman's life. To have your name on a boat.

"There's girl fishermen too though, right?" asks Hazel.

Billy says, "Yuh. We let a few in." Matty can't tell if he's joking or not.

"I would say that it's probably also an honor to be the most important man in a fisherwoman's life," Hazel says. "Right?" She looks at Matty and smiles.

"Right," says Matty.

The orange overalls Billy gives them are too big on both of them; they look like kids dressing up on Halloween. He hands them each a pair of gloves that make Matty think of the gloves Pauline wears to wash the dishes.

"This here's my skiff," Billy says, pointing to one of the small boats tied up at the wharf.

"We row out to the *Pauline*," explains Hazel. Billy swings a foul-smelling bucket into the skiff—bait—and motions for Matty and Hazel to climb in first. "Can I row, Granddad?" asks Hazel, and Billy tells her maybe on the way back, when they're done hauling. She is so comfortable, so self-assured, that something in Matty's heart clenches and unclenches. His breath snags in his throat. He is not worthy.

On the boat, Billy fires up the radio, uncoils some ropes, checks the engine. (Should Matty offer to help? What if he does and Billy says okay? He doesn't know how to help!)

"I'll give you a tour," says Hazel. "Pot hauler." She

points to a pulley contraption on one side of the boat. "Radar antennae. Gunwale." The rail along the edge of the boat. "That's where we'll rest the traps when we pull them up. Let's see. Bathroom." She motions to an empty bait bucket.

Matty blanches. "Bathroom?" he manages.

"Only in emergencies. You can just go over the side if you need to. Benefit of being a boy. Me, I'll hold it all day."

Matty is 150 percent sure he's not going to go to the bathroom in front of Hazel or Billy.

Hazel pours coffee from a big sliver thermos into three Styrofoam cups. "We drink it black out here," she says. "Hope you can handle it." A joke, or a challenge? He isn't sure.

"I can," he says.

"Hazel," Billy says. "Here's a trap I need to take back for repair. Forgot to bring it with me last time. Want to show your young friend there what's what on it? So's he knows the drill?" The trap is metal: yellow and green. Hazel slides it between them and squats down beside it. Matty squats too.

Hazel points to the different parts of the trap. "This here is the bait bag. This is where we're going to put the herring. See how the trap is made up of two compartments? The lobster, let's call him Fred, comes in through this first part—it's called the kitchen." She walks her fingers into the trap. "Then he smells the bait in the bait bag." Hazel's voice goes high and she says, 'Yum! Herring!'" Matty laughs. "He gets a little taste and it is *delicious*. So then Fred is like, I would *love* some more of that herring. Or maybe he's thinking, I'm super full, time to get out of here. Either way, he goes through this netting into this second part here, which is the parlor. And, there's no going back from the parlor, because the netting is wide where he enters, see, but narrow where he'd try to go back. Fred is trapped." She grins at Matty. "Then we pull up the trap, and we say hello to Fred."

"That's it," says Billy approvingly. "Tell him about the eggs."

"Oh! Yeah. So let's say Fred was actually Frederica, and she was pregnant. We'd flip her over and we'd see these eggs attached to her belly. They look like a bunch of little black berries spread all over. You can't miss them." Matty feels slightly sick to his stomach at this part. "Then we make a notch in her tail with this thing here, it's called a V-notch. We toss her back into the water, so she can go out there and have all of her happy little lobster babies and nobody else will bother her. It's illegal to keep a female with eggs. Got it?"

"Got it." Matty can't believe that in addition to being

an absolute goddess Hazel knows everything there is to know about lobstering, and she's not scared of anything. It's official: Hazel is perfect.

"The most important thing," Billy says, "is to always know where the ropes are." He points to the deck of the boat, and the neat coil of ropes. "Know where your feet are relative to the ropes. *Always.* You get your feet caught in the ropes and I don't know about it and I throw a trap overboard or turn on the hauler, that's it for you. Straight overboard."

"People die that way all the time," says Hazel. "Don't they, Granddad?" Matty shivers.

"Maybe not all the time," says Billy. "But, yuh, I've known my fair share. There's hardly even enough time to cut someone free of the ropes before they drown." He looks out to the horizon and furrows his brow, then looks at Matty like he can see all the way into the very depths of his soul. "Ready, crew?"

In Matty's grandparents' dining room Billy Pelletier sometimes looks out of place, his hands too big for the silverware, maybe, his voice too loud or too gruff for the room, his accent too strong. But here on the water Matty can see how he fits in. Everyone has a natural habitat—Matty's is the cross-country course, his mother's is the classroom, his father's the podcast studio—

and clearly this, the open water, the wheelhouse of the *Pauline*, is Billy's.

"Ready, captain," says Hazel. They both look at Matty until he repeats, "Ready, captain." Billy starts the engine.

The sky is at first ablaze with deep oranges and reds; the colors get brighter and brighter until suddenly they become paler, the strips of white overtaking the colors, until the sky is uniform. The engine is loud. They round the corner by Monroe Island—Billy points this out—and off in the distance are the islands of Vinalhaven and North Haven. Except for that there's nothing to see but the blue-black ocean. Matty chokes down his coffee and puts the cup in the garbage bag Hazel points to. He eats a muffin and contemplates the peace and beauty of life at sea. After some time Billy cuts the engine, and everything quiets. Hazel points to buoys bobbing in the water. She explains that every lobsterman has his own buoy colors. Billy's are blue with a black stripe and a red stripe.

"Same color my dad had, and his dad before him," says Billy. "Now let me show you the what's what of how this all works. This hook thing here? This is called a gaff. I'm going to catch the buoy with the gaff, then hook the rope onto the hauler, this pulley thing here.

Then I press this button here on the hauler to wind up the rope, which raises the trap. See that?" Matty nods. "The trap comes up—"

"That's called 'breaking the surface,'" interjects Hazel.

"And we balance in right here on the gunwale to look through it," says Billy.

"That's our job," says Hazel. "We're the sternmen. So we open the trap, we toss back the ones that aren't keepers, and put the others here—" She points to a black bin in the middle of the boat. "Then we're going to rebait the traps and toss them back over. That's the best part. I *love* that part."

Hazel snaps her gum at him and smiles. She has put sunscreen on her face and a small streak remains on one of her perfect cheeks. Matty wants nothing more than to wipe it off. He is definitely in love.

All at once the boat springs into action. Billy grabs a buoy using the big hook, pulls it up, loops the rope into the hauler. And there, coming out of the water, rising, rising, is a lobster trap.

"Got it!" calls Hazel. She grabs it easily, guides it onto the gunwale. She opens it, and reaches inside. "We got some keepers, Granddad!" she says. She throws back a few that are too small. The keepers go into the holding tank. The trap goes to the other side of the boat, near the bait bucket, to be rebaited and sent back down.

"Nice work, Haze," says Billy. "You getting to be a real pro, aren't you? Soon enough you'll be captaining your own boat."

"I wish," says Hazel. "You can get the next one," she tells Matty. She moves out of the way. Billy gets the hauler going once again. Matty feels about as nervous as he does before the start of a race. His heart is hammering. His palms are sweating. He trains his eyes on the water. It's so dark, anything could be in there. Anything.

Then, as the next trap breaks the surface, something terrible happens. There's a hunk of seaweed hanging off the end of the trap. Matty knows it's seaweed—his *mind* tells him it's seaweed—but in the depths of his *heart,* or wherever it is that his deepest fears live, he sees a person's hair. He imagines a body, coming to the surface right after the hair. He can't look any longer. He turns away. The trap almost hits him in the head.

A hand reaches out and grabs it. Billy's.

"Whoa," he says. "Look alive, boy. What happened to grabbing it?"

"Sorry," Matty whispers. "I'm really sorry. I missed it. Wasn't paying attention."

He glances at Hazel. She's watching him, but when

he meets her eyes she turns away, looking down at the bait bucket.

"Don't think too much, boy," says Billy. "You just gotta do." Matty's body is on the *Pauline,* but his mind is swimming in a sea of his own mortification. "S'all right," says Billy. "It happens. But don't let it happen again. There's one more trap in this string, you stay right there and try once more."

This time, when the hauler winds the rope, and when the trap breaks the surface, Matty is ready. He grabs the trap, rests it on the edge of the rail. Hazel opens it and together they go through the findings. Four keepers. One pregnant female. A sea cucumber.

"That's good," says Billy. It's only two words, but each one feels to Matty like a gold-wrapped gift. "Now you two rebait these traps, and down they go."

"I don't know why I love this," says Hazel. "It's so gross. But it's also sort of appealing, you know?" She reaches her hand in the bait bucket like it's popcorn and they're at the movies. "See here? You just take some like this, and you put it in the bag." She look at him expectantly.

"Okay," he says. He hesitates, but only for a second. He will *not* be undone again in front of Billy. He reaches into the bucket, picks up a slimy handful, and packs them into the bait bag.

"Now we toss them overboard," says Hazel. "Just watch your feet, and the rope." Matty checks to make sure his feet are clear. Hazel lifts the trap, rests it on the rail, and pushes it off. "Go get 'em," she says to the trap. "Bring us back some more lobster." Matty watches the trap disappear into the water.

The sun rises higher. Matty gets lost in the rhythm of what they're doing: catch the trap, check the trap, rebait, send it back down. He is dead tired, so he tries to recall the feeling at the end in the last quarter of a race, when you're so depleted you think your body can't carry on but somehow it does anyway.

At last: "Think we'll head back now. What do you say, Haze? Think your grandma's made a batch of that chowder for lunch?" Billy says *chowdah*.

"Hope so," says Hazel.

Billy consults the instruments in the wheelhouse and turns the boat around. They've been heading back for fifteen minutes or so when Billy says, "Take the wheel."

Hazel nudges Matty. "He's talking to you."

Matty jumps. "What? Oh, but I don't know how—"

"Just take the wheel. Keep it going straight. Not much more to it than that."

Billy steps back from the wheel, and Matty takes his place. Deep breath. Okay. He is doing this. He takes one hand off, putting it nonchalantly near where a pocket would be, if the fishing gear had pockets, which apparently it does not. The open ocean, the wheel underneath his fingertips, the blue sky stretching out in all directions above him . . .

Billy barks, "Both hands on the wheel!"

He whips his hand back onto the wheel.

When the pickup truck pulls into the driveway at Ships View, Billy pulls a roll of bills from his pocket, peels off two twenties, and hold them out to Matty.

"Oh, no, sir. I can't take that." Matty knows that's what he's supposed to say, even though to be honest he wants very badly to take the money.

"You worked, didn't you?"

He glances at Hazel. "I guess. Yes." If spending the morning in the presence of an angel is considered work then yes, he worked.

"Then take what you earned."

"Take it," Hazel whispers, hitting her hand against this thigh.

"Thank you, sir," he says. He opens the door of the truck. "Thank you for everything."

"No sir. Just Billy will do."

"Billy. Thank you."

Hazel snaps her gum and winks at him. "See you around," she says.

"Yeah, sure." He's trying to play it cool. "See you around."

The sun is fully bright now, high in the sky. He can see where the edges of the grass are starting to turn brown—it's been a while since they've had rain. Danny is working in the far garden, but Matty doesn't hear anyone else on the porch or in the water. His legs and arms are quivering with fatigue, or with relief, or with some combination of the two. The morning he's had is enough to send his heart soaring up, up, up, out of the truck and toward the cottony threads of cloud above.

30.
Louisa

Dear Daddy,

When are you coming? Mommy says she's not in charge of your schedule, she has plenty to worry about with the schedules of everyone else in the world. The lobster festival is only nine days away, so you'd better hurry up and get here. August starts the day after tomorrow!

Matty and Hazel went out on Hazel's grand-dad's lobster boat and even though I am POSITIVE there was room for me and for Claire too Matty told us that there wasn't and me and Claire had to stay with PAULINE because Granny went shopping and Mommy was in town working on her book and PAULINE wouldn't let us go in the water so we had to stay there and play UNO for the six hundredth time. When you come can you please bring two games from my room that I forgot to pack? They are: RAT-A-TAT CAT which is in a small white box with a cat dressed like the Statue of Liberty on the cover and also TICKET TO RIDE which is in a bigger box with a picture of a train on the cover.

Love,
Abigail

Annie is taking the children on the ferry to Vinal-haven for the day; they will have lunch at Surfside, and a doughnut after at Sea's Bakery. Louisa had wanted to go to Vinalhaven this summer but she asks if it would be all right if she went instead to the library in Camden, where there is more space to work than there is at the Rockland library.

It takes Annie about a third of a second to answer that it's fine if Louisa chooses to work—the part she doesn't have to say out loud is that she's just as irritated with Louisa as Louisa is with her.

"Great," says Louisa. "It's not a choice, though, just so you know. It's work."

"Wonderful," says Annie. "I wish you a fruitful day."

Camden on a summer Monday: hot, but with a cool

breeze sauntering in from the harbor. Crowded, sure. Always. Part of the charm, Louisa supposes, even as she fights a Subaru with Vermont plates for a parking space, and loses.

Eventually she finds a spot along Elm Street, in front of her favorite Camden coffee shop, Zoot; she starts her day with an iced mocha. She walks with her coffee toward the public library and sits on one of the benches facing the water. The park near the library is full of happy people walking dogs and calling out cheerful greetings. Locals, it seems, because all of the dogs appear to know each other. When she's finished with her coffee, she decides, she'll stop into The Smiling Cow and maybe pick out a sweatshirt for each of the children. She feels bad that she's not the one taking them to Vinalhaven. Matty has outgrown last year's sweatshirt—his arms and legs look like strands of spaghetti poking out of the thin cardboard box of his body. And then she will absolutely, no question, get down to work.

In The Smiling Cow she spends an inordinate amount of time perusing the mugs and the penny candy and the earrings and kitchen magnets before she makes it to the sweatshirts. She's holding up a navy-blue hoodie with a picture of a moose on it, wondering if Matty would ever wear it, when she hears her name and turns, and then she knows what Steven was trying to tell her on the phone the day she cut him off, because she is looking into the liquid brown, heavy-lidded, carefully made up eyes of . . . Aggie Baumfeld.

"*Aggie?*" says Louisa.

"*Louisa?*" says Aggie.

"What are *you* doing here?" Louisa asks, unable to keep the accusatory tone out of her voice.

"Visiting!" cries Aggie.

Aggie's blond (can't be real, not anymore) hair is artfully beach-wavy, and she's tanned in that perfectly even way that Louisa's Irish roots would never permit. Dress: resort casual.

"I thought Minnesota was the Land of the Ten Thousand Lakes," says Louisa. "Why are you visiting Maine?"

Aggie sighs. "All lakes and no oceans make Aggie a dull girl, Louisa." Inwardly Louisa groans. She had forgotten Aggie's habit of talking about herself in the third person. "Also," Aggie continues, "I have *such* fond memories of being in the area at your wedding. I've always wanted to come back here. It's been on my bucket list forever."

Frankly Louisa is surprised Aggie had retained any memories of their wedding at all. She'd gotten very drunk and had gone back to the Samoset, where most of the guests stayed, with one of Steven's groomsmen, sullying, Louisa worried, her family's decades-old sterling reputation at the resort. Although surely Aggie wasn't the first person—nor would she be the last—to show up green at the gills to a morning-after champagne brunch.

"I've been saying to Ernie for such a long time: We have *got* to get to Maine. I told Steven we were going to be up here! Didn't he tell you? I told him to tell you!"

Louisa shakes her head. This is her own fault. Steven wanted to tell her one more thing about Aggie. And Louisa, stung about the money, hadn't wanted to hear it. *Serves you right,* she tells herself. Serves. You. Right.

"I was hoping you and I could get together," Aggie said. "I asked him to pass along my number to you. Did he not?"

"He did not."

"Oh, Steven." Aggie rolls her eyes and gives Louisa a conspiratorial look, as though Steven is a mischievous child and they are the parents, trying to outsmart him. "But look, here we are now, anyway! We've just had six *glorious* nights at the Inn at Ocean's Edge, and tomorrow we head down to Portland to fly back home. Do you know the Inn at Ocean's Edge?"

"Only by name," confesses Louisa. The other half of the "we" must be Aggie's husband, Ernie, whom

Louisa has never met. Louisa and Steven had been unable to make it to Aggie's wedding almost three years ago—it was in September, too close to the beginning of Louisa's school year.

"Well. It's wonderful. If you ever get the opportunity to go you should take it."

Louisa thinks, but does not say, that she probably won't get the opportunity. A week at the Inn at Ocean's Edge would eat up her book advance.

"This trip has sort of a special reason," Aggie continues, apparently not noticing that Louisa hasn't responded. "A *sad* special reason." Aggie's eyes fill almost immediately with tears, which stop at the edges before they spill over and threaten her makeup. "If I start talking about this I may lose it."

"You don't have to tell me!" *Please*, thinks Louisa, *please don't tell me.*

The foot traffic in The Smiling Cow is picking up; Louisa begins to worry that they are blocking people from reaching the lobster buoy Christmas ornaments and the dish towels that say things like NEVER TRUST A SKINNY COOK and BE GRATEFUL, with a drawing of a cheese grater. But every time she attempts to move away from Aggie, to build some space around them, Aggie moves forward and creates a new block—a pawn challenging Louisa's opening gambit.

"Oh, I don't mind. There's no shame in it, after all." Aggie releases a world-weary sigh. "We finished our final round of in vitro and it didn't work. So we decided to drown our sorrows in luxury."

"Oh no!" says Louisa. "I'm so sorry, I didn't know."

"How would you know?" asks Aggie. "I haven't seen you in ages." She presses her lips together and shakes her head, and Louisa can't help it: she does feel bad for Aggie. She'd never pegged Aggie as someone who wanted children; she imagined her like one of the characters on *Succession,* cruising exotic islands in a yacht the size of Louisa's Brooklyn neighborhood without a care in the world except for when the Veuve Clicquot would be chilled enough to drink.

"I know, but I have friends who have been through that. I know it's rough. I really am sorry."

"Thank you," says Aggie. She turns, looking over the sea of tourists between her and the door, and says, "There he is! My love."

Instead of what Louisa was expecting—a Hugh lookalike, maybe, Jackman or Grant—she sees a man at least two inches shorter than Aggie, with a balding pate and a wildly unfashionable pair of sneakers. "Ernie!" calls Aggie. "Over here!" Ernie makes his way over and Aggie kisses him in a way that stops *just* this side of inappropriate—the kiss almost makes

Louisa blush! "Ernie's my heart and soul," says Aggie. "Ernie, Louisa. Louisa, Ernie. Louisa is Steven's better half." Louisa searches Aggie's voice for signs of irony but finds none at all. Next to Ernie, Aggie looks like Princess Kate posing for a photo with a commoner. "Ernie's going to look in The Leather Bench. And *I'm* looking into becoming vegan, so I won't go in there. I've been reading up on the meat industry and global warming, and honestly I don't think I ever need to eat another burger in my life. Hey—if you're free, why don't we get a drink?"

Louisa looks surreptitiously at her watch. It's just past eleven-thirty; her iced mocha has barely made its way down her digestive tract. "I should be getting back," she says. "I left the kids with my mom." She doesn't say that she left them with plans to be gone all day.

"Oh, come on," says Aggie. "It'll be fun! Like old times."

Louisa squints at Aggie. She's not sure she and Aggie have experienced enough old times together to relive them. *Steven* and Aggie, for sure. But it appears that Aggie is not taking no for an answer. Before Louisa has a chance to say more, Aggie has grabbed her by the wrist and is pulling her toward the door. Over her tanned shoulder Aggie calls out, "Louisa and I are going to Peter Ott's, okay, sweetheart? We'll be on the deck. You go ahead and enjoy the leather, and meet us there when you're done."

Aggie leads Louisa down the street to Peter Ott's and asks for two seats on the deck. They are given a corner table under a dramatically flourishing hanging flower basket. "Dark and Stormy?" asks Aggie. "That's my favorite thing to drink on vacation. Now that I'm not trying to get pregnant any longer." She sighs.

"Sure," says Louisa. "Dark and Stormy it is."

"It's so nice to sit with a friend," says Aggie. "Now tell me what you're working on. A book about Fiji or something? Is what Steven said?"

"Pitcairn," says Louisa.

"Pitcairn. Of *course!*" says Aggie, like Pitcairn is her favorite dog breed. Louisa feels like she's living in some alternate universe. Aggie Baumfeld isn't scary or threatening, the way Louisa has always thought of her, the way she's been thinking about her in particular since she found out about the money. She's *nice!* Sure, she's the richest person Louisa will ever have a Dark and Stormy with, and her makeup is flawless, and her dress is gorgeous, but like everybody else walking around on God's green earth she's harboring legitimate heartache. Besides that, she's in love with her homely husband. There is absolutely no indication *whatsoever* that she's trying to appropriate Louisa's.

Directly in front of them one of the old-fashioned schooners prepares to take on a boatload of passengers for a harbor tour. Mount Megunticook rises in the distance. Maybe it's the dark rum talking, but the last thread of resentment Louisa has toward Aggie begins to wear thin, and then, finally, to break. "It *is* nice to have a drink with a friend," she agrees.

"I don't have a lot of friends," says Aggie.

Steven has said as much to Louisa, but still she has trouble believing it. "You don't? I picture you out every night, living the high life."

"Oh, sure, we're out a *lot*," Aggie says. "When you have money you can't throw a stone without hitting someone who wants you to attend a benefit. But those people aren't friends. They're benefit friends."

"Different from friends with benefits, huh?"

Aggie's laugh is loud and genuine—so loud that the couple at the table nearest them turns to look. "Right," she says. "You're really funny. Steven always talks about how funny you are. I bet *you* have lots of friends." Below them, in the harbor, a woman wobbles as she steps into the bow of a red double kayak.

"Sure," says Louisa. "I have friends." She thinks

about Franklin, and her childhood friend Chloe, and her Brooklyn friends, and her Fordham girls.

"I bet you have tons of mom friends, and professor friends and college friends. I only have a couple of friends from college. Most people at BC except for Steven thought I was obnoxious." She bows her head for a split second, then looks up with a wicked grin. "I *was* obnoxious, I guess. I don't blame them. Not Steven, though. He could see through all the drinking and the throwing around of money. He's the only one who ever could. Until I met Ernie."

Louisa notices that this narrative conveniently leaves out the part where Steven found Aggie in bed with another man, but her Dark and Stormy is halfway gone and she's certainly not going to bring that up now. "We sort of got in a fight, you know," she says. "When he told me you gave him that money."

Aggie narrows her eyes at Louisa. "I didn't *give* him that money. It's a loan. I expect every penny back, with interest. I had Steven give me the exact same presentation he gave any other investors. I would *never* give away money like that, no strings attached. Are you kidding me? My grandfather would shoot me and then truss me up like a Thanksgiving turkey. And when he was finished my father would take a turn at me. I may *look* like a trust fund baby, Louisa, but believe me,

I'm a businesswoman. I see real potential in All Ears. I listen to a lot of the podcasts, and they are *phenomenal.* That's why I was willing to help." She glances behind Louisa. "Hey, babe!"

Louisa turns around. Ernie is walking toward them. He's wearing a giant leather hat, and he's smiling to beat the band. "Ladies," he says, and tips his hat. Louisa can't help grinning back at him.

"I should go," says Louisa. "Here, Ernie, take my seat." She's definitely a little drunk! She's going to have to get a sandwich at the Camden Deli and repair to her bench before she goes to the library to finally, *finally* get to work. She stands to give Ernie her seat, and Aggie stands too.

Aggie reaches out and hugs Louisa, pulling her tight, boob to boob. She smells like roses and limes and freshly dried laundry while Louisa is certain she herself smells like summer sweat ineffectually masked by the crumbled dregs of the Secret deodorant she's dropped on the floor at least a half dozen times and keeps using anyway. "All of those children of yours," muses Aggie. "I hope you know how lucky you are." She touches her perfectly flat stomach, unmarred by childbirth and convenience food, and says, "You take care of yourself and your brood, okay? And tell Steven to keep knocking 'em dead."

As Louisa regains her seat on the bench and eats her sandwich she thinks about how many different levels of wealth there are. There is Aggie wealth: impenetrable, incomprehensible, never-have-to-worry-about-paying-for-anything wealth. Then there is Martin and Annie wealth: solid wealth, not showy, and apparently not bottomless. This is silver-haired, old-home-on-valuable-land, frayed-carpet wealth. But isn't there actually another level of wealth above Aggie's? Private plane wealth? Private *island* wealth? And then, of course, there is a level below Martin and Annie. This is Steven and Louisa wealth, which doesn't feel like wealth at all, not to Louisa, because there are tax bills, and there are braces and glasses and clothes and college for three children, and there are houses one cannot save, and there are safety nets that turn out to have holes in them, holes big enough to fall through. But what feels like non-wealth to Louisa must look like wealth to Kristie, who works for an hourly wage. And below Kristie, there is a whole other level of people with no jobs and no homes.

Before she gets back in the car she texts Steven. Ran into Aggie, she says. She almost stops there, but she continues. And I get it now. About her investment. It's the right thing.

You don't have to be a history professor to know that this might lead to a détente.

31.
Kristie

Tonight, Kristie will tell Danny about the baby. She'll tell him about the bill collectors, too. If he doesn't want to stick around once he knows the whole story, well, that's his choice, and she's prepared for it, and she won't blame him. She'll call upon her inner reserves of strength, the ones she built watching Sheila strong-arm her way through hard times, and she'll be okay. She really will.

When Elaine offers her a ride home Kristie asks if she can drop her off at the corner of Park and Main. She hooks a left on Main and walks to Main Street Markets, where she picks up two baguettes, good salami, a jar of the spicy mustard Danny likes, two kinds of cheese (Gruyère and cheddar), and a package of chocolate cookies for dessert. It's an extravagant purchase, but it's a special night. On the way home she hugs the trail by the water and breathes the harbor smell. It's just past six o'clock and there are two hours to go until sunset, but the color of the water is beginning to shift in that subtle twilight-y way she has come to love.

The lobsterman's daughters are playing hopscotch in the street, tossing a little key onto the squares. Tatiana waves at her and the other one keeps her gaze mostly down, peering up just a little bit through her bangs.

Kristie knows something is off as soon as she opens the door. Danny is home, but he doesn't greet her. He's sitting on the couch with his chin in his hands, and he barely looks up. She sets down her Main Street Markets bag. "Babe?" she says. "What's wrong? I brought dinner."

Then she sees it.

Her Ships View collection is spread out on the rickety coffee table. Here is the printout of Louisa's bio from the New York University website. Here is the press release from the court, announcing Martin Fitzgerald's retirement. Here are the directions to the house from downtown Rockland, and the Google Earth printout of the aerial view, and the Zillow page. Here is the photo of Matty McLean winning a cross-country race. Here is the check for one thousand dollars, made out to Kristie Turner from Annie Fitzgerald.

"I was going to bring our laundry to the Laundromat," says Danny. "I looked in your backpack for some quarters. I didn't think you'd mind—" Kristie's heart is beating so hard she feels like it's going to jump out of her rib cage. "And then I found all of this. So I've been sitting here, trying to figure it out."

There is nothing to tell him, after all, but the truth.

So she tells him everything. She tells him about her mother, and the letter, and her bus trip from Altoona, and how the day they met she'd ridden her bike there, just to get a sense of things. Just to see. She tells him that she didn't expect to meet Danny. How even after she met him she didn't expect to fall for him. And how no way did she expect him to fall for her in return. The whole time she's talking she's watching a muscle move in Danny's cheek. In, out. In, out. It's so pronounced that she wants to reach out and touch it. When she does, he pulls away.

"You can stop talking," he says. "I get it." He rises from the sofa.

"No, Danny. That's what I'm telling you. You don't get it. You're misunderstanding me. I'm just telling you how all of this started."

"I don't think I am misunderstanding. You've been using me, Kristie. All of this—" He makes a gesture that takes in her and the apartment together. "All of this was just a way to get close to the Fitzgeralds. It was nothing to do with me." And then he's packing his things into his own backpack—his toothbrush, the extra pairs of boxers he keeps in the dresser, the beer mug from the 2011 Lobster Festival. His sneakers by the front door, his razor. "All those questions you had about the family," he says. "I get it now. That time you said you came to tell me about your new job, when you were standing by the garden. You weren't there to see me, were you? Don't answer that. I know you weren't. You were there for them." He chews on his bottom lip and considers her. "I knew this was too good to be true."

"It's not! It's not too good to be true! It's just true! Danny. Danny. Sit back down. It's more complicated than you're making it sound. Let me explain. Let's talk about it."

"I don't feel like talking, Kristie. I just feel . . . disappointed. I feel really, really sad."

When he walks out the door he doesn't even slam it. He just closes it.

Kristie sinks down on the couch and kicks at the bag from Main Street Markets and wonders how many more pieces her heart can break into.

She sits there for a long time. She considers having a good cleansing cry, but then she thinks about how she's planning for two now. She's got to hold herself together. She picks up her phone, and she texts Louisa.

I need to talk to you. Can you meet me in town?

She paces while she waits.

The three dots appear immediately, and then the answer: Now???

Now.

This time at least two minutes go by with no dots at all. Then the dots come back, then this text.

I can't leave now. My mom is at her book club and I need to stay here with my dad and my kids. Kristie waits, and then another text arrives. You could come here?

Kristie calculates the cost of an Uber there and back, and then she adds in the emotional cost as well. Will Martin Fitzgerald be there? Is there any chance at all that Annie will see Kristie? What if Annie's book club ends early, or Kristie's Uber is late?

Her phone pings again. You have to come now if you're coming. Book club usually ends around nine.

It's twelve minutes past seven.

OK, she answers. I'll come.

By the time she contacts the Uber, waits for it to arrive, and makes the trip it's seven forty-seven. Kristie doesn't know how far away this book club of Annie's is, but she is sure as heck going to be out of there before nine. Earlier, if possible. What if the book being discussed is terribly boring and Annie decides to leave before the meeting is over?

Louisa meets Kristie on the grass when the Uber pulls up. She's barefoot, and holding a giant glass of white wine. "I thought we could sit out on the porch," she says. "My dad goes to bed early most nights, so he's in his room."

Kristie doubts Martin Fitzgerald goes to bed quite this early, but she gets it—Kristie is being hidden from the inhabitants of the house. She follows Louisa across the lawn to a set of steps on the side of the porch and then up them. It's almost the end of July—the days are growing shorter, and sunset is probably only twenty minutes away. She notices that all of Danny's gardens are thriving—the dahlias are tall and proud, the ornamental grasses are performing a light dance in the breeze, and the vegetable garden, safe behind its wire fencing, looks pristine and luscious, with a giant almost-ripe tomato bowing on its vine. Thinking about Danny makes her eyes well up immediately, so she tries to shepherd her thoughts elsewhere.

On the porch, Louisa gestures for Kristie to take the love seat that faces the water. She flicks a switch to turn on the lights in the porch ceiling, then sits in a chair turned three-quarters of the way to face the love seat. "Can I pour you a glass of this?" she asks, holding up her wine. "It's a really nice one. I brought out a glass for you." On a low table in front of the couch is a half-empty wine bottle (or maybe, Kristie thinks, it's half full!) and an extra glass. Kristie looks at the bottle. It's a Pascal Cotat Sancerre, which she knows sells for over $120 at a restaurant so must be close to $70 to buy in a shop.

"No, thank you." (She'd love to taste that wine, though.)

"Something else, then? Water, or seltzer? Whiskey?"

"I'm all set." She thinks about telling Louisa why: I'm on the wagon because I was on my way to becoming a raging alcoholic when I lived in Miami Beach. Oh, also, I'm pregnant. The father is your lawn guy, Danny, who just tonight left me, because of what he found in my backpack, which has to do with you.

But she decides against it. Better to ease into the conversation than to wallop Louisa over the head with her troubles.

"I hope you don't mind if I keep drinking," says Louisa. "Let me tell you, I've had a day." She takes a long pull of the wine and regards Kristie over the edge of the glass with Martin Fitzgerald's eyes.

"Of course not," says Kristie. "Drink away." *You've had a day?* she wants to say. *I've had a life.*

"So . . ." says Louisa. She leans forward toward

Kristie, and something about her posture and expression make Kristie think of long-ago middle-school-aged Twyla, with her fancy family tree and her rec room, rolling her eyes at her parents with their dishes of ice cream—Twyla, who never fully understood how lucky she was to be placed so firmly in her own particular orbit; Twyla, who always expected to move within that orbit, without question or examination.

"So," says Kristie. "I opened the envelope. With the check. And I really appreciate it, the gesture and all of that. But." She pauses and looks out at the rapidly darkening sky. The fog has moved in, and between that and the time of day she can't make out the break-water, even though it's just across the harbor. "But. I don't think it's enough. I mean, it's not. I don't think; I know. It's not enough." She turns back to face Louisa. She watches as the familiar spots of color appear on Lousia's cheeks, and then as they flatten and spread into a full flush. Kristie sees a pad of paper and a pencil on the side table, next to the wine bottle and the glass. She picks up the paper. It's a grocery list. Olive oil, says the list. Cabernet. Peaches. Brie. Kale (farmer's market?). It's a rich person's grocery list. She takes up the pencil and turns the page to reveal a fresh sheet. She writes down the $27,000 that she owes the bill collectors. She writes down her Linden Street rent, then multiplies that by twelve, then writes down that number. She writes down her estimated cost of a new stroller, a crib, a year's worth of diapers. She's guessing, because she doesn't really know. There are so many more things she could include—premiums for health insurance, formula, utilities. But she stops there. She adds everything carefully, taking her time, because math was never her best subject. "This," she says when she's done. She pushes the paper toward Louisa. "This is closer to the right number."

Louisa takes the pad of paper. Her eyebrows shoot up. "That's a big number," she says.

Kristie stands her ground by staying silent. A long moment passes, then another one. She resists the urge to explain herself. She'll let thirty seconds go by, the way Sheila taught her. She stares out at the water, and at the sky, turning orange now.

Louisa drains her wineglass and sets it down on the low table. Kristie can see her contemplating pouring the rest of the bottle. "You know, Kristie. I'm really sorry about your mom. I am. I'm so, so sorry. But this—this is practically extortion."

"It's not extortion," says Kristie. "I'm just trying to get my feet under me."

"But I don't—we don't necessarily have . . ." Louisa's voice trails off, and she looks around the porch; it's possible, from her expression, that she is realizing how ridiculous that must sound to Kristie. The foghorn on the lighthouse sounds. *Hello!* The foghorn seems to be saying, *Here I am, just across the harbor from your big fancy house!* "I mean, I hate to trot out a platitude, and I'm not sure exactly what all of your problems are, but money won't fix everything."

This statement infuriates Kristie so much, and so quickly, that she can feel the flame of anger licking at her everywhere—the tips of her fingers, her toes, the top of her head. She almost loses it. She stands up, walks to the railing of the porch, turns around. "Can I tell *you* something, Louisa? That's bullshit."

Louisa stares at her. "Excuse me?"

"That's complete and absolute bullshit. The fact is that the only people who say that money can't fix problems are people who have plenty of it! Because guess what? Besides the fact that my mom is dead, every single one of my problems is connected to money. All of them. And all of my mom's problems were connected to money too. She didn't have any money saved for medical emergencies. How could she? She was always just trying to survive. If my mom hadn't met your dad, if she hadn't gotten pregnant and decided to keep the baby—decided to keep me!—she would have gone to law school instead of being an assistant forever. She would have been a lawyer. Maybe *she* would have been a judge. But she didn't have the money. And she had to take care of me." Kristie takes a deep breath. "My mom's life changed in every conceivable way after she met your dad. And your dad's life didn't change at all."

Louisa flares her nostrils and her voice gets cold. She crosses her arms. "My parents sent money to your mother four times a year until you were eighteen. My father didn't shirk his responsibilities. He did what he could."

Kristie snorts.

"He *did*, Kristie. He didn't just walk away without a backward glance."

"Maybe not. But it wasn't enough," Kristie says. She's leaning back on the railing now, facing Louisa. "It was never enough. I mean, the checks, yeah, I'm sure they helped. But we still struggled. We *always* struggled. And he never had to *really pay*, not the way my mom paid. He didn't give up any of his plans. He didn't get thrown off track. *You* didn't even know about me—what does that say about how much his life changed when I was born?"

Now Louisa does pour more wine. She takes a small sip and puts the glass down too hard. "What should he have done, Kristie? Deserted my mom and me, two people who didn't do anything wrong, who would have been worse off without him? Left us to figure it out? So maybe things would have been better for you and your mom but they would have been worse for us."

Obviously, thinks Kristie, *obviously I would have preferred that.* But she sees Louisa's point. "Yes. No. I don't *know,* Louisa. I don't know what the answer is."

Louisa sighs. "I guess the answer is that there is no answer. But I bet you don't have any idea, Kristie, what he accomplished in his life, in his career. He wouldn't have done any of that if he'd left his marriage, or if it had come out that he had a daughter with another woman. He helped a lot of people as a judge. A *lot* of people. His mantra was, *Leave the world better than you found it.* And that's what he worked toward, every single day. He helped create these drug courts—"

"I don't care about drug courts!" says Kristie, too loudly.

Louisa stares at her, and then she says, "Maybe you don't, but that's probably because you don't understand them. He kept so many people out of jail, got them treatment, got them back with their families . . ."

"Maybe. Sure, okay. That's great. But he didn't leave *my mother* better than he found her! He didn't leave me better!" Kristie takes a deep breath. "And if you don't want it getting out that *our father* hasn't always been the perfect saint everybody thinks he was, then I would really appreciate it if you'd take this check back to your mother and ask her to write another one because it's a nice gesture and whatever but it's just not enough to cover what we gave up."

"Getting *out*?" says Louisa. "Are you threatening us? What are you going to do, go to the *Portland Press Herald* with a tip?"

"Maybe," says Kristie. (Is this how blackmail works? She's not sure; she's never blackmailed anyone.)

Louisa shakes her head. "No. No, you're not going to do that. You don't know everything you think you know. You're getting it all wrong."

Now Kristie walks to the end of the porch, and back again, before she speaks. "Only from your point of view. From mine, I know a lot. I know it's easier to be you than to be me. I know it's always been easier. I know you went to private school, then college, then graduate school. I know you have both your parents, and I have no parents. I know what your *summer house* looks like. I mean, come on. Just the fact that you *have* a summer house . . ."

"It's not my house!" Louisa cries.

"It will be one day."

Kristie can see the change move over Louisa's face—her own rage moving in to battle Kristie's. Louisa takes a bigger sip from her wineglass. "You think you have me all figured out, Kristie, from a couple of glimpses of this house, but you don't. You don't know anything about any problems I might have. You don't know anything about my marriage or my job, or how hard I've worked for any of it. And you think I have both my parents? I don't have my father, not anymore. Every single day he's slipping a little further away. So maybe I've known him all these years and you haven't, but that also means I can see what's disappearing." Louisa's chest is heaving, and there's a tear snaking its way down her face.

"I'm sorry about that," says Kristie. "I really am sorry. But I still—"

"I'll see what my mother says." Louisa cuts her off. She glances at her watch. "She'll probably be home soon."

"Thank you," says Kristie.

"Good night."

It's eight forty-five now. Time to go. She'll schedule the Uber while she's walking around the side of the house, and she'll wait for it at the top of the road, where nobody will be able to see her.

32.
Pauline

"Like this, Grandma?" Hazel takes one of the strips of pastry Pauline cut and lays it across the top of the pie.

"That's right. Just like that, gentle, like you're putting a baby to bed."

Hazel laughs. She sounds so much like her mother that Pauline's heart nearly stands still. Sometimes, absent these reminders, Pauline can hardly believe that she shares any blood at all with this creature, so different from the girl of ten who visited three years ago—this girl who is now tan of skin, long of limb, throwing out "y'alls" and "I reckons" and "fixin' tos" like they're trap ropes. But then Hazel laughs, or tilts her head in a certain way, or crosses her ankles just so, and Pauline sees Nicole's genetic stamp all over her.

"There you go," says Pauline approvingly. "We're going to put these ones all in a row, just like this, see? Now unfold every other one back in on itself. And put the long one here, perpendicular to the others."

It's a blueberry pie, with blueberries from Weskeag in Thomaston. Pauline sees Hazel struggling to place the second strip of dough, putting it too close to the first. She sticks the tip of her tongue out when she's concentrating, just like Nicole used to do. "Here now," Pauline says, showing her. "Like this." Some people just throw the top piece of pie dough on top of the pie, cut a few slits, and call it a day. But not Pauline. In Pauline's opinion a lattice crust is the only way to go. "Now watch, I'm going to teach you how to make an egg wash. Anybody ever taught you about egg wash on a lattice crust?"

"No, ma'am."

"You don't need to call me ma'am. Grandma will do just fine."

"Got it," says Hazel. "Grandma."

Pauline mixes the beaten eggs with a little bit of water. "This is what's going to give it a glossy finish." She shows Hazel how to brush it on carefully, not letting too much of the wash get on each dip of the pastry brush. Pauline's pastry brush is old, with some of the bristles sticking out like a person with bed head. Still she'd no sooner replace it than she'd replace her own big toe. When that's done, she washes her hands and wipes them on the dish towel on the counter. Hazel does the same, then slides her hand—warm, still a little damp, with long graceful fingers, inside Pauline's.

"Grandma?" she says. "I love visiting here with y'all. I wish I could stay longer."

Pauline feels an inconvenient tear take shape in each eye. There's something grandkids can do to your heart nobody else can. She holds on to the hand for a long second before releasing it, giving the pie one last check, and sliding it into the oven. "*Y'all* this and *y'all* that," she says. "You sound like a southern girl."

Hazel's eyes go very wide and deep like a great round pool Pauline could wade into. "But that's what I am, Grandma. A southern girl, born and bred."

Pauline's heart feels like it's been put in a paper shredder which has then been switched on, without a thought in the world for what might be inside. She remembers Nicole's little starfish hands, slapping at the bathwater. She remembers Billy holding up a live lobster to her and Nicole reaching out to touch it, then pulling her hands back away from the claws, shrieking, Billy saying, "He won't hurt you none, Nicole. He won't hurt you none," and all of them laughing. Now that it's over, Pauline remembers Nicole's childhood as though it was yesterday, every piece of it scored in her memory like marks along the trunk of a tree. She remembers moments in the lives of her sons too, but, yes, it's different with a daughter. It just is.

There was that old dog they had once, Gus, with the long hound's ears, soft, like pieces of silk, and more patience than four saints put together. Nicole used to play with those ears, lying down next to the poor thing and spreading the ear across her face like it was a blanket. They don't have a dog now, but sometimes at the Fitzgeralds' house she watches the kids with Otis and she thinks about Nicole. Some way, somehow, it seems like a corner of her mind is always thinking about Nicole. She watches Matty and Hazel too, from the house when they're out on the rocks, for hours, sitting next to each other, not touching, but talking, Hazel with her knees pulled up to her chest.

Pauline sets the timer on the oven and thinks about how happy it will make Billy, this pie, when he comes back from the airport with Nicole, and how he'll ask to have a slice of it before supper, and how Pauline will think about saying no but in the end, of course, she'll cut him a slice, because he works hard, out there on the water all day, and neither of them is getting any younger, and so why the hell not eat pie before supper if you're lucky enough to have a working mouth, and a piece of pie to put into it?

"How long will it take?" asks Hazel.

"Fifty minutes or so. We'll check it in twenty-five, maybe put a shield around the edges then, so they don't get too brown. I'll show you. You want a glass of lemonade while we're waiting? Maybe play a game of gin rummy?"

"Yes!"

Pauline takes the pitcher from the refrigerator and Hazel fetches the glasses from the cabinet and Pauline thinks about the first day she was here when Hazel asked if they had any sweet tea in the refrigerator. Sweet tea! Of all things.

Hazel drinks half her lemonade in one gulp, and when she puts the glass down she wipes her mouth with the back of her hand and Pauline thinks about handing her a paper towel but decides to let it go, and then Hazel says, "Matty told me that Mama and his mom used to be friends."

"Used to be, that's right. A long time ago."

"But they're not anymore?"

Pauline opens the drawer in the kitchen that holds all manner of things, rubber bands and extra scissors and Scotch tape and buttons and spare change. Organized chaos, is what this drawer is. She extracts from the drawer the deck of cards, worn soft by years of playing, and begins to shuffle them. She taught Hazel gin rummy her second day here—the girl didn't know a single card game! Pauline couldn't believe it. "Not anymore," she says. She deals out the cards, ten each.

"Why not?"

Pauline concentrates first on grouping her cards and then she says, "Oh, lots of reasons. People grow apart. You think your life is going in one direction, and then—wham! Bam! Off it goes in another."

"Matty says they got in a fight about a boy." Hazel giggles. "Did you know about that?"

"Oh, sure," says Pauline. "I knew about that, all right. Your go."

"So what happened? With the boy?"

What happened, thinks Pauline, is what always happens—what's been happening since the beginning of time. What happened is that the rich girl won. What happened was Nicole crying in Pauline's lap—sobbing, really, brokenhearted in the way you can really only be when you're sixteen and think you're in love. Or maybe Nicole *was* in love. Sixteen-year-olds are allowed to be in love, same as anybody else. There's no law against it.

"Nothing worth talking about," says Pauline. "Just silly teenage stuff. And it's hard being human." She considers the ace Hazel has just discarded and decides to take it. She thinks about Marilyn in the hospital bed in her front room. "It's hard having all those feelings, not always knowing where to put them."

"I don't think it's hard being human," says Hazel. "I think it's nice."

Pauline watches her—this golden beauty, the product of landlocked southern sun, cheese grits, green grass without snow on it. She's so tired suddenly that she wants to crawl inside the blueberry pie, pull the lattice crust over her like a blanket, and fall asleep. "Well, sure," says Pauline, trying to keep her voice from sounding gruff, because it isn't gruffness she's feeling, not exactly. It's more like a depletion of her emotional reserves: the well is running dry. "Sure, you would think that, honey. I don't blame you at all."

"Can I go over to Matty's after we're done with this game?"

"Of course." Pauline knocks on the table and says, "Knock."

"Already?" Hazel wrinkles her perfect nose.

"Yup," says Pauline. She was lucky this time; she dealt herself a good hand. She lays down her cards.

33.

Louisa

Louisa can't believe it's August tomorrow. Where has July gone? Poof. Into the past. Another summer almost over. One hundred forty-three pages still to go. That's a lot of pages! She's sitting on her bed, laptop warming her thighs, watching the light shift outside, turning the seaweed-studded rocks from brown to a golden purplish-mauve, when the doorbell rings. She waits to hear if someone else is going to get it and when she doesn't hear anyone she sighs and pads down the stairs.

She squints at the person outside the door: a petite blond woman, very pretty, with big brown eyes, perfectly made up, and a knee-length printed belted dress.

"Louisa," says the person. "It's me." Louisa squints harder. "Nicole Pelletier!"

Yes! Of course it's Nicole. Nicole, from the summer they were sixteen; Nicole, from Mark Harding's Whaler—Nicole, who was always first into the water because she lived here year round and wasn't scared of the cold.

"Nicole!" cries Louisa. "Hey! *Hi!* You look *fantastic!*" Nicole's hair is blonder than it used to be—Nashville blond, Louisa would venture—and she's thin in a way that bespeaks barre class or Pilates or another form of exercise taken up by women of means. Her dress is the sort that Louisa has never been able to pull off but that looks endlessly adorable on Nicole, and she is smiling. She has the same dimples she always had. "Your mom isn't here," says Louisa. "Didn't she take today off because you were coming? Isn't that what my mom said?"

"I know," says Nicole. "My mom's at home, finishing up dinner. I'm just here for tonight. I came to fetch Hazel home." There's a trace of southern in her voice, and for sure in her word choice. *Fetch Hazel home* sounds so delightful. Why does nobody in Brooklyn ever fetch anyone home? "I came to say hi to *you*. You know, since your Matty and my Hazel have been hanging out, and since, I don't know, we're never here at the same time anymore . . ." She falters and touches the belt on her dress. She's flustered, realizes Louisa.

"Of course!" says Louisa. "Of course. I'm so glad

you did. Come in. Do you want to come out on the porch for a drink?"

"Oh no," Nicole says. "Thank you. I should get back. We're having dinner at home. My mom and Hazel baked a pie . . . but I just wanted to say, hey, you know, it's been so long. Maybe give you my phone number? I'm just here so quick this time, up and back, but my mom's cousin is doing poorly so there's a chance I'll be back before summer's over . . . if I am, I'll look you up. Maybe we can talk a little bit."

"I hope you do," says Louisa. She gets—*fetches*—the pad of paper on the telephone table and hands it to Nicole, who writes down a number and hands the paper back.

Nicole is halfway up the little hill to the driveway when Louisa remembers something. "Nicole!" she calls. "Your girl. Hazel. She's a *great* kid. Really great kid."

Nicole smiles again; even from the doorway Louisa can see her dimples. "Thank you for saying that, Louisa. She's the best thing I've done with my life." She turns and squares her shoulders and seems to walk with a new purpose.

While she is putting Nicole's number in her phone, Steven calls. Louisa scarcely has time to greet him before he blurts out his news: "We got nominated for five Poddies!"

"Really? Steven, that's fantastic!" A Poddie is like the Emmy of podcasts; Steven has been hoping for a Poddie since All Ears' inception. (They've been twice nominated, but never won.)

"And one of them is for one of my shows, *The Fabulous Life of Mrs. Jean Dunn!*"

"That's so great, Steven!" *The Fabulous Life of Mrs. Jean Dunn* tells the story of an eighty-eight-year-old Black woman living in Baltimore. It aired in nine parts, each part focusing on one decade of Jean Dunn's life, moving from the Great Depression through the Civil Rights era and culminating in the Black Lives Matter movement. Jean Dunn is neither rich nor famous— she worked for most of her life in the cafeteria of the Johns Hopkins Hospital and raised four children. She's an Everywoman, and that's what makes her life so interesting. "Jean Dunn is my very favorite thing you've ever done. It's really brilliant."

"Thank you. *Thank* you! I really think we have a good chance of winning this year. It's my favorite too. I wish I could kiss you! I wish I could kiss Jean Dunn!"

"Well, I wouldn't go *that* far," says Louisa, but she's laughing. She hasn't heard Steven this happy in a long time.

"If we get this award," says Steven, "it will all have been worth it."

Louisa feels a shift in the air as she says, "All what will have been worth it?"

"All of the work, and the sacrifice, and, you know— everything."

What Louisa says is, "Okay. Sure." What she *doesn't* say is, have I sacrificed my work, my sabbatical, at least five-eighths of my sanity, our time together this summer, and, if you'd had your way, our Emergency Fund, for a *podcast award?* She doesn't say this because she is a good and supportive partner and of course a good and supportive partner wouldn't say such things.

The air must not have shifted in Brooklyn, because Steven says, "We're going out to celebrate! I'll call you after, okay? But if it's late and you don't answer right away I'll hang up, and we'll talk tomorrow."

If you keep poking the bear, thinks Louisa, the claws are going to come out. She checks in first with Annie, who returned from Vinalhaven the other day acting less frosty toward Louisa than she had been. Then she looks at her newly edited contact list and starts a text.

Nicole! Louisa here. Not sure what time you're eating but any chance you want to grab a quick drink in town tonight after dinner?

The answer comes back so fast it seems like their texts could have collided in the air. Yes please. Just got home and already dying to get out. (The text is heavy on the emojis: winky face, smiley face, party hat.) I'll pick you up at seven-thirty.

At seven-thirty sharp, Nicole appears at the door. She has changed out of her belted dress and into teeny-tiny shorts and a flowy silk tank top. Her legs are firm and tan, and she's pulling off wedge sandals and shorts with aplomb. *Southern ladies*, thinks Louisa, feeling pallid and flat-haired. Her summer dress, which looked bohemian in the Pink Room mirror, now feels stodgy and maternity-like.

"You want to drive?" says Louisa. "Or should I?" She's not sure if Nicole is a big drinker or not. Back in the day, sure, neither one of them said no to some purloined vodka mixed with lemonade. But Nicole might have turned into a health nut. Look at her skin—it's glowing!

"I figured we'd take an Uber. Girls' Night Out, right?"

"Oh!" says Louisa. "Oh. Got it." So not a total health nut. And this is not merely a night out, this is a Night Out. She recalculates. The air has that feel particular to Maine in summertime—the sudden cooling of the day, the fog like a curtain over the water, the change in atmosphere that feels like teenage promise even though Louisa hasn't been a teenager in two decades. She thinks about Steven out celebrating the Poddie nominations and she says, "What the heck? Let's do it, all the way. Girls' Night Out."

Nicole whips out her phone.

In the Uber they decide on Myrtle Street Tavern, because it's one of the only places in town with live music. Sure enough, there's a band setting up, and a massive group of fortysomething women, mostly blond, in white jeans and tank tops; they look like they're ready to take over the dance floor as soon as the music starts. Nicole and Louisa sit at the bar and order two vodka tonics. One of the white jeans ladies comes up next to Louisa and leans on the bar. "Another round of the same tequila shots, please," she says. "Thirteen. Put it on my tab. You have my credit card. Sherri Griffin." She lowers her voice and whips her head around toward her friends and back again and then she says, "How much will that be, by the way?"

"Ninety-one," says the bartender.

"Okay." The woman looks worried. To her hands she says, "I think we're splitting it up after . . ."

"You still good to go?" asks the bartender. "Or you want to go lower shelf?"

"Oh, no, gosh no. The ladies wouldn't like that. I'm good to go." She produces a wobbly smile and glances at Louisa. She's pretty when she smiles, although the worried divot remains in the center of her forehead. "We all have thirteen-year-old girls home in Massachusetts, and we're on a two-night getaway. Trust me, we need these shots."

"I have a thirteen-year-old girl!" says Nicole.

"*I* have an almost thirteen-year-old boy!" says Louisa. "And they *like* each other," she adds, motioning back and forth between herself and Nicole. "Her girl and my boy."

"Awwww," says Sherri. "That's adorable." She looks more closely at Louisa and Nicole, as if trying to decide if they are people she can confide in, and then she says, "I'm the newest member of this group. It's the first time I've been invited overnight. I don't want to do anything wrong."

"Fourteen shots," says the bartender. He starts to put them on a cocktail tray. "Here's the first bunch. You might need to come back for the rest of them."

"Oh, I—" Sherri starts to say something, but the bartender has already turned away to line up the rest of the shot glasses.

"Excuse me!" calls Louisa. "Bartender!" He turns around. "She only ordered thirteen. Make sure you don't charge her for the fourteenth."

"Thank you," whispers Sherri. She palms the tray

and steadies it with her other hand—clearly this is not this woman's first time in a bar—before making her way back to her group.

The bartender shrugs. "Got it." He pushes the extra shot toward Louisa and Nicole. "One of you two want this?"

"Definitely not," says Louisa.

"*I'll* take it," says Nicole. She throws back the shot, then looks at Louisa expectantly—she looks like one of Louisa's students, waiting for her to start the lecture.

"Soooo . . ." says Louisa. (What do you say to someone you haven't seen in twenty-three years?) She settles for, "Tell me about Nashville."

Almost instantly, Nicole starts crying. "Sorry!" She plucks a napkin from behind the bar and blows her nose with an indelicacy that contrasts heartily with her silk tank top and expensive perfume. "Sorry. It's not really all that bad. Nashville is a great town! Amazing music. Amazing food, blah blah, just like everyone says, super hot in the summer but the flowers bloom just about all year long. I'm going through some things with my husband, and oh, who am I kidding, I know we're headed for a divorce, and that'll be *three* divorces, and I'm not even forty. But it's fine. It's totally fine. I'm sorry." She lets out a big puff of air and says, "To be honest, Richard thinks the sun comes up just to hear him crow.

I think it'll be good for me, once we're separated. Good for Hazel too. But three divorces! I just can't get over what a failure that makes me feel like."

Louisa slides a clean cocktail napkin in front of Nicole and says, "Mark Harding has had two divorces. And he's our age. He seems pretty normal. Sometimes things just happen, and they may not be your fault. Sometimes you have to go easy on yourself."

"Mark *Harding?*" says Nicole. She blows her nose and dabs at her eyes and somehow, due to magic mascara or a lot of practice crying in public, her makeup looks just as fresh as it did in the driveway at Ships View. "Holy smokes, there's a name I haven't thought of in years. Mark Harding, huh? You keep in touch with him?"

"No. I haven't been. But I ran into him this summer, sort of randomly. He's up here full-time, you know. He's a *detective.*"

"A detective!" Nicole whistles. "Impressive."

"Not what I would have guessed for him."

"Me either. I would have thought, I dunno. High school principal?" Nicole finishes her drink and signals the bartender for two more. Louisa, realizing she's behind, tries to drink faster without gulping. "That was my first heartbreak, when Mark chose you over me. Oh, I cried and I cried over that."

"If he saw you now," says Louisa, "he'd think he chose wrong."

The smile Nicole gives Louisa is filled to the top with rue. "No way. Never. I'm a mess. Clearly. But you— My mom's kept me updated on you, over the years. A professor! I mean, wow. She said you're writing a book! And you have three kids, I only have one and I can barely manage. How do you have everything so together?"

Louisa nearly spit-takes her drink. "Are you kidding me? I don't have anything together."

"Well, you could have fooled me. My mom talks about you like you walk on water."

"Just that one time," said Louisa. "And to be honest I didn't go very far." Nicole cracks up at this, which Louisa appreciates. "For real, though. You've only been around me for what, like forty-five minutes? An hour? It takes a little longer than that for the cracks to show through. But believe me, they're there." Louisa ticks her problems off on her mental fingers. Sick father. Strained marriage. Unfinished book. Newly discovered love child, badly done by. Hole in the safety net big enough for a dead seal to fall through.

"I think you're just saying that to make me feel better. I can't seem to do any of it right," says Nicole. "I don't know why I'm always messing things up." She lets out a weight-of-the-world sigh. "Maybe I shouldn't have left in the first place. Maybe that was my mistake, looking for greener pastures when I had the pasture in front of me all along."

"The way I figure it," says Louisa, "we spend about half our lives trying to get away from our roots." She shrugs. "And then we spend the other half trying to get back."

"Ha! That's so true, right?"

Louisa thinks about Aggie: *I hope you know how lucky you are, Louisa.* She thinks about Nicole asking her how she has everything together. She thinks about Pauline, who has told Nicole things about Louisa, good things, that Louisa didn't even know Pauline was aware of. Maybe, just maybe, it's time for Louisa to start feeling as lucky as she looks to other people.

The bartender wipes down the bar next to them with great attention, and then he rearranges the napkins and the lemons and limes, which do not need rearranging. Two men come in and survey the available seats. They choose to sit next to Nicole, even though at least six other bar seats are open. They look like fishermen, brawny, tanned faces, tattoos.

One look from Nicole and the men are introducing themselves. They are Captain Jeff and First Mate Noah. They run a tourist boat out of Camden in the summer, and in the fall they pull traps out of Rock-port. In the fall, they're in bed by 7:00 P.M. "But in the summer we live it up," says Captain Jeff, wagging his eyebrows at Louisa. She must be getting drunk, because she wags her eyebrows back. Louisa watches Nicole slip on a coat of pure charm as she acts like a fisherman is an exotic creature, like she hasn't grown up around three of them. Before she knows what's happening, Captain Jeff and First Mate Noah have bought them a *third* round of drinks.

"I don't know if I can," says Louisa when the fresh drink appears in front of her.

"Of course you can," says Nicole. "You just drink right up, Louisa. The band is starting. The night is young."

"It's not *that* young," says Louisa. "It's middle-aged at best." But she picks up the third drink anyway and swivels in her chair to watch the band. They're good! They cover some old stuff—the Ramones, some Stones, which the fishermen really get into. All of the band members are older than Nicole and Louisa. Maybe fifty, or even sixty; they have weathered faces and long, out-of-style hair. They look happy. When the lead singer starts the chorus of "Satisfaction" he tips his head back and sings to the ceiling and Louisa imagines she can see what this guy would have looked like in high school, the girls going crazy for him.

"Satisfaction" ends, and Louisa looks around for Nicole. She's walking toward the band! She's talking to the singer! He's bending his head toward her to hear, and Nicole has her hand on his shoulder. She's speaking directly into his ear. When she gets back to Louisa her smile is as wide as the day is long.

"What'd you do?" Louisa has to yell to be heard.

"Nothing." Nicole's dimples deepen.

The music starts again. Two bars, then four. The song is "I'll Melt with You" by Modern English. Nicole and Louisa scream. They were both babies when this song came out, but that doesn't matter: they recognize it for the happy high school dancing romantic anthem that it has been forever and ever. They take over the dance floor at the Myrtle Street Tavern on the last night in July, as summer turns the corner in Rockland, Maine, and they dance like two friends with everything ahead of them and nothing behind.

August

34.
Matty

Eight o'clock in the morning, the first day of August, Matty is in the deepest, darkest sleep, his shades pulled all the way down, the covers over his head.

"Matty?" It's Claire's voice, and then the door opens a few inches and then it's half of Claire's face peeking at him. "Matty! Sorry, I'm sorry I woke you up, but Hazel is looking for you."

"Hazel? For what?"

"*I* don't know," says Claire, irritated. "She didn't tell *me*."

"Did you ask her?"

"Nope," says Claire. Her face disappears and the door closes.

Matty gets out of bed, pees, brushes his teeth, looks with a critical eye at his hair, and then grabs his Yankees hat from the bathroom doorknob it's hooked over. He can hear someone clattering around in the kitchen so he slips out the front door, barefoot. Hazel is standing in the side yard. She's not looking at her phone; she's not shifting her weight or playing with her hair or anything. She's just standing in the grass, very still, facing the water, waiting.

"Hey," says Matty.

"Hey! Did Claire wake you up?"

"Yeah."

"Sorry."

"Don't be."

"I wanted to make sure to say goodbye, that's all."

"Goodbye?" His heart clenches.

"I'm leaving," says Hazel. "Going home." Adorably, she wrinkles her nose. He notices that there are more freckles now than there were at the beginning of the summer. Each freckle is beautiful to Matty; each one like a tiny gift.

"Now?" says Matty. His voice comes out like a croak. Stupid voice, so unreliable: too high one second, too rough the next. "I thought you were leaving at twelve." It can't be true. He's wasted all of his chances—he's wasted the whole summer, and now Hazel is leaving, right now, this minute. Even though there's fog shrouding the water and the morning is cool, the grass still damp with morning dew, his palms start to sweat.

"I know," says Hazel. "That's what I thought too. Our flight doesn't leave from Portland until four. But my granddad has to do some things along the way so he wants to go early. He's got to stop in Bath for something to do with his traps." She shrugs. The gum flashes at him. She's wearing shorts with one of her crop tops, a flannel shirt over the top in concession to the morning chill. His eyes fall to her thighs, and he can see a layer of goose bumps.

"I guess you'll be happy to get back home again," says Matty. "See all your friends and all."

"Yes and no," says Hazel. "Mostly no."

It's Matty's turn to say something or do something but he doesn't trust his voice not to betray him if he speaks. So he nods and kicks at the grass with his bare foot, sending out droplets of dew.

"Well okay then," says Hazel. The Tennessee is returning to her voice, as if it's preparing: *will okay thin.* "I'd better go. My granddad wants to get an early start. He worries about traffic." She peers at the sky. "Also, I think it's going to rain. So, bye, Matty." She hesitates for a split second and then turns, walking quickly up the small hill, stumbling briefly on an uneven patch of grass and then righting herself.

"Wait!" says Matty. "Wait! Hazel!" Hazel stops, then turns, and Matty starts up the little hill, jogging, then running, until he gets to her.

"What?"

"I forgot something," says Matty.

"What'd you forget?" She puts a hand on her hip, cocks it. Tosses her hair. He steps closer to Hazel. He's close enough to touch her, although he hasn't yet. He can smell the mint of her gum, see again the green flash of it in her mouth. Then she takes the gum out of her mouth, bends down, and sticks it to a rock. Matty is momentarily alarmed by this gesture. If a bird picks up the gum in its beak, or if another animal does—"Did you forget to kiss me?" She grins.

Just like that he stops thinking about the gum and the birds and the animals. He remembers Billy on the boat: *Don't think too much. You just gotta do.*

And he takes Hazel's face in his hands, one hand on either cheek. He's not sure if this is exactly the protocol but he's seen it happen this way in the movies and all in all it feels pretty good. Okay then. Next steps. Turn the head. There is a terrifying moment when he thinks they might both turn their heads in the same direction— but, no, at the last second Hazel corrects course, and their lips are touching, then moving together, and there is even a quick flick of Hazel's tongue inside his mouth, and she tastes like mint and strawberry lip gloss. And none of it lasts forever but it lasts long enough.

Hazel pulls away first. Matty would have stayed there all day and into the night, but he knows not to give Hazel a reason to cross her granddad. Then she does the best thing ever, which is to bury her face in his neck for a fraction of a second and whisper, "I'll see you around, Matty McLean," before she turns to start up the gravel driveway and toward her granddad's house.

Then the skies open.

Matty stands in the rain and watches her go but not for too long because he feels something rising in his throat, what is this, a *lump* he has to *swallow* around because, what, now he's going to *cry* about Hazel leaving? He squares his shoulders and moves toward the house, not even registering the movement of the curtains in one of the upstairs front windows, the lowering of the ship-watching binoculars.

"*I knew it,*" whispers Claire.

35.
Louisa

There is not enough caffeine in the world to soothe Louisa's hangover. When she wakes, the doors to the kids' bedroom are still closed. Her mother has taken her father to Camden for a doctor's appointment. Pauline isn't coming in today—she has to help with her sick cousin, and get Hazel and Nicole out the door to Portland—so Louisa pulls out her laptop and her notebook and lays them both out on the dining room table. She has made progress this summer, yes. But not at the rate that she should have.

She imagines Phoebe Richardson sitting at some sleek desk in some nearly empty apartment, probably wearing a silk robe tied gracefully over matching silk pajamas. Possibly drinking a mimosa. She imagines the words are flowing from Phoebe Richardson's pen like water from a faucet, while she, Louisa, can do nothing more than stare at the rain dashing against the picture window.

Instead of transcribing her latest writing in the notebook into her computer, she spends some time drawing palm trees and Pitcairn's craggy shoreline. She adds a longboat with a muscled crew. One of the crew is smiling, and the other is grimacing with the effort of rowing the longboat into the waves. It takes an incredible amount of strength to row a longboat.

She pours another cup of coffee—her third. Now she feels hungover *and* strung out. She should eat, but she's not hungry. She'll wait for the kids to wake up. She'll make them a big breakfast.

After an eternity she gets into a little bit of a rhythm. She starts to write about the very first magistrate of Pitcairn, Edward Quintal, whose father, one of the original *Bounty* mutineers, was killed by a hatchet before Edward was born.

She hears the front door open. This can't be her parents already, can it? Her back is to the front door; she turns around. It's Matty, looking like a drowned rat. His hair is plastered to his face and water is pouring off him in actual rivulets.

"Matty? Your door was closed. I thought you were sleeping."

"No, I was outside."

"What were you doing outside? What are you doing *up*?"

Matty shrugs. He's not wearing running clothes. There's so much water in his shoes that she can hear them squishing. She points to the towel they keep near the front door for Otis and says, "Not another step. Take them off. Dry yourself before you go upstairs."

Matty says, "Mom, I—" He pauses. She has lost her train of thought: it was already so slender, so ephemeral, and now it has disappeared altogether.

"Yes?" She tries to make her voice tender and patient. "Yes, Matty?"

"Nothing," he says. This comes to her: *Here is a boy who needs his father.* Every thought the girls have comes somersaulting out of their mouths at top speed, like a gymnast taking its turn on the tumbling mat. But boys are different. Talking to a boy can be like picking tiny stitches out of a hem: you need time and patience and excellent eyesight.

"Are you sure? Come sit down. Talk to me."

"That's okay," he says. "You're working." He goes up the stairs.

She turns back to her work. The view outside the picture window is obscured by the rain and fog. If there are any boats out there she can't see them. *The sea was angry that day, my friends,* she thinks. *Like an old man trying to send back soup in a deli.* Vintage Seinfeld.

After a time Abigail and Claire come down, warm and sleepy-eyed and hungry. They press into Louisa's side and she kisses each one on the top of the head and tells them that Granny and Grandpa and Pauline are all gone for the morning, and it's just them. "Breakfast soon," she says. "I'll make pancakes."

"Pancakes!" says Abigail.

"I'm just going to do a little more work first. Why don't you go play for a bit."

The girls set up a game of Clue in the playroom, but Clue is only good with three or more people, so before long they are yelling for Matty to come join them. The volume of their voices does battle with Louisa's hangover. "Go upstairs and ask him instead of yelling," she suggests. She puts on headphones and turns back to Pitcairn.

More time passes. It's no use. The most dire parts of the hangover are beginning to recede but the headache is here to stay, like the houseguest who spreads the newspaper all over the living room and doesn't fold it back up. She can't get a handle on what she wants to say in this chapter. She thinks about Phoebe Richardson, who by now has changed out of her silk pajamas, completed a Pilates class, and donned one of those elegant, expensive blouses whose ads fill Louisa's Instagram feed. (When she clicks on the links, she often learns that they cost north of $300.) Why can't she imagine Pitcairn as clearly as she can imagine Phoebe writing about Pitcairn?

Even through the headphones she can hear the children's voices. Why did she promise pancakes? Pancakes are messy. Her mother doesn't stock mix, so she'll have to make them from scratch. There will be a lot of cleanup. By the time she's finished with that, the day will be half over and she'll have nothing to show for it but this silly drawing of the longboat.

She looks up, startled, when she hears the door from the screened-in porch to the inside open. It's Claire, with a sopping wet Otis. How did Claire get by her? She whips off her headphones. "Where'd you come from, Claire?"

"From outside. Otis really needed the bathroom. I tried to tell you but you had your headphones on."

Claire is dripping all over the good dining room carpet. She is still in her nightgown, a careworn pink hand-me-down from Abigail, which is stuck now to her bony little body. Louisa can see each individual rib.

"*Claire.*"

"He had to go. And he didn't want to go alone." Claire juts out her lip.

"Towel," says Louisa, pointing to another Otis towel by the porch door. Claire either doesn't hear or hears but doesn't listen and Otis steps closer to Louisa, then closer, almost like he's about to tell her a secret. "Towel, Claire!" Otis gives one of those giant golden retriever shakes and every droplet that was in his fur is now on Louisa's notebook, the screen of her laptop, her color-coded index cards.

"Claire! There's water all over *everything!* I told you to *towel him off.*" Louisa is trying to keep it together, but there's water on the walls too.

Claire's lip wobbles. "But I couldn't . . ."

Without the headache, the lip wobble might have been enough to force Louisa to speak more softly. But then Matty pokes his head around the corner, and says, "I heard there were going to be pancakes," he says. "Is that still happening, or—" And now she's sort of screaming.

"You have to respect the house, Claire. This isn't our house! And all of you, you have to respect my time. I. Am. Trying. To Concentrate!" Each word comes out like a firecracker, lit with its own fuse, ready to explode.

It feels like it's beyond her control, though, because her head is pounding, and her heart is pounding, and it's not just about the water, of course. The water is merely the conduit for all of Louisa's other problems: The house. The book. Her mom. Her dad. Steven. Kristie. The money that she hasn't the guts, or the heart, to ask Annie for on behalf of Kristie. The house again. Her dad. Then back to the book.

Matty stares at Louisa. Louisa looks at Otis, who is frozen in place, ears down, tail low. Is there any worse feeling than scaring a dog? Yes, thinks Louisa, scaring your own child. Claire fixes Louisa with such a look of disenchantment, of disappointment, maybe even wound through with a shred of hatred, before she turns and drips her way across the dining room, down the hall, and up the stairs, drip drip drip, each footfall on the hallway like an affront to Louisa, like a stab in the center of her rotten black heart.

36.
Matty

Today is Matty's long-run day. He's been building up to this all summer. Twelve miles. Six out, all the way up North Shore Drive, to Route 73, continue on where it turns to Main Street, through town, passing the restaurants, the shops, the breakwater. Main Street will become Route 1 and he'll keep running, almost to Rockport, practically to Camden! The turnaround point is at Glen Cove. Then the whole thing in reverse.

Thoughts of Hazel and the kiss buoy him through miles one and two. Around mile three and a half the rain stops and the sun struggles out from behind the clouds. At a stoplight on Main Street he sees a girl in a car who reminds him of Claire. He runs in place and looks more closely but the girl whips her head around and begins talking to the driver of the car, a grandmotherly woman in a pink shirt. He's not even halfway and already he's hallucinating. The light changes, and he keeps going.

He turns around at a red house with a turret when his watch tells him he's hit six miles. Behind the red house he can see the water winking at him, and he considers finding a spot for a dunk. But, no. He's stronger than that. He's tougher. He turns around.

Because Main Street through town is one way, he's facing traffic on the return trip. Some guy yells, "Run Forrest run!" at him out of the window of a car.

Mile seven. What if he did the kissing wrong and Hazel was laughing at him on the inside? What if now, driving down to Portland with her granddad, she's texting all of her friends in Nashville to tell them about their awkward encounter?

Mile eight the shirt comes off. He tucks it into the waistband of his shorts.

He's positive he did the tongue part of the kissing wrong. He's not sure if he should have used more tongue or less tongue, but definitely erred on one side or the other. Mile nine he spends trying to re-create the kiss in his mind to figure it out. Wasn't Hazel's tongue venturing into *Matty's* mouth first? Yes, for certain it was. So maybe he had been right to allow his to travel as well.

Women. It all seems so difficult. What's the point, really? Then he thinks of the way Hazel's skin felt, the sides of her face in his hands. The way she looked back at him when she said, *I'll see you around, Matty McLean.* That right there. That's the point.

Miles nine, ten, and eleven are hell on earth.

One mile to go. He passes a yard on North Shore with a sprinkler set up in the yard. Yes! Shamelessly, he runs across the yard, tilting his face up to take in some of the water. This respite is enough to propel him all the way home. He consults his watch and calculates his pace. Just under seven minutes per mile average. Solid.

He drags himself inside. In the playroom he sees an abandoned game of Clue. He fills a water glass in the kitchen and finds his mother still sitting at the table, her hair even wilder than it was when he left. She's squinting hard at the screen of her laptop. Otis is lying at the very far edge of the room. Usually he sits on Louisa's feet as she works. His eyes are open, and wary: they follow Matty. No sign of the pancakes, but obviously he's not going to bring them up again.

"Mom? Where is everyone?"

Louisa looks up distractedly. She looks awful. The skin under her eyes is gray. "I don't know," she says. "Upstairs? I'm not sure. I've been working. Matty?

Could you run up and grab me the bottle of Tums from the medicine cabinet? My stomach feels terrible. Thank you, sweetie. I'm sorry I yelled at you—I'm just. I'm just tired."

"That's okay," says Matty. "I get it." On the way back from the bathroom he conducts a quick search of the upstairs. Claire's bed is empty. Abigail is lying in her bed reading *Bridge to Terabithia*.

"Go away," she tells Matty, not unkindly. "And close the door behind you please."

Matty closes the door. He delivers the Tums to his mother, and fills a glass of water for her too. She looks up and says, "Oh, perfect. Thank you, sweetie. Breakfast soon, I promise." He doesn't mention that it's almost time for lunch. He slides open the screen door—Otis slinks through—and lies down on the porch swing, utterly spent. He closes his eyes and thinks about Hazel.

He should get up and eat something. He'll do that in a minute. Peanut butter. Apples. A big glass of milk. A slice of Pauline's famous blueberry bread, if Claire hasn't snuck away with all of it. Or maybe his mom will make those pancakes after all. But probably not.

He might just close his eyes first.

He wakes with a start who knows how much later. Louisa is standing over him with her hands on her hips.

"Where's your sister? I can't find her."

Matty blinks and sits up. "Reading. In her room."

"Not Abigail. Claire. I don't know where Claire is."

"Maybe in the downstairs bathroom?" Claire has been known to spend inordinate amounts of time in the half bath near the kitchen, hoping to pick up useful secrets.

"She's not anywhere." Louisa rakes her hands through her hair. She bites her lip so hard it turns white. "I wouldn't blame her for being upset. I was just trying to concentrate and—"

Her sentence stops there, cut by an ear-splitting wail. Louisa and Matty both jump and start toward the sliding screen door. Before they get there Abigail flies through the door and onto the porch. She is still in her pajamas, and her hair is almost as crazy as Louisa's.

"What happened?" says Louisa. "Where's Claire?"

Abigail holds up her copy of *Bridge to Terabithia*. "I don't know where *Claire* is." Tears are running down her face in rivulets. "But Leslie *died*, Mom."

"Oh geez," says Louisa. "Holy hell. You scared me to death, Abigail. We can't find Claire."

"She *died*. The rope they used to swing to Terabithia broke and—" Abigail cannot go on. She holds the book to her chest and gives in to the grief.

Oh, brother, thinks Matty. He really, really, really needs his dad back.

"I know, honey. I know." Louisa opens her arms and into them goes Abigail. "It's one of the great tragedies of children's literature, it really is. And I promise we'll talk about it later. But you guys, I need your help." She taps Abigail on the back, one, two, three, as though signifying that her allotted time to be sad has run out. "Fan out, okay? Let's find your sister. Otis? You can help too. I'm sure she's just hiding somewhere, but I'll feel better once I know where."

37.
Kristie

Kristie is stocking shelves in the grocery section when Diana, her manager, tells her, "There's someone here to see you."

"There's someone here to see *me*?" Kristie lines up the boxes of Oatmeal Squares perfectly. She loves it when one carton's worth of boxes fits exactly on one of the shelves. Last night, for the first time since Danny left, she got a good night of sleep; she and her baby, which is now the size of a kumquat, are ready to take on the day.

"Yup. She's up front."

Kristie wipes her hands on her Renys vest and thinks, *she?* She hoped it would be Danny. Is *Louisa* here to see her? She hopes not.

"She's very small," Diana adds.

Kristie thinks, *small*? Louisa isn't particularly small. Thin, sure, but of medium height. Certainly not "very small."

Kristie walks to the front of the store. There's a little girl sitting on the bench by the entrance, swinging her legs back and forth. Oh, sure. It's Claire, Louisa's youngest daughter, the one who wasn't allowed to get the Connect Four game.

"Claire?" says Kristie, and Claire hops off the bench. She's wearing pink shorts and a white T-shirt that says NOTORIOUS R.B.G.

"Yes," she says. She makes a motion with the top of her body that is almost like a bow. Her voice is squeaky and adorable. "Hi."

"Hi." Kristie squints at Claire. Her sneakers are white, dirty, but on top of the dirt is an overlay of sparkles. They look like the sneakers of a girl who's had a lot of fun this summer. "What—to what do I— what are you doing here?"

Claire's skinny shoulders move up and down in a shrug. "I just came to visit."

Kristie looks around for Louisa or another adult. The store is empty—the early rain kept people away. "How'd you get here?"

"A nice lady drove me."

"What nice lady?"

Instead of answering Claire says, "Do you have any water? I walked a really long way before the lady picked me up."

"Sure," says Kristie. She takes a bottle of water from the cooler near the register. She'll charge it to herself after. She wonders what kind of lady would drop a little girl off at Renys without asking any questions. When Claire finally lowers the water bottle—she's almost panting from drinking so much so fast!—Kristie asks, "Who's that on your shirt?"

Claire looks down and pulls the shirt out from her stomach to get a better look. "A very famous lady. Ruth Baby Ginsberg. My mom bought it for me. She says you're never too young to honor a liberal icon."

"Facts," says Kristie. When Claire speaks, a little furrow pops up between her eyes, the furrow of a much older person. Kristie wonders if Claire is a worrier. Kristie worried a lot when she was a kid. She gets it. She asks again, "What nice lady drove you?" and again Claire doesn't answer. So Kristie says, "Did you really just come for a visit . . . ? Or, for some other reason?"

Claire says, "Mostly for a visit."

"Okay," says Kristie. Claire's hair is cut in a way that from the back she might be mistaken for a boy but from the front there's a long swoop that tucks behind her ear and looks decidedly feminine. It's a good haircut.

It's actually a great haircut. "Well, I'm always happy to have visitors. But I do have to get back to work. Before I get in trouble."

"Who would put you in trouble?"

"My boss. Diana. She's really nice, but she's still a boss. My cell phone's in the back. Can you tell me your mom's phone number? I'll call her from the store phone and have her pick you up." She doesn't relish the thought of speaking with Louisa, but she'll do it if she has to.

"Nope," says Claire.

"Nope you *can't* tell it to me, or nope you *won't* tell it to me?"

Claire shrugs and RBG's crown moves up and down with the motion. "A little bit of both." Then she gets the little furrow between her eyes again and says, "I'm not going home. I ran away."

Kristie tries to keep her lips from turning up. Running away seems like something an old-fashioned kid might do. She imagines Claire holding a long stick, a bandanna filled with her possessions swinging from the top. She nods gravely and says, "Sure. I get that. I'm sure you have your reasons. But you probably won't stay run away forever, will you?"

"I might." Claire tucks her lips in toward each other, making them almost disappear.

"How come?"

"I'm not—" She pauses, and Kristie can tell she's taking care to pick out the exact right words. "I'm not *interested* in returning home right now."

"I see," says Kristie, fighting even harder to keep her lips from turning up. "So where will you sleep? This store closes at nine P.M." She recalls a long-ago story about a bear who spent a night in a department store, trying out all of the different beds.

Claire jabs a finger in Kristie's direction and says, "I could stay with you?"

Kristie feels her heart warming to the melting point. Corduroy, that was the name of the bear. He was looking for the missing button to his overalls, not trying out all the beds. Sheila had read that book to Kristie when she was a kid. "That would be really fun." She chooses her next words as carefully as Claire seemed to have chosen hers. "But I don't have much extra room in my apartment. It's pretty small. I'm not sure where you would sleep."

"I can sleep anywhere," offers Claire. "It's one of my talents. I can sleep sitting up, or outside on the ground without a blanket. I can fall asleep on a pool float."

"That's a good talent," says Kristie.

"My other talent is untangling knots."

"Another good one. Very handy."

"Yeah," agrees Claire, sighing, like both of these talents are also heavy responsibilities to bear.

There is a scab on Claire's knee and Claire starts to pick at it. Kristie finds herself saying, "Don't do that!" and Claire immediately lets her hand fall. *Wow*, thinks Kristie, *I just sounded like a legit mom*. She touches her belly and thinks, *See, kumquat? We might be okay after all*.

Claire's hand finds the scab again. "Seriously," says Kristie. "You have to trust me. Don't pick at it."

"Mommy says I have summer knees," says Claire. "I fall a lot. Not because I'm clumsy, just because I'm not scared to try stuff."

"Summer knees," says Kristie. "I like the sound of that. But if you keep picking at the scab, you know, it's not going to heal right and you'll end up with a scar."

"I don't mind that," says Claire.

"You may not now. But maybe when you're older, you'll mind. Maybe you'll want to wear a short skirt or a dress and you won't like your scar then."

"I don't wear dresses."

"Fair enough."

"Do you have a scar?"

"I have a lot of scars." Oh, does she ever have scars!

"Can I see them?"

Kristie sighs. "They're not all visible to the naked eye. Some are on the inside." Her newest scar is Danny.

Claire nods like she gets it. She points at Kristie's ivy tattoo. "Is that a scar?"

"No. But it's covering all sorts of scars."

"Oh." Claire considers this. "I think it's really pretty. Can I touch it?"

"Sure." Kristie holds out her arm and Claire traces her finger along the vine. Her touch is soft. Her nail— all of her nails—are bitten way down, ragged along the edges. Kristie sits very still as Claire traces a leaf. It feels nice, having a little kid's hand on her like this. It feels innocent and sweet.

A shadow falls over them, breaking the spell. It's Diana. She looks from Kristie to Claire and back again, and then she says, "Cute kid. But you need to get those boxes done. I've got a delivery coming in at noon."

"Got it," says Kristie. She reclaims her arm and stands. "I'm on it. Hey, Claire. I need to get back to work."

Claire hops off the bench. "I'll just come with you, and watch you work. Maybe I can help you."

"Um, okay," says Kristie. She glances at Diana, who is pretending not to listen. She's pretty sure little girls aren't covered under the store's insurance policy. "Sure, okay, why not? Maybe for a little while. But then we're going to have to call your mom."

"Let's cross that bridge when we come to it," suggests Claire. She walks next to Kristie, and when her arm swings into Kristie's neither one of them moves away from the other.

Back in the food section Kristie gives Claire a carton of Goldfish bags to shelve; she's moved on to the Dilly Green Beans, locally made and pickled. Claire is chockfull of questions. She points at a row of jars high on the shelf. "What's that?"

"Blueberry preserves."

"And what's this?

"Spicy mayonnaise."

"How spicy?"

"Very."

"And when all of this food gets delivered where do the trucks pull up? Front of the store or back of the store?"

"Back," says Kristie. "There's a loading dock." She anticipates Claire's next question. "Before you ask, you're not allowed back there."

Claire holds up her hands, palms out, traffic-cop stance, and says, "Okay, okay."

Kristie puts a hand on her kumquat again, and Claire

asks, "Why do you keep touching your stomach? Do you have a stomachache?"

"No," says Kristie, dropping her hand. Claire tells a story about how her brother once threw up after riding the roller coaster at Six Flags Great Adventure.

"Did you throw up too?" asked Kristie.

"Too small to ride it," says Claire regretfully. After a minute of concentrated shelf stacking she adds, "But I wouldn't have."

"I believe you."

Next Claire tells Kristie about a video of a gorilla she saw online. The gorilla was in a zoo, and a four-year-old boy somehow crawled or fell into the enclosure. Claire's voice gains strength and steam as she tells the story. She's at the part where the gorilla is dragging the little boy through the water, maybe trying to protect him, maybe trying to hurt him, when they see Diana marching back toward the food section. Behind her is a fortysomething man with brown hair and a navy-blue polo shirt. Behind *him* is an older woman with glasses, a soft belly, and a T-shirt that reads WORLD'S BEST GRANDMA.

"Uh-oh," says Claire. "I'm outta here." And in a flash she is gone.

Diana jerks her thumb at the man and says, "This is

Detective Harding. He's looking for the little girl who came to see you, Kristie."

"Little girl?" says Kristie, like she's not sure what the phrase means.

Diana says, "She was *just* here! She was helping you stock the shelves. Sort of a boy haircut?" Diana is in her middle sixties; she hasn't received the message that there's no such thing as boy haircuts and girl haircuts anymore. There are only haircuts. "She was talking to you!" says Diana. "She was right here."

"Hmm," says Kristie.

"I'm the one who drove her here," says the self-proclaimed World's Best Grandma. "Picked her up on the side of the road. I said to myself, what's this little peanut doing all by herself on North Shore Drive? There's not much of a shoulder on that stretch. You wouldn't catch *me* walking there. So I slowed down and asked her what she was doing. She said she needed a ride to Renys, wouldn't tell me anything else. I've been keeping my eye on her the whole time, since I dropped her off. She's a *very* determined little girl. I let her get out of the car, but I didn't let her out of my sight. I would never. I've got three grandbabies myself." She points to her shirt, for proof. "And I called over to my brother who works for the Rockland P.D."

"At the very same time I spoke with the child's

mother," says the detective. "I—ah, I know the family." His cheeks pink up ever so slightly when he says that. He turns to Diana and says, "I'm going to need to conduct a thorough search of the premises. And I'm going to have to ask you temporarily to lock all doors leading in or out of the store."

Diana says, "Certainly, Detective." Diana never uses words like *certainly* so this makes Kristie giggle on the inside, even though her stomach is also knotting up on Claire's behalf. Where *is* she?

Off goes Diana to comply, and the detective turns to Kristie and smiles. She tries not to smile back, out of loyalty to Claire, but she can't help it. The smile is contagious.

"Let me look for her too, okay?" says Kristie. "I think she trusts me." When she says *trusts* she imagines her kumquat turning over, like it's lifting its face toward the sun.

The World's Best Grandma makes a sudden noise and points enthusiastically behind the detective and Kristie, and there's Claire, standing at the end of the pajama aisle.

"You don't have to look for me," says Claire. "I'm right here." Somehow a streak of dirt has landed across the face of the Notorious R.B.G. "You can lower your weapons."

"No weapons," says Detective Harding. And then he says, "Hello, Claire. It's nice to see you again."

"You called the *police*?" says Claire, stricken, looking at Kristie.

"*I* didn't," says Kristie.

"I didn't," says Diana.

"Guilty," says the World's Best Grandma, raising her hand. "I did. If this was one of *my* grandbabies, running around town without supervision—"

Then there is a banging on the front door of the store, and a woman's voice yelling.

"I locked it, just as you said," says Diana.

Claire turns and looks at the door and then says, "Oh, brother. That's definitely my mom."

38.

Louisa

They look for Claire absolutely everywhere. Louisa checks to make sure both kayaks are still under the deck. Abigail crawls underneath every one of the upstairs beds. Matty goes down to the rocks with the ship-watching binoculars and checks to make sure there's no body floating in the water.

They put Otis on the case, sending him all around the yard. He comes back empty-pawed, wagging his tail apologetically. The panic is starting to rise in Louisa's throat. Her parents won't be back from the appointment for at least an hour, maybe longer. She calls over to the Pelletiers' house, using the number from the list on the refrigerator, but there's no answer, and Matty tells her that Mr. Pelletier has gone to bring Hazel to the airport and do some lobster trap errand on the way.

Louisa knows that Pauline is with her cousin. Oh, realizes Louisa when Matty tells her about the airport. Hazel is gone. This is the reason for Matty's long face. But there's no time to dwell on that now: they need to find Claire.

Louisa is searching her secret upstairs bathroom when her phone rings. It's Mark!

"Louisa," he says. "This is really strange but we just got a call in about a little girl without a parent or caregiver at Renys, who was picked up on North Shore Drive, not far from you. I'm heading over there now to check it out. Is there any chance she could be one of yours?"

"We can't find Claire," she whispers. Her heart is hammering. "And we do know someone who works there, somebody Claire might have tried to visit."

"I'm heading over there now," says Mark.

"I'm heading over there too," says Louisa. "Matty!" she calls up the stairs. "You're in charge of Abigail. We think we might have found Claire. I'll be back." She can feel one hundred different emotions course through her body: fear, relief, anger, shame. What if it isn't Claire? What if it is Claire?

Louisa's phone rings again when she's still on Route 73, before it turns to Main Street.

"It's Claire," says Mark Harding. "She's perfectly

safe and happy. There's no rush for you to get here. I've got my eye on her."

"How did *Claire* get to *Renys*?"

"The details are only now becoming clear. When you get here, I'm sure we can sort it all out."

Louisa curses the summer traffic all the way. Stop and go along Main Street; every crosswalk presenting a pedestrian with the right of way. When she gets to the store the door is locked and she has to bang on it until a woman with an enormous bosom comes to open it. She follows the woman to the back of the store, and there is Claire. And Mark Harding. And Kristie.

"Claire!" she says. "Claire Bear. What the—? I mean, how did you—? I don't even—" She crouches down so that she is level with Claire's shoulders. "I don't know whether to shake you or hug you."

"Hug me," says Claire.

"Of course," says Louisa, and she does.

"I'm sorry," says Claire, breaking down. Tears come out fast and furious and she cries on Louisa's shoulder. "I'm sorry, Mommy."

"It's okay," says Louisa into Claire's neck. "It's okay. The important thing is that you're safe."

The World's Best Grandma wipes the corner of her eyes with a tissue and says, "She's a very determined little girl."

"She is," says Louisa.

"A real firecracker. I'm just glad everything's okay. I said I would drive her here, but in my head I said I wasn't going to leave until I knew that everything was okay. And I sat right outside in that parking lot and watched her from my car. It was clear that she knew this one—" She jerks a finger at Kristie. "But I was keeping an eye just the same. Then I thought, well, I'll just call down to my brother, who works for the Rockland P.D., and inquire if anyone has put in a call about a missing child. Just in case, you know."

"Thank you," says Louisa. She's about to start crying herself.

"All's well that ends well," says Mark. "I just need to take a few notes, since a call was placed regarding this case." He has pulled out a little notebook and is busily writing in it with a small pencil, the kind you might use for recording mini golf scores. "And I'm sorry," he says to Kristie. "I didn't catch your name?"

"Kristie Turner," she says.

"And your relationship to—to the family?"

"She's the love child," says Claire, swiping at her face.

"I'm sorry?" Mark says.

"You see," continues Claire. "When two people love each other—"

The World's Best Grandma says, "Oh, my," and puts her hand to her throat.

"Claire," says Louisa, half sharp, half laughing. "Not now." To Mark she says, "It's complicated."

"It's not that complicated," says Claire.

"I can explain, if you need it for your records," adds Louisa. "But maybe in private?"

"I'm Frances, by the way," Best Grandma says, nodding at the detective's pencil. "In case you need to note that down. I can give you my phone number too. Do you think you'll have further questions? I'm very happy to participate in any investigation that may occur."

Mark hesitates, then, maybe seeing how badly Frances wants there to be an investigation, he says, "Certainly. Why don't you step over here with me. I'll gather the relevant details." Frances beams. Claire asks if she can look at the candy, and Louisa says yes, but they aren't buying any, and this leaves Louisa and Kristie alone, face-to-face. Louisa readies herself to speak but Kristie beats her to it.

"I know you think I'm trying to infiltrate your family, Louisa, but she came to me."

"I know that. And I'm sorry. I really am. I'm sorry if Claire disturbed your workday, or got you in trouble—"

"She didn't," says Kristie. "It's fine. I mean honestly, she's a great kid. You're lucky."

"She is," says Louisa, sighing. "And I am. This is all my fault. I was stressed-out this morning, and I yelled at everybody, like *really* yelled—I don't blame her for running away. The real surprise is that there's anyone left who didn't run away." Kristie half smiles, and this gives Louisa the encouragement she needs to continue. "Really what I'm lucky about is the fact that she picked you to run away to. And not some, I don't know, some logger from Lincolnville in a murder van."

Kristie crosses her arms over her Renys vest. Her expression is inscrutable. A long moment passes, and finally Kristie says, "What'd your mom say? About the money?"

Louisa clears her throat. "So, listen—" she says. "I wasn't able to ask her about the money. I'm sorry." The half smile disappears. Kristie raises one eyebrow. (Louisa has never been able to raise one eyebrow without the other going along for the ride. She has heard this ability is passed on genetically; she supposes Kristie must have inherited it from her mother.)

"I guess I'm not surprised," says Kristie.

"No, it's not like that."

"What's it like, then?"

"I—she—my dad. I mean." If this conversation is a minefield, Louisa is aware that she's very close to triggering an explosion. "There are some other things going on, with money. She doesn't have the money right now, to help you out. Not in cash. I can't ask her, Kristie. I can't do that to her right now."

"With all due respect," says Kristie, "your mom is not my concern here, just like I wasn't her concern when I was born. My concern is getting myself on my feet, and paying off the money I owe from my mom's medical bills, and taking care of my baby."

"Your baby? You're *pregnant*?" says Louisa.

Kristie nods. "I guess you knew what you were talking about in the bathroom in Archer's that day."

Louisa has so many questions. How far along is Kristie? Is Danny the father? (She assumes Danny is the father.) What does he think about this? Does Kristie know what kind of baby she's having? Is she planning to have the baby here in Maine, to put down roots? Before she has a chance to pose or even really think through these questions Mark Harding, World's Best Grandma, and Claire all come trooping back from their various corners of the store.

"I think we've finished up," says Mark. "Frances here has been kind enough to give me some very valuable details." Frances nods importantly.

"Can we go home?" says Claire. "Mommy? I'm tired.

Can we go home now?" She appears to be hiding something behind her back. Louisa gently draws her arm out into sight; it's a large bag of gummy lobsters.

"Uh-uh. No candy," says Louisa. "Honestly, Claire, after what you've put everyone through, don't even think about it. Go put it back, please."

"Got it," says Clare resignedly. "I just figured it was worth a try."

"It's always worth a try." Frances winks at Claire. "I admire your pluck."

"What about Connect Four?" Claire asks Louisa.

"Fine," says Louisa. "Okay, *fine*. Connect Four."

Claire trots off to return the contraband to the candy section and pick up the game, and Mark and Frances walk toward the front of the store, leaving Louisa and Kristie alone once more, save for the few shoppers who came in once the doors were opened.

"I'm sorry I can't help you more," Louisa says. "I mean that. I'm really sorry."

Kristie closes her eyes—Louisa's eyes, Martin Fitzgerald's eyes, Kristie Turner's eyes—for several seconds, and when she opens them she no longer looks hardened and tired but warm and disheveled, like a child waking from a nap. "I can't say I'm shocked," she says. "But I was—I am—desperate, and like Claire says, I figured it was worth a try."

When they get home from Renys Louisa sends Claire straight up to her room with instructions to stay there until dinnertime. Yes, they hugged, and yes, they shed tears, and yes, of course, Louisa is overcome with gratitude that her daughter is safe—but Claire still did something very dangerous.

"You're going to be in trouble for a good long time, young lady," she says. When she passes Claire's door on the way to her own room to retrieve her Pitcairn notebook she can hear Claire's mournful sobs. You think that when your children aren't with you they're gliding along in solitude, like one does on the flat moving staircase at an airport. But life doesn't work that way! The second you let your kids loose in the world they immediately begin bumping up against other people, seeing things, saying things and having other things said to them, all of which contribute to the completeness of their human experience.

Louisa will think of a reasonable punishment soon; for now, Claire needs to stay put. She walks down to the rocks and sits there for a while, staring out at the water and thinking. She hears a scratching behind her. It's Danny, scraping at the little wooden gate that leads down to the water. *For the love of all that's good and holy*, thinks Louisa, *does every single piece of wood on this property need a new coat of paint?*

"Sorry!" he says, noticing her turn around. "Didn't mean to bother you."

"No bother!" she says untruthfully. "I was heading back up to the house."

Danny opens the gate he's been scraping and stands aside to let her pass. Louisa thanks him and almost keeps on walking, up to the house, to her sobbing daughter and her two other children who probably need things from her she's not even aware of yet. But something makes her stop.

"Hey, uh, Danny," she says. She stands awkwardly for a moment. Today he has forgone his broad-brimmed hat in favor of a pair of sunglasses, which he pushes up now. His eyes are big and olive colored and there are laugh lines radiating out from them. He wears his hair a little long, and it curls around his ears. "I have a question for you."

"Sure," he says. "What can I do for you?"

What she wants to say is, Do you know that your girlfriend, Kristie, is my father's illegitimate daughter? But what she actually says is, "I just wanted to thank you. For all the things you do for my parents. For everything you take care of, you know. All the—things. Around the house." This is not a question, she realizes.

He smiles, and the lines deepen. "Sure thing. Someday they might even start paying me."

"*What?*"

"I'm kidding," he says. "Oh, man. If you could see your face. Of course they're paying me. I make more here than I make landscaping for Gil. But I want to own my own landscaping company one day, so working for Gil is good experience."

"Ha!" Louisa tries for a chortle but it comes out like she's choking on a crouton. "No, of course. I mean, obviously, you're kidding. Good one. You got me!" She pauses, then forges ahead. "I do have a question for you. About your girlfriend. About Kristie. I'm not sure how much you know about this, but we're sort of related. Not sort of. I mean, I'm sure Kristie has told you that she's my . . ." Her voice trails off while she searches for the right word. She's not quite ready to say "half-sister."

Danny gives a tiny shake of his head and says, "She's not."

Louisa pauses. "She's not what?"

"Not my girlfriend."

Louisa's face warms. "I'm sorry." Is the baby not Danny's? Did they break up because of that? "I must have misunderstood. Please forget I said anything." She should take her notebook and her big, incorrect mouth and go back to the house.

"You didn't misunderstand. We—ah. We broke up." Is she imagining it, or is that a tear in each of Danny's big olive eyes? "About a week ago." Yes, those are tears. "We didn't even know each other that long. But we got along really well right away, you know? Things moved fast. I miss her. I miss her so much. But I guess it just wasn't meant to be."

Louisa is moved by these statements, by the be-seeching, sorrowful look in Danny's eyes, and also by the memory of Kristie standing next to the World's Best Grandma as Louisa and Claire left the store. Kristie had looked so very alone, and thin, and tired. Early pregnancy is no picnic, even when one isn't going through it solo.

"I don't know why it's hitting me so hard. I've lived with someone for much longer . . ." Danny's voice trails off mournfully, then picks back up. "But there was something about her. About *us*. About us together, you know?"

Louisa is gleaning from Danny's presentation of this relationship that Danny doesn't know Kristie is pregnant. Plot twist. *Major* plot twist. "I know," she says. "I get it." Then she asks, "Want to know what I think?"

"Sure." Danny slides his sunglasses back on; his voice is affable once again.

"I think that if you miss her, she probably misses you too."

"She did something that I thought—well, and then I—" He shakes his head. "There are some things I said that I don't think I can take back."

"Oh, Danny," Louisa says. She lays her hand on his arm. The gesture surprises them both. His skin is warm from working in the sun. "I'm sure that's not true. Pretty much everything can be taken back, you know."

At dinner Louisa pours herself a big glass of the pinot noir Annie has set out to go with Pauline's baked haddock, and she lets the wine's warmth spread through her. Her hangover is no longer raging, but it is still grumbling. The pinot helps to send it back into its lair.

Abigail and Matty have a small quibble over whether or not Abigail's elbow—she's left-handed—has crossed over into Matty's territory, but it's minor. Annie tells a funny story about the receptionist at the doctor's office and then, looking at her husband, says, "Remember that, sweetheart?" The tenderness in her voice brings quick, hot tears to Louisa's eyes. Her voice is telling the story, but it's clear that her heart is saying, Please remember that. Just that one little thing.

Martin says, "Montserrat," and they all turn toward

him, alarmed. "Montserrat," he says, again, pointing at the picture window. The sun is setting so much earlier than it did when they arrived in June. Now dinnertime is the golden hour, with the daylight redder and softer, and the sky preparing for the big sunset show. Passing in front of the window is a glorious yacht, all white, gleaming in the last rays of the sun.

Matty leaves the table to get a closer look. He lifts the binoculars to his eyes. "The flag," he says. "It's got a British flag and a person with a harp . . ."

"That *is* Montserrat," says Louisa. "Tax haven." She looks at her father in wonder. "How'd you recognize that one, Dad? From so far away?"

"Don't know," Martin says. He shrugs and gets back to his haddock. "Lucky guess, I suppose."

"Mommy, what is your face doing?" asks Abigail.

"What? Nothing. Why?"

"You were doing something funny with it. Like smiling, but not really."

"Oh," says Louisa. "I don't know. I was just thinking, I guess."

Louisa imagines, looking at her children, that she can see through their hair and skin and bones, all the way to their hot, pulsing cores: she can see Matty's first love and Claire's wish for connection to her newfound aunt and Abigail's desire for Steven to come up and make them a whole family again.

"You're still in my spot," Matty grumbles to Abigail.

"That's literally impossible, Matty, I'm all the way over here."

"Hang on," says Louisa. She stands and moves Abigail's place mat and dishes to the other side of Matty's, then she motions for her to stand and moves her chair over too. Abigail sits down and Louisa asks, "Better?"

"Sort of," concedes Abigail.

"Not really," says Matty. "But a little bit."

Once Louisa regains her seat next to Claire she reaches over and gives her leg a squeeze. Claire smiles at her plate. Another boat crosses in front of the picture window—a schooner on a sunset sail, probably chartered out of Camden. For a moment they are all silent, watching, eating. Even Claire is taking down her haddock with a surprising amount of gusto, and Claire always, *always* complains about Fish Night.

Later that night, everyone in bed but Annie and Louisa, Louisa debates the wisdom of what she wants to do. Con: It will really piss off her mother. (Pro: It will really piss off her mother.) Pro: Kristie has a right to stand face-to-face with her own father, the man who relinquished her in favor of a storied career, a story-book family: Papa Bear, Mama Bear, and Baby Bear, three seats at the table, three beds in the cottage, no room for anyone else.

Martin has good days and bad days, happy enough hours and wretched ones, and if Kristie comes during the bad or the wretched things could really turn into—well. Con.

There's also this. Each time Louisa and Kristie have met it's been accidental or awkward or governed by parameters beyond Kristie's control. Send this sandwich back, I can't eat mayo. Come over, but stay on the porch, and leave before my mother gets home. Please put down the cardboard boxes you carry in service of your minimum wage job and entertain my errant daughter. Each interaction has been unbalanced, tipping every time toward the Fitzgeralds. And that's what finally decides it for Louisa.

She finds her mother at the long dining room table, laying out a game of solitaire.

"Want to play doubles?" Annie asks Louisa. "There's an extra deck on the hutch."

Louisa fetches the deck, shuffles, sits across from Annie and lays out her own game. They begin, slowly at first, then picking up speed and momentum, getting into the rhythm of it, ace then two then three, finding comfort in the order and symmetry.

Louisa waits until she is stuck, waiting for Annie to make a move that will unstick her, and says, "Did you know Kristie was dating Danny?"

Annie pauses, a seven of diamonds in her hand, and says, "Kristie? Our Danny?"

Louisa smiles at that. "That's exactly what *I* said. But obviously he's not our Danny."

"No, of course not." Annie touches the chain at her neck, tucks her hair behind her ear, lays down the seven. "I didn't mean it like that."

"He's his very own Danny."

"He is," says Annie.

"But they broke up, I'm sorry to say. Danny told me that."

"I had no idea you were so friendly with Danny."

"I'm not. I mean, I'm not *un*friendly with him. I just haven't talked to him much before today. He's really nice. And also, there's one other thing, about Kristie." Louisa pauses for dramatic effect. She's back in the game now, which gives her something to focus on. "She's pregnant. I don't think Danny knows yet."

"Oh, for heaven's sake," says Annie. "Like mother like daughter, I suppose."

"*Mom!*"

"What?" says Annie.

"You can't say that." Annie doesn't respond; she's biting her lip, studying the cards.

"I think we should invite her for dinner," says Louisa. "I think she deserves to meet Daddy."

Now Annie glances up. "I believe she met him in the garden, when she brought that strange note."

"To meet him for real, I mean. To be *introduced* to him, properly. And if you don't want to be involved, I understand that completely. We can do it on a book club night."

"Book club takes August off," says Annie frostily.

They go on like this for a time, card upon card upon card. Then Annie lays down her final card; they haven't finished, but neither can make a move.

"Stalemate," says Louisa.

"I'll say," says Annie. They begin to count the foundation cards to figure out the winner.

"You win," says Louisa. Annie smiles thinly. "You can go out to dinner with Patty Miller!" says Louisa. "You can go to Primo, or into Camden. You deserve a night out. Go to Peter Ott's! Have a nice cocktail."

Annie takes a long breath. Louisa tries to figure out what's in her eyes. Stubbornness? Fear? Vacillation? "I can have a cocktail right here," she says. "I don't care to be displaced from my own home. If you must go ahead with it"—she pauses, giving Louisa time to say she will *not* go ahead with it, but Louisa doesn't claim the chance—"I think I will attend this . . . *dinner.*"

Annie rises and walks to the kitchen. Louisa follows her. Counters gleaming, dish towels laid out to dry. Annie looks at the calendar hanging next to the refrigerator. She chews her lip and doesn't meet Louisa's gaze. "I think the tenth will work fine," she says. "Why don't you ask her for the tenth."

Louisa says, cautiously, "Danny too? I got the feeling there's a chance for them still—"

"Why the hell not," says Annie, who *never* curses. She throws up her hands. "Danny too."

39.

Kristie

The World's Best Grandma stays so long at Renys that Kristie thinks Diana may have to offer her a job. "I heard you say you're pregnant," she says to Kristie, after Louisa and Claire have left, after Detective Harding has packed up his tiny pencil and his small notebook and his chin dimple and departed.

"Yes," says Kristie. The cat is already out of the bag, may as well set it loose around the neighborhood.

"To me, you look thin," says Frances.

"I'm small-boned," says Kristie. "Always have been." (Not true: she's actually pretty curvy.)

"How many weeks did you say you were?"

"Ten." Kristie returns to her station to continue unpacking the boxes. Frances follows. Kristie wonders where the World's Best Grandkids are; Frances seems to have nowhere else to be.

"Well, we're going to have to plump you up a little, aren't we?" She roots around in her giant bag and pulls out an aluminum-foil-wrapped oblong shape. "Here," she says. She points the shape at Kristie. "It's a sandwich. Turkey and swiss."

"Oh, I couldn't," says Kristie.

"Of course you can." Frances pats her bag. "I always travel with a few extra sandwiches. You never know when you might run into someone who needs a meal. Take it, okay? It would mean a lot to me if you'd eat it."

Then the funniest thing happens. Kristie's stomach *rumbles*. Her stomach hasn't rumbled—hasn't expressed actual, legitimate hunger—since the day she took the pregnancy test. Suddenly she is ravenous. Suddenly nothing sounds better to her than Frances's torpedo of a sandwich. She takes it.

"Thank you, Frances," she says. "It sounds delicious. I'll eat it at my break, I promise." Impulsively, she reaches her arms out, and Frances steps into them, and they hug. "You really are the World's Best Grandma," Kristie tells her. "You really are."

Frances beams.

Later, at home, Kristie boils some pasta and eats it

with a little bit of salt and butter, sitting cross-legged on the blue denim couch. It has been a long day. A very long day. "I know you need more vegetables," she tells her kumquat. "I'm sorry. Today was a rough one. Tomorrow it's one hundred percent spinach and broccoli, I promise." For the first time since he left, Danny's absence takes on the feel of a background throb rather than an all-out screaming pain. She watches a little TV, not really paying attention to it, and then crawls into bed.

"Good night, kumquat," she says. She lays her hand on her stomach.

Just before she drifts off, her phone buzzes. She jerks awake—Danny? Please, please. Let it be Danny.

Hey. It's Louisa. You should come to dinner at the house. Bring Danny. How's the tenth?

Kristie stares at the phone for a long time, her heart pitter-patting. She doesn't know how to respond. She turns off her phone and goes to sleep.

She lets two days go by. In the middle of the night on the second night, she wakes. Her stomach is cramping something awful. She lies in bed for a few minutes, gripping her midsection, hoping the feeling is a dream and that it will go away.

It gets worse.

No, she thinks. No no no no no.

She doesn't even know where the nearest hospital is. She knows she's supposed to be setting up prenatal care, but so far all she's done is take the giant vitamins she bought at Walgreens. She's been planning to figure out how to go about the rest of it soon, on her next day off, as soon as she has the money.

She drags herself to the bathroom and is horrified to see that there's blood in her underwear, blood on the toilet paper after she wipes. No no no no no. She sits for a minute staring at her phone, but she doesn't sit for too long, because she doesn't know how long she has. She presses the call button.

She says, "Danny. There's something wrong. There's something wrong with the baby. There's blood. Danny, I need help."

For the rest of her life Kristie will remember how everything Danny does at that point is perfect. *Perfect.* He doesn't say, What baby? He doesn't say, I thought we broke up. He doesn't say, I'm with another woman, a more honest, better woman. He sounds like his normal calm self, like someone who wasn't woken out of a deep sleep, like someone who isn't surprised and bewildered. He says, "I'll be right there." He says, "Kristie, stay where you are. Don't move. Don't hang up. Stay on the phone with me, I'll talk to you while I'm driving." He says, "I'm coming, Kristie."

While they are waiting for the doctor in one of the partitioned-off emergency room cubicles, Kristie thinks about the story Claire told her about the gorilla dragging the kid through the pen at the zoo. She never found out what happened, and she needs to know. She asks Danny to google it. She sees a range of emotions cross Danny's face as he watches the video. At the end he frowns.

"What happened?" she asks. "What, Danny? What happened? Did that little boy die? Please tell me he didn't die." This suddenly seems like the most important thing in the world. "Please, Danny."

"He didn't die." He shakes his head. "The boy didn't die. The *gorilla* died. They had to shoot the gorilla to get the boy away safely." He sounds immeasurably sad about this, and looking at the downward pull of his mouth, his clouded expression, Kristie thinks: *I love this man.*

"But what if the gorilla didn't mean any harm? What if he was trying to help the boy?"

"I don't know," says Danny. He squeezes her hand. "I guess they couldn't take that chance."

When they get home it's almost morning. The black nighttime sky, turning now to navy blue, with lighter blue around the edges, is going to give way any minute now to stripes of light. At this hour most of the other cars on the road are pickups, many with lobster traps in the back.

The lobsterman's truck is not in the driveway. Danny leads Kristie upstairs and tucks her into bed. She can hear him rattling around in the kitchen as she drifts in and out of sleep. At one point she wakes up and discovers a cup of hot tea on the nightstand by her bed. She doesn't even like tea! But the gesture is so kind, so without judgment or condemnation, so *Danny-like*, that her eyes, which she thought were empty, all cried out, fill up once again. She's been crying all night. She cried while they waited in the emergency room. She cried her way through the exam, and she couldn't stop crying when the doctor told her that the cause of her bleeding was a "subchorionic hematoma." (She'd had Danny write this down so she wouldn't forget.) "*Bleeding behind a portion of the developing placenta,*" the doctor had explained. "Plenty of women with a subchorionic hematoma in the first trimester go on to have a perfectly normal pregnancy," she'd added, and Kristie had cried some more, this time tears of happiness. If the bleeding stopped, which the doctor had every reason to believe it would, the rest of Kristie's prenatal care could be routine.

(It's time, she realizes, to acquire a prenatal routine.)

She cried oceans and rivers and creeks and streams

when the tech hooked up the ultrasound machine and squirted the cold gel on her belly and showed her the little blob that is her baby. Of course she cried when she heard the heartbeat, which was, after all, sure and strong. She sits up and takes a sip of the tea. Danny has added milk and a little bit of sugar and it turns out Kristie *does* like tea: it turns out this mug of tea is the best thing she's ever tasted. The tea warms her from the inside out. She starts to cry, because the tea is so wonderful.

Danny whips his head around the doorway and says, "What is it? Why are you crying? Does something hurt again?"

She shakes her head and holds her tea and more tears leak out of her eyes. "I'm just so happy you're here, Danny. I just—it's just—" She hesitates, and the weight of all the bad years and the mistakes and the regrets lifts right off her shoulders. "It's just that things like this don't happen to me."

He is drying his hands on a dish towel; she bets he went to town on the dirty dishes she'd left in the sink. "Things like what?"

"Things like this. Like you. Like this tea." She points to her belly. "Like this *baby*. Like everything looking like it's going to turn out okay." Of course there are still so many obstacles. There is money, for instance. There is the bill she's going to get from the emergency room, and all the other bills that are going to come on top of that, bill after bill after bill, all piled on top of her mother's bills. There is the question of whether Danny is here for the moment or for the long haul.

He takes her hand in both of his and examines it. Then he wraps his fingers tightly around hers. "Maybe things like this didn't used to happen to you," he says. "But now they do. I'm not leaving you, Kristie. We're going to do this together."

Her eyelids are so heavy. "I have to call Diana," she says. The doctor told her to take it easy for a couple of days. "I have to tell her I can't work tomorrow."

"Not just tomorrow. You're not going back to work there," says Danny. "No way, no how. You're not doing a job that requires any heavy lifting. Not with *my* baby in there." He grins to show her he doesn't mean that in a misogynistic way and puts his hand on her belly. "I'm making good money from Gil right now, and with what the Fitzgeralds pay me on top of that, I can cover us, Kristie. For a while anyway."

"But what will I do?"

"You'll be a lady of leisure."

The thought of herself as a lady of leisure makes Kristie laugh out loud, as tired as she is. She's worked her whole life, from her first job taking pizza orders at age fifteen. She'll never be a lady of leisure—it's not in her DNA.

"I can work," she says. "I want to work." Maybe she'll look for a job that doesn't require lifting boxes or being on her feet all day. Maybe she can be a receptionist at the YMCA just down the street. She's walked by there and seen all the exercise equipment lined up along the floor-to-ceiling windows looking out on the harbor. Maybe she could sit at the desk and check people in. "Anyway. Your jobs are seasonal," she whispers. "This baby is coming in the winter."

"I can save up though. I have been saving up. That's how we do it in Maine. We work really hard all summer, and we hibernate all winter. Or!" His voice gets excited, like he's a little kid off to the circus. "Maybe we'll go somewhere where there's no winter."

"No way," she says. "I tried that in Florida. I'm all done with that. All that—" She can't keep her eyes open anymore; she lets them fall closed, and her own voice sounds very far away, like she's speaking into a tunnel. "All that sun all the time. It's kind of awful, after a while. Relentless." Even when it's sunny in Maine it's a paler kind of sun, cooler, less intrusive. She feels more protected here. She is learning to appreciate water so cold you have to brace yourself just to get your feet wet, and a craggy shoreline in place of endless hot sand.

Her fingers are still intertwined with Danny's. He's rubbing the knuckle of her thumb back and forth, back and forth. "You know where I want to go?" he says.

"Where?"

"Portland. Not the Portland here. Oregon."

"That sounds nice," she says groggily. "Tell me about it."

"I've never been. But man it looks amazing. Online I saw pictures of a Japanese garden, with a teahouse and a waterfall and everything. Want me to show you?"

"Tomorrow," she murmurs. "So sleepy."

"Okay. I'll show you tomorrow. There's a gondola that takes you into the clouds. There's a giant rose garden too. They call Portland the City of Roses. It's basically a landscaper's dream. We can get a little bungalow."

"Bungalow," she repeats. It sounds like a magic word.

"And you know what the very best part is?"

"What?"

"No snow. You know what that means?" She moves her head on the pillow a tiny bit to approximate a shake. "It means a *lot* of people need their lawns mowed. *All year long.* Nothing seasonal about that."

She falls asleep imagining her and Danny and the baby in a covered wagon, Kristie in a bonnet and floor-length plaid, Danny in a wide-brimmed hat, heading west, seeking their fortune.

When she wakes up she answers Louisa's text.

40.
Matty

Here's Matty, on the old ten-speed that's lived in the detached garage at Ships View forever. It's so old, from, like, 1978, that it has the curving handlebars that look like a ram's horns. They're covered in ripped and peeling foam. The gearshift is so rusted that it's a miracle it still works. Matty has to use an old rag he finds on the garage workbench to clean the cobwebs off it.

Matty cannot believe how messed up his family has become this summer. A few days ago, Claire went missing and they all had to look frantically for her and it turned out she had hitchhiked to Renys. *Hitchhiked!* She could have been kidnapped, and cut up into little bits and left by the side of the road. Luckily, she came home all in one piece and with a new Connect Four game to show for it.

If Matty has to play another game of Connect Four with Claire he thinks he might lose his mind.

He puts a beach towel and his water bottle and a ten-dollar bill from his allowance money into his backpack. Before he gets on the bike he checks his phone to see if Hazel has texted him back. He waited twenty-five hours after her departure, and then he sent the following:

How's it going?

So far there's been no reply, and the panic is beginning to mount.

Then there is the matter of his parents. Because his father hasn't made it to Maine for even one second of the summer he's worried his parents are going to get a divorce. Yes, he knows his father is busy at work, and he knows the company is trying to raise money or whatever, but still it seems like an enormous betrayal on his dad's part not even to try to come up.

He rides the bike east on North Shore Drive, toward the post office and the lighthouse, past the little pond where his mom has told him a moose once stood still for a whole day. Back in Nashville Hazel is getting ready to start high school; southern schools go back earlier than those in Brooklyn. He pulls in at the general store next to the post office and orders an egg sandwich. He puts it in his backpack along with the towel and the water bottle.

His biggest worry as the bike flies down Main Street is that Hazel will forget—maybe has already forgotten—that she ever knew Matty, and while he is reliving the glory of their kiss over and over and over again she will be presenting her smile, *her heart,* maybe even a glimpse of her perfect stomach, to boys who are not him.

Should he send another text?

Left on Lighthouse Road, past the pretty houses that are spaced far apart, and into the parking lot for the lighthouse. The grass between the parking lot and the water, which is a gentle downhill slope, is dotted with picnic tables, and he chooses one to sit at while he eats his sandwich. He looks out at the little strip of sandy beach and Owls Head Bay beyond that, and even farther out, Monroe Island. After he's done eating he spreads his towel out on the grass and lies down on it.

He checks his phone. There is a missed call from his mother, but nothing else. He counts his ribs. They are all present and accounted for. He has never known Hazel not to be holding her phone, so the thought that she may have just, like, put it down is unimaginable. She must be ignoring him on purpose.

He does fifty sit-ups and twenty-five push-ups in the grass, staving off the urge to check his phone again. When he's done with the push-ups he sits up, panting. A little boy is staring at him. He's maybe four or five, with chubby cheeks and a cowlick and a little golf shirt with a collar.

"Hey," says Matty.

"Hi," says the boy. Then he puts his thumb in his mouth and, talking around it, says, "What were you doing?"

"Nothing," says Matty, embarrassed that he had an audience. "Just some sit-ups."

"Why?"

"To get strong."

"But why?"

Matty considers the boy. He's wearing little boat shoes too. He looks like a miniature Wall Street guy on vacation. *To impress an angel named Hazel* doesn't seem like the right answer, even though it's partly true. "Because I want to be strong," he says. "So I can run fast."

"Why do you want to run fast?" Matty remembers when Claire was in this phase. You never got to the end of the questions: there was always another *why* waiting in the wings.

He's trying to think of an answer to this round when

he hears a lady calling, "Miles! *Miles!*" A minute later she appears, jogging down the hill from the parking lot. When she reaches them she says, "Miles. You *can't* run away from me like that. Do you see all that water down there? That water is *very dangerous* for little boys like you. The currents are strong! And it's cold."

"Okay," says Miles equitably. The woman guides Miles's thumb gently out of his mouth, and, yeah, Matty was just thinking that he's a little old to be sucking it, but *he* wasn't going to bring it up.

"Sorry," the woman says to Matty. "Sorry if he was bothering you. He has this habit of just *taking off* lately when my back is turned."

"He wasn't bothering me." Matty smiles at the little boy and says, "Bye, Miles."

"Bye." Miles and his mom move up the hill away from Matty.

His phone rings again. His mom. Decline. Hazel had said, *I'll see you around.* But what did that mean? Was Matty supposed to call her? Or will she call Matty? The thought of calling Hazel and having to suffer through her potential declining of his call is too much to bear. If he asked his mother she would most likely spout something about Ruth Bader Ginsberg and female equality without really answering the question.

He'd like to ask his dad.

The way back to Ships View has a lot of uphills. He pedals very slowly by the Pelletiers' house. Billy's truck is gone; he's probably hauling. When he gets to his own driveway he's sweating and his leg muscles are quivering. Matty's water bottle is empty, so his plan is to wobble his way right through the playroom and into the kitchen, avoiding whoever is eating in the dining room (there's always someone eating in the dining room), and refill it. Then he'll go up to his room and stare at his phone some more, until he decides to swim.

Not so fast, though. From the dining room he hears, "Matty? Is that you? Where've you been? I've been calling you!" His mom.

Then he hears: "Hey, buddy. Come in here." He turns off the faucet without filling his bottle. Only one person in the world calls him *buddy*.

His dad is there, sitting at the table, drinking a glass of iced tea. Claire is in his lap, even though she's way too old to do that, and Abigail has her chair pulled close on his left side.

"There he is!" says Steven. "Nobody knew where you went!"

"Look who surprised us." Louisa's cheeks are pink, the way they get after she's been drinking wine, but she's not drinking wine. "Look who found time to come up after all! I couldn't believe it. The phone rang a little bit ago, the house phone, and you know nobody ever calls me on the house phone, so I didn't think it was for me. But it was this guy, wondering if anyone could pick him up at the Owls Head airport!"

"Smallest plane I've ever been on," says Steven, grinning.

"Olivia is taking care of Gavin," says Abigail. "So he's in good hands." She turns to Steven. "You told her not to overfeed him, right? You definitely definitely told her?"

"Definitely definitely."

Matty can't believe it either. His father is *here*! Right here in front of him, like it's the most natural thing in the world. He steps toward Steven. He'd like to hug him, but that would be hard with Claire in his lap.

Steven seems to read Matty's mind. He raises his hand for a fist bump. Matty fist bumps back like it's not a big deal. Then Steven spills Claire from his lap and stands and opens his arms, and into them goes Matty, and he doesn't stay there too long, because after all he *is* almost thirteen, but he stays there long enough.

41.
Pauline

When Billy comes home from hauling, Pauline is sitting in the easy chair in the living room, looking over the small east-facing vegetable garden. You can't see the water from their house the way you can from Ships View. The trees lean too thickly toward each other here, and even if they didn't the distance is too great; you'd only catch a glimpse at best. That's okay. It's enough to know sometimes that the water is there. It doesn't necessarily need to be in your face.

"Darlin'?"

She starts when she hears his voice. He'll know something is up, finding her idle like this. She's never idle, unless she's sleeping, and sometimes not even then. Billy always says she sleeps like she wants it to be done so she can get up and cross it off her to-do list.

"It's Marilyn," she says. She'll keep her voice steady, because she's already cried her tears. She prefers to do that in private. She got the news when she was at the Fitzgeralds' and all she did was swallow hard and keep on working, folding dish towels into perfect rectangles and stacking them in the drawer. Then once she got home she got her crying done. She continues looking out at the vegetable garden, which still has some life in it. There are the broccoli and cauliflower still to come in, the big tomatoes. The radishes too. Pauline has always loved a radish straight from the ground. "She's gone," she says. "I called Nicole already, let her know. She wants to come up for the funeral. Says Hazel wants to come too, but I suspect that has more to do with Matty Fitzgerald than with Marilyn. Too close to the start of school though. Nicole won't hear of it."

"Oh, Pauline." The best part about Billy is that he doesn't say anything after that, he doesn't try to find the right words, because there aren't any, and he has sense enough to know it. He sits on the arm of the easy chair and she takes in his familiar smell—the soap he uses to wash the smell of bait off his hands, maybe some oil from the boat, the brine and salt of the ocean itself. Sometimes, when she goes a long while without looking at Billy directly or looking in the mirror herself, she believes they're still the earlier version of themselves, eighteen, smooth skinned, crazy for each other, their hearts and souls without a blemish on them.

Billy puts his rough hand over her rough hand—his calluses come from traps mended and pulled, ropes wound and unwound; hers from potatoes scrubbed and carrots peeled and dishes and dishes and dishes. She reaches around with her other hand to lay it on top of his.

Let them have all the secrets in the world over at Ships View. Not that they are as secretive as they think; Pauline's known for years about the love child—she knew exactly who that was in the garden that day in July. You're invisible when you work in someone's kitchen, but that doesn't mean you're not watching and listening. She's been waiting for this drama to unfold for years. But never mind any of that: leave the drama to them, those with energy for it. Pauline's got what she needs right here, and she knows it. How lucky she is to have him, and to love him, and to be loved by him too: this man beside her, this man whose heart is as big as the sky.

42.

Louisa

She finds her mother in her cross-stitch station. The Owls Head Lighthouse piece is almost complete. Louisa sits next to Annie on the wicker bench to get a closer look, moving over the basket of thread and needles. It's not just the lighthouse itself on the fabric but also the former keepers' house with its red roof and red door and the set of stairs leading up to the door. The two pines stand tall and proud to the left of the lighthouse.

"It's so pretty, Mom," Louisa says. "Really."

Annie holds the cross-stitch out in front of her and turns it this way and that. "I think it will be," she says. "When I'm done." She puts down the fabric and rubs her eyes. "I feel like I've been working on this one forever." The light coming in the window, its angle so specific and unwavering, shows the fines lines around Annie's mouth and the deeper furrow in her forehead. "We haven't even been to the lighthouse this summer," she says. "There's still so much to do."

"I know," says Louisa, thinking about her secret trip there when she found out about Kristie. She thinks about all of the anger she had with her that day, a tight little ball of it, pulsing like a heart. "There's still time, though. Summer isn't over." (Almost, though, it is.)

"I forgot to tell you!" says Annie, suddenly brightening. "You and Steven have a reservation tonight at Primo. Seven o'clock. I gave them my credit card when I called. It's my treat." Annie is *so happy* to have Steven here. The kids are too. Later he's going to take them into town for a pirate ship tour as part of the Lobster Festival, further cementing his father-of-the-year status. He's also promised to take Abigail to see the Oreo cows, to paddle Claire across the harbor in the double kayak, and to make sure Matty eats at Wasses at least three times before they go home. But because she was already ensconced in the Pink Room, with the single beds, and Steven fell asleep reading to Claire in the girls' room the first night, some of their marital issues remain . . . untended to. Is that okay for now? She thinks so. But she's not positive.

"Are you sure? Primo is so expensive, Mom!"

"I'm sure. You two have a lot to talk about, and you don't need an audience. You know the walls here have ears."

It's true. They *do* have a lot to talk about, and they *don't* need an audience. And the walls here definitely have ears. Yet still Louisa hesitates. It still feels so wobbly between her and her mother, and the money thing feels wobbly too. "I don't know——" she says. She chews at her ravaged thumbnail. Primo feels like an extravagance. "Maybe we shouldn't go."

"For heaven's sake, Louisa, it's a dinner, not a house—it's not going to make or break my bank account. Put on a dress, do your hair, have a lovely meal. I hear the menu at Primo is fabulous this summer. Well, of course, it's fabulous every summer."

Annie's gaze is pointed toward the Samoset. Louisa wonders if she's thinking of her own wedding there, all those years ago. Annie puts her cross-stitch into the basket, along with the extra thread and the tiny magnifying glasses she attaches to her glasses, and she folds her hands in her lap, and she turns her head to look at Louisa.

Louisa reaches over and takes one of Annie's hands. "I'm sorry, Mom. I'm really sorry. About everything you're going through."

"I know," says Annie, squeezing Louisa's hand back.

"I'm sorry for you too, of course." She pauses. "Do you want to know the craziest part? It's too soon. To me, it feels too soon. I've loved your father for—how many years? A thousand. A million. And I'm not ready to not have him here to love anymore. I'm just not ready. And sometimes I'm mad at him, and sometimes I'm frustrated, and sometimes I want to scream, wake up! Get up and *do* something, won't you? Get up and be yourself. Stop torturing me like this. But most of the time, it all just seems too soon."

Before Louisa can respond the screen door slides open, and suddenly the room is full of children. Wet, and yelling, and laughing, and punching.

"Ow," says Abigail, rubbing her arm. "Claire, you hit me."

"Sorry," says Claire. "I got too excited."

"Everybody in the car," says Steven. "Lobster Festival time."

Louisa wants to tell him not to fill up on ice cream because they have a seven o'clock reservation at Primo; she wants to tell him that she's happy he's here and she's still mad at him but she's also *not* mad at him; she wants to tell him to drive carefully in the summer traffic because everything, her whole life, her whole heart, is about to climb in the minivan with him and suddenly that seems like the scariest thing in the world.

But she just says, "Have fun, you guys," and rubs the top of Abigail's wet hair.

Louisa has been to Primo only once, years ago. That's where Steven took her when he proposed to her. Primo was just a few years old then, and it was a big deal to have a farm-to-table restaurant with a James Beard-award-winning chef in a little coastal town. Annie is setting up make-your-own pizzas for the children; Pauline is taking a few days off. Her beloved cousin died. Claire is over the moon about the pizzas.

Primo is in a gorgeously redone Victorian house. Steven and Louisa's reservation is in the formal dining room, at a small table near the window, where they can look over the wildflower garden and the greenhouses. Beyond those, farther from the main road, are the acres of farmland that make up the farm-to-table part of the equation. The mere act of stepping onto the wide-planked front porch, where tasteful jars of flowers sit on floating shelves above reclaimed picnic tables, puts Louisa at peace. The whole setup makes her want to move to the country and host dinners for poets and artists in flowing homespun clothes. While they wait for their table they make their way to the back bar for a cocktail. Steven has a Spanish Gin Tonic and Louisa an Aperol Spritz. By the time the hostess—supermodel

willowy, beautiful enough for New York but too nice
for it—finds them to tell them their table is ready they
are both a little buzzed. (Aperol Spritzes are no joke.)

Their waiter, Thomas, who has a soul patch, really
good posture, and an attitude that says he's *very serious* about the food he's going to bring them, goes over
the specials. They order a bottle of Henri Bourgeois
Sancerre. When Thomas has opened the bottle and
poured a bit for Steven to taste, and when Steven has
given his approval and Thomas has filled both glasses,
Steven and Louisa look at each other for a long moment.

"Well, cheers," says Louisa, finally. Their glasses
go tink against each other. "I'm glad you're here." She
means it. Matty's face when he greeted his father: it
was enough to break her heart. Louisa has been here
all summer, but she hasn't been *here here*—she blinked
and missed the fact that Matty was growing and changing and falling in love.

"Me too," says Steven. "But. Or, *and*. We need to
talk, for real. Right? We have a lot to talk about."

"We do," says Louisa. She puts down her drink and
folds her hands on the table.

"I know we've had some disagreements over the
money."

"That's putting it lightly."

"Do you want to go first on the specifics, or should I?"

"You."

"Okay. What hurt me the most . . ." He pauses, and Louisa is surprised to see that his eyes are damp. He takes a deep breath, begins again. "What hurt me the most when I brought up the money is that you didn't believe in me enough to give me a chance. You wouldn't even discuss putting down the Emergency Fund as an investment toward All Ears. As an investment toward me. You wanted it for the future of the house, when that came up. But what about *my* future? Which is your future too. I mean, All Ears is probably going to sell in the next two or three years. We'll have that money back a few times over. Why wouldn't you entertain the idea of investing in me?"

"I *have* invested in you," Louisa says. "I've invested in you for such a long time. After I gave up the Reed job I never even considered positions that would take you out of New York—especially once you started in podcasting. Do you know how hard it is for a professor to confine herself to a single geographical area? I've published far less than other professors my age"—she thinks of Franklin, with his seersucker and his sweet tea; she thinks, basically, of everyone but her—"partly because your job takes up so much time. I've juggled and backflipped my way through the last five years so you could get All Ears off the ground. I'm behind on my book because I invested my time in you. *That's* been my investment, Steven! That was me investing in you. Don't you see?"

"I know that, Louisa. You know I know that. But this time I needed a different kind of investment. And when I tried to broach that with you, you didn't even give me a chance."

Laughter, the tinkling of glasses from the other rooms. The best restaurants give you a beautiful setting, a strong cocktail, and space to think. Thomas arrives to take their order. They are going to share the chicken liver mousse and the oysters two ways (which two? She doesn't know! But it's Primo, so both ways will be fantastic). Louisa orders the steelhead trout with butter-poached lobster and Steven orders the grilled sturgeon. After she watches Thomas's back disappear through the doors of the dining room Louisa rounds up every square of her obduracy, every scrap of pride and stubbornness, gathers them together, and stuffs them where the sun don't shine. The time for honesty is now.

"You're right," she says. "You are right. I didn't want to invest the money in the company."

Steven grimaces. "I know. But why not?"

She sighs, plays with the napkin in her lap. Why not indeed? "It's complicated, but let me try to explain it.

I *didn't* see it as an investment in you, not the way you're seeing it, or the way you saw it earlier in the summer. I mean, you wanted to use *our* EF to float the business—when, like I said when we talked about it, there are so many other ways for a business to get money. It took us so long to save that money. And we might need it. My dad's care is going to cost so much— the house . . ." The thought veers off trail and she stays quiet for a moment before she retrieves it. "There are so many things that qualify as emergencies. And I didn't think a business loan was one of them. I mean, look, ultimately you were able to get it from Aggie, so, see there *were* other ways—"

"You say that now," Steven points out accurately. "But at the time that's not how you felt about Aggie's money at first."

The appetizers arrive, and that gives them some- thing else to concentrate on for a few minutes: sauce, slurp, sip. But yeah, Steven is right. Two oysters in, Louisa continues, "At the time, I was just mad. I was mad about everything. I was mad about my dad being so sick, and mad about the fact that you got all this time to concentrate on your job while every day I was get- ting more and more behind on my book . . . and you didn't even realize what that meant for me." She tries to do book math to calculate the pages, but the cocktail and the wine are making the numbers swim in her mind. "I think I have like—I don't know. I have a *lot* of pages left. So many pages, Steven."

Steven says, "I know you do. At least from now until when we go home, I can take the kids on an outing or something every day while you work, to give you a few dedicated hours a day. Would that help?"

"Yeah. Yes, that would help a lot."

"And when we get back, we'll figure out more ways to split the time until school starts, because when the kids' school starts yours also does. We'll figure it out, I promise."

Louisa squints at him. "You mean it?"

"Scout's honor." Steven and his brothers were all Scouts, so she takes him at his word.

"Thank you," says Louisa. She eats her final oyster. "And by the way. You never told me what the catalyst for coming when you did was."

"Hang on. I can show you." Steven reaches in his pocket and pulls out a piece of paper. "We have this missive to thank for it."

"What's that? Is that a letter? Is it an Abigail letter?"

"It's not a letter. It's an email from Matty's email."

"*Matty* sent you an email?"

"Abigail did," says Steven. "From Matty's phone." He reads aloud:

Dear Dad,

You had better get up here right now. As in, imme-
diately. Everyone is losing it. Matty got his heart
broken. Claire hitchhiked to Renys. I heard Pauline
on the phone saying that Grandpa's marbles are
officially gone and won't be coming back. Leslie died
when the rope swing broke so as you can imagine I
am distraught. I know that Mom thinks we can all
do this without you but trust me. We can't. She. Is.
Losing it. We need you. This is the last time I am
going to ask you before I stop being nice about it.
WHEN. ARE. YOU. COMING?????

Love, Abigail

Louisa is laugh-crying by the time Steven gets to the end of the email. She wipes her eyes with her fancy Primo napkin. "I can't even," she says. "I just can't. Abigail!"

"I know," says Steven. "So, long story short, it was right after this that I bought a plane ticket, packed my bag, and found a home for Gavin." After a pause he asks, "Did you notice anything about this letter, compared to all the others?"

Louisa takes a healthy gulp of her Sancerre. "I noticed she didn't pull any punches," she says. "She hung us all out there, warts and everything."

Her children used to tell her every little thought in their heads. My elbow itches. I saw a spider. I had a dream about ice cream. My poop was so big. I want. I need. I am. I am. I am. Now their interior lives are developing—or developed! They have secrets; they have thoughts and desires and regrets she'll never know about. They have *opinions*, and plans, and in some cases they have the power to put those plans in motion.

"Yes, that's true, she didn't pull any punches," says Steven. "But there's something else."

"What? Let me see, I want to read it for myself!" Louisa drains her glass, and holds out her hand. "Oh!" she says softly. "I see it. I see it now. You're Dad, here. You were Daddy in all the other letters."

"And you were Mommy."

"Now I'm Mom."

"Now you're Mom."

The food arrives, looking every bit as perfect as Louisa remembers her meal being all those years ago. Thomas kindly doesn't acknowledge Louisa's wet face. He pours what's left in the bottle into each of their glasses, then backs away like an actor taking a bow then making room for the rest of the cast to come onstage.

"Listen," Louisa says. "I want to apologize about being mad about Aggie and the money. She's really nice and super smart, and, man, she *really* loves that Ernie."

"She does," says Steven. "Loves him. God bless Ernie. And the part *I* want to apologize for is not seeing how important the house is to you. I mean, I've always known it's *important*, of course. But I was getting back at you for not supporting me, and I was being petty about the Emergency Fund, and honestly it took me getting up here and seeing everything you've been seeing all summer, the kids and your dad and all of that, to realize. And now, I think we should do whatever we can to keep the house in the family, Louisa. In fact, I can't think of a bigger emergency."

"You can't?"

"I can't."

Louisa takes a bite of her trout. It's so tender that she can't believe it's not made entirely of butter. Now that the sun is beginning to set, the farmland is shimmering in magical evening light. She takes another bite, and another. She has just taken her final blissful bite, and she's thinking about what Steven said—she's thinking that maybe in fact she *can* think of a bigger emergency, but she's not ready to talk about that yet—when she hears someone say, "Louisa!"

She turns. Detective Mark Harding is standing in the doorway to their small dining room. With—*Nicole Pelletier!*

"Hi!" says Louisa. "Mark! Nicole! Come over, come

say hello. Steven, this is Mark Harding. And *this* is Nicole Pelletier. Hazel's mom! Hazel, of Matty and Hazel fame. Nicole, what are you doing here?"

"My mother's cousin died," says Nicole. "I came back for the funeral. I was going to call you, Louisa, or text—but things got busy. You know how it is."

"Marilyn," says Louisa. "I know! I was so sorry to hear about that."

"Yeah," says Nicole. "Yeah, thank you. Your mom sent flowers and everything, and a really nice note."

"And you two . . . ?" asks Louisa. She motions with her eyebrows toward Mark.

"Oh, *us* two!" Nicole flushes, and Mark Harding smiles. "We just ran into each other in town, and we got to chatting . . . And here we are!"

"Here you are," says Louisa.

"Actually I'm thinking of moving back up here," Nicole says. She ducks her head. "You know how we were talking, Louisa. I might be ready for a change."

Mark clears his throat and says, "Changes are good." He squeezes Nicole's hand. "I'm a big believer in change."

"Me too," says Louisa. "Where's your table?"

"We don't have a reservation," says Mark, shrugging. "We're taking our chances as walk-ins in the Counter Room." He points to the staircase. "Upstairs."

"Good luck," says Louisa. "I wish you guys the best. For the table, and for—whatever else."

"Roger that," says Mark. He gives a little salute, then he and Nicole turn to go, and Louisa gets the funniest feeling, like the universe had been tilted all summer and now suddenly has righted itself.

"Louisa," says Steven. "There's something important I have to say." He takes her hand across the table, threading their fingers together. Their plates are gone, magically whisked away while they were talking to Mark and Nicole. Steven looks deep into her eyes and says, "I don't know how your mother is going to feel about what I'm going to say next. This decision is going to affect her more than anyone, you know."

She steels herself. It'll be okay. She's strong. She can handle anything. "What?" she whispers.

"I really think we should get a second bottle of Sancerre." He signals Thomas.

While they're waiting for the wine a memory tiptoes into Louisa's mind. When Claire was a newborn—opinionated more than colicky, but almost clinically opinionated—Matty was five and Abigail three. Matty had to be picked up from half-day kindergarten at noon every day, which was right when Abigail, who stubbornly refused to give up the security of Pull-Ups, even though she could use the toilet perfectly well, typically unleashed her daily bowel movement. Louisa was teaching only two classes that semester, but it was two classes too many, and the part-time sitter, a student at Parsons, was more artsy than reliable. If Louisa was anywhere in the children's orbit, they (or anyway the two who could successfully perambulate) would prowl the apartment, looking for her. She graded an entire stack of midterms on the floor of her closet with the aid of a flashlight she hung from the clothing rod because for a short time nobody could find her there. And it wasn't a big closet.

One time Steven came home from work and found Louisa draped across the kitchen counter, weeping quietly into her sleeve. Matty and Abigail were building a tower out of pasta boxes, and Claire, in her baby bucket, was just beginning to stir.

"Glass of wine," he said. "Bath. Go. I've got this."

"But Claire will need to nurse—"

"Claire can wait twenty minutes. Go. Use bubbles."

At the mention of bubbles Abigail perked up and said, "I come too."

"No," said Steven gently. "No, no. You stay with Daddy, Abigail."

It was only one night, out of a thousand messy, chaotic ones. And yet she can't stop thinking about it all of a sudden. Louisa, who has never liked baths, who probably hasn't taken a bath since then, had soaked for forty-five full minutes, until the skin on her fingers and toes was wrinkled and pinked. When she'd finally come down Steven had set the table for two, fed Abigail and Matty, and was soothing a bereft, hungry Claire while overseeing a pot of pasta on the stove. (He had even tidied up the pasta tower.) Remembering this now, and looking at the printout of Abigail's email, Louisa feels like there's a tiny fist squeezing her heart very gently. She has to dab at her eyes again.

Louisa sleeps *so late* the next morning. It's nine-thirty when she opens her eyes. Louisa hasn't slept until nine-thirty since she was pregnant with Matty, almost fourteen years ago. After Primo she and Steven had gone into town for a nightcap at Fog Bar. After that, worried that they were too tipsy to drive home safely without waiting a bit, they'd walked down to the sandy beach near Archer's where they'd made out like a couple of teenagers before eventually going home and sharing one of the twin beds. She blushes now, thinking about it. Until last night she hadn't shared a twin bed with a man since *college!*

She lies in bed for a few more minutes, listening for sounds in the house. She hears—nothing. No quarreling in the upstairs hallway, no running of water from any of the bathrooms, no washing machine chugging away with the endless loads of bath towels and beach towels and kitchen towels and running shorts. She tiptoes down the stairs, worried that she'll find that the whole family has been murdered in their sleep and that she, for some unknown reason, has been spared. The dining room is empty; so too the living room and the playroom and the kitchen. The kitchen counters gleam.

She calls out an exploratory, "Hello?"

"Out here," says Steven from the porch, where he is sitting in one of the wicker chairs. Abigail is kneeling on an ottoman in front of him, her back to him. The water is calm; the harbor looks scrubbed clean.

"Daddy's braiding my hair," says Abigail. "You slept late," she adds accusingly. "I had three big knots."

"Ouch. *Three?*" Louisa watches Steven working the comb through Abigail's mane. His patience is baffling. "I'm sorry! I can't believe how late it is. Where is everybody? Does anyone need breakfast?"

"Everyone's had breakfast. Your mom went into town, and she brought Claire with her. Your dad's sitting over there—" He nods toward the water, and Louisa sees Martin in one of the Adirondack chairs, maybe watching the boats, maybe dozing, maybe lost in the distant past or the near past. "Barbara's due in half an hour. Matty is running, of course."

Louisa sits on the arm of Steven's chair.

"How's it look?" asks Abigail. She's always anxious about her hair. Louisa supposes this instinct will get worse, not better, with age.

The part is off center in the back, zigging and zagging like a broken zipper. "It looks *perfect*," says Louisa. She waits for Steven to wrap the elastic around the second braid so she can take his hand in her own. "It looks absolutely perfect."

43.
Matty

Matty falls asleep on one of the large flat rocks at low tide. When he wakes, his father is standing over him.

"Hey, buddy, want to put on a shirt? I'll take you out for happy hour in town. I could use a beer, and they only have wine and cocktails here." He rolls his eyes in an exaggerated way.

"We have beer here!" Louisa calls from the porch, where she is inspecting the herb pots. "But go ahead."

Happy hour? Matty puts on a shirt. They go to the Time Out Pub. The interior of the pub is dark and cool, a direct contrast to the sunny day.

"Hey loves," says the bartender. "Boys' night out?" She has an accent. Irish, maybe. Could be Australian. Something about her reminds Matty of Hazel: it might be the freckles across her nose, or it might be the tiny gap between her two front teeth, which you can see that Hazel's braces are working to close.

"That's just right," says his father. "Boys' night out." He claps Matty on the back, too hard. He pulls out a barstool for Matty and one for himself. "What'll it be, Matty? Beer? Cocktail?"

The bartender smiles and says, "I'll need to see some ID for that."

Matty stays quiet. Grown-ups making jokes for other grown-ups, using Matty as the straight man, are endlessly confusing. He asks for a Coke. His dad doesn't bat an eye and orders a Rock Harbor Storm Surge.

When the bartender brings the drinks, pressing each into a square napkin she's laid out, she says, "Enjoy, lads." She leans her hands on the bar and smiles. "I'm Fiona. Let me know if you need anything else, okay?"

His father is studying his phone, but when he catches Matty's glance he smiles and says, "Work thing, sorry. I'll put it away now." He puts his phone into his pocket and takes a long drink of his beer. Matty does the same with his Coke, trying to match his dad's timing and gestures.

"Anything you want to talk about, Matty? Or do you want to sit here and just drink our drinks?"

Matty looks at the bubbles in his Coke and says, "Well. Actually. Yeah."

"I'm All Ears," says Steven. "Pun intended."

"It's about, like . . ." He squirms. He doesn't know how to say it, or even really what to say. "It's about, well. There's this girl I met this summer. Hazel. She's gone now."

Steven nods. "Mom mentioned a Hazel."

"I think I—we—I mean." Matty can't figure out how to put it. "I'm just not sure how to do it."

"Do what?" His dad glances around, then moves his face closer to Matty. "Hold on. You're not talking about sex, are you?"

"*No!*" says Matty, horrified. Sex! He only just barely survived his first kiss. "No. *No.*"

"*Phew.* Okay." Steven pretends to wipe fake sweat off his forehead.

Matty thinks about Hazel's cool strawberry lips. "No. I'm talking about, just. How to be. How to be, like, a man. That sounds stupid, doesn't it?"

"Not at all. It's a good question." His father leans back on his stool. "It's different for you than it is for your sisters. Girls, they're hearing all sorts of empowering messages. Which is great. I want your sisters to grow up strong and confident."

Matty snorts. "I'm pretty sure that's not going to be a problem."

Steven laughs. "But for you . . . it's complicated. I think what we need to do is not think about how to be a man but think about how to be a *person*. Does that make sense? Treat people with kindness. Think about how your actions affect them. Everything we do in life has an impact on someone else, sometimes on purpose and sometimes inadvertently. And so the best thing we can do as men—but also just as people—is to try to leave the world better than we found it. That's something your grandfather used to say, actually."

"Yeah," says Matty. He thinks about the photograph of the court in the library, and about the fact that his grandfather had a baby with someone else and didn't tell Matty's mother, and about how that baby turned into the person who left the note Matty found. He used to think that grown-ups had everything figured out, that you reached an age where, pop, suddenly things made sense, and all the math added up correctly, but if he's learned anything this summer it's that nobody has it figured out. But what his father is saying makes sense, yeah, it definitely does.

"And it seems easy enough to do. But if I'm being honest I don't think I've done a very good job of listening to your mother over the past year. I think I've been thinking about myself a lot and not thinking about how my actions affect her, and affect you kids. I think I can do better."

Fiona is back then, smiling. "You boys staying for the music?"

"Wish we could," says Steven. He reaches for his wallet in his back pocket. "We've got dinner waiting at home."

"Well done, you two. Lucky boys." Fiona takes Steven's credit card.

"Yup," says Steven. "We sure are."

When they get back to Ships View the dining room is abuzz with activity and nervous energy. Abigail is helping Louisa set the table, and Claire is clowning around with one of the lobster bibs, tying it around her waist like an apron. Annie is in the kitchen, mixing a drink.

Louisa smiles when she sees them, and she lifts her face up to kiss Steven on the lips. Matty looks politely away, but it still makes him happy. "Oh, this came for you," says Louisa. She hands Matty an envelope. He studies it. The envelope is square and plain and white. There is his name, Matty McLean, and this address. Ships View. Hidden Beach Road. Owls Head, Maine. No return address. He looks more closely at the envelope, where the postmark is partially worn off. He sees an *A*, an *H*, the letters *VILL*.

His heart skips at least seventeen beats.

Nashville.

Matty McLean has run pretty fast in his young life, but he's never run so fast up those stairs as he does right then.

Dear Matty,

I lost my phone! I got a new one but I didn't have my contacts or messages backed up so I lost EVERYTHING. I'm sorry! If you texted me I never got it.

I am **SO NOT AT ALL HAPPY** *to be back in Nashville. School has already started. It's really really hot here, like ninety-five degrees and humid, and obvs there's no ocean. Every day I wake up and wish I was standing on the rocks right now or out on Granddad's boat. I'd rather pull a hundred lobster traps than spend ten more minutes here. All anyone here wants to do is make TikToks and buy more makeup. My mom went back to Maine because my grandma's cousin died but she wouldn't let me go with her because of school. I was SO MAD.*

I wish it was next summer already. Next summer I am going to go to Maine for as long as I can. Next summer cannot come soon enough.

*If you want to write back to me my address is at
the top of this notepaper—see? Send me your number
again.*

Xoxoxo
Hazel

Matty reads the letter again, more carefully the
second time around, parsing each individual word for
meaning, and then he puts it in his pocket for safekeeping. He floats down the stairs, wondering if he can
score something to eat before dinner. Floats into the
kitchen, where Pauline is considering a blueberry pie
resting on the counter—she's considering it so hard
that Matty wonders if the pie is about to say something.
She looks up when she hears him.

"Looking for a snack?" He nods. "You can have
some of those crackers over there. Or fruit. Dinner's
not too far off." He nods and selects a plum from the
bowl on the counter. He turns to go, and Pauline says,
"Matty?"

"Yeah? I mean, *yes?*"

"Make sure you don't break Hazel's heart, okay?
She's a good girl."

"*Me?*" (*Hazel's* heart?) "No, ma'am. I would never
do that."

"Good." She turns back to the pie.

He wants to say, Could you please ask her not to break *my* heart? No doubt that is the greater danger. He can still feel the silk of Hazel's cheeks between his palms, hear the ring of her voice in his ears. Music. "Pauline?" he says. She turns. Her face is watchful—wary. He clears his throat and says, "Granny told me about your cousin. I'm sorry. I'm sorry for your loss."

The smile Pauline releases is like a river winding through a canyon: slow and deliberate, but here and there moving in unexpected bursts. "Thank you, Matty." Then she is coming toward him, and then she's hugging him, and for an instant he is allowing himself to lean against her. This is different from receiving a hug from Granny—with Granny your head presses into the sharp plane of her clavicle, and the swing of her hair is like a whisper on your cheek. Pauline's hair is pulled back, with pieces falling out of the bun, and her body is soft, the bones hidden well beneath the flesh. If you had asked Matty at the beginning of the summer if this was a hug he'd ever be inside of, he would have said, *absolutely not,* but now that he's here it's sort of nice, and worth staying for a moment.

When Pauline releases him from the hug she says, "Hazel's a good girl. But I'll tell you what. You're not so bad yourself, Matty. Not so bad at all." She swipes at her eyes, which Matty can see are damp. "Damn onions. Been chopping them all day." When Pauline opens the refrigerator door and pokes her head inside, Matty looks all around the kitchen. He doesn't see a single onion sitting out. He pats his pocket with Hazel's letter in it and he thinks, *grown-ups*. He'll never understand them.

44.
Louisa

When the night of the dinner arrives Louisa is nervous. Matty and Steven go out for happy hour, and the girls help Louisa set the table. She tries not to think about the example she is setting, the men going out while the women do the housework. But Matty really needed time with Steven. Tomorrow night they can do the dishes.

They'll have lobsters, and corn chowder, and rolls, and one of Pauline's blueberry pies. Pauline had three days off for the funeral of her cousin, but now she's back at it, solemn and thoughtful. Annie offered her more time but Pauline wanted to come back. Claire lays out the metal nutcrackers, and Abigail sets out the plastic bibs and the wooden bowls for the shells. Pauline is in charge of the pie and the chowder, and Steven is going to steam the lobsters in the big pot on the porch as soon as he's back. Louisa has given herself the bartending role. They'll have wine, but also the option of cocktails, and plenty of seltzer or ginger ale or lemonade, for Kristie. Beer for Steven and Danny if they'd prefer. Milk or water for the children. Claire puts a lobster bib on like an apron and Louisa has to chase her down to get it back.

Matty and Steven return. Louisa smiles and gives Matty a letter that arrived for him. She has already noted the postmark, and she watches him note it too. She can practically see his heart burst out of his chest. He dashes up the stairs. The ice cubes in Annie's gin and tonic clink; the air is festive and late-summer cool; the water is blue-gray, with plenty of boat traffic. Louisa surveys the table and reassures herself that hosting this dinner was the right thing to do. Everything is ready. Her hands are sweating. She pours a glass of white wine, drinks it too fast. She wonders if she should have gone for the hard stuff instead. Probably not. Annie goes upstairs to freshen up. She already looks plenty fresh. She's going to check on Martin too. Just before Kristie and Danny are due to arrive Annie descends the stairs. Her eyebrows are knitted together. Her glass is empty. She shakes her head, and the hand holding the glass is shaking a little bit too. "He's not up to it, Louisa."

Louisa's heartbeat picks up. "What do you mean?"

"It's not a good evening, for something like this. See for yourself, if you don't believe me. You can go on up."

Louisa studies her mother. Her lipstick is perfect. She smells like Shalimar. The air thickens between them. "I believe you," she says levelly. "I don't need to see for myself."

"It can't be helped," says Annie. "The timing of things."

"I know, Mom, I know."

"He's not in his own head right now. Pauline can bring him a plate upstairs."

"He can't crack a lobster upstairs."

"Of course not. The chowder, then. The bread."

"Okay. Okay, Mom." It's not about the lobster or the chowder—obviously. It's about Kristie, who's expecting to sit down with Martin Fitzgerald after twenty-nine years—who's expecting to be acknowledged.

The doorbell rings and Annie and Louisa jump and stare at each other alarmed.

"It's okay. It'll be fine," says Louisa, as much to herself as to Annie.

Kristie has brought a bottle of Whispering Angel—

she remembered, from the day at Archers. She hands it to Annie.

"Lovely," says Annie graciously. "Thank you." Introductions or reintroductions all around, then a review of the beer choices for Danny from Steven.

"Come with me into the kitchen," says Louisa to Kristie. "Let's see what you want to drink." Kristie glances at Danny, then follows Louisa. "We have ginger ale, seltzer, water, lemonade," says Louisa.

"Ginger ale. Please."

Louisa fills one of the tall frosted glass with ice, then, while her back is half turned, says, "Listen, Kristie. My father is having one of his bad days. He's not coming down to dinner." Louisa turns fully toward Kristie and watches a complicated expression cross Kristie's face, watches her let out a breath. Surely Kristie noticed that Louisa said *my father* and not *our father*. "I'm sorry," Louisa continues. "I'm really sorry. We can try another time. I know I told you he has good days and bad days, and I was hoping that this would be a good day. I really, really was. I wish I had some control over it."

A beat, then Kristie sets her shoulders back and smiles. "That's okay," she says. "I understand, really." Louisa watches her slip on invisible armor; her face makes Louisa think of her children attempting bravery after a hard fall on uneven pavement. How valiant it is, the way humans get hurt and just keep going.

Dinner proceeds. It goes okay, considering, and despite Martin's absence. Lobsters are good for keeping people busy. Children make excellent distractions in any circumstances. Claire spills her milk and Louisa pretends not to mind; she wipes it up cheerfully while delivering a joke, like a sitcom mom, even though she had told Claire to move her elbow away from her glass, and on the inside she is irked. One thing that helps the meal move along is that Steven and Danny get on immediately—Steven is full of detailed gardening questions for Danny. Louisa supposes it is this natural curiosity that makes Steven such a good podcaster, and she remembers to be grateful for it. Kristie is clumsy with the lobster, and Claire helps her get the meat out of the claws. Annie is quiet, concentrating on her plate, or passing this and that, making sure everyone has enough melted butter, plenty of chowder. Louisa drinks more wine.

It goes on like this: a meal like any other, except it's not; it's a meal built up to over the summer, brick by brick, hour by hour. The water and the sky visible from the picture window do their part by changing gloriously as the sun descends. Louisa looked at the sunset calculator online before dinner; the sun will set just after seven-thirty. It set at nearly eight-thirty when they arrived in June. Summer is marching toward fall.

And then, partway though dessert. A change in atmosphere; an alteration. The night seems to shake itself out, a dog after a swim.

"Oh, sweetheart," says Annie. "Hello." They all turn. In the doorway to the dining room, framed in the last rays of the sun, which settle around his shoulders, the imposing crag of his chin: Martin Fitzgerald. Annie half-rises, and there's an expression on her face, a *tenderness*, that brings tears to Louisa's eyes.

Louisa says, "Daddy?" and Claire says, "Hey, Grandpa," and even Danny dips his head and says, "Chief."

"I'm feeling better now," says Martin Fitzgerald. He looks around the table, taking it all in. "I thought I'd come down."

45.
Martin

"I'm feeling better now," he says. "I thought I'd come down." And that's all it takes to get the room moving, all of them fussing.

A chair is pulled out; a napkin appears, then a glass of water, a piece of pie.

The chatter picks back up, but Martin isn't listening to it. He's lost in his thoughts, sinking into them. That's what people don't understand, that sometimes it's confusing and disconcerting, where his mind goes. But sometimes it's comforting and irresistible, when he's in the past, and the past is like a warm liquid pool, and you can sink into it, down, down, down, but you never drown. You can float on the past forever.

———————

"I thought we'd go up to the house for the weekend," says Annie over breakfast.

Martin looks up from his paper. It's early, seven, and Annie is dressed already, jeans, a blouse, ballet flats, earrings, hair styled. Louisa is still in her pajamas, her glorious hair—hair that old ladies used to stop Annie on the street to comment upon when Louisa was a baby—messed from sleep.

"It's only Tuesday. Are we already planning the weekend?"

"It's never too early," says Annie. "The weekend will be here before we know it! That's how it goes."

It's October, and he'd thought their last visit of the season was behind them. "I can't this weekend. I've got to work late all week, and I'll probably be back at it on Sunday." He turns back to his paper. Bill Clinton thinks George Bush wants to be best friends with the world's dictators.

"You can work at the house. My parents won't bother you, I'll make sure of it. You can have the downstairs bedroom all to yourself as an office. Or you can work in the living room, looking out at the water! We'll set up that folding table."

"I can't work at the house. I need to be near the office. The papers—" No matter how much Annie claims that nobody will disturb him at Ships View, the fact is that somebody always disturbs him at Ships View. It may be just to see if he needs anything—a blanket, a snack, lunch, a cocktail, a break—but it is a disturbance nonetheless.

"Bring the papers," suggests Annie equitably. "Can you sneak out a little early on Friday, do you think?" Fenway has lain down just to the side of Louisa's chair. "You've been working so hard I think it would be good for you to have a rest, maybe go out on the boat with my father. Clear your head. The season's over, you know. They'll be closing up next weekend. This is our last chance. I know this case is big, but can't you just bring the papers with you?"

The feminist wave that swept across the country seems to have missed his wife entirely—a blessing, Martin can easily admit, but also often a bewilderment. Annie seems as though she truly doesn't need or desire anything more than home and hearth, child and husband and parents, a windswept bit of rock, a cocktail and a garden and an occasional new dress. She sees her job as smoothing the way for his job, laying out soft, thick carpet to cover any bumps that he may encounter as he sets his own feet down.

"It's more than the papers," he says. "It's the time in the office."

"It'll be winter before we know it, and we'll wish we had done it."

"You go ahead without me," he says. "Spend time with your parents. Go out on the boat with your dad, enjoy the beautiful weather."

Annie has a wet cloth; she's wiping something from the floor. She straightens up and smiles at both of them. "You know what?" she says. "I think we might just do that, if it's really all right with you. Is it really all right with you? Louisa?"

"Sure." Louisa is nine—easygoing, except when her temper rears up.

You have a bright future ahead of you, people have been saying to Martin since his high school days, and earlier than that too, really since he got to this country, a boy of twelve, with his brogue and his foreign parents and his unfashionable clothes, determined not to let anyone pass him. Yale undergrad, Harvard for law, private practice, his eye one day on the state supreme court, and here he is, in a city, in a kitchen, at a table, holding a paper, wanting nothing more than for his beautiful wife and his sunny daughter to leave him alone so he can grasp at the brass ring as his horse moves around and around on the carousel.

"Of course it's all right," he says. "It's more than all right, I'd feel terrible if the two of you were stuck back here when you could be up there, breathing in all that ocean air, being tended to by your mother."

"All right," says Annie. "If you're really sure about it, I guess we'll go. We'll go! Should I leave Fenway with you, or bring him with us?" Annie considers the dog, who raises his ears affably and looks back and forth between the two of them with his black button eyes.

"I'm sure I don't mind either way," says Martin. He folds the paper, stands, kisses his wife on the cheek, his daughter on the forehead. Fenway presses against his leg and Martin pats him on the head. "He'd get more chances to run up there, and he'd be nice company for Louisa."

Martin doesn't know the rest of it that morning— how could he? Later that week he'll meet Sheila Turner. In three years Annie's parents will be dead, and the Owls Head house as well as a significant amount of money will go to Martin and Annie. In four years, he'll be a district court judge, then superior court; in ten, a state supreme court justice, black-robed in front of the famous red curtain. Fenway will be only the first of the golden retrievers, followed by Gremlin, by Bentley, by Winslow, by Otis.

By seventy-three he'll hardly know that any of this happened.

He says hello and goodbye to his daughter Kristie on the very same day. Kristie is two weeks old. She grasps Martin's thumb in her little fist, and her eyes meet his. Louisa's eyes had stayed in a milky state for some time before resolving into their startling sapphire blue, but this baby's eyes are clear and bright already. It's like looking into his own eyes, and he has the feeling that Kristie knows that, that she's looking into his very core, that she knows what's coming next.

Martin touches his lips to Kristie's silky forehead. She smells like baby powder and Ivory soap and innocence; she smells just as Louisa did as a baby. Kristie closes her eyes and he stares at her gossamer eyelids, the tiny lavender veins snaking their way across.

Sheila is going to take the baby and go back to Philadelphia, where she has family. She'll live with her sister. That makes him feel better. Where there's a sister there's help and hope. She'll put off the rest of her education now, but not forever. Of course not forever.

He has to pull over on the drive home—he can't see, for crying so hard, and he can't stop crying, thinking of the gossamer eyelids and the baby powder smell.

It's a workday and Annie isn't expecting him home at this hour. He catches her humming as she goes about her business in the kitchen, measuring, chopping, washing. The radio is on: Eric Clapton.

"I have to talk to you, Annie," he says. He pours two glasses of whiskey and hands her one. Louisa is at school—the bus drops her off at three o'clock.

"Martin! It's two in the afternoon. What on earth?"

"I've made a mistake," he says. "And I need your help to put it right."

A rustling under the table. He puts his hand down and feels the square head of the dog. "Fenway," he says.

Louisa clears her throat. "Daddy, that's Otis. Fenway is long gone, remember?"

"Ah," he says. Well, no matter—one soul carries the soul of the dog before it, which carries the soul of the dog before it. In the end, maybe, it's only the dogs that remain.

He looks around at all the faces, and beyond them, to the picture window, and beyond that there's the water meeting the sky, the tangle of colors as the sun is setting. A sailboat gliding by, a glimpse of the far-off Samoset.

At the opposite end of the table is Annie, the love of his life, his North Star, silver hair catching the last of the sun, as beautiful now as she was the day she was his bride. And Louisa, and her children, and her husband. And the young man who mows the lawns and weeds the flower beds.

And Kristie.

They all think he doesn't understand; they think he doesn't know, and sometimes he doesn't. Sometimes he's lost, swimming through the murky past. Can't tell the surface from the depths. But in moments like this, when the thoughts unsnarl and the memories slot themselves into the right places, he knows. Oh, for certain, he knows.

Louisa raises a glass and every person at the table follows suit, even the children with their glasses of milk, Matty with his water. Martin catches Annie's eye across the table and she gives him a tiny nod, because she knows too.

"To family," says Martin. One by one they echo him. The word bounces off the walls, pings off the picture window. To family. To family. To family.

46.
Kristie

Danny takes Steven out to see the black knight flowers and the hydrangeas, his August bloomers, and Kristie begins to help Louisa clear the table; she heard Annie tell Pauline earlier to go ahead and go home. But Louisa shoos Kristie away and says the kids will help her. Otis exits after Danny, and then it's only Kristie and Martin and Annie left in the dining room. Kristie lingers there for an awkward moment, unsure where to go or what to do. Annie, standing, leans over Martin, seated, and says something too quietly for Kristie to hear. The intimacy of the moment propels Kristie straight out of the dining room and into the adjacent living room.

The living room is longer than it is wide, with pink-and-green floral couches that look like they've seen better days but also look like, yes, they've seen some *really amazing* days. The windows on the back wall, which reach from behind the couch to nearly the ceiling, look directly onto the porch and by extension onto the yard and the water. The room has the haphazard, premium look that most of Ships View has: a table in the corner with a jigsaw puzzle 30 percent completed, an antique coffee table stacked with books, another faded Persian rug. Everything in the house seems to be saying, *You could replace me if you want something newer. But you'll sacrifice quality to do it, and whatever you choose instead won't look nearly as nice.* The walls are covered with family pictures in plain wooden frames.

Kristie turns and runs her hand along the back of one of the armchairs. Her mother had been in this house! Had her mother been in *this* room? Had she sat on *this* chair? Had she touched *this* flower on the fabric? What about this one? This couch, this table, this book about the building of the Rockland breakwater? Kristie remembers again the family tree project in seventh grade. *Leave it blank. Put deceased.* She sits on the couch; she closes her eyes and opens her heart and her soul. She tries to imagine her mother here, as a young woman, a hopeful woman. A woman with a married lover; a woman with a secret. A woman who still thought anything was possible. When she opens her eyes, she's not alone any longer. Martin is standing in the doorway, watching her.

"Ohmygod," she says. She puts a hand flat on her chest. "I'm sorry, I—you startled me. Sorry."

"I didn't mean to startle you. My apologies." He does a funny little formal bow, then he says, "May I?" and gestures to the end of the couch farthest away from her. She nods, and he sits. She catches a whiff of aftershave. Kristie tilts her body to look out the window, where she sees shadows moving across the grass, too fast to be Danny and Steven. The kids must have abandoned the dishes. Maybe they're catching fireflies. Do contemporary kids catch fireflies? She and Twyla did, long ago. "I'm glad you came tonight," Martin says.

Kristie waits a beat, to see if anything more is coming, and when nothing does she says, "I am too."

After that there are a lot of things Martin Fitzgerald doesn't say. He doesn't say, I'm sure that by now you understand my predicament upon learning about your anticipated birth. He doesn't say, The good I accomplished in my career has far outweighed the loss of you as a daughter, and I'm sure you understand that too. He doesn't say, That is exactly how it had to go, the greatest good for the greatest number. He doesn't say,

Your mother was the love of my life and her absence is like a canyon through the center of my heart.

He stands, walks to the wall of photos, and motions for Kristie to join him. One by one he points and explains. Here is Annie in a graduation cap and gown, standing between two people: her parents. Here is Louisa with Annie and Martin in front of Ships View. Louisa is six or seven, grinning widely, no front teeth. Kristie is able to follow Louisa's life by looking at these photos as Martin points: here she is as a teenager, still smiling, but more guarded than in the younger photos. Here she is at her wedding, stunning in a simple strapless gown and a flower crown. Here she is holding Matty as a baby. Matty is impossibly small and is wearing a tiny blue cap. Here is Abigail, here is Claire.

Kristie thinks, This man is a stranger, showing me photos in the lives of other strangers. Nothing about him is familiar, not his spotted, veined hands, not the slight forward curve of his shoulders, not his gravelly voice nor the smell of his aftershave. What had she expected? That something about him *would* seem recognizable in some way—that upon seeing him there would occur some ancient, tectonic shift, that plates would slide apart and reveal *father?*

He turns toward her and looks at her for a long, long time, and she looks back at him, and it goes on for so long, one set of blue eyes staring into another. There is an instant—quick as a caught breath, the beating of a butterfly's wing—when Kristie panics, wondering if he's forgotten why Kristie is here, or maybe even who she is, until he says, "Kristie."

She waits. Then, cautiously, "Yes?"

"You seem like you're happy. Are you happy?"

She thinks about it and realizes she is. Danny outside, so proud about his flowers. The dark times with Jesse in Florida behind her. The loss of her mother beginning to feel like a weight she can bear rather than one that will pull her under by the ankles. The new life inside her. Happiness on her own terms. For the first time in she doesn't know how long there's more promise ahead of her than behind her. "Yes," she says. "Yes, I'm happy."

He nods. "I hear you're going to have a baby."

"Yes." It comes out in a whisper, like a secret.

Martin Fitzgerald's smiling face reveals his age more than his face does in repose: deep fissures appear along the sides of his cheeks and around his eyes. "A baby is a wonderful thing," he says. "A wonderful, wonderful thing. A blessing."

"Daddy?" says Louisa, who is suddenly in the doorway next to them. "Mom is looking for you, in the playroom. Okay?" She points.

"I know where the playroom is," says Martin, somewhat irritably.

"I know you do, Daddy."

Martin walks out of the living room without another word, without a glance backward, forward, or sideways. Kristie tries to figure out what she's feeling. Is it disappointment? Heartache? Longing? Then she figures it out. It is relief. It's over. She met him, and she talked to him, and the world didn't implode, and she didn't implode either.

Louisa pushes her hair out of her face and then allows it to fall back exactly where it was. One of Louisa's eyebrows, the left one, has slightly more of a natural arch than the right one. Kristie's eyebrows are like that too. She wonders: Does Louisa have one foot bigger than the other by about half a size, as Kristie does? Do her fingers go numb when she's nervous? When she sneezes, do her sneezes blow the roof off, like Kristie's, or do they come in a dainty trio, three puffs of air? These are things she may never find out.

"Listen," says Louisa. "I have something to give you." She pulls something out of her pocket and unfolds it. It's a check. She holds it out, and Kristie takes it. In the corner she sees the names Louisa and Steven McLean, and a Brooklyn address. The check is for $150,000.

She says, "What?"

"It's for you," says Louisa.

It's more money than Kristie has ever held at one time—it's more money than she's even thought of at one time. She closes her eyes, to test if they're working correctly. Maybe it actually says $1,500, which is still a lot of money. Even $500 is a lot of money. When she opens her eyes, the check is still there, with her name on the *PAY TO THE ORDER OF* line, and *One hundred fifty thousand and 00/100* on the next line.

"But your mom—" she says. "You said that your mom couldn't do this. I wasn't going to tell anyone about your dad, you know. I know I said I would, I know I threatened. But honestly, I wouldn't do that. I wouldn't even know where to start. I'd be such a bad blackmailer." She holds the check back out to Louisa and says, "You don't need to do this. Please, take it back. This is too much money. Take it back. Tell your mom thank you, but I can't."

"My mom doesn't know about this," says Louisa.

"She doesn't?"

Louisa shakes her head. "This is mine and Steven's money, and we talked about it. We agreed on it. It's the first thing, moneywise, we've agreed on in months. And I'm not doing it because of the . . . uh, the attempted blackmail." She twists her lips—it's a half smile that tells Kristie she didn't have much faith in Kristie's blackmailing either. "I'm really not. Danny said you want to move out to Oregon. Or maybe you haven't decided—maybe you want to stay here. Either way, you'll want to lay down roots, pay off your bills, and get a start in your new life. You can put down a solid down payment on a house out there, and get you and your baby on the right track."

Kristie looks again at the check. Her eyes fill with tears, thinking about how good it will feel to get the bill collectors off her back. (She hopes Sierra will get some sort of a bonus once Kristie pays up.) "You must need this money. I mean, three kids . . . ? College and all of that?" Her voice trails off. She has no concept of Louisa's finances, what she needs or what she has, what anything costs for someone like Louisa.

"You've paid enough," says Louisa. "I've done a lot of thinking about safety nets this summer. You never had one. I always did. And if it's time for me to live without one for a little bit—well, I'm ready to do that. Steven and I need to be each other's safety net for a while."

Kristie has to wipe at her eyes, because the tears are starting to leak out. Louisa reaches out and squeezes Kristie's hand just as Danny appears in the doorway. The doorway has now apparently become the wing where all the actors take a turn entering, while Kristie remains onstage.

"Come in," says Louisa. "I was just leaving."

Kristie is so taken aback by everything that she has to sit back down on the couch. Danny sits next to her, scooches closer, and puts his hand on her knee. "How's it going? You hanging in there? Strange night, right?"

She shows him the check. All this *money*. For her, and her baby, and Danny if he's going to stick around, which she believes now he really will. Like Kristie said to Louisa on the porch that time, the only people who say that money can't fix problems are people who have plenty of it. Because this money would fix some real problems. This money would equal solid hope, and she breathes easier just holding it.

Danny whistles. "Holy shit," he says.

"Louisa gave it to me. What do we do? I don't know if we should take it. What do you think?"

He doesn't answer right away.

"Danny? It's not like anyone *owes* me this." She so badly wants that fresh start that Louisa talked about, though. She really does.

She can tell he's getting his words in perfect order before letting them out. "What do I think?" he says at last. "I think on one hand you are owed everything you didn't get because your father made a mistake and a bad decision, and you are the one who suffered from that decision."

"And my mom."

"And your mom. But on the other hand—you aren't owed anything, not really, because the universe doesn't work like that. The universe doesn't make everything even for us." He gestures to the shadows running across the grass, the wide expanse of water, as calm and flat as a dinner plate, the crescent of moon on the rise. "Without that guy you wouldn't be here at all, for one thing. For another, this family was never yours and it isn't yours now. One lobster dinner isn't going to change that. One check isn't going to change it. But that's *okay*. It's really okay. We don't need *this* family, Kristie.

"What we need is, we need to go off and start our own family. You and me and this little chicken." He hovers his hand over her belly. "May I?" She nods, and he rests his hand on the baby. "I think if you take this money, and we take what I have saved, and we head out west, we'll be in good shape to make a really good life together. But if you don't take it, we're going to be okay too."

"Yeah," she says. She lays her hand on top of his hand on her stomach. She squeezes. "We're going to be okay."

Danny excuses himself to use the bathroom before they find their hosts and say goodbye, and Kristie lingers for another moment, watching out the window as the sky darkens completely. She thinks about all the turns her life could have taken but didn't, and all the turns her life has taken but easily could have missed. She could have followed Jesse down his dark path. She could have wasted her whole life in Miami Beach and had nothing to show for it in the end. She could have gone home to Altoona sooner, and had more time with her mother, or gone later or not at all, and had none. She could have never left Altoona in the first place. She could have read her mother's letter and decided to let bygones be bygones, never getting on that Greyhound. Then there would be no Danny, no baby, no future in Oregon.

She could spend her whole life lamenting the fact that she started out behind—or maybe, maybe, she can recognize the areas where she's ahead, and understand that she's going to do *so right* by this baby, starting now, with the money to help her, and going all the way through. She's going to do so right.

Outside, the foghorn on the breakwater blows. All summer Kristie has thought of that sound as mournful, but now she wonders if it might be more hopeful than she gave it credit for.

47.
Louisa

Departure day. Louisa packs her bathing suits and her shorts; she packs the water shoes she wears on the rocks because she lacks the bravura and balance of her children; she packs her Pitcairn notebooks, both empty and full; she packs her carefully cushioned Damariscotta mug, and her jar of Blue Razz Conserve from Nervous Nellie's in Deer Isle, and her laptop. She zips her duffle and carries it down the stairs and sets it outside the door with the other luggage. How they will fit everything they brought here plus all of the items they've accumulated over the summer *plus* Steven is anybody's guess. Luckily, Steven packed light, and car packing is his superpower. She supposes Matty is leaving a piece of his heart behind, so that might account for some extra room.

The day before Kristie and Danny came to dinner Louisa told Steven what she wanted to do with the Emergency Fund. She expected a fight, but instead of raising his verbal fists Steven nodded, as though she'd told him that some of the glasses in the dishwasher didn't get clean and they'd have to rerun it. Then he took her hand and knotted his fingers through hers and she thought that she had maybe never loved him as much as she did in that moment.

"It's the right thing," he said. "It's okay."

"But the house," she says. "Now we can't help keep the house."

"Not yet. But if All Ears sells, maybe we can then. We'll have to wait and see. Or maybe the Pitcairn book will be a runaway bestseller."

"I don't think so. I'm pretty sure not, in fact."

Now that Louisa has given the check to Kristie, the window for making excuses has slammed shut. She'll have to finish the book while starting up the school year. She's made her own bed, with sheets woven from procrastination, and now she will have to lie in it.

She finds her father on the back porch, sitting in the rocker, though not rocking, looking out at the water. Not so far from them a sailboat glides by. Beyond the boat, on the far side of the harbor, hangs a curtain of fog, turning the outline of the Samoset ghostly and ethereal, even in midmorning.

"Daddy?" She slides the screen door closed behind her. "We're almost all packed up now. Steven is just putting the last few things in the car. I'm sure we've left a hundred other things behind." Hair elastics, paperbacks, bottles of nail polish—who knows what? There's always a package from Annie the week after they get home, filled with the left-behinds dug out from underneath the couches, behind open closet doors. "You'll come out and say goodbye, won't you? The kids will want to say goodbye, and Steven too."

He turns and faces her then, and his eyes are clear and bright. He's in there right now, the real Martin Fitzgerald, the Chief, present and accounted for.

"Sit with me," he says, indicating the love seat beside the rocker.

She sits.

"I remember something," Martin says.

"What's that, Daddy?"

"I remember the first time you came here after Matty was born. He would have been how old?"

"Just a month," she says. "It was fall, before you closed up for the year."

"The two of you sat right here," he says. "I remember coming down one morning, early, and you had fallen asleep holding him. You looked like Madonna and child. The sun was just starting to come up—" He pauses and studies his hands. "It was so beautiful," he says. "So beautiful."

"I remember that visit," Louisa says. She remembers being elated, exhausted, overworked, overjoyed. She remembers Matty's little fists, beating lightly at her while he nursed. "That was a good visit," she says. There's so much else she wants to say—about Kristie and Danny, about Sheila's death and Kristie's baby, about Annie holding the secret for so long. But when she opens her mouth, what comes out is this: "I think Matty got his heart stomped on this summer. By Nicole's daughter. Hazel."

Her father raises his eyebrows and chuckles. "Happens to the best of us, I'm afraid. He'll recover. He'll be grand." A trace of the Dubliner he once was comes out in that phrase. *He'll be grand.* She imagines her father as an impish schoolboy with a cowlick, a sweater vest over a bow tie, short pants.

"I think he will too." After all, sometimes it takes the younger generation to atone for the missteps of the parents' generation. But she won't get into that now. Louisa knows that these moments of lucidity of Martin's won't last; she knows that the disease will continue its endless march through her father's brain until his memory bank is wiped entirely clean. Toward the end of his life Ronald Reagan no longer knew that he'd been president of the United States! This conversation with her father, this temporary clearing of the neural pathways, is an unexpected gift.

Be in the moment. Connect.

This will be the final time she sits like this with her father. She had thought at one time they'd all be here forever on this porch, summer after summer, winding the memories around their fingers in an endless game of cat's cradle. There was the time that. How about that day. Do you remember when. But this is it. It all goes so fast, no time to look around.

Steven will be itching to go; they'll have to leave soon if they have any hope of avoiding traffic through Queens and into Brooklyn. They will need lunch and at least three bathroom stops—nobody will coordinate, and Claire will need to go twice.

Louisa stands and holds out her hand to her father. "Come on, Daddy."

He stands, using her weight to steady his. "Where are we going?"

Before they walk through the screen door she turns and looks again at the Samoset across the way. She can see it fully now. She can see the breakwater and the rolling swaths of emerald grass that stand between the harbor and the resort's pool. It's amazing she can get any words out with her voice clogged this way, clogged with all of the things she'll never say. "We're going out to the car so you can say goodbye to everybody before we leave. How's that sound, Daddy?"

"Good," he says. "That sounds good."

The sun is dancing off the water in the most lovely way. Miraculously, at least for now, the fog has cleared.

Acknowledgments

The Santa Maria, Dunn, and Hare families have been allowing me into their home in Owls Head, Maine, as a guest for so many years that it almost seemed indecent to use their house as a setting for a book—but I couldn't help myself, because I love their home as much as a nonfamily member can. The fact that they continue to open their door to me, feed me lobster, and give me stretches of quiet waterfront writing time is a testament to their extreme hospitality and generosity. Margaret and Wally Dunn, Priscilla Hare, Lainé Santa Maria, Mark and Denise Santa Maria, and Mary Stroot, thank you for letting me be an honorary member of your household. I may have taken a couple of liberties (the house has a *name?* And *what* downstairs office?) and I hope you can forgive those.

Sue Santa Maria left us in 2020, before I'd completed a draft, but it is my wish that her soul, spirit, and love for Damariscotta Pottery (which I briefly resurrected for this book) are throughout. (If other establishments closed between the time I started writing *Vacationland* and its publication, I chose to keep them as they were at the time of the book's conception.)

Answers to various queries came from Valerie Piana and Dr. Jackie Lee. Chris Young of the Rockland Police Department replied to endless emails about plot points that mostly ended up coming out of the book—but someday, when I write my murder mystery, he'll be my first call. Dominique Walk, assistant stranding coordinator of Marine Mammals of Maine (I can't imagine a better title) shared her enthusiasm and expertise with me. My good friend Stacy Gediman talked to me about her family's experience with Alzheimer's and I'm grateful for her openness and honesty. Renee Heath helped me understand the world of a professor. The staff at Primo gave me a wonderful tour of their top-notch restaurant in summer 2020. The Hon. Leigh Saufley, former chief justice of the Maine Supreme Judicial Court, generously shared large and small details about her years on the court.

Margaret Dunn and Jennifer Truelove gave me early and valuable feedback (and Margaret gave me the book title!), and they always provide me with unflagging friendship and endless laughs. (I've never thrown Jennifer Truelove a research question she didn't throw right back with an answer attached.)

Most of my close friends (hey, Newburyport ladies!) are not writers themselves, but over the years I've been lucky enough to find a community of writers and book bloggers online and in person who have made my writing world wider, richer, and infinitely better. Elin Hilderbrand in particular has been incredibly generous in spreading the word about my books to her many, many devoted readers. Being part of the Newburyport Literary Festival committee the past few years has enriched my writing world as well.

To call my editor, Kate Nintzel, *exacting* is perhaps an understatement—but then again so is calling her brilliant and insightful. She is all of those things and more, and with each "you're not done yet" email she sent me, this book got better and better and better. Every writer should be so lucky. Everyone at William Morrow—Liate Stehlik, Jennifer Hart, Amelia Wood, Julie Paulauski, Molly Gendell, and Shelly Perron—has taken such care when putting my books out in the world. If this book is in your hands right now it's because of their hard work and the hard work of the sales team. Elisabeth Weed of The Book Group has been in my corner for so long I can't imagine what the corner would look like without her. In fact, I don't think there would be a corner at all, and I'm beyond grateful for her.

My parents, John and Sara Mitchell, and sister, Shannon Mitchell, are constant sources of love, support, and guerilla marketing. We lost my mother-in-law, Cheryl Moore, as I was finishing this book. I hardly ever saw her without a book in her hands, and I so wish *Vacationland* could have been one of them. Brian Moore is a willing early reader and my biggest champion. I always say he is coach to many, father to three, and husband to one. I'm so lucky to be that one. My daughters, Addie, Violet, and Josie, don't always get to this last page in my books, but if you do, Moore girls, I hope you know how proud I am of you every day, and how much you teach me—and not just about what not to do on social media. I love you all.

About the Author

MEG MITCHELL MOORE worked for several years as a journalist for a variety of publications before turning to fiction. She lives in the beautiful coastal town of Newburyport, Massachusetts, with her husband and their three daughters. *Vacationland* is her seventh novel.